BILL BROADY is the auth
and *Eternity is Temporary*
 In This Block There Lives A Stag, won the 2002 Macmillan/
PEN prize. With Jane Metcalfe he edited *You Are Here: The
'Redbeck' Book of Contemporary British Short Stories* (2006).

BILL BROADY

THE NIGHT-SOIL MEN

SALT

SHEFFIELD

PUBLISHED BY SALT PUBLISHING 2024

2 4 6 8 10 9 7 5 3

Copyright © Bill Broady 2024

First published in Great Britain in 2024 by
Salt Publishing Ltd
18 Churchill Road, Sheffield, S10 1FG United Kingdom

www.saltpublishing.com

Salt Publishing Limited Reg. No. 5293401

A CIP catalogue record for this book is available from the British Library

ISBN 978 1 78463 318 9 (Paperback edition)
ISBN 978 1 78463 319 6 (Electronic edition)

Typeset in Neacademia by Salt Publishing

Printed and bound in Great Britain by Clays Ltd, Elcograf S.p.A

To Jane and Mignon

"Is fiction which makes fact alive, fact too?
The somehow may be thishow."
        – ROBERT BROWNING: *The Ring And The Book*

CHAPTER ONE

CONFERENCE (1893)

A S THEY CROSSED the square the town hall clock was striking nine. Once more the sun had neglected to rise over Bradford: two faint smears of light that did relieve the gloom were in quite the wrong quarters of the sky. Whenever it snowed Jim Sharp was reminded that the stone of the civic buildings was not black at all but mossy green. However lightly he stepped, the scraping of his clogs through the slush almost drowned out the words of his companion.

Jim swung round: they were still not being followed. This was the morning of the inaugural meeting of the Independent Labour Party; the world was about to be turned upside down but nobody seemed in the least concerned. Outside the Law Courts two policemen, lighting each other's clay pipes, did not give him a second glance. Under one arm he was carrying a large bale of soft-leaded pencils: it could have been dynamite for all they knew. He leaned a shoulder against one of the Doric Columns but it wouldn't budge. He was no Samson: the tubby peelers could smoke on in peace.

"There's smallpox passing through the ward again," Fred was saying. "Three streets a day, one house in four, like the plagues of old Egypt. The council says there's nothing it can do but all the necessary powers are right there in the Housing of the Working Classes Act. The Liberals put things on the statute book then join the Tories in ignoring them."

Fred Jowett's voice was slightly slurred, as if he was a toper, but Jim had never seen him go beyond a single half of dark mild. Fred's mother came from Devonshire but although he had often sat in the Jowetts' parlour, Jim had never heard her utter a single word.

"Smallpox in January! It's the privy middens. The colder it gets, the worse the smell: even after a frost the air is full of flies. The ash freezes solid so that it can't absorb and then the dirt piles up until the streams of urine carry it down the yards right up to the back doorsteps."

Once Fred got on to sanitation there was no stopping him. How often Jim had wished that he would find a more elevated hobby-horse to ride! As Fred became excited his thick black hair ridged up like the hackles of an angry dog. Although the down that shadowed his upper lip gave him an adolescent look he was already silvering at the temples. Jim knew that he didn't fuss about his appearance but he still contrived to have an almost dandyified air. He wore a baggy grey suit with a red ribbon tie that was always on the point of coming undone. Jim could actually see the thoughts and emotions passing across those pale features: it was like prising open a fob watch to reveal the cogs and wheels whirring round inside. Even so, Jim had never glimpsed the least trace of meanness, fear or calculation. He wasn't sure whether to envy Fred or to pity him: perhaps a man without weaknesses was not really a proper man at all?

"And all they ever say is, 'Why can't you turn your thoughts to higher things?'" Fred continued. It's true what Kipling said about William Morris: that one decent primer on sanitary engineering is worth all the tomes of sacred smut ever written." Jim took his cue. "But I thought that Kipling was a jingo while Morris is on our side."

"Yes," said Fred triumphantly, "but even good Socialists can act like ninnies and even a jingo is sometimes right."

Jim decided not to enquire where he could obtain some of this sacred smut in order to reach a properly informed judgement.

Before they had set out together he had wagered Fred that in crossing the city they would not see on a single face anything approaching a smile. First they had encountered, trudging from somewhere to somewhere else, half a dozen swaddled figures who appeared to have no mouths at all. Then there had been a skeletal woman driving before her a pack of feral children. These had teeth aplenty but no lips to speak of. Everyone was blighted: even the peelers had seemed to be disgusted by the taste of their own tobacco. Now, beneath the statue of Forster, 'The Great Educator', a brindled terrier was busily worrying an obviously long-dead rat. On seeing them, it dropped its trophy and danced a little jig, revealing that it was missing a foreleg, then put its ears back, opened its jaws and rolled out its scarlet tongue.

"Nay, Fred," said Jim, before his companion could speak, "Dogs don't count."

At the bottom of Chapel Street the gates of the mills burst open and they were engulfed by a great flood of humanity. The night-workers had reached the end of their shift. Perhaps it was only to be expected that as the two men approached their appointment with History they should find that everyone else was heading in the opposite direction.

The first wave had separated them. Jim watched Fred forging up the hill as he himself was jostled sideways. His friend's mouth was still moving, even though he was no longer at his side. Jim was bigger and stronger but stiffer and slower and bandy-legged, the result of childhood rickets. In the event of his meeting a pig in a passageway, perfect strangers were always taking it upon themselves to inform him, it was unlikely that he would be able to stop it. Even when he was not carrying two hundred pencils he would walk, for the sake of symmetry, with his elbows pointing outwards.

Crowds terrified him: he felt swallowed, like Jonah in the belly of the whale. There had been rumours of kidnappers who, taking advantage of the press, would roll their victims up in carpets. Surely even the clay-pipe policemen would notice gangs of roughs lugging wriggling lengths of Axminster?

He saw that Fred had stopped and was peering through his chipped eyeglasses. Everyone found this myopia endearing rather

3

than comical. It was as if he could never get your face into focus: it made Jim feel somehow blurred, not quite there. Although Fred was always talking about 'The People', Jim wondered if he had ever been able to see them properly. Perhaps a stronger pair of spectacles might modify his Socialism? The faces in the crowd were sullen or downright hostile: they walked in silence, save for a curious hissing sound as they drew deeply on cigarettes or pipes, like a fuse burning down to an explosion. It would be just Jim's luck to be in the middle of them when it finally happened. Even though they were working men like himself, he still could not think of them as brothers.

"We need to begin again," Fred was saying when Jim, fighting for breath, finally rejoined him. "To raze Manchester Road and Longlands to the ground and build municipal terraces, wide straight streets with trees and lawns, where people can work and live with dignity. And we need new schools with proper teachers, in which every child is guaranteed at least one nutritious meal a day."

Sometimes Jim wondered if he secretly disliked Fred: he felt like giving him a good shaking to waken his ideas up. But this was the whole point of Socialism: unlike religion, you did not have to pretend to love everybody, merely acknowledge a mutual interest. Now, however, he felt Fred's right arm hook through his left, with the slightest squeeze, and he looked into that open face with its strangely wavering smile, the eyes swimming behind the dusty lenses as if filled with tears. On these rare occasions when he and Fred touched, a sweet glow would spread through his body and his perpetual restlessness would ease. And so the oft-told tale of how Councillor Jowett had scuppered the Sanitation Committee, forcing them to conduct weekly inspections of every privy midden in Manningham, would suddenly seem the most fascinating thing in the world.

More people were emerging from the side streets. There were lost children seeking their parents, ragged pickpockets pulling off their mittens and evangelicals brandishing cheap tracts but mostly they were lonely souls in search of companionship. There were no

4

carpet-roll kidnappers but Jim could see looming ahead a couple of unusually tall mill-girls, also arm in arm, like a distaff mirror image. The tiny heads bobbed on their goose-like necks while their hips swung sideways and forwards at the same time. The younger one's features were heavily pitted but smallpox scars could be an adornment to some faces. She looked to have been hewn out of sandstone: Jim imagined that his stubble might strike sparks against those cheeks. Her companion resembled a ship's wooden figurehead, salt-stained and faded. Their chins were tilted as if they got a clearer view down their nostrils and their shawls were pulled back to display expanses of blueish throat and chest.

Jim already knew that there would be no pairing off: they were only interested in Fred. Women liked thick hair that they could get their fingers into and they seemed to prefer little men, perhaps because they were more agile, less of a weight or, if it came to beating, less likely to do a girl serious damage.

Fred was trying to focus but the glasses had slid to the end of his nose. It was apparent that to him the women were nothing more than a pale obstruction.

"Excuse us, gentlemen," he muttered as, stretching out a hand, he parted them like saloon doors. Jim caught a sweet, cider-like smell as they passed.

"Nay, nay," he was protesting. "They're lasses, Fred, ladies!" – but it was too late. Looking back, he could still see the women's faces bobbing above the crowd like backstroke swimmers on a choppy lake. They did not seem to have taken offence, however. From those black and yellow flashes, he could swear that they were actually smiling. He wasn't going to tell Fred, though: a bet was a bet.

Women! There really was no accounting for them. Every time he tried to raise the subject Fred would merely laugh politely as if at a joke he did not understand. Had he never noticed the women who continually sighed and brushed against him? It made no sense: if Jim had been a woman he certainly would not have fancied Fred. It was something you were born with: you either had it or you hadn't.

And whatever Jim did – whether he smiled or scowled, however he dressed or combed his hair – they never noticed him. Nor could he blame the rickets or the stammer: even sitting down, with his mouth shut tight, he remained utterly invisible.

Some of the older ones in his weaving shed had showed faint signs of interest but he could tell from the bitter twist of their lips that they were considering him as a last resort. Jim had his pride: if he could not be anyone's first choice he was damned if he would be a consolation prize, better than nowt but only just. Nor was he prepared to patiently woo through steadiness and dependability. He wanted to be *desired* – at first sight by a total stranger – before any financial or social considerations could enter in. He would have settled for just one of those looks that Fred attracted a dozen times a day and never noticed. He had entertained one last hope that under Socialism women might begin to feel for him what he felt for them but the movement's few eligible spinsters had shared the prejudices of their less enlightened sisters.

Now the masses convulsed again, clearing a path for a group of tall-hatted figures. Half a dozen under-managers were marching two steps behind their manager who in his turn remained four steps behind the mill-owner, Behrens. You could have divined their relative status by the silkiness of their hats and the length of their watch-chains. It appeared that God had given Gustav Behrens the right to move in a six-foot radius of empty space, like the prime grave plot next to his father that awaited him in Undercliffe Cemetery. In the three years since Sir Jacob's death, blithe young Gustav had somehow aged three decades to become the spitting image of his evil papa. At least he had the courage to show his face: Soapy Sam Lister had not been seen in public since his glorious victory over the Manningham Mill Strikers.

With their unblinking eyes and bloodless lips, their hands gripping their coat lapels and their shiny toe-caps pointing at ten to two, the men reminded Jim of bad actors – or perhaps actors who, all too well cast, had descended into caricature. Since he became a

Socialist he saw them in a new way, with contempt and even a little pity. "Poor devils," Fred had once commented, as the millocratic clan had rattled past in their great black and silver coach drawn by Shorts and Damages, those famous high-stepping geldings. "It must be an awful strain having to be wicked all the time."

They had recognised Fred. Jim saw the familiar consternation as they wondered why anyone would choose to be on what was obviously always going to be the losing side. It was common knowledge that Jowett had recently turned down the offer of a partnership in Leach's Mill: could there possibly be something that he knew and they didn't?

". . . And if the Liberals and Tories won't agree to realistic taxation or fair rents" - Fred looked up, vaguely aware of another obstacle to their progress - "We shall be compelled to take the land, with or without compensation, into public ownership." Once again his left hand, fingers spread wide, was extended in that hesitant yet peremptory gesture.

"Excuse us, ladies."

The under-managers became all tangled up with each other, skittling the manager and forcing Behrens to plant one immaculate foot in the filthy suint-clogged gutter. As Jim and Fred passed through, that shockingly-wizened face, almost swallowed up by an astrakhan collar, turned even whiter than before.

Jim was certain that Fred was unaware of what had happened. Some cynics claimed that it was all an act, intended to raise Jowett's asking price beyond the regulation thirty pieces of silver when he finally, inevitably, allowed himself to be suborned. But Jim knew that if he told Fred, he would go back and apologise: he would rather have died than insult anyone. Such squeamishness would not do when the Day of Retribution dawned - unless a way could be found to cut Behrens' throat without hurting his feelings.

During the five years that he had worked with Fred, life had gradually come into focus. Fred made everything seem just as it should be, logical and inevitable instead of a pointless, bloody mess. Even an apparent disaster like the failed 1891 strike was merely a necessary pause for retrenchment before the steady march of Socialism was resumed. Jim recalled how his friend's lunch had always come wrapped in the pages of the *Sunday Chronicle* so that instead of eating he would end up reading aloud the articles of the notorious radical Robert Blatchford. Fred had never seemed to notice when the ever-hungry apprentices filched his bread and scrape.

Fred had been the first person to whom Jim had confided his great dream of emigrating to America: a dream that was gradually becoming a reality at the rate of sixpence a week. A new life in the New World! But Fred had just shaken his head: "Wasn't it Goethe who, when his friend told him that he was going to America to start again, replied '*Here* is America – or nowhere!'?" What had convinced Jim were the accompanying gestures: Fred had spread his arms wide and then with clenched fist given his chest a double rap right above the heart. Jim had promptly abandoned the project but, out of sheer habit, had continued to set the money aside.

At the mill, Jowett had risen from warp-slayer to whitening-licker and then, at the unprecedented age of nineteen, to overlooker. Everyone had suspected a cruel joke: Fred certainly had the delicate fingers for loom work but how on earth could he carry the warps up and down the steep staircases between sheds? He was a mere seven stone while each beam weighed at least twice that. But Fred had been practicing for years, building up his arms and upper body in readiness for that moment. Although the tiny form disappeared beneath its burden, the beams then proceeded, seemingly of their own volition, to fly dizzyingly around the building. It was not Fred's outspokenness or election to the council that disturbed his enemies – it was the memory of those beams. A recent public meeting had been addressed by the sitting Liberal MP for Bradford West, Briggs Priestley, who had just talked out another feebly reformist Factory Bill. Fred had risen and silently pointed his finger at the wretched man who – as if a warp loom had been launched unerringly towards his head – had flinched so violently that he fell off his chair. Jim had begun to wonder whether such power was only incidentally to do with Socialism.

At last they reached the brow of the hill and turned left into Peckover Street. Here the silent men before them kept pausing to spit or stamp the snow off their boots, while surreptitiously checking the pavement behind. Unlike Fred, they appreciated the need for discretion. Under the pulled down cloth caps were faces different from the nightworkers, displaying the even deeper tiredness of hard toil overlaid by equally hard strivings against it. One by one, after a final scan of the street, they ducked inside the Labour Institute, except for the familiar figure of Horner, the Keighley delegate who – drunk even at this hour – was throwing up against the tannery wall. Keighley was a peculiar place: even its Temperance fanatics were alcoholics.

Despite its dilapidated facade, the Institute was a relatively recent building. Originally a Wesleyan Chapel, it had then become a Salvation Army barracks before being leased to the party at an extortionate rate, presumably making the point that although God could be bought he did not come cheap. Jim saw that the two Sugdens from Laisterdyke were manning the door: although identically squat, dark and unsmiling, they were not in fact related.

"Comrades, Mr Sharp here is supernumerary," announced Fred. "He will be attending to refreshments and clerical needs and restoring order should it need to be restored." Jim thrust out his chest and tried to look fierce even though this reputation of his had been lightly come by. Although he had indeed recently ejected two lackeys of the Duke of Devonshire for disrupting a branch meeting at The Royal Oak in Shipley, the men had been, even for gamekeepers, thoroughly soused.

The doormen's attention, however, was focussed on a tall red-bearded Irishman in an obscenely tight russet-brown suit of scratchy-looking wool. Whatever could this strange Paddy have to do with Socialism? Jim wondered. Universal brotherhood was all very well but a line had to be drawn somewhere.

"There's only one delegate from the Fabian Society on this list," Sugden One was saying, "and that's a Mr De Mattos."

"That's me," said the Irishman.

"I thought you said your name were Shaw," said Sugden Two.

"No," crowed De Mattos/Shaw, "I said that my name was De Mattos, to be sure."

The Sugdens pointed to their list. "This mark shows that Mr De Mattos has already arrived."

"And that black line below is where my name's been crossed out," said Shaw, "Everyone knows me. I've been up here for three days and I've spoken at eight meetings already."

"Aye," sighed Sugden Two. "we walked out on you at Laycock's last night. Permeation! Permeation! Permeation! We thought you were never going to stop."

"But I've come all the way from London." Shaw somehow contrived to bestow four syllables on the capital.

"If coming from London had owt to do with it," said Sugden One, "then Dan Leno, Jack The Ripper and the bloody Queen would be writ down here an' all."

And so it was that on this very last step Jim lost his bet. Shaw's smile was dazzling, like someone throwing open a canteen of cutlery. Wherever had the fellow got hold of such teeth?

"What's all this permeation?" Jim asked Fred, as they went inside.

"It's the Fabians' great new scheme. Instead of forming our own party we join the Liberals and gradually radicalize them. As Aveling says, such a process would have to be measured in geological time."

"That Shaw looks like a police spy." Jim spoke softly for the Irishman was bigger than the gamekeepers and seemed to be mad rather than drunk.

"He's a writer of some sort," said Fred. "completely harmless."

Once the delegates were off the street they tore away their mufflers to reveal bright red ribbon-ties: a couple even perched eye-glasses on the end of their nose. Much though Jim admired Fred, he had never thought to copy him.

At the inner doorway, Keir Hardie was greeting each delegate in turn. He had a reputation for never forgetting a face or a name, although this was hard to confirm because everyone was 'laddie' or 'lassie' to him. Jim had to admit, though, that when those tiny black eyes locked on to his he felt that this was a man he had known and trusted all his life.

Hardie had recently been elected Independent MP for West Ham South, although the Cockneys understood hardly a word of his broad Lanarkshire. He was wearing the same outfit that had so scandalized the House of Commons: rough tweed jacket and dogstooth check knickerbockers with a ragged purple comforter tied in a hangman's knot and white canvas shoes. His left sleeve was rolled back to reveal the famous watch that bore the teeth marks of a pit pony from his years down the mines. Jim suspected that the soft metal casing displayed the configuration of the man's own scanty fangs. With his matted hair and shaking hands it seemed that he had arisen from his death-bed to utter some terrible final prophesy but apparently he had always looked this way. The puffy grey lips did not move when he spoke: "There's a problem with the pencils, laddies." The voice was breathless, as if he had made a perilous journey across country, pursued by packs of hounds.

The wide high-ceilinged hall was filled with long trestle tables draped with bolts of scarlet cloth. Each delegate's place was laid with a stack of vellum flanked by two pencils. Hardie's eagle eye had seen from the gold lettering that these had come from a notoriously anti-union firm. On Fred's signal, Jim sent his bale of properly Socialist pencils rolling along the Executive Committee's dais.

"Here's two gross, ladies and gentlemen," he announced, "But I'm afraid you'll have to sharpen them yourselves."

The sweet smell of cut wood filled the air as the hundred delegates whittled away. As Jim gathered up the rejected pencils he regretted that his own suggestion of having just one huge round conference table had been ignored. They could have told the papers that they were founding a Second Camelot. He had to admit, however, that it was difficult to imagine Hardie as being able to even lift Excalibur and harder still to see sturdy Mrs Bullock from the Women's Labour Union as Guinevere. And Merlin and Lancelot had apparently declined to attend. There were no flagons of mead or silver wine goblets, only chipped and various jugs and carafes, brimming with well-boiled but still turbid water. Most of the delegates had followed Hardie in signing the Temperance Pledge.

The two Sugdens had taken their places, locking the doors behind them, but Shaw could still be heard outside. Although the plain glass lancets were a full seven feet off the ground, his flat-topped head kept appearing. "Affiliated delegate!" It was wonderful how he was able to jump and shout at the same time.

A full two-thirds of the assembly were from the northern textile areas, with half a dozen Scottish Labour Associations and a smattering of small trade unions. Only four had come from south of Birmingham. "London's a broken reed, laddies," Hardie was always saying. A few of the Social Democratic Federation's Lancashire branches were represented but its inner circle – Hyndman and his anarcho-Communists – had remained in the metropolis.

Jim recognised Ben Tillett, an old comrade from the Manningham Strike. He was Alderman Tillett now. Fred always maintained that he had a sanctified air but with his broadbrimmed black hat and long poker face he reminded Jim of the man who parts you from your money at a cock-fight. Next to him was chubby Ben Turner who was always laughing, even when no-one else could see the joke. The press had styled him 'The most dangerous man in Britain' – a professional agitator, moving from strike to strike, dispensing funds from bottomless bags of gold – but Ben presented himself as a simple wandering weaver and versifier who by chance kept fetching up in all the wrong places. Jim prayed that he would not try to read one of his dreadful poems.

The befuddled Horner had lost his pencils. He disappeared under the table for a full two minutes before returning empty handed. The delegate from Keighley would not be taking notes. Across the aisle, Edward Aveling, Karl Marx's son-in-law, was watching in appalled fascination. He was swarthy, with a pronounced squint and there was something horribly wrong about the way his shoulders joined his neck but he was said to be irresistible to women. The more you wondered about such things the less sense they made. Aveling's legs were as bandy as Jim's own.

The warm fug of tightly-packed bodies had awakened an enormous bluebottle which began to fizz around the room. Perhaps this was the fraternal delegate from the Amalgamated Society of Dunghill Workers? Every time it passed, the normally gentle Fred flailed wildly but Jim himself did not move: his responsibility was security, not flies.

Up on the executive table a tiny figure struggled to its feet: W. H. Drew was opening the conference. He was so shrill that you would have taken him for a woman if it had not been for his enormous soup-strainer moustache.

"Mr Shaw has been going round town saying that this conference is premature. So we've decided not to waste any more of his valuable time." Pausing, he took a violent pinch of snuff which caused his voice to drop to a bass rumble before racking back up to its usual level. "It's not us that's too early but him and his permeations that's too late. The blows he thinks it will take a century to strike are already being struck."

As the cheers subsided, Fred rose to his feet. "Point of order, Comrade Drew. In the light of revised circumstances, I move that Delegate Shaw be readmitted to this conference."

"What revised circumstances?" squeaked Drew.

"It's snowing again."

Shaw's cries were getting fainter and his now white-capped head no longer appeared. Tellers were appointed and the hands went up. Forty-nine were for readmission and forty-six against. Scottish voices called for a recount and when the result was unchanged demanded another but the Sugdens were despatched, with obvious bad grace, to admit the permeationist.

"Before I cede this chair to Comrade Hardie," Drew continued, "I have been instructed to notify delegates that after the meeting you are all invited to a tea in Temperance Hall. It'll be nowt fancy though" – his near-scream drowned out the applause – "soup and buns is all we can run to by way of a feed."

Shaw entered at a trot, huge boots clattering as if shod with steel. Taking his place next to De Mattos – who did not noticeably welcome him – he ignored his unsharpened Socialist pencils, producing instead from his capacious pockets a green baize notebook, ink bottle and a beautiful silver-topped pen. Then he cracked his finger-joints and looked expectantly around. He resembled Mephistopheles, ready to draw up a contract for any souls that might be going cheap. Jim was sure that he could hear a forked tail thumping upon the floorboards.

❧

"For the right moment, you must wait, as Fabius did most patiently when warring against Hannibal, though many censured his delays; but when the time comes you must strike hard, as Fabius did, or your waiting will be in vain, and fruitless . . ."

Without raising his eyes from the page, Philip Snowden tracked his mother's progress around the living room. In the twenty-three months since his accident he had developed this intermediate sense, somewhere between sight and hearing. How he pitied the rest of humanity who, not being paralysed, would never even suspect the existence of such superhuman but useless powers! Mrs Snowden grasped the faded curtains, shook them violently, then let them fall.

This made no difference to the amount of light entering the room; it was merely a habit. And now she was going to do the furniture, moving each piece a few inches to the left then back again. She was still a strong woman, pushing and pulling the worm-riddled side-board with one arthritic hand. Philip saw, heard - no, felt - her lips slide over her teeth in a terrible smile: everything was in its proper place. And now she would polish the glass case of stuffed birds - a dingy pea-hen and a half-sawdust thrush - proudly displayed in the window to identify theirs as a Temperance house. Sometimes Philip's rascally uncle, and landlord of The Grinning Rat, would threaten to pot them with his fowling-piece, but only when his termagant sister-in-law was out of earshot.

It was fortunate that Mrs Snowden had a sense of humour: her God liked his little jokes. Just when the years of struggle had seemed to be over - with the girls married and Philip off to his new civil service career - Jack, her husband, newly promoted to overlooker, had dropped down dead. He had never had a single day's illness in his life. And now Philip had come home again, bed-ridden and helpless in his prime, unable to reach the door, let alone the earth-closet half-way up the fellside. It was as if the son was dying the father's death. The lines around her mouth and eyes had deepened and the skin tightened, turning her habitually mild expression into a sardonic mask. She had learned that no matter how bad things got, the worst was yet to come. This was not to punish your sins or test your faith: it was merely God's little joke. Now she appeared utterly content: if she herself had been a god she would have ordered things in exactly the same way.

He could feel her standing behind him, one hand on the door-knob, staring at the back of his head. Would she try to shave him again? He still insisted on doing it himself: as a result, his cheeks and chin were a patchwork of cuts and rusty fur and a hedge of beard ran under the jawline. Slowly he lowered the book until it touched his nose, then let the pages close around his face. The door's hinge and his mother's piercing laugh sounded the same resigned note.

Being alone was best. At first there had been a regular procession of former schoolmates, ex-colleagues, uncles and aunties, ministers and their congregations. Dutiful, well-intentioned folk, emanating sympathy and simple human kindness: every sentence they uttered was more idiotic than the one before. Even their breathing sounded stupid. Until his accident he had not been fully aware of such things.

Last week, after two years of sick leave, the Civil Service had invalided him out with a gratuity of £31. At first they had treated him as a malingerer, then as if he had, by some unspeakable sin, brought down these tribulations on himself. Yesterday, four policemen had come to repossess his bike: they acted as if he had stolen it and they were expecting him to put up a fight.

Philip had no idea how the accident had happened. There had been some rain and a light cross-wind, but nothing unusual. One moment he was on the bike, the next he was off. There had been no other traffic or passers-by. He had got to his feet, brushed himself down, tied a handkerchief round his barked shin, then remounted and cycled on. Still shaken, he had tried to ease down but his legs had insisted on pedalling away at their accustomed speed. That evening, after a hot bath, he had felt fully restored: it was a full two days before the paralysis gripped him while he slept.

You never got used to the pain. Sometimes it was dull and slow, like a hymn tune, but at others it tripped along like a Gilbert and Sullivan patter song. Pressing his palms against the offending areas provided some relief: they sopped it up like bread in gravy but then the ensuing finger cramps were even sharper, with every phalange and metacarpal having its own distinct ache. It stabbed, then it throbbed, then it stabbed and throbbed. He almost felt sorry for his pain: if he had no respite from it, then it had no respite from him.

Even worse than the pain was the stink, like a dead ewe left rotting in a ditch. It was unnatural to be aware of your own smell, let alone to be disgusted by it. He had taken up his father's old briar pipe: when the acrid black twist smouldered it was as if he was smoking away his own useless body.

He lowered *Fabian Essays* on to his chest. He had been reading so much that he was no longer aware of turning the pages: the words seemed to pass across his illuminated palms. Now his groping fingers found the shaving mirror, interposing it between the roughly-plastered ceiling and his own face. The eye-sockets were purple and the cheeks and forehead seemed to have been scorched. The tip of the nose – how long and narrow it had become! – glowed a drunkard's fiery red, although he had never touched a drop in his life. The chin had also changed shape, sharpening to resemble the blade of an adze. If the glass had not been cracked already, then that phiz would have done the trick.

The sofa on which he lay had been the bane of his childhood. It had protruded or sagged in all the wrong places, at once rock-hard and horribly enveloping. But now its contours perfectly fitted his broken frame: all these years it had been patiently awaiting his accident. The walls and ceiling felt to be expanding then contracting: one moment he was out on a vast empty plain, and the next narrowly confined, as if already in his coffin.

By twisting his neck he could trace, against the skyline, the jagged shape of Cowling Crag. He closed his eyes and imagined himself up there once again . . . First, he gazed across the valley to the Craven Highlands, then turned to the North West where sharp-prowed Ingleborough and Pen-Y-Ghent stood like twin men 'o' war exchanging broadsides. Then he dropped his gaze to scan the three hamlets of Cowling – Stotthill, Ickornshaw and Top End – until he had picked out, on the last terrace before the fells, the final house with its crooked chimney. He capped his view until he could see through the window a grotesque figure stretched across a shapeless sofa. And then he shrugged and turned away from himself, heading sure-footedly towards the mountains, without looking back.

At school Philip had always been the cleverest, especially in those subjects that did not appear on the curriculum. When, on his signal, pandemonium broke out in the classroom, he alone remained head down at his desk, piously scribbling away. The teachers had never suspected that he was the Top Lad, the one behind it all. They had even paid him to stay on as an assistant but unfortunately he had disciplined the pupils so much that they had been too terrified to learn. Now, he feared, he was never going to be behind anything again.

Having dodged the mill, the forge and the army, Philip had landed the best job of anyone in the whole parish. He had become a revenue man, surveying and gauging for the Excise at £50 a year. "Na' then, here's the scurvy gouger!" they would jeer on his infrequent returns to the village. And he had scurvily gouged from Liverpool to Plymouth, from Carlisle to Aberdeen. He'd even spent three fruitless months in the Orkneys: where, whenever they entered a harbour, flotillas of boats were just casting off. Sometimes it had been exciting, when smugglers fought or tried to run away, and he had stayed in proper hotels with chambermaids and silver jugs of warmed milk on the breakfast tables. He had cycled through thousands of miles of countryside: everywhere the leaves had their own distinctive rustle, each meadow was a slightly different green and endless varieties of wild flowers would come bursting out of the hedgerows.

Ting-ting! Parp-parp! How he had loved that bike! On particularly fine days he would find himself unnecessarily sounding the bell and horn simultaneously. He could ride with no hands: on long slow descents he would sit up with his fingers laced behind his head, whistling the Hallelujah Chorus. The whistling days were behind him too: his mouth was always dry and it was all he could do to breathe, the air dribbling in and out hardly reaching those congested lungs.

He recalled one particularly idyllic afternoon, pedalling across Salisbury Plain. Just beyond Western Camp he had espied three shotguns blasting away into a cloud of red grouse. He had already passed similar groups but something about this one caused him to stop. After a while you developed an instinct for such things. He propped the bike against a convenient gate which he then effortlessly vaulted. The hunters had ceased firing: he could see that their own instincts were telling them who he was.

"Revenue and Excise," he said, displaying the seal. His Yorkshire accent vanished whenever he was in his official capacity."May I please see your shooting licences" – he paused slightly – "Gentlemen?"

"I seem to have forgotten it," said the one in the too-small deerstalker, patting his pockets, while the oldest began spluttering.

"Look here, young man, don't you know who you're talking to?"

Yes, he had actually used those words, while his face had gone from puce to crimson.

"I could have sworn that I had it here in my wallet," said the youngest, in a surprisingly high-pitched voice. He was leafing through a thick wad of banknotes. First he held out a brown one, then a yellow one, then both together. But Philip merely smiled. Although that smile looked all right in the mirror it had a curious effect on folk. The man hurriedly put them away.

"This is sheer effrontery," said the splutterer. "Sansculottism run mad!"

"Your licence must be carried at all times," said Philip, examining their visiting cards."If it is not on your person then it cannot be said to exist. Nor is it valid retrospectively".

Two were baronets and the squeaky one turned out to be Sir Walter Long, Chief Secretary to The Treasury: so *that* was why he was carrying so much cash! Deerstalker's shotgun was twitching like a divining-rod: Philip could tell by the glitter in his eyes that the man really wanted to shoot him. All he had was the penknife in his pocket but he still felt in complete control of the situation. When those twin barrels finally touched the ground he knew that the man had acknowledged it too.

"You will be receiving your summonses in due course" – he smiled during the even longer pause – "Gentlemen".

And away he had cycled, as the grouse and cock-pheasants

mocked the impotent guns below. "Good-bye!" they clucked – "Good-bye! Good-bye!"

At least there had been one such perfect moment in his life! When he got home he had looked up 'sansculotte': they needn't have worried – he was too shy to ever take off his shirt in public.

Once more Philip took up his book. That grating sound was coming from his sternum: he would chant the words of Shaw's 'Transition' until it stopped.

"The Young Socialist is apt to be catastrophic in his views – to plan the revolutionary programme as an affair of twenty-four lively hours, with individualism in full swing on Monday morning, a tidal wave of the insurgent proletariat in the afternoon and socialism in complete working order on Tuesday."

This was reassuring: Philip had indeed feared that he might miss the whole show. Who could tell what might be happening in the world beyond Cowling? Every Saturday, when Mother brought his newspaper, he was relieved to find that the revolution had not yet taken place.

He had been working through his father's surprisingly wide-ranging library. The poets had been pleasant companions – who would have thought that Burns and Swinburne could be so racy? – but it was the political and speculative writers – Ruskin, Morris, Kirkup, Henry George – who had hooked him. It had been like tunnelling through to Australia and discovering that all was indeed turned on its head. So many heretical doctrines and so calmly and judiciously argued! Such anathemas against industrialism, ugliness and waste, against poverty and disease, against monarchy, bad sanitation and the Church! Most wonderfully, it was as if he had already known but had somehow forgotten all this, as if the true nature of his own mind was now revealing itself to him. He had been born a Socialist but had slumbered on unawares until the accident had awakened him. Perhaps it was a spirit, some socialist Ariel, that had overturned his bike, but miscalculated the impact and the extent of his injuries?

After the funeral Philip had discovered *Fabian Essays* down the side of his father's bed. The familiar bookmark – a faded postcard of Niagara Falls – was six pages from the end. He had worried that Dad, wherever he might be, would be vexed at never finishing it.

John Snowden had died four years before. He had arisen in the middle of the night, gurgled and expired without a word. Philip was not sure whether his mother had said 'gurgled' or 'giggled' but thought it callous to enquire further. Try as he might, he could no longer recall Dad's face even though he could picture every last one of his schoolmates taken off by the diphtheria epidemic fifteen years ago.

Philip was surprised at how extensively his father's pencil had been employed in the margins of his books. Exclamation and question marks were interspersed with lines of Xs large and small. He had ticked passages that he agreed with and scored out those he didn't. His comments were indecipherable, except for those baffling capitals – SULPHUR VALVE – above the Unearned Increment section. The final essay, the one that he had never finished – 'The Outlook' by Herbert Bland – was particularly heavily marked, with the pencil sometimes driven right through the paper. Unlike the other contributors, Bland called for the formation of a new party, a working-class alternative to the Liberals. Everything was in place, he argued, except for the necessary leader. "The eye expectant searches in vain for such a man now among the younger brood of the new democracy. He is possibly at this moment in his cradle and equitably sharing out toys and lollipops to his comrades of the nursery." His father had underlined the word 'lollipops' and filled the margin with squiggly vertical lines. Could he have found it amusing? This suspicion was hard to credit because Philip had never seen him crack a smile.

His father had never talked much about anything, least of all the past. Only once, visiting relations in Calderdale, had he let slip that the last time he had been in Halifax was as one of the eighty thousand Chartists converging on Skircoats Moor. That was eight times the strength of Henry V's army at Agincourt, four times that of Wellington's at Waterloo. "What was it like?" Philip had asked. "It were a bit of a crush," came the laconic reply. "And who won the battle?" At this his father had made a curious snuffling sound. Apparently they had listened to some speeches, applauded, sung some songs and then gone home. Philip gathered that the enemy – whose precise identity remained unclear – had declined to engage.

As a child Philip had wanted to be a preacher. He felt no vocation or burning faith, merely liked the idea of being looked at with respect and listened to in silence. After leaving home, however, he had discovered something even better. Acting: it was like a cathedral organ compared to a leaking harmonium. Even Pastor Grimshaw could only take his flock down to Hell then up to Heaven, whereas Henry Irving or Barry Sullivan, in one short speech, could bounce them half a dozen times between ecstasy and despair. Such dreams could be forgotten now, unless he confined himself to Richard Crookback and Caliban, but there was still another way of being listened to and looked at. In Aberdeen he had seen Kropotkin address a street corner meeting: the princely anarchist had hardly finished clearing his throat before the previously apathetic crowd were in a frenzy. Then, in Nelson Town Hall, there had been Charles Bradlaugh, 'The Iconoclast', debating in favour of atheism – but with such authority, good humour and grace, that he had seemed himself to be the very embodiment of the Divine. And there was Dad's old favourite, the American economist Henry George: he had spoken haltingly, almost inaudibly, but the rapt crowd were almost finishing his sentences for him.

You didn't need to be able to move in order to read, think and speak. Folk could carry you onto the platform and afterwards lift you down again. Philip's memory had always been sharp but now he could recall every word he read. Some untapped part of his brain was synthesising all the information into logical and accessible arguments, suitably adorned with similes and metaphors, quotations from the Bible and the poets, homespun jokes and ironies. He had no illusions that he might be an original thinker, but he was sure that he could proselytize, expressing and embodying the ideas of others, setting them to his own pain-racked inner music and before giving them thrilling utterance.

Now, to his relief, the grinding bones were no longer audible, but his spine jarred every thirty seconds as if he was being dropped from a considerable height. Each impact triggered a volley of sneezes: his head seemed to be trying to rip itself from his condemned body. At least the doctor had told him straight: he was a hopeless cripple with only a few, doubtless miserable, years to live. But even as the man had been pronouncing this sentence, Philip had felt a great surge of hope. It had risen from his solar plexus, filling his lungs, constricting his throat and then bursting in his brain as an utter conviction that a great, unimaginable future lay ahead of him. And the more common sense told him that this could not be, the more certain he became. He would never be the man he had been before – the top lad and the scurvy gouger were gone for good – but he could feel each word he read moving him closer to his rebirth. He was no longer waiting for death. Even though he could hardly lift this book, let alone a standard or a sword – he was waiting like the original Fabius Maximus for the right moment to strike. The next thing to do was to work on his smile.

಼

The voices droned on and on. Jim could no longer follow what was being said: the words were merely flickering patterns like the snowflakes in the rising wind. His face was burning and sweat dripped on to the still blank paper but from the waist down he became increasingly chilly until his feet felt to be encased in ice. He had finished snapping the non-union pencils between forefinger and thumb; the fly had dashed itself to death against the windowpane. If he had been granted wings he might have done the same.

At least he had some excuse for moving, stamping across the room to gather the empty water carafes. Horner was apparently trying to sluice himself back into sobriety. Although there had been no break in proceedings, not one delegate had left their place: even their bladders were committed to the cause.

As if being boring was not enough, most of them were ugly as well. Ears and noses were either huge or vestigial and heads and limbs seemed to have somehow attached to the wrong bodies. Horner apart, everyone was unnaturally pale: the executive committee were decomposing before Jim's eyes. At least his own ugliness was of an individual and striking nature.

Shaw was not exactly ugly but he had some curious mannerisms. He would grip his ankles then force his knees up to touch his jutting chin. He took from his pocket handfuls of nuts and raisins, wadded with fluff, which he would cram into his mouth and – despite those remarkable teeth – swallow without chewing. Jim's attentions switched to a small man dressed in light grey except for a high-collared shirt of dazzling whiteness. The hair had been cut close to the skull but the black moustache, gleaming like a well-tended piece of ordnance, was so enormous that it shadowed the lower part of his face. It was 'Nunquam' – Robert Blatchford himself, editor of *The Clarion*, voice and conscience of the movement, whose words, declaimed by Fred, had cut through the frowsty air of the weaving shed. The head and neck never moved but the man's dark, liquid eyes, expressing a mixture of amusement and scorn, ceaselessly swept the room. Although silent so far, he seemed to be on the point of saying something truly momentous.

For the last half hour Conference had been debating what their new party should call itself. Carson and Smillie of Lark Hill – in accents even thicker than Hardie's – favoured 'Socialist Labour Party'. What did it matter? It might as well be called 'The Schlis-La-Ba-Pa-Da' as anything else. 'The Will of the People', someone suggested. "No, the Cause of the People," said someone else. "The Sword!" a beefy lad from Lilycroft shouted, while his neighbours

24

ducked his flailing arms. "The People's Sword!" All of these had to be proposed and seconded before they were voted down. "Why not . . . 'The Future'?" came a deep voice from the back. Fortunately, no-one would even second this. Then one of the SDF contingent got to his feet, clenched his fist and said, very slowly and emphatically, "S . . . D . . . F!"

This was too much for Ben Tillet. The very thought of Marxism was enough to set him off. He launched a tirade against "hare-brained chattering magpies of continental revolutionists," looking pointedly at Aveling who was reportedly the eyes and ears of Friedrich Engels. When Ben had exhausted himself Hardie gave the right of reply to an ex officio journalist from *Vorwarts!*, a German radical paper. Jim was delighted to see that this individual – with oiled black hair and long pale face, protruding eyes and a manner at once timid and aggressive – did indeed resemble a magpie crossed with a hare. Anyone more calculated to raise the hackles of an honest English working man could scarcely be imagined.

After Herr Bernstein had finished, Aveling rose. He was the same height standing as sitting down.

"May I suggest that for now 'Independent Labour Party' be retained. The name is immaterial, comrades. What matters is the programme and the constitution." Now Jim understood the secret of his allure: there was a whole orchestra in that voice. It was as if the sound were descending from heaven, reaching a crescendo as it passed through Aveling's larynx, then floating up again to exit through the skylight. The three women in the room seemed initially unaffected but then Jim saw a scarlet tide slowly spreading up Katharine St. John Conway's long, long neck. She was one of those frightening Girton girls, so devastatingly smart and sweet that he did not dare look into her face. Now vast Mrs Bullock had begun to wriggle and tiny Mrs Reynolds to languorously stretch her limbs. Why was Aveling wasting his time on politics? If Jim had been in his shoes he would have swept up all three of them and been off to bed until Spring.

Now Conference was away again into a maze of motions and counter-motions, proposers seconded and seconders proposed, composites, points of order and references back to references back. Jim had a panicky sense of time passing, as if when they got outside they might find themselves in suddenly unfamiliar streets, with everything having changed without them. "I can't take much more of this," he muttered but Fred merely nodded vigorously, as if he took these words to be an enthusiastic endorsement of the proceedings.

Fred would put up with any amount of faffing about if there were the slightest chance of achieving something at the end. He was usually right, but the more Jim recognized this, the more uneasy he became. Their friendship had been the making of him but he was not sure that he liked having been made. True, Fred would listen respectfully to him, but after a couple of minutes Jim would become aware of the inadequacy of the words coming out of his mouth. He would stutter, then fall silent, and Fred would gravely resume his monologue.

It was not only politics that Fred had revealed to him. Before they met, Jim had been oblivious to Nature. He was astonished to find that there were wild places so close to the heart of the city. Fred took him down to Heaton Woods where, under the shade of the trees, all smells and sounds of industry vanished. Here Fred's vision was curiously restored, his eyes catching the tiniest bird on the highest branch, the merest shadow of a squirrel's tuft. He moved quickly and silently, blending into the greens and browns despite his dark suit. The undergrowth seemed impenetrable but wherever Fred set his foot, a path would obligingly appear.

Jim recalled how the young rabbits did not seem to hop but to be gently tipped forward by invisible hands. When their soft noses had sniffed at the toes of his boots he had resisted the urge to stamp on them, suspecting that this would not be the Socialist thing to do. A line of bristling jays had perched on a branch, screaming warnings to which they themselves paid no regard, while two young kestrels, under their parents' unblinking gaze, plummeted from the rocks above, flattening out at the last moment to claw their way back up, as if the air was a solid thing to them. Each time the birds fell, it was straighter and more slowly until, at last, they began to swoop.

Jim had found it disturbing that all these creatures needed to learn how to run and fly and hunt and be afraid of men. Apparently everything had to be taught how to be itself.

"All of Creation starts out the same," Jowett had said. "Alone. Helpless. Lost."

"And most stay that way an' all." Jim had been surprised by the strength of the grip on his arm when Fred replied. "Not for much longer, Comrade!"

Who would have thought that there could be such variety of butterfly and moth? Each appeared equally miraculous, as if it were the first he had ever seen. And so many songs and cries, that seemed only to deepen the silence behind them! But according to Fred, this was not even the half of it.

"Our chatter scares away the deer, foxes, badgers and wolves. You should come down here on your own some time."

"Wolves?" Jim was not sure whether he was excited or scared.

"Not real ones," Fred laughed, "just a pack of feral lurchers from Laisterdyke way."

When Jim returned a few days later it had been a disaster. Everything was grey and dripping, although he had not been aware of any intervening rain. Fred's tracks now led into deep bogs or impossible gulleys. The stepping stones by which they had blithely crossed the beck had become slimy and unsafe. The water was stagnant and discoloured: everything smelt of rot and decay. Nothing stirred, no birds sang and the only insects were black flies that darted into his face. The silence was no longer magical but a menacing absence of sound. He had the sense of being watched, malevolently: perhaps the dogs were sizing him up? He turned and ran, churning through the mud so that, as he sobbed with exertion and shame, the whole bank seemed to be shifting beneath his feet.

Before, he had been able to share Fred's delight but now, alone, he had been given the woods he deserved. At last the great square-topped chimney of Lister's Mill had risen before his eyes. It was the first time that he had regarded it with anything other than loathing.

"Hum culneys," a Scottish voice was saying. "Hum culneys." Opening his eyes, Jim realized that his head had tilted right back. He hoped that he had not been snoring: his brothers said that it sounded like a hen fighting with a sow. Perhaps this explained his failures with women: they could pick out the snorers. "Dignity in work for all our people," Hardie continued. This Home Colonies scheme – mass road construction for the unemployed – was his hobby-horse, equivalent to Jowett's sanitation. Jim had never understood how navvying could be ennobling. Why not just put the money in their hands and send them off to the pub until it was time for them to be digging graves, with the rich making their own contribution by filling them?

In the New Jerusalem there would be an eight-hour working day, with overtime and piecework abolished. Children under fourteen were to be banned which seemed a good idea until Jim realized that it was merely a raising of the working age. For a moment it had seemed that university education would be compulsory for all but Conference were divided on whether it should be secular or non-sectarian. The executive wanted to extend suffrage to women. As far as Jim was concerned, women were welcome to all the suffrage they wanted, so long as no-one was stupid enough to give them the vote.

"The chair recognizes Comrade Blatchford," Drew squeaked. For the first time in the day there was a smattering of applause as the man, apparently savouring the drama of the moment, rose slowly to his feet. He cleared his throat, looked around the room, then cleared his throat again. The well-tanned face turned pale and his papers slipped from his grasp. The pronounced Adam's apple bobbed alarmingly and the eyes seemed to have rolled back into their sockets. Three times he tried and failed to balance his

28

gold pince-nez on the bridge of his aquiline nose. His trembling hands poured a glass of water but he did not attempt to drink it. The silence only lasted a minute but it felt like forever. Fred's face showed genuine distress, his lips moving like an unheeded prompter at a play. At last Blatchford sat down or, rather, seemed to plummet a considerable distance back into his chair.

If this man had not written 'Merrie England', if he had not somehow drawn those words from his heart and soul, then this conference would almost certainly not have been taking place. Not one of these delegates – not Hardie, not Tillet, not even Fred – would have been the men they were. And there he sat, head in hands, a lord of language who now could not form a single syllable. He was said to be a great drinker who held forth in crowded taprooms for hours on end, but take the glass out of his hand and set him on his feet before a seated audience and he was paralyzed. All these nondescript little men around him were utterly self-assured, certain of their opinions and their right to be here. As Jim watched, Blatchford became Blatchford once more: the noble head rose, the broad chest expanded and he let out a great guffaw at the sheer absurdity of the thing. Why was their main polemicist called Nunquam – the Latin for 'never'? Why not Nunc – 'now' – or at least 'brevi' – 'soon'? With Nunquam you were buggered from the start.

Now Shaw was speaking again. Any hope that he might be cowed by the general hostility and hold a watching brief had proved to be ill-founded. With Hardie and Drew tacitly ceding the chairmanship, he had taken over the meeting. The room seemed to be filled with contending Shaws. Everything flowed through him: he summed up each debate, putting the conclusion into simply-worded resolutions that were also strangely memorable, almost musical. "To secure the collective ownership of the means of production, distribution and exchange": Shaw had almost sung the words.

Jim was struck by how even the Scotsmen and the SDF were allowing this to happen. They obviously did not admire the man's talents: in fact, they seemed to despise him all the more, as if what he was doing were beneath them. Jim was reminded of the racing on the Knavesmire when the Dukes and Earls emerged to congratulate their victorious jockeys – half-starved, mud-spattered midgets whose legs were even bandier than his own. The expressions on those florid faces had been exactly the same.

Only Drew had put up some resistance. "Does the delegate from the London Fabian Society" – he shrilled – "Actually believe in anything he is saying?"

"Whether I support these measures or not is beside the point," Shaw replied patiently. "We owe it to the language to ensure that everything is clearly expressed."

And he proceeded to define the conference's fiscal stance: "Abolition of indirect taxation and taxation – to extinction – of unearned income." Every hand was raised in approval. Or almost every hand, for when Hardie did call for any dissenters, a single, unusually long arm was seen punching towards the ceiling. Shaw was voting against his own proposal.

೭೫%

When the wind got up and the rain turned to snow, Victor Grayson took shelter beneath an enormous roadside oak. The swaying branches were laden with dead leaves but even over their rustlings he could still hear the howling of the wolves. Digging his fingers painfully into the wet bark he began to climb. The wolves seemed to be no nearer but now their sounds were coming from every direction at once. Victor's grip began to slacken, then an agitated branch swept him up and deposited him within scrambling distance of the tree's central fork.

Although it was only four hours since he had set out he was already desperately hungry. He had taken the last apple from the dusty fruit-bowl and wrapped it in a cleanish handkerchief which he then lashed to the thickest splinter of his shattered cricket bat. He didn't much like fruit but without an apple and a hanky on a stick a boy could not be considered to be properly running away from home. Unfortunately, when the factories and houses had given way to woods and fields and he had stopped to rest, he discovered that - although he had heard no sound and felt no easing of his burden - the apple had gone. It looked as if something had chewed through the cotton: only the granny-knot remained. He had re-traced his steps but the apple had made good its escape. Although the stick might still serve as a cudgel it would be of little use against his pursuers. Why had no one warned him about the wolf-packs of West Lancashire?

Pressing his ear against the trunk he could hear a deep regular throbbing: the sound of the heart of the tree. Under his breath he began to sing:

> "Hearts of oak are our ships
> Hearts of oak are our men"

His voice gained strength as the branch beneath him creaked its encouragement.

> "We are always ready
> Steady, boys, steady.
> We'll fight and we'll conquer
> Again and again."

His own body felt as if it was full of hearts - beating away in chest and head, in his palms and the soles of his feet, in kneecaps and ankles and between his legs - as if he was not one person but an assembly of different creatures.

Victor Grayson - The Little Roamer. "He runs away that often," his mother had said, "that whenever he *is* at home, the rest of the world sends out search parties for him." Today his destination was not Dickens' London or the glens and peaks of Sir Walter Scott but the furthest and most fabulous of all - America. Although he

31

knew that there at the bottom of the hill was the Mersey which led to the sea which then became an ocean which would in time wash him up in New York Harbour, he had found himself walking in the opposite direction. Victor had long ago learned always to trust his own feet. Perhaps the maps had all been designed to keep small boys from running away and you should go East when they showed West, go North instead of South? Perhaps those blue parts were really land and the red parts water?

The more it snowed, the warmer he became. The howling continued but, up in his tree, he was feeling very much at home. He had always loved to hide. At home, whenever he heard footsteps approaching, he would dive under the bed, now that he was too big to fold his limbs inside his father's chest of drawers. There was a delicious pleasure in the waiting: wondering who might find him and how long it would take them-even though it was usually a matter of seconds and almost always his mother.

Victor realized that he had begun to whistle and that the wind seemed to be trying to join in. It was the tune that Professor Sweeney's Cowboy Band had been playing just six months before as Buffalo Bill Cody and his Congress of Rough Rides of the World entered the sawdust ring at Newsham Park: 'There'll Be A Hot Time In The Old Town Tonight'.

The touring company had arrived at Lime Street Station in three long, long trains - one for the scenery, one for the cowboys and Indians, one for the horses, buffalo, elk and deer. The large bright posters on almost every wall in town promised "An absolutely original and heroic enterprise of inimitable lustre." When Victor had asked a teacher what the word 'lustre' meant her lips had twisted and her ruler had rapped his knuckles even more loudly than usual.

On their way into the enormous tent his father had bought him a paper cone filled with hot, soft, salty buttered husks. They called it pop-corn: the more you chewed it the more it grew until your mouth was crammed.

Dad was still moaning about the cost of the pop-corn: "A whole bloomin' ha'penny" – when a voice from the heavens, booming over the music, had cut him off.

"Colonel William H Cody, Greatest of the Indian Fighters, Buck-skinned Bayard of the Old Frontier, Defence and Succour of Womanhood And Children" and there in a crimson shirt and fringed cream buckskins was Bill, galloping his white horse, Charlie, through the smoke and dust, twirling his lasso so that the loop hung steady above his head, like a halo.

He had proceeded to rope and hog-tie three wild Texas steers before Victor could empty his mouth, then teased a succession of drunken-looking buffalo before giving way to 'The Peerless Lady Wing-shot', Annie Oakley. She was less than five feet tall, her angelic face framed by dark brown curls. Her smile never wavered as she loaded, aimed and fired her Springfield Rifle, unerringly drilling a series of playing cards that her assistant held sideways on, next to his right cheek. Then, while Professor Sweeney and his boys went into a breakneck version of the 1812 Overture, a vast elk ambled out of the shadows, fixed the audience with a long disapproving stare and ambled off again.

Now Victor's tree suddenly decided to rid itself of him but he stayed on the bucking branch like one of Bill's bareback riders. He wished that he could understand the leaves' rustling but perhaps they were only saying help, help, we're going to fall. He told himself that he was always going to remember this moment even though he had felt the same way on hundreds of occasions and had subsequently forgotten them all.

His had been a strange childhood. As a toddler he had nearly drowned in a fast-flowing spring stream. He wasn't sure whether he had fallen or jumped or even been pushed. The world had watched helplessly from the bank as he was borne along until the waters reached a mill-race where he had passed miraculously unscathed through the mill-wheel's spinning blades. As he lay recovering in bed half of Liverpool had shuffled past, touching his forehead for healing, protection or good luck.

Then for two and a half years he had lost his voice. There had been so much to say, so many questions to ask, that it all got tangled up so that he was left trying - with only one thick and furry tongue - to express a thousand things at once. When your tongue was tied you could only communicate through actions: it was no longer enough to merely dream about something, you had to go out and do it. Nothing had seemed to be beyond him: he had discovered that if you act as if what you want is your rightful due, then it often falls out that you get it. It was true what The Bible said: "To him that hath shall be given and from him that hath not shall be taken away even that which he hath." This was why he was whistling up in his tree. If he ever stopped making a noise he might be silenced for ever.

He recalled how in Liverpool the elk and deafening cannons had been succeeded by the surviving veterans of the Charge of the Light Brigade. Too old to ride, they had marched stiffly past under a tattered and faded union jack. Then the arena had exploded with men, fighting. The Sioux were finishing off the Seventh Cavalry at Little Big Horn. Brandishing General Custer's long yellow scalp, the redskins rode around the ring at breathtaking speed only to be ambushed in their turn by Buffalo Bill, leading another cavalry troop. They were augmented by Prince Ivan and his Ukrainian Cossacks and a bunch of gorgeously-attired gauchos who just happened to be passing. Much retributive slaughter had followed. In a ferociously convincing knife fight, Bill killed Yellow Hand, then crouched over the body to spring upwards, clutching a red-dripping pigtail with a great shout of "The first scalp for Custer!" At the last, the mutilated corpses had dragged themselves to their feet, joined hands with their murderers and, smiling broadly, advanced on the wildly applauding audience.

From fully thirty yards away, the glittering eyes of the Indians - introduced as Little Bull, Cut Meat, Black Elk, Poor Dog, Rain-in-the-Face - caught and held Victor's own and he felt a spark of recognition passing between them. Now he understood that the cowboys and the Indians were on the same side and that their real enemies were the audience, the good people of Liverpool, as they cheered to the echo something that they could not even begin to understand. America! America! Victor had glared down on the mayor and corporation who – together with their golden chains of office – were occupying the front two rows. Cut Meat and Rain-in-the-Face would have polished them off before they could even bleat, only they were not worth killing. How could you scalp a bald-headed man? He had glanced at Dad who, purple-faced and choking, was having another of his coughing fits.

This bent and broken man was not his real father. Mum was not his real mother. He looked nothing like either of them. Liverpool was not his rightful home: its air would never fill his lungs. Victor dreamed of a bigger, hotter sun and of rains that fell more softly on his skin and of strange people who seemed to be neither male nor female. Yesterday, on John Brown Street, a couple of middle-aged men, notably well-dressed but unshaven, had fallen silent as he passed. Although they were men they had smelt strangely fragrant, just like his headmistress. Stopping at the corner he had seen that they were still standing there, staring at him. Then he had turned and run away, although he had really wanted to be running back towards them.

The wolves were very close now, although their cries kept breaking off for longer and longer periods. Every time they stopped Victor realized that he was praying for them to take up their song again. It had a curiously soothing and sentimental tone, like the Saturday night drunks singing on Scotland Road. Perhaps they didn't want to harm him but to save him, to carry him like Romulus or Remus off to their own wolfish world. For some reason he imagined those two smart and silent gentlemen throwing back their heads and howling.

Victor had always known that he was not like everybody else. He had been christened Albert Victor after the eldest son of the Prince of Wales and had often wondered if he was not himself some kind of Lost Prince. He had read how Bill Cody, supposedly the child of poor Irish emigrants, had always felt the blood of Milesius and the First Kings of Erin pumping through his veins.

If he really was a Grayson, then he could console himself with the knowledge that he was the seventh son of a seventh son. A gypsy at the fair had told him that this would give you unimaginable powers. You were so unlucky that you became lucky, misfortunes turned to your advantage, and your weaknesses all became strengths, as if an enormous hand had seized the earth and turned it upside down.

At school the bullies left him alone. At first this had upset him: how vile and insignificant you must be if even they wanted nothing to do with you! Then one of the girls had told him that they were all terrified of him – that they could see by his eyes that he was not afraid and that if they were to start a fight he was the one that would never stop. Victor was unsure about this but thought it best not to disabuse her.

Until the Rough Riders all his secret games had been drawn from The Bible. In David and Goliath he would play both parts, clutching at himself until it really did feel – in that mixture of triumph and exhilaration, humiliation and terror – that he was sawing off his own head. He loved the way that Samson smote those Philistines but where in Liverpool could you obtain the jawbone of an ass? He often tickled the ears of the coalman's donkey: how could so deadly a weapon be drawn from such a gentle beast?

The crucifixion was his favourite, though. He would stand on the low playground wall, head on one side, eyes shut, while all the girls looked up at him adoringly. None of the other boys could balance on its rounded top for more than a few seconds but he had once remained there for a whole lunchtime. For so long, in fact, that his admirers had become bored and, in the order of their prettiness, drifted away, until only Lorrie – silent, shapeless, almost a cretin – had remained.

But now all his dreams and fantasies were about Buffalo Bill. 'The Defence and Succour of Womanhood and Children'. Victor wondered why he needed to *suck* them. Presumably they had been bitten by rattlesnakes and Bill was pressing his lips to their wounds, drawing back the venom and spitting it out. Victor could actually feel that sharp, wagging beard scratching insistently at the crook of his elbow.

"Bill Cody! Bill Cody!" he cried into the teeth of the gale. As if in answer the howling started up again but it was somehow different now, with a vulgar, yelping note. Looking down, Victor could see that a swaddled form resembling an enormous bandaged thumb was being drawn through the snow by two shivering lurchers, straining on the ends of long pieces of rope. Other dogs and well-wrapped men came ploughing after them.

"I said there were! I said there were!" – the high squeak seemed to be coming through the wire muzzle of the smallest dog rather than from its master – "I said there were a little lad up in yon tree!"

꩜

Point of order, reference back. What a contrast between this snail-like progress and the restless energy that Jim had sensed on the street! The meeting was more like an attempt to negate it. He suspected that every shade of political opinion would be united by contempt and fear of the crowd.

Point of order, reference back. Jim was beginning to feel sick. Perhaps Socialism was like the purple medicine that his mother would ladle out for all ailments? It had made him vomit and brought out his hair in handfuls: apparently these had been sure signs that it was doing him good. Tom Maguire from Holbeck caught his eye and grimaced, then mimed tightening a noose around his neck, lolling out his blue-black tongue. Every few minutes Tom was seized by a fierce coughing fit but fortunately he was able to smoke and cough at the same time. He kept spitting into what Jim had at first taken to be a red-spotted handkerchief.

For the last half hour Conference had been discussing the

Central Election Fund. Should individual contributions be tuppence or tuppence ha'penny? The aim was to exclude larger, anonymous payments such as in the Tory Gold Scandal, when their enemy had stumped up for the deposits of SDF candidates standing against Liberals in marginal seats.

"What's wrong with Tory Gold?" Maguire's patience was exhausted. "Why shouldn't we take money from Satan himself so long as it's used for the cause? We have one thing in common with the Tories: we need to destroy the Liberals. And when they're out of the way we can move on to the real task. Why shouldn't the Conservative Party pay for its own funeral?"

The other delegates had been openly contemptuous of Shaw but they looked as if they hated Maguire. He had organized the gasworkers', clayworkers' and tailoresses' strikes and was now submerged in the shadowy world of the Jewish radicals. Strangely, he still professed allegiance to William Morris' Socialist League, even though it had collapsed three years ago and not even Morris himself had remained a member. No employer would hire him so he was trying to eke out a living as a photographer. His camera and tripod were propped against the wall behind him.

Conference seldom referred to the Liberals or Tories and then only in neutral terms. They had also retained a vestigial respect for the aristocracy and if anyone mentioned the Queen, the words "God bless her" seemed to hang in the air. Their real hatred was reserved for one another. Jim found this strange because the various factions looked and sounded alike. They had the same mirthless laugh and the same sneer, as if their upper lips had been snagged by an angler's line. There were a few identifying characteristics: the London group sat with their legs crossed, the Christian Socialists all had colds, the Labour Army had the biggest ears but otherwise, interchangeable grey men spouted the same platitudes in identical flat voices. At least they could have been given differently coloured uniforms with gold braid and rows of medals, with sabres to rattle and well-polished boots to stamp.

Now Drew was proposing that the new organisation should remain a federation. He fiercely upheld the autonomy of the region, the city and the district branch, but above all he upheld the autonomy of W. H. Drew. This was carried, to be followed by a second motion that Conference should be supreme, electing an executive committee to implement its instructions. This was passed with equal enthusiasm.

"But you can't have both!" Shaw was actually slapping his knees with mirth. "A federation is one thing and an executive committee is another. They're opposites. You've created a two-headed freak of nature: one head is a dog's while the other is a cat's – they will either tear each other to pieces or run off in opposite directions." Conference, however, was not in the mood to be persuaded. Wasn't it the whole point of Socialism to make the seemingly impossible a reality?

And now silence fell. The agenda had been completed. There was no further business. Nothing more could be said. No-one dared to look up in case they saw their own consternation on other faces. What on earth was going to happen now?

Then Hardie's voice yelled: "Where is the Labour Party?" Some delegates actually flinched, as if they were being accused of stealing it, before realizing that this must be a rhetorical question.

"We are here," Hardie continued, "Such as we are, such as circumstances have created us, the expression of our inborn, or undying determination on the part of the democracy of this land to assert itself in its own spirit and through its own methods."

Jim had no idea what this might mean and nor, he suspected, did anyone else.

"But after all has been said," Hardie wagged a bony finger, "We maun gang oor ain gate." This broke the tension: everyone knew that they must laugh whenever dialect was employed.

"Nothing is more conducive to spirit-breaking, than a snarling, querulous, frivolous criticism of everybody and everything." Was it Jim's imagination or had Hardie's gaze lingered on him on its way from Maguire to Shaw? "The eyes of the country are on Bradford," he continued, pausing until a cheer went up, so faint that it might have floated across the valley as City scrambled a last-minute consolation goal.

"The party politicians are looking – and looking longingly – in the hope of seeing the apple of discord embedded in your midst. But behind these are the wailing voiceless millions whom we specially represent." An eerie sound could be heard – "Wooo! Wooo!" It was Shaw, delightedly exploring the possibilities of voiceless wailing. Jim was beginning to warm to the man.

"If we go forward in this spirit I am convinced that – to slightly adapt a couplet from an old Scottish ballad –

> 'Children yet unborn shall bless
> The concord of that day.'"

With a little nod of satisfaction Hardie resumed his seat. Even before the stormy applause had died away Jim could hear Shaw haranguing De Mattos. "Why should this mysterious apple appear in 'your' rather than 'our' midst? Is the man himself above such temptations? And can we anticipate an influx of contending Greek goddesses? 'Aphrodite Vainly Importuning Comrade Hardie For The Apple Of Beauty' – now there's a subject for Mr Watts' brush! But surely an apple – even a discordant one – cannot be embedded, otherwise we would be unable either to eat it or bestow it. And whatever could it be embedded *in*? Such things do matter." – De Mattos had clapped his hands over his ears – "They matter more than anything else."

Shaw Maxwell was now saluting Hardie's chairmanship and, as a memento of the occasion, presenting him with the conference bell. Grasping it with both hands Hardie gave it a vigorous shake but no sound issued forth. Closer examination revealed that the clapper had been removed. "How very appropriate," crowed Shaw, "Ding-Dong! Ding-Dong!"

Then Conference sang 'The Red Flag', a new song written by an Irish comrade. Everyone caught the tune but only Shaw seemed to know all the words.

> "Though cowards flinch and traitors sneer,
> We'll keep The Red Flag flying here."

"Bravo!" Shaw was clapping his hands. "That sounded like the funeral march of a fried eel!" He seemed determined to get himself assaulted before the meeting broke up. Now he was grabbing the arms of two SDF men for the singing of 'Auld Lang Syne'. When they struggled he only clutched them tighter, like a benevolent python.

"That felt more like six years than six hours." Jim was surprised to hear an unfamiliar whining note in his own voice.

"But it was worth it," said Fred, slowly, "Because that might have been the most important political event of the century."

"Nay, Fred," Tom Maguire called across the room, "There's still seven years to go."

"This is how change happens," Fred continued, unabashed. "A small group of people sitting talking in a shabby room. Real history isn't like Cromwell seizing the mace or Alexander cutting the Gordian Knot."

"But why does it all have to take so long?" Jim was sounding even more plaintive.

"I'm afraid that your patience is going to be severely tried." They moved towards the exit, "But when the great day dawns it will be well worth the wait."

Why was Fred talking about patience when they had not even given impatience a proper try? Why were self-styled Socialists advocating consolidation when there was nothing to consolidate, negotiation when there was nobody to negotiate with, and falling out with each other when the rest of the world was already ranged against them? Why didn't they fight for a little while – take to the streets, open the prisons, set up the guillotines – if only to see what happened?

Maguire, shouldering with difficulty his camera and tripod, led them outside. The commemorative photographs would be taken in front of the cathedral, Maguire having been talked out of storming the millowners' gothic Wool Exchange. Most of the delegates, however, were shunning posterity in favour of the Temperance Hall's soup and buns. Some were already off down Chapel Street, led by Shaw, his arms and legs pumping, and Ben Turner, who was picking up speed like a runaway piano. Jim suspected that there would be precious few buns left when the rest of Conference arrived.

The snow had stopped and the sun had come out at last, a scarlet disc balancing on the horizon. It seemed to be delaying its departure in order to accommodate Maguire and his camera. Hardie, Drew, Aveling and the rest were shuffling towards it.

"Fred, when do you think Socialism will come?" Jim was relieved that his voice was back to normal.

"Well into next century. By 1930, if I had to make a guess. But sometimes I fear that I may never see it, not even if I live to be an old man."

"So what is the point? Why are we doing all this?"

"For The People. For our grandchildren. For their grandchildren. For people that we will never know, living lives we cannot even begin to imagine."

"And they'll remember us," Jim had begun to stammer, "There will be streets and towns with our names. And we'll be holidays: there'll be no work done on Jowett Mondays and Sharp Fridays. And they'll even put up statues of us." – he glanced down at his own legs – "Equestrian ones."

"I hope not," said Fred. "If we are remembered it will only be to be blamed for our failures. If they forget us it will mean that we have discharged our duties."

Outlined against the sunset, the Cathedral looked more like a fortress than a place of worship, rearing above the mills as if to warn the delegates that if they did get rid of Mammon they would still have God to contend with. Everyone was slipping on the slush. Each saw the man before him fall but then helplessly planted his own foot in exactly the same place. Only Horner, still partly drunk, could keep his balance. None of them thought to follow Fred and Jim in stepping off the path and ploughing through the virgin snow.

Jim was heartily sick of hearing about The People. Fred spoke of them in the same hushed tone that others reserved for saints and heroes. It was almost as if he believed himself unworthy to be numbered among them. Jim could have understood his being enthusiastic about what The People might one day become but there was surely little to be said in favour of what most of them actually were. It was not as if The People had elected to be The People. Being The People required no effort at all. Unless, of course, Fred was giving them the credit for padding out their stupid bones with muscle, nerve and skin, or closing their eyes when they slept, or putting one foot in front of the other when they walked.

By the way Maguire deployed his equipment it was apparent that he had come to love his new trade. His hands ran over the tripod's brass and wooden legs: he seemed to be whispering into the shutter and then listening for a reply. When he finally set himself in readiness, it was hard to tell where the man ended and the camera began.

On the cathedral steps the delegates, like a soccer team, had formed three ragged lines. Their heads seemed to be trying to shrink away inside their collars. Their hands were clasped in front of them. The angelic figure of Katharine Conway materialized in their midst. "Hands behind backs, Comrades," Maguire ordered, "And feet well apart. Now open your mouths a little – but whatever you do, don't smile."

As he took the final picture the sun, having done its duty, plunged down behind Ilkley Moor. The others moved off but Fred remained standing in the porch, lost in thought, his right hand absently stroking its blackened stone. Jim glared at an enormous and elaborate memorial cross: he did not recognize any of the names carved along its base.

America! This was the moment he had been unconsciously waiting for: it was time to go. Perhaps it truly was a pitiful fantasy of escape but surely it was better to ruin your life than to miss even the slimmest chance of transforming it? And perhaps America really would be like it was in Walt Whitman: everyone singing all the time with the earth and sky taking up the chorus? America! Where no-one knew or cared where you came from or what you might have done there. Where you could move on forever and never run out of space. Where if you were too hot you could always console yourself that in another part of the country people were freezing to death. And where, when things did get bad, the policemen would at least be wearing different uniforms and have differently-shaped truncheons to hit you with. If Jim was going to die in a gutter then let it be on The Bowery, not Manchester Road. At least he would have got there by a route of his own choosing.

As he turned away from the cross he felt that he was no longer looking down on the streets of Bradford but already out to the open sea. He was no longer Jim Sharp – millhand or socialist – but a nameless man about to walk bandy-legged and unafraid into an unknown future. America! With any luck The People would not have reached there yet. And if he had anything to do with it they never would.

Maguire had finished folding up the camera: his own legs were as stiff as the tripod's. Fred took Jim's arm. The three men inched down the steps and then turned back towards the road. It was impossible to remain angry with Fred for long. If only Jim could persuade him to come with him! But he knew that it would be a wasted effort. Jowett of Bradford would never leave his privy-middens for a place that did not exist.

Round the corner, parallel with the nave, they came across the other delegates, lined up facing the wall, wreathed in clouds of

44

yellow steam. Those heroic bladders had finally given out. In the window above, a stained-glass patriarch was threatening them with his staff: Jim was relieved that Katharine Conway had evidently vanished back into the ether.

"Hell and damnation, Comrades," said Tom Maguire, straightening up from his coughing fit, "There's the picture I should have taken."

CHAPTER TWO

IN THE BRAIN ROOM (1897)

JOWETT WAS STANDING outside The Jollity Theatre, watching the audience arrive. It was a flimsy but ornate building deep in the valley's cleft where copper-hooped barrels and filthy wool had dammed up the waters of Bradford Beck. When things began to rot they were said locally to be stinking of jollity. On Sundays it was no longer a mere music-hall but home to the Labour Church Debating Society. The singers, comedians and dancing girls were still sleeping off their hangovers. There would be no further jollification until first house tomorrow.

He leaned back against the blackened wall. It felt to be vibrating, as if it had somehow stored up the hopes and dreams of thousands of people. These stones were even more alive than those of the Cathedral, as if laughter might be a higher form of prayer. The statues in the parks were the best, though: you got a powerful jolt when you touched the rounded kneecaps of those two bare-shouldered nymphs who flanked a scowling Sir Robert Peel. In contrast, the crumbly bricks of Fred's own house were lifeless and so were all the other ones in his street.

Folk came streaming down the terraces: there would be a good turnout today. Fred's attention was caught by one particular group, aligned like rugby forwards, who were pushing an unusual conveyance, part-handcart, part-perambulator. On it reclined what appeared to be the corpse of an emaciated man. As they passed, however, the eyes flickered open, bloodshot but piercingly blue. One bony hand clutched a small black notebook to its chest, whilst the fingers of the other scraped the pavement. The old Chartists used to place a cripple at the head of their demonstrations: Fred had imagined that this was a placatory gesture but now it struck him that it had been a reproach, an accusation or even a declaration of aggressive intent. The attendants were red-faced and sweating, despite the apparent lightness of their load, as if they had drawn it over the tops from Keighley.

This ominous figure could only be one man. Advance reports of new arrivals in the movement were usually exaggerated – the dwarf and the giant would be separated by a few inches, Adonis and Quasimodo could pass for brothers – but in this case they had not told the half of it. Philip Snowden, The Lazarus of Cowling: a red-hot jingo who had fallen and hit his head and then woken up, a week later, as a fire-eating radical. He was said to live on roots and berries in a cave up on the moors. He would answer any question on history or economics and could do amazing sums in his head. He wrote a column in *The Craven Pioneer* under the by-line 'Robin Redbreast', in which he dismissed everyone not in the ILP as 'parasitical murderers'. Above all, he was a spell-binding orator, although Fred could not imagine anything more than groans issuing from those thin grey lips. Once, a group of parasitical murderers had gone to give him the thrashing he deserved, only to retreat in disorder, shaking in every limb. They said that he had given them the Evil Eye, although surely nothing could be more intimidating than what was presumably his habitual expression. At least Jim Sharp would not have been able to make his customary observation that each new hope of the Labour movement looked and sounded exactly like the previous one.

Jim had left last Spring, without a word. A comrade working at Liverpool Docks had seen him – "I'd have known them legs anywhere" – negotiating the gangplank of the *Ivernia*, bound for New York. Now Fred dreamed of his friend drowning – the face distorted, with streams of bubbles issuing from the mouth – even though his ship had safely arrived. So many of their best men had already been lost to drink or to the colonies or, like Tom Maguire, had died. Fred's head would still turn, only to find that Jim was no longer at his side.

There were unfamiliar faces in the Jollity queue: older people, unusually well-dressed, and more clergymen – not just the Unitarians but a good half of the Bradford diocese. Fred did recognize a group of small millowners from Lancashire with their managers, overlookers and wives: the Sugdens would never have let them in.

There was a distinct sense of anticipation: whenever the line surged forward he was almost engulfed by two well-upholstered ladies. "We've come for Mr Snowden," the smaller informed him. "We saw him at Haworth last week and at Silsden and Bingley before that."

"And he's different every time," the other winked and dug him in the ribs, "Even though he always says the same things."

Inside the hall the smell was more pronounced: the crimson carpet was suspiciously damp and even the dust had begun to mould. Although Fred could have perched up on the platform with the other luminaries he preferred, if he was not speaking himself, to occupy a centre aisle seat halfway back. Horner had seen him, though, and jumped down to shake his hand. The firmness of the clasp indicated that the man was almost sober. "You'll have to look to yourself, Jowett," Horner was now trying to crush his fingers, "Our lad's after your crown."

"I haven't got a crown." Fred easily broke his grip. Why did people always think that there was some competition going on? Why ever should a comrade's success be a source of chagrin for him?

Everyone in the stalls was talking at once, while ribald laughter and whistling issued from the gods. Perhaps the usual Variety crowd had turned up by mistake? If they didn't get their two dozen choruses of 'Down At The Old Bull And Bush' there was no telling what they might do. Directly across the aisle Fred recognized

48

Johnny Coe, a retired weaver from Wibsey. He was always in Laycock's Temperance Hotel, his small tortoise-like head swaying as the political arguments raged back and forth. He never said more than 'aye' or 'nay' or ''appen' and his graveyard expression did not vary. Now, however, he was all smiles, chatting to his neighbour and actually puffing away at the clay pipe that usually protruded redundantly from his top pocket. Then Metcalfe, the Chairman, massively cleared his throat and began to lever himself in stages to his feet: a complete silence fell.

"Ladies and Gentlemen," - his unusual animation showed that he too had been possessed by the music-hall spirit - "Bonnie Scotland has its Ben Nevis, wild Cumberland has its Scafell Pike and all Wales lies under the benign shadow of Mount Snowdon . . . but we have here, in the heart of the West Riding, our very own mighty and majestic eminence, that fourth peak, the greatest of them all, which - unlike its unfortunate Welsh namesake - is day by day growing in stature and reputation. Ladies and Gentlemen, I give you . . . Brother Philip Snowden!"

The applause surged, then slackened: redoubled, then died away. There was still no sign of the speaker but now the crowd could hear a hollow double thud, followed by a loud metallic scraping. As Fred turned, Snowden came past. The attendants had disappeared and he was now supporting himself on two walking sticks: although weirdly knotted and twisted, of different thickness and length, these somehow contrived to keep him on an even keel. He cast them forward to spear the carpet and then dragged his body after them. He wore enormous boots heeled and soled with steel plates: Fred was surprised that they did not leave a double furrow in their wake. On the next row the two friendly ladies had produced a stopwatch and were timing their hero's progress.

Only now did it register that the small black notebook was clamped between Snowden's teeth. Under a domed forehead, the face was tiny, with pinched, delicate features: seen from behind, the head was almost square. Although the lower half of the body had wasted away, the shoulders were wide and powerful. The overall impression was not of weakness but of a colossal strength somehow out of its element, as if a kraken or leviathan had been plucked from its oceanic trench and deposited in a Bradford music hall. His every step was a triumph over the laws of gravity and motion: Fred could feel the audience silently willing him on.

Snowden managed the steps up to the stage surprisingly well, with a sort of scissoring action, the sticks seemingly rowing through the air. Then, with a slow swing of the shoulders, he turned. The sticks rattled to the floor as the body toppled forward until those bony hands fastened like raptor's talons on the top of the lectern. The air could be heard rasping and whistling in the dry windpipe: it seemed that Snowden was the only one in the place that was breathing. The bowed head shook itself in a spray of perspiration then the sharp chin rose. There was a collective gasp: those eyes! They seemed to change colour from grey to green with a distinct flash of scarlet on the way. But outside, surely, they had been blue?

"So it is true that people are rising up from under the yoke of oppression." Snowden spoke in a low voice, as if resuming an interrupted conversation. "And it is also true that even our opponents no longer seriously attempt to justify that yoke."

Although Fred had been expecting a howl, a snarl or a serpent's hiss, the voice could only be described as pleasant. It had an unusual resonance so that each word seemed to remain hanging in the air, joining the others to create a soft but swelling descant.

"It is true that the word socialism is not only on the lips of working men but on those of poets and philosophers and the movers and shakers of the temporal world. It is even being whispered in the conclaves of the great palaces and cathedrals of Europe."

The man's body was gradually realigning itself. The lolling head had settled securely on the neck and the strength of those shoulders had somehow worked its way down to the hips. First one hand came off the lectern, then the other: the face was no longer chalk-white but putty-coloured.

"It is also true that the Liberals and Tories have stopped their slanders and are now offering us bribes of money and power. Whatever their offer, it will never be enough. Already they resemble those Russian travellers pursued by wolves across the endless Steppe, trying to tip each other off the back of the sled."

The volume never varied, so that a whisper was as loud as a shout. All the dynamics, all the colours, were in the pauses and emphases and the increasingly expressive gestures of those long-fingered hands.

"For it is indeed the truth that we are ready to take power. And it is also true that those who rule are tired and broken and know that they are doomed. But it is also true that they will fight and that we will hesitate and err and that our victory might be tomorrow or not for a hundred years. And as Russell Lowell has said –

"Truth is forever on the scaffold, wrong forever on the throne.
Yet that scaffold sways the future, and behind the dim unknown
Standeth God within the shadow, keeping watch above his own,"

Looking round the hall, Fred saw that every face was rapt and tilted upwards, every gaze apparently directed towards a particularly threadbare patch on the russet curtains, ten feet above the speaker's close-cropped head.

※

Victor Grayson – much against his will – finally had to admit it. They were heading through the thickening mist in quite the wrong direction. By now they should have reached the grim little town glimpsed yesterday down a side valley a few miles to the north but here they were, climbing once again. The carpet of pale spiky grass had given way to mud, then to stone before the horizontal seemed to lurch abruptly to the vertical and they had found themselves crawling up a jagged rock face. Even now that they were back on their feet they were still being drawn remorselessly upwards . They must have slipped to the north west when tacking across to a field-gate to avoid climbing the ninth sharp and slippery dry stone wall of the morning, after which the fog had seemed to come billowing out from under their feet, streaking their ragged clothes with yellow foam. And so they had blundered – inevitably, it now seemed – into those lowering peaks that they had been skirting for the last two days. At least the rain had stopped and there was no wind to hinder them, although there was none to help them either.

Every time they were on the point of turning back Victor would see a little pyramid of stones or a faint arrow scratched on a boulder. Such marks must have been left by shepherds or pedlars or even brutally-moustachioed brigands, like in the Alps or Pyrenees. It meant that they were heading *somewhere*, moving from one named place to another. He was determined to keep going: not once during the last week had they retraced their steps. At least if you were climbing you could not be going round in circles. He turned to check that Mikey's pale face was still floating along behind. Although the younger boy's wits had been addled by their recent experiences he still managed to be always silently there at Victor's heels.

Little Mikey was now the last of the bootblacks – that had a nice Fennimore Cooper ring to it! There had originally been five of them – Lanky, Jacky, Davy, Mikey and himself: all stowaways on the *Ardendee*, a cargo boat bound for Chile. Three days out, when the captain had discovered their presence, they had been ignominiously dumped on a passing homebound vessel. At Tenby dockside they had been greeted by an enormous policeman. Lanky, under the impression that they had just arrived in South America, had been horrified: "I didn't think there'd be peelers here as well". With a series of well-aimed kicks the man had directed them to a freezing lodging house in Saundersfoot.

The next morning they had been turfed out with no breakfast, penniless and without a map, over a hundred miles from Liverpool. All they could do was to begin walking away from the sea. After a couple of hours the policeman had reappeared and arrested the frailest of them, Lanky, for vagrancy. "I'm doing him a favour," he said, "But the rest of you dirty little sods can get out of Wales on Shank's pony." Victor's companions had momentarily brightened up, being under the impression that the man was going to lend them a horse.

There had been few passers-by and these were all men, small and furtive. When asked for directions they merely pointed back towards the coast. Like the captain of the *Ardendee* they seemed to be not so much speaking as singing a bitter and sarcastic song. A large bird circled above: Victor hoped that it was an eagle which would swoop down to his shoulder as if it were Napoleon's but it looked more like a vulture, waiting to pick their bones.

In Aberystwyth workhouse they had been put on to stone breaking but had gone supperless because when their pitiful rubble had stuck in the mesh of the regulation sieve the smirking overseers had refused to shake it. Then, in the middle of the night, they had been awoken by a navy recruiting officer, resplendent in cocked hat and braid, who had been followed out by a seemingly hypnotized Davy. Victor, with difficulty, had held back Jacky and Mikey

After they had escaped they stopped talking. If they had tried to speak they would probably have burst into tears. Then they had given up singing and whistling which, instead of lifting their spirits, now depressed them. A black, fast-flowing river had driven them eastwards and then the mountains had blocked their way: these seemed to have appeared out of nowhere, as if at their approach huge policemen had wheeled them into position. Jacky had immediately sat down and refused to move. They could not shift him: it was as if he had taken root. At last they left him and when they looked back the hunched figure was nowhere to be seen. Victor had thought of these boys as his first disciples: now, apart from the idiot, all had already betrayed him.

One of their few possessions was Davy's rusted pistol with which he claimed his grandfather had shot three Frenchies in the Crimea. Victor suspected that in that particular war they had been on our side. As their leader – the one who pretended to know the way and, going first, tested the ground for sphagnum bogs – he had insisted on carrying the weapon. It had weighed heavily on the band of his trousers, as if the earth was exercising a magnetic pull: whenever he stumbled he was terrified that it would go off. Just before he threw the useless thing away he had pointed it at a bedraggled hill-sheep and pulled the trigger. The unexpectedly loud click had evidently enchanted the creature: it had been following them ever since. Its distinctive face – chipped left horn, wildly rolling eyes, black lozenge on the muzzle – kept looming out of the murk. Although the lamb was a Christian symbol and the Devil was supposed to be a goat, Victor felt that *his* sheep had no significance and was simply annoying. Napoleon had his eagle of destiny but Victor would be attended for the rest of his days by a scraggy old ewe.

It was hard to see their current predicament as "an heroic enterprise" unless the more exhausted and wretched you got the more heroic you became. His thin shoes had long since worn right through but he still retained their flapping uppers, for appearances' sake. Perhaps other people would subsequently attribute an appropriate degree of heroism? If you were sitting in a nice soft armchair, reading about this, it might all seem very different.

❧

"A political democracy animated by our social ideals will be nothing less than the second coming of Christ to rule the nations in righteousness."

Fred was fascinated by Snowden's hands. The left seemed to be wringing the neck of an invisible goose while the right smoothed down its feathers. He had heard that audiences cowered before the man's jabbing forefinger but this notorious digit had yet to make its solo appearance. Nor had there been much of that fabled invective. Even when Snowden called anti-reform Liberals "The men who crucified Christ," it was with a raised eyebrow and a rueful shake of the head, as if to say 'Hark at that!' And those clenched fists were surely not menacing, more like a sign of resolve or a pledge.

The first part of the speech had been punctuated by statistics which bore little relation to the argument, like chunks of vegetable bobbing to the surface of an otherwise turbid soup. And some of these had been dubious: Haworth's IMR could never have been *quite* so high unless there had been more infant deaths than pregnancies. And surely working men could not be consuming such volumes of beer and spirits – not even in Keighley.

He had been told that Snowden shared his concern for sanitation but there had not been a single word on the subject. And where did he stand on electoral reform, working hours or the minimum wage? Jowett had always been hurt when people disparaged his own oratorical attempts when he was usually the only one on the platform prepared to engage with practical matters. What folk wanted – just like a Saturday night Jollity crowd – was a *turn*: someone who would rant or croon, alternate pawky jests with hair-raising threats, and wipe away imaginary tears while banging – not too loudly – on the table. Changing the world wasn't enough, it seemed: they wanted to be entertained. Snowden was yet another speaker who aimed at the heart or the gut while completely by-passing the brain. His gestures conflicted with his words, so that peace and brotherhood seemed the direst of threats, while suffering and conflict might be holiday-tide outings to Whitby or Brid.

The listeners continued to applaud, craning forward or leaning back together, all laughing at what he assumed must be jokes – although without Jim to confirm this he could not be sure. How respectable they all looked! The movement was growing in numbers but it felt to be declining in energy and drive, as if it had passed from youth to senescence in a mere five years. In contrast, he recalled, most of the mourners at Tom Maguire's funeral had been children.

"Human perfection," said Snowden, slowly and emphatically. "The great example of human perfection is the life of Christ." He began to speed up: "His precepts are widely accepted as the supreme guide to the attainment and practice of personal righteousness." The words came faster and faster: he pronounced 'Him' and 'His' with great exhalations of air, as if he was being punched in the solar plexus.

On hearing Snowden compared to John the Baptist, Fred had wondered for whom or for what he might be preparing the way. Now it seemed that the triumph of Socialism was to be The Second Coming of Christ, in person. What had begun as a political creed would soon be incarnated in flesh, bone and holy spirit. Snowden had obviously been reading Renan's *Life of Jesus*: there was always a book of the moment that was holy writ to every socialist until the next one came along.

Fred had nothing against religion – although he had shared Jim Sharp's aversion to the Pope – but he thought of it as utterly separate from the political world. Christ seemed to have been managing pretty well without their help: they should render unto socialism what was socialism's, and unto God what was God's – whatever that might be. Neither did he accept that anything could be achieved through music or poetry or architecture or landscape gardening. Nor did he subscribe to the comforting notion that the great establishment figures – Archbishops, Prime Ministers, Poet Laureates, even the Queen herself – were all, in their heart of hearts, "really socialists". They knew that they were wrong, right enough, but that was not the same thing.

"And now I see 'as through a glass darkly'," said Snowden, in a tone of mild wonderment. "A vision of what the world will be when this spirit of love and sacrifice shall animate all men." He kept stressing the words "I see . . . I see . . . I see": the more obscure his vision became the more he asserted its tangibility. And for one moment

Fred seemed to see it too: like some strange French painting in which everything pulsed with life, as if trees and sky and even people were composed of swarms of brightly-coloured insects.

Snowden groped for his carafe and glass. The sharp chin dropped on to the chest and the twisted features disappeared. He could be heard lapping, his long red tongue like a dog's. Then the head came up once more to reveal a face transformed by the radiant smile of a child anticipating its mother's enfolding arms. Fred saw that answering smiles were breaking out on every face. He himself was smiling too: there was nothing to be done about it – the corners of his mouth felt as if they had been pulled up towards his ears.

> "Ring in the valiant man and free,
> The larger heart, the kindlier hand."

Tennyson's *In Memoriam* would surely never be out of favour.

> "Ring out the darkness of the land
> Ring in the Christ that is to be."

Tears were pouring down Johnny Coe's furrowed cheeks and audible sobs were coming from that still-smiling mouth. Perhaps this *was* politics after all – politics at its deepest level. Snowden's magic had not worked on him directly but through the medium of the audience. Once again The People had been right. Now he was feeling what they were feeling: part of one great single organism – like a benevolent army marching perfectly in step – while simultaneously floating alone in some hazy realm with that sweetly reasonable voice sounding in their inner ear. Snowden seemed to be catching his eye but that great head kept swinging to and fro: everyone else in the theatre would be under the same impression. Now Fred saw the young people he had previously missed: mill-hands with their sweethearts, as rapt as all the rest. There were more and more, as if they were springing up in response to the words.

"No reaction will prevent us from attaching ourselves in religion to the great intellectual and moral ancestry at the head of which we see the name of Jesus, shining. In this sense, we are Christians, even when we separate ourselves on almost every point from the Christian tradition which has preceded us."

This was the first person Fred had encountered who believed as much as himself not only in the righteousness of their cause but in the inevitability of its triumph. He thought of Hardie's hectoring tones and the look of terror in those black eyes, as if he might at any moment be dragged back to his Lanarkshire coal mine. Other speakers did exhibit some degree of confidence but usually – as with Aveling or Shaw – only in themselves.

To Snowden it was evidently not a matter of winning but of winning in the right way, preserving one's own decency and humanity in the process. He was forgiving his enemies long before he had beaten them. The great change would be managed firmly but kindly: only Jim Sharp would be disappointed by the absence of throats to cut. Although he looked like Robespierre, Snowden was that rarest of things – a *good* man. The People had seen beyond appearances to his true nature, his real message: The People, as always, were right.

"But the only way to regain the earthly paradise is by the old hard road to Calvary – through persecution, through poverty, through temptation, by the agony and bloody sweat, by the crown of thorns, by the agonizing death."

Snowden's shoulders sagged and he bowed his head, then it rose once more to display that seraphic smile.

"Cheerfully we face the thumbscrew, rack and fire . . . For after that is the resurrection to the New Humanity – purified by suffering, triumphant through sacrifice."

The applause did not begin until Snowden had taken up his sticks and turned away. It was tumultuous, of course, but surprisingly short-lived, as if the audience felt it to be an inadequate response to what they had just experienced.

"I've never seen him clench his fists like that," the two ladies were standing in the aisle, "I liked the way he looked surprised, as if his hands were doing it off their own bat."

"I do miss the finger, though," said her friend, "But you can't beat him for a good peroration."

Only Johnny Coe was still in his seat. No longer crying, he appeared to be kissing a creased and faded photograph. Fred recalled that the man had lost his wife a few months ago.

Snowden had tucked one stick under his arm and was shaking hands, modestly averting his head from the more fulsome congratulations. Some people were lightly touching his rounded back - for good luck, perhaps, or to confirm that he was real.

Two queues were forming. One towards the stage, where the branch secretaries were signing up new members, the other for the top table on which - flanked by gleaming tea-urns and pyramids of sliced bread and butter - there sat an enormous, well-crumbed ham.

Abruptly, Snowden's head swung towards Fred. The eyes bulged like a frog's, while the jaw muscles clenched so that the cheeks grew even whiter, while those thin lips appeared to bleed. This must be the evil eye that Fred had heard so much about. The effect was disconcerting but he extended his hand nonetheless. "Sorry, Councillor Jowett" - the face relaxed into a smile even more disarming than the platform version - "That was just our Keighley way of saying hello." The handshake was unexpectedly strong but, unlike Horner, he did not try to crush your fingers.

"May I crave your indulgence" - Chairman Metcalfe had started shouting again. "For the Orpheus of Undercliffe, The Little Wonder, The Nightingale's Chick. Your own - your very own - Percy Jennings!" On the stage a huge bland-faced man seemed to materialize out of thin air: he launched himself into "The Sailor's Grave," leaving his pianist trailing far behind.

"I'm speaking again in two hours" Snowden gave Fred's forearm a gentle squeeze," Can we get out of here and find somewhere to talk? The rack and the consuming flame may hold no terrors but I can't bear to watch them scoffing that ham."

"We could go to Laycock's but it would be a fierce uphill push for your lads." "Oh, they're all in The Cock and Bottle," Snowden laughed, "Some nights I have to wheel them home. But I can make it under my own steam. For a few hours after I've spoken I feel as good as new. I only do this for my health, you know: the doctors keep telling me to rest but they're Tories to a man."

They had gained the street with surprising ease before a terrible sound blew them up the hill.

> "Guests refreshed in joy's new-rising morn!
> Come and swell the song
> Silent now so long –
> England is risen and the Day is here!"

The Undercliffe Orpheus was grappling with Edward Carpenter. Snowden's movements were now utterly different from when he had entered the hall: hunched over his sticks he progressed in a series of spritely hops. The source of his Robin Redbreast *nom de guerre* was now apparent.

⟡

Even in July there were still traces of snow on the mountain, as if the two boys were climbing into a different season. A deep gully was filled with ice, dirty grey streaked with yellow: it reminded Victor of the foul-smelling sinks at the workhouse. At least there were still signs of human passage: a twist of brown paper, a frayed tether, a blackened farthing. There was even a white lace-edged ladies' handkerchief with the blue initials 'RN' sewn into a corner. Although it had no smell, it was slightly salty to Victor's tongue. A ball of hard slush struck the back of his neck. He turned, but Mikey was fully twenty yards away. The idiot did not have the

60

co-ordination to gather and throw with such accuracy: nor, surely, did the sheep. Perhaps it had been 'RN', the beautiful leader of an equivalent female gang of runaways?

It all seemed like a dream. One moment he had been sitting by the Mersey, dozing in a patch of sun, and the next found himself being pitched about in a mid-Atlantic storm and now here he was blindly scaling some awful Welsh peak. It took an effort to recall the sequence of events in between.

Once he had learned what little school had to teach him he had begun to steal away to spend his time down at the docks. The ships fascinated him: he would sit for hours, waiting for them to sink. How massive they were, lying at anchor, but how tiny and insignificant they became when you watched them sail towards the open sea! Huge seagulls would surround him: with their unblinking eyes and razor-sharp bills he never dared to refuse them a share of his meagre lunch. He saw emigrants herded on to the biggest ships bound for America, his eyes filling with tears as he waved farewell, imagining that people he had not yet met – the sweetheart, the irreplaceable friend – were being carried away forever. Men in important-looking hats bustled about, shouting orders that were seemingly ignored by lean, weatherbeaten longshoremen, who calmly went about their business.

Victor would sit on the low wall in front of a crumbling red brick building with boarded up windows. It looked so derelict that it was some time before he noticed a small silver plaque on which was engraved, SAILORS' HOSTEL. No-one entered and no-one left but on investigation he found that its occupants preferred to use a rusting fire escape round the back.

At first the sailors themselves had been a disappointment, slouching up or down their gangplanks as if they wanted to be on neither sea nor land. Victor liked to imagine himself as Jim Hawkins but none of them had parrots on their shoulders and all had a full complement of legs and eyes. Nor did they carry cutlasses or pistols and they tossed their empty bottles away instead of sliding tiny carved ships inside. After a while, however, he began to understand the way they were living during their brief periods ashore.

It was almost like watching the pigeons in City Square. The men would strut around in small silent groups and then, for no apparent reason, rush off, singly or in pairs, in every direction at once. Sometimes a lone sailor would stand on the corner, turning slow circles, seemingly oblivious to the people he forced into the gutter, until he would slip into one of their passing shadows and be drawn away out of sight. After nightfall they would flit in and out of the hostel with bulging sacks over their shoulders. Victor was sure that one had actually *wriggled*: perhaps being toted around inside a sailor's sack would be even more exciting than hiding?

At first he would walk past the building then duck into the alleyway and count slowly to fifty before retracing his steps. Then he would repeat this on the opposite side of the street. Alternating between a saunter and a brisk trot, he would change the angle of his long-peaked cap and then remove it on every fourth pass. After a while he abandoned all pretence and just stood there, propped against the lamp-post. Still no-one paid him any attention, except for a gang of filthy urchins, evidently bootblacks in the hostel, who jeered and spat, apparently under the impression that he was after their jobs.

The sailors were always smiling but whenever they actually laughed their faces became oddly serious. They liked to swap clothes with each other, regardless of differences in size. The tobacco in their pipes was darker and more pungent than landlubbers' and they drew the smoke more deeply into their lungs. Their speech was half-growl, half-song, with the words seeming to issue from the stomach and the nose: it was exactly the way, Victor thought, that Poor Dog and Rain-In-The-Face would sound.

He now felt so relaxed, so much a part of things, that he had at first been unaware of the hand that had fallen on his shoulder and the breath that was tickling his ear. MacBride, the man said his name was, although he had hesitated as if he had almost forgotten it. Victor had never seen anyone like him before. His sun-blackened skin was beginning to flake and he smelt like the inside of a rusted kettle. Dark hairs swarmed like insects over his forearms and his wide nostrils looked to have been stuffed with the same shag as his Churchwarden pipe. Although the arms were unusually long, the legs were stunted, with the feet pointing outward like a clown's. It seemed as if moving his eyes might be painful because the whole body would turn to change his angle of vision. The other sailors seemed to be afraid of him while he himself seemed equally afraid of them. Nevertheless, Victor had no doubt that Providence had brought them together. There was something that he needed to know and here was the man who could tell him. He had been waiting for MacBride and when he looked into those unblinking eyes he knew that MacBride had also been waiting for him.

His other new friend was a very different type. Attilio Verona was only a few years older than Victor but he had already sailed three oceans and half the larger seas. He was as handsome as MacBride was ugly, as young as MacBride was old. His hair was black and glossy, whereas MacBride always wore a ribbed woollen hat pulled down to his eyebrows. Attilio loped – in contrast to MacBride's rolling gait – but his feet were also splayed at ten to two. His voice was low and his arms were held close to his sides. He regarded the world with a level, neutral gaze and the world looked back in the same way. Strangely, whenever MacBride left, Attilio would almost immediately appear. Victor had never seen them together: it was as if knowing one was the price you had to pay to know the other.

MacBride's body was undecorated, while Attilio's was heavily tattooed. Victor loved to trace the lines of the small but gruesome crucifixion in the crook of his friend's right elbow. The biceps were adorned by lines of poetry in a foreign language: Attilio, declining to translate, said that he did not think that equivalent words or sentiments could be found in English. In the centre of his burnished back was a mermaid who turned fish only just above the thighs.

Instead of nipples, wide and long-lashed eyes were set on the tips of her breasts. She was seated – or, rather, coiled – scraping back her long straight hair with a cuttlebone, smiling at her own reflection in a mirror of oyster shell.

Everyone liked Attilio but he also had two special lady friends. One was tall and very grand in her white gloves, chaperoned by her cross-eyed elder sister. The other was older, always flushed and hectic as if she had been running away from something. Her bright clothing kept slipping to reveal unexpected expanses of flesh. Attilio seemed like a different man with each: Victor, whenever he encountered them, somehow knew not to approach or even acknowledge him.

Through Attilio and MacBride, Victor had met many sailors from America-bound ships but not one was prepared to help him. "No room for stowaways," he was told. Every inch was accounted for, with even steerage stacked up like those good old slavery days. Add just one small boy and the great ship would founder. MacBride, however, about to sail for Australia, had offered to smuggle him on board. By the time they reached Brisbane, he assured Victor, he would have learned enough seafaring to command a berth on any ship, to anywhere he wanted to go. Although America was indeed a bully place, why not see the rest of the world on your way?

He had gone to say goodbye to Attilio. His friend would be heading out on the same day as bosun of the *Ardendee*, a full-rigged barque bound for Coquimbo on South America's farthest coast.

"Come with us," said Attilio, "At least you'd be in the right hemisphere. That's typical MacBride: to New York via Australia, Atlantis and Hell. His ships are never lucky. The cabin boys" – his hands clasped to mime diving – "They have a habit of falling overboard."

Victor had never heard of Coquimbo or even of Chile. "What is it like?" he asked.

"I've never landed there but I was laid up in Valparaiso just down the coast. There's a thick forest, then a desert, then sheer mountains that no-one can climb. They have red and yellow parrots that will speak only Spanish. All the insects sting and all the women are small and squat. Whatever you do, you'll never get them to smile. I didn't like the place much at the time but I've never stopped thinking about it since."

And so, instead of meeting MacBride, Victor had trudged up the coastal road to Southport where the *Adrendee* was lying at anchor. He had left home at midnight, on tip-toe, carrying his shoes, even though his so-called parents had long since stopped listening out for him. This time he was taking *two* apples and an orange, in view of the distances involved. He was wearing his best clothes - Eton jacket, long trousers and a deep-collared shirt with a short blue necktie. He had learned that you could get away with anything if you looked respectable enough.

Attilio, in his romantically hooded cape, was already waiting. Victor was led along the deck and then down into the ship's dark interior: he banged his head and scraped his shins on things he could not see. At last Attilio pushed him on to the farthest bunk and proceeded to pile sailors' bags and pieces of tackle on top of him. This continued long after he had been completely hidden from sight. There was some skill to it because he could still breathe easily and felt not in the least constricted or weighed down.

The next twenty-four hours had been blissful. Being concealed in a strange place, first in silence, then surrounded by the sounds of men engaged in unknown activities, with the smells of leather, smoke and sweat - Victor prayed that it would never end. Perhaps Heaven would be like this: being hidden forever, while the cherubim and seraphim searched for him in vain.

He had become aware of his own regular heartbeat and various tickings and pulsings all around his body. Behind these, however, there was an insistent warbling sound, as if he could hear his own so-called mother calling from ten miles away. He still did not want to piss: he had a cast-iron bladder. When MacBride had given him beer it had retained every drop. Nor had he felt tipsy, merely as if his fingers and toes belonged to somebody else. "It's like mother's milk to you," MacBride had said, with evident disappointment.

After a while he could hear voices but could not make out what was being said. The jangling chains and creaking wood reminded him of the melodrama that was the only play that he had seen. There was a regular drumming of hooves, but surely they wouldn't have horses on a ship? Periodically, Attilio's long arm would work its way through the coverings to pass him ship's biscuits that crumbled in his fingers but nearly broke his teeth.

When the ship finally moved it seemed to be along the vertical rather than the horizontal plane, as if it were rising into the heavens or sinking into fathomless depths. He did not feel in the least seasick and, to his relief, his mother's cries had finally been stilled. Now he was sure that he could smell and taste the salt of an ocean breeze and so was not too disappointed when chinks of light at last appeared in his cosy prison. Attilio was removing each piece with as much care as he had piled it on.

After the last kitbag had been pulled away, Victor realigned his aching limbs and levered himself to his feet. He was surrounded by a ring of faces, grotesquely shadowed by the swinging oil lamps. There were a couple of Chinamen, closer to green than yellow, and a huge man in oil-stained overalls whose face and chest were covered with thick black fur. Perhaps it really was a bear? Most of the others were shiningly bald but had grown long beards to compensate, so that their heads looked to have been twisted upside down. They were not like anyone from the Liverpool Hostel – even stranger than MacBride. He realized that these must be the sailors who were never allowed ashore. Even Attilio looked different: that habitual grin now seemed predatory and cruel. They were all just staring, as if waiting for Victor to do something but he had no idea what that might be.

The silence was finally broken by a faint rhythmic tapping from beneath their feet. The ship's cat, a massive tabby, sprang forward to scrabble at the panels with its great flat paws. With metal hooks the Chinamen tore open the hatches to reveal a quartet of small, filthy, semi-human figures.

One by one, they emerged. The hissing cat still seemed to take them for rats but they were Victor's old enemies, the bootblacks. Lanky, Jacky, Davy and Mike: they seemed pleased enough to see him now, crawling forward until they had joined him in the centre of the circle.

"After my own candidacy fell through," Snowden was saying, "I went to Colne Valley to support Tom Mann. At the main rally in Slaithwaite all the men just stood aside, too scared to attend. Finally I called on the women to set an example and they came shuffling over, faces muffled, cringing and squinting up at the sky, as if expecting a thunderbolt to strike them down."

"When we got in here last time, hundreds of people were openly showing our colours."

"They probably think that the doings of Bradford Council are beneath God's and The Gaffer's notice." Snowden took Fred's arm: when they had reached the top of the hill he had stopped using his sticks. "Parliament is the only thing that matters. Until we are there – in numbers – we are nowhere. Only then will our actions be of any significance. Even if we merely walk into the Chamber and then walk straight back out in protest: whatever we do, they will have to report it."

For the first time since Jim Sharp's defection, Fred no longer felt that nagging emptiness on his left hand side. Somehow none of his other friends in the movement had sufficed. They had been too tall or too short, silent or over-garrulous and he had difficulty keeping them in focus, as if they were only half there. Now, with Snowden in place, everything was once again as it should be. He glanced down: Jim's bandy arch had been replaced by Philip's stiff and wasted limbs. For some curious reason it seemed necessary that his closest comrade should have difficulties with walking while still being able to keep up.

Philip was recounting his Keighley debacle: the experience did not seem to have embittered him for he was laughing. As a local candidate he had been reckoned to have a fighting chance until it came to paying the £160 advance poll costs, when it was discovered that the party funds long since put aside had mysteriously dwindled to less than half this amount.

"Horner said that there had been some . . . unexpected expenses." Snowden's free arm made a vigorous quaffing motion. "Still, Keighley wouldn't have been easy to represent: you wouldn't be able to turn your back on it for a moment."

They paused. There to the East, clinging to the slopes, lay the great slum of Longlands. Wreathed in a yellow haze, the houses looked to have been cobwebbed by enormous spiders. People were living eight to a room and the mortality rate was three times the city average.

"Ah, Longlands!" Snowden's raised claw swept along the horizon. "It makes even Keighley look good." Such disgust was in healthy contrast to Jim Sharp, who had taken a perverse pleasure in degradation.

"In our lifetimes Bradford will have become The City Beautiful." Many times Fred had said those words to Jim who would always reply, "But it's beautiful already – the Rome or Athens of filth."

"Then it will be needing a new name," was Snowden's response, "Jowettsberg has a nice ring to it."

"Last week I told the Sanitation Committee how, after the rains, Longlands' privy middens were draining into the houses. And the Liberal aldermen complained that talking about such things only shows our city in a bad light." Fred was too embarrassed to repeat what else the man had said: "If your people haven't yet learned how to shit in the pot, it's their own lookout."

With relief they turned away towards the city centre. "I wish I shared your optimism," said Snowden. "But that election has set us back ten years. It's all Hardie's fault. He was never in the House and when he was, he just provoked everyone, especially the Irish. Then he picked a fight with the miners with the result that our candidates in South Yorkshire were pelted with stones. He completely neglected East Ham and, when he finally did speak there, stormed off the platform after his constituents demanded that he say it all again, in English. And after he'd lost, he immediately embarked on a lecture tour of America. The National Executive Committee has not met in over a year. And now he's threatening to resign because the Aberdeen party won't stand down their own by-election candidate in his favour."

None of this affected Fred's morale. He had his own ways of measuring the progress of the cause. The sound of his feet on the pavement and the way he felt inside his own skin confirmed that everything was going perfectly well.

"At least we've heard the last of permeationism. Having been elected on the Fabians' Newcastle programme, the Liberals shelved it and did nothing for the full four years. And when it came to the election, they effectively conceded to Rosebery and turned all their guns on us. When Hardie lost, you know, it got the biggest cheer of the evening at the National Liberal Club: they flagged it up as their gain rather than the Tories'. And the Fabians are finished, too: a pity, because my old Dad had great hopes for them. Hyndman and the SDF are the real danger to us – that's if they ever discover that there's life north of Peterborough."

On Westgate a tingalary man was pushing his mechanical organ, followed by a jeering gang of urchins, throwing stones and handfuls of mud. His thick curls appeared to be full of pale dust and the green of his shirt scorched the eye. A mangy monkey was perched on his shoulder, biting at his ear. The tune they were playing was unrecognisable. The whole scene was utterly degraded.

"We'll soon be having no more of this," Fred muttered.

"Nay, our Fred," Snowden had broken into broadest Yorkshire. "No more barrel organs? No more monkeys – or Italians?"

"No more music," Fred was laughing for the first time in over a year. "And no more kiddies, neither."

Laycock's Tea Room was a lump of sticky black stone wedged between Westgate and Sunbridge Road. It appeared to be derelict: all the sound, heat and light was sealed away inside. The brass doorknob was stiff and shiny and set so low, that when it finally did turn you fell forward over the threshold. There were no dignified entrances at Laycock's.

"All right, our Phil?" Fred, holding the door, saw that his friend was leaning on his sticks again. The legs stiffened, the shoulders hunched and the head twisted sideways. "Sorry, our Fred," One eye winked up at him, "I don't like to disappoint anyone."

Word of their coming had evidently preceded them. Snowden levered himself in to a storm of applause. Fred wondered if there might be an element of irony in this unprecedented display but every face exhibited delight, admiration – even awe.

"Nay, silence is the best I ever get." Fred was relieved that he felt not the least twinge of envy.

"That's because you're local. I get the same in Keighley. They'll never put their hands together for one of their own."

Laycock's interior was like a Second Empire ballroom crossed with a Wild West saloon. The gas lights were flickering and the pipe smoke was so thick that you could hardly make out the other side of the room. A silver hardboard moon slowly revolved above: it had been installed after the *Yorkshire Post* had dubbed the place "a hot-air factory where the balloonatics of sansculotteism pilot their leaking dirigibles of revolutionary moonshine towards the shrinking heavens". Although the place was strictly temperance, hip-flasks and bottles circulated openly. Many of the regulars were freethinkers or downright eccentrics, like the man with the long grey tongue and his friend who claimed to live off omelettes containing live and wriggling worms. The rest were 'just ordinary folk' who, when you got to know them, turned out to be even stranger. Argument and debate raged to and fro: rules and procedures were said to exist but even after ten years Fred had no idea of what they might be.

Each packed room had its own brass nameplate. Snowden and Jowett passed through the House of Commons and the House of Lords, then skirted Theology And Religion where a shock-haired man appeared to be beating himself up. At last they reached the deepest and darkest: The Brain Room where, under a dusty etching of Millais' *Bubbles*, they found an empty table.

"And all Hardie can do is to blame 'traitors in the party'." The presence of an audience did not make Snowden tone down his criticisms. "Did you read his latest editorial in *The Labour Leader*?" – he assumed a grating Scottish accent – "'The fibre of the Socialist movement has been almost totally destroyed by a spirit of irresponsible levity'. When Hardie walks down Fleet Street and hears the *Clarion* boys in their pubs, he thinks they're laughing at him, when it's probably about cricket or horses. He shouldn't worry about such things: no-one cares what Blatchford and *The Clarion* say."

"It has a circulation of a hundred thousand," said Fred, "And the penny edition of *Merrie England* has sold three quarters of a million copies."

"But that's just entertainment. And Hardie, to give him his due, is at least a serious man. What people laugh at and applaud and what they actually think and do are very different things."

At this everyone laughed and applauded. The crowds were pressing into The Brain Room: at the back some were even standing on each others' shoulders. Young Willie Leach had been pushed forward so that he was now kneeling on their table: sheepishly, he reached out to shake Snowden's proffered hand.

Willie had been Fred's second convert but he had never matched Jim Sharp in his affections. Leach regarded him with rather too doglike a devotion while treating everyone else with a condescension that betrayed his origins as a mill-owner's son. Now the glance he gave his mentor was hard and cold: it was sad but Fred felt no resentment – he had known that this would happen, sooner or later. As ever, Willie's sisters and cousins were in close attendance. They were markedly fresh and pretty young women: all the regulars appeared to be terrified of them. Now they only had eyes for Snowden and did not seem to register Fred's presence at all. It was most curious: he had not realized just how they had been looking at him until they had stopped doing it.

Even before the ship had reached the open sea it was violently assailed by wind and waves. Victor had imagined being rocked to and fro at varying speeds but instead they seemed to be spiralling upwards and downwards simultaneously, as if a typhoon and a whirlpool were fighting over them. His brain banged against his cranium while his stomach made leaden plunges towards the heaving deck.

The tempest seemed to be facilitating the various couplings of sailors and boys, throwing them together and then pulling them apart. At least, unlike the bootblacks and some of the men, Victor had not vomited yet – not even when the second Chinaman's cock had been thrust halfway down his throat, flooding it with thick, tepid liquid. He was surprised that the semen of Chinamen, Lascars, Irishmen and bears tasted exactly alike and their breath and skin smelled neutral, except for a faint salty tang. Perhaps sailors all took on the odour of the sea? Similarly, laughter sounded the same in all languages and he could tell that each man was muttering the same mixture of endearments and threats.

The sailors liked to double up. They would set their boy on all fours between them and then kneel in prayerful attitudes to penetrate mouth or anus. One wild-eyed man was always left out. He kept jabbing his semi-erect penis into Victor's ribs, as if seeking some concealed orifice until, admitting defeat, he turned to punch the bulkhead's splintered panelling. The others chattered away as if waiting at a tram stop – mainly about women, left behind or

72

waiting for them in the next port. Victor suspected that these men spent their lives at sea precisely because there were no women there.

"You know why they call it Coquimbo?" asked the man in front. "It's because there's nothing there but cock and quim."

"And bo," said his friend, squeezing Victor's buttocks and thrusting even harder than before. "There's always room for a bit of bo."

Their conversational tone did not vary as they speeded up and ejaculated. Although the sailors obviously wanted to climax together they never quite managed it. They were surprisingly coy, never lowering their trousers beyond the upper thigh or unfastening more than the top and bottom buttons of their shirts, and constantly shouting at the boys to shut their eyes. When they had finished they would hop backwards, clutching at themselves, desperate not to stain their clothes. Something told Victor that laughing at them would be a serious mistake.

Their beards felt surprisingly soft, whereas back on shore Attilio's apparently smooth skin had always sandpapered Victor's chin. It was Attilio - now wearing the white lace gloves of his younger lady friend - who was organising everything that happened, while taking no active part himself. Perhaps - being young and handsome - he felt it to be somehow beneath him - or did holding back give him an even deeper pleasure? He set them up in ever more elaborate and uncomfortable poses, seemingly under the impression that a body could bend from the waist as far backwards as forwards and that heads could turn full circle. Sometimes he would turn away to consult a thick volume that Victor guessed must be an instruction manual of some kind.

"You're the Devil, Attilio," whined a sailor who was trying to support his full weight on one hand while thrusting through an apparently ownerless pair of legs towards an ever-receding mouth.

"Not really," said Attilio, thoughtfully. "I'm just naturally curious about things." He surveyed the tangled bodies and sighed. "This should really be seen from above to get the full effect."

Victor had never thought much about his arsehole. Once, with the aid of two mirrors, he had managed to inspect it but the thing had merely stared dumbly back at him. Now it nagged and pulsed but its rawness was not that of a wound, more like a newly-discovered and developing extra sense. His brain teemed with images that grew clearer with each thrust. It was as if all these humiliations were somehow bringing him fully to life. Instead of sliding in and out, each cock felt to be wrenching sideways or downwards, as if there were gold and jewels locked inside and they were trying to jemmy him open. The worst pains, though, were up along the spine and across the shoulder blades. His jaws had also begun to ache and his teeth felt loose: the back molars rattled like dice in a cup whenever he dipped his head.

The men never touched each other and nor did the boys. For sailors to go with sailors or for boys to go with boys would evidently be against all laws of God and man. They ignored Victor's erection, while the other boys displayed no signs of arousal. He suspected that they were part-pretending that the boys were girls, denying any mutual sensations, reducing them to complete passivity. When Victor made to frig himself, Attilio pulled the hand away and knocked the burning embers of his pipe out into the palm. It was obviously best not to show any sign of pleasure or pain.

Attilio now ordered him to feed a coil of knotted rope into the bear's anus. He was startled at how much disappeared into that dark, distended hole, half-expecting the tip to come poking out like a cigar between the creature's teeth.

"When he shouts 'Madre!'," Attilio tied the other end round Victor's wrist, "You must haul it out – fast!"

When his shipmates began to flag, the wild-eyed man finally got his chance. He reeled from one partner to the next, twitching and jerking as if electricity were passing through his bones, but all to no avail. The face turned red, then purple, then almost black whilst those eyes bulged wider and wider. At last he shrieked and, clutching his right calf, fell to the deck, overcome with cramp.

One of the Chinamen expertly massaged the leg, while the other prised the teeth apart to grab the tongue. After a while they were able to hoist him back into position once again. As the struggle resumed, the wind stopped howling and the sea grew calm. It was as if everything in the world had stopped and was waiting for the benighted soul to gain relief. Finally, Attilio took off his broad leather belt and belaboured the skeletal back until - as if fired from a cannon - the man flew backwards across the deck. A blue-white tear was trembling at the purple tip of his member: each drop was cheered as it slowly fell, to be soaked up by the thirsty wood.

There were thirteen sailors involved, but sometimes others would pick their way across the stage. They scowled or spat and one even threw his sea-boots at Attilio with a snarled "I signed up for a barque not a bum-boat!" But none thought to intervene. Sea-boots took up an ocarina to squeeze out a jaunty little tune and everyone broke off to shout and stamp along. The song was about a ship floating in the doldrums whose crew had drawn lots to discover which of them might be the cause of such bad luck. The lot fell on Brown Robin who admitted:

> "It is nae wonder
> Although I dinna thrive
> For with my mother I had two bairns
> And with my sister five."

So his mates tied him to a board and threw him overboard. But then Christ and The Madonna came walking over the placid waters and bore Robin up to Heaven - "All for the fair confession you made upon the sea" - leaving his more virtuous fellows to their fate. Everyone liked this so much that they sang it all through the second night.

For a few hours, when most of the men had been called above deck, Victor was able to lie down and rest. The bootblacks, like puppies, snuggled up to him and immediately fell asleep. They didn't expect much from the world: at least they were dry and warm and safe – well, safe from anything worse that might have been happening. Whenever the ship lurched, Mikey's eyes would open and he would ask mechanically, "There yet?" The hatches were unfastened but Victor did not attempt to leave. There was nowhere to hide and, besides, how could you run away from running away?

The Bear turned out to be the cook. He ladled out a delicious stew with tiny morsels of very pale and spongy meat. Victor wondered if this might be a cannibal feast of leftovers from the stowaway boys of previous voyages. If anything, this gave his appetite a keener edge. Grog tasted weak and watery until it ignited in the pit of your stomach. He had watched in fascination as the Chinamen ate his running-away apples: sucking rather than chewing, they took over an hour to consume them.

On the third day the sailors finally showed themselves naked. None could match Attilio's tattoos: there were merely a few ink and pen hearts and anchors although one man was covered by blue serrated lines, reminding Victor of the plaster of Paris pig which hung outside Garnett's Butchers with all its joints mapped out. Their nakedness had not relaxed them: they had a surly and disappointed air. Whatever they had been hoping for had not taken place: any pleasure they had felt only left a bad taste in their mouths. For all their huffing and puffing, for all Attilio's ingenuity, they were left unsatisfied. Victor thought of the magical visions – guns, trees, knives, wolves, princesses in towers, flying ships – that he could summon up by simply touching himself. Perhaps what these sailors lacked was imagination?

You could see the shame in their eyes but that only made them even crueller than before. He had long since learnt that people would show no mercy when they knew they were in the wrong. When a teacher entered the noisy classroom and picked out a culprit at random, Victor had often been the chosen one. The resultant beating was always worse than when you were caught red-handed for a more serious offence. At first the sailors had hit him for meeting their eyes, but now they hit him when he looked away. From the bootblacks he had learnt to ride the blows: a punch could only land properly on a cringing target. Exceptional brutality was always followed by exaggerated kindness, as if to restore some natural balance. How concerned they had been when Davy began to bleed! It was as if they did not realize that they themselves had been the cause.

Even Attilio's enthusiasm had flagged: the balance of power was shifting. When Victor's hands stretched out to finger the arseholes of two surprised sailors, not even Attilio, delightedly clapping his hands, had suspected that he himself was now instigating proceedings. Once you fully understood a situation – no matter how bad it was – you could gradually take control. Now he felt as if he was leading them on, towards a point where they would suddenly find themselves exhausted and defenceless, when the oppressors and the oppressed would change places.

Nothing that had happened on that ship had felt strange to him. Somehow he had already known what to do: how to lie, bend, tense, relax, breathe, when to move and when to keep still, how to employ lips, tongue and teeth. Surely no-one could have been born corrupt – not even the seventh son of a seventh son? He had the feeling that he had done all this before – like the Hindoos believed – in other lives that he could never quite remember.

He had not been altogether surprised when, on the fourth morning, Attilio had betrayed them. The first indication came when the sailors suddenly became blind and deaf to the boys' presence. They started playing cards – a loud variant of Snap – with a pack so worn that the values could hardly be discerned. Then Attilio, dressed in his smartest rig, had come off watch and made a great show of 'discovering' them. With enthusiastic applications of his rattan cane, he had driven them up the hatch, across the deck and into the Captain's cabin.

Captain Clay was sitting reading at a desk with a long pipe in his mouth. The effect was somewhat spoiled by the book's being upside down and the pipe unlit. It was obvious that he was Captain because his hands were small and soft looking, with well-shaped but filthy fingernails. Victor did not like to see them turning the pages of that fine-bound volume. The man's grizzled beard was so thick that it stood a full three inches out from the face: it looked as if he was trying to swallow a badger whole, with his tight little mouth corresponding to the creature's fundament.

"And what have we here?" His tone indicated that he knew very well just what they had there. Victor recognized the dry cough, the unnecessary pause, the tilt of the head and the stiff movement of the neck as the mannerisms of every person in authority that he had met. "Good work, bo'sun," Clay continued, "No matter how we plug and caulk, the rats will always find their way in." Victor was not in the least intimidated but what did disturb him was Attilio's manner – humble, even fawning, without a trace of self-mockery.

Clay looked them up and down in turn. He saved Victor for last, appraising him for a full half-minute before speaking.

"As long as I am Captain" – the voice was almost a whisper – "I will permit no lowering of the moral standards on this ship. Only my consideration for the fishes keeps me from throwing the whole damned pack of you overboard."

And now Victor recalled where he had heard those half-singing, half-choking tones before. On that first night, just before three bells, the lights had been abruptly extinguished and all the sailors had drawn back. Then from out of the darkness that voice had sounded close to his ear: sobbing, cursing and praying whilst its owner kept thrusting and missing, finally forcing his way inside only to feebly flop back out again.

Now Clay was pacing about, expounding on what he still had half a mind to do to them. Victor had often wondered what keel-hauling might be and this man evidently had a thorough knowledge of the subject. His attention strayed to the Captain's book, laid face down on the greasy table top. GIBBON'S ROME, read the gold letters on the spine's red band. He was sure that he had heard of this: could it have been the one that Attilio had consulted? Curiously, eleven identical volumes were lined up on the bowing shelf above the Captain's scabby head. Victor determined to obtain his own copy, although in the jungles of Chile it might prove hard to get. As his forefinger was lifting the corner there was an explosion of blue and silver stars and his head rang like the town hall bells. Captain Clay had pitched one of his old-fashioned buckle-shoes unerringly across the room. Sea-faring men evidently did not like people touching their books.

"Twenty years ago you would have been on the business end of five hundred lashes." He breathed out a great blue cloud of smoke, having finally coaxed the pipe back to life. "And another fifty on that five."

After searching them thoroughly for concealed money that might enable them to buy their passage, Clay announced that they would be returned to England on the next homebound ship. Even though the traffic was heavy at this time of the year, a full dozen passing sails had been hailed in vain before the schooner *Eclipse*, low on salt and fresh water, had agreed to accept a supplementary cargo of small boys.

At this point, the crew of the *Ardendee* had become agitated. Concerned that Victor and the bootblacks might dive off the long-boat and swim below the ship to hole in its hull, they insisted on binding them hand and foot.

"Give my regards to the ladies of Liverpool," Attilio called to Victor, all the old gaiety back in his voice. "And tell them I said they're to keep you entertained until my return."

Their bonds were not untied when they were hauled aboard the *Eclipse*. They had spent the next two days and nights lashed to the foredeck. Fortunately the seas were calm and the skies clear but there was no respite from the sun. Even at midday the sailors would not drape a tarpaulin over them. Victor wondered what Clay had told them. When he thanked them for the water they had clapped their hands over their ears, as if he might have been a siren, singing alluringly from its rock.

꙾

Snowden was entertaining his listeners with tales of Keighley. In order to be near the railway station he had left his mother's cottage and moved in with Horner and his brothers in Queen Street.

"The first thing I noticed was that someone had chiselled Her Majesty's 'N' into an 'R'. It's a rather rackety establishment. Once I found my room full of hens: when I told Horner he smiled and asked 'were they green or blue?' And last week, returning late after proselytizing the length and breadth of Calderdale, I fell into bed only to discover a pair of bare feet on the pillow next to me. They were as cold as death but what really worried me was that there was no matching head at the bottom. Fortunately, next morning the feet had gone. When I told Horner his only response was" – he broke off and conducted the audience as they chanted – "'Were they green or blue?'" Truly, Our Phil could have topped the bill at The Jollity for the other six days of the week.

"Breakfasts are the worst. I'm the only one who eats. The others hold their heads and groan until someone shuffles to the corner for a gallon jug of porter and it all starts again." Snowden's smile vanished and he glared around the room. "For some reason they feel they *have* to do it, as if drinking is the main qualification for being a Socialist, for being a man." The biggest soaks in the room, Fred observed, were the ones tut-tutting the loudest.

The girls' heart-shaped faces were clustered together, as if about to burst into song. The middle one's arm, bare almost to the elbow, thrust out a large lace-bound autograph book festooned with coloured ribbons. Snowden, in bold but slanting italics, inscribed his name right across one rose-pink page. Fred had never been asked to sign anything but petitions and manifestos. Returning the book,

Snowden raised his other arm so that his forefinger – at last that renowned digit was putting in an appearance! – extended itself to trace, without quite touching it, the girl's long jaw line. She did not react and no-one else seemed to think this was out of the ordinary. Unlike Aveling or Hyndman or the movement's other Don Juans, there had been a curious innocence to the gesture – like a baby reaching out for things as they moved in and out of focus.

"We'll make no more progress without a proper leader," Snowden resumed. "He should be tall, with good skin and a level gaze, a deep voice and preferably a black moustache. In short, he should look and sound like a Conservative: a man who cannot be dismissed as just another navvy with a grievance, who even those that would never dream of voting for him would still respect and trust. But he should be more than a figurehead: he should seem like a father, a king or even a sort of God. So that when Fred here has finally cleaned up Longlands, its grateful inhabitants will instead attribute it to the efforts of that mighty and distant figure who watches benevolently over their lives. It's all there in Carlyle's *Heroes and Hero-worship*: without our own hero, without our Truly Great Man, this movement will remain in the shadows."

"Our Truly Great Man": Snowden, stamping his crutches for emphasis, had almost barked the words. Fred had never understood Carlyle's enduring appeal to Socialists. He recalled reading the book while lying on the bluebell bank in Heaton Woods: the print had swum before his eyes and even when the sun came out he continued to shiver. How could Dante and Luther both be Heroes? How could one's Catholicism and the other's Protestantism both be right? It was as if nothing mattered except individual talent and dramatic, decisive actions: who cared whether The People were led to famine or plenty, victory or defeat, so long as The Truly Great Man was there in the van, fulfilling his destiny? When he reached page 144, where The Chartists were described as 'ignorant' and 'unwashed', he had thrown the damned thing clear across the beck. Then he had retrieved it – for books should be respected, after all – and placed it in the hollow of an oak tree. Jim Sharp had observed that if some Truly Great Squirrel should subsequently sally forth to challenge man's hegemony, it would be all Fred's fault.

"I thought that, as Socialists, we were going to get rid of kings, lords, masters and bosses," said Fred. The girls were still not looking at him. "So why should we have to produce our own variants? Why do people still need to be *driven*, even if it's with new whips and in a different direction?"

"Of course no-one should be driven," Snowden put his hand on Fred's, "But we all of us – even you and I – still need to be led."

"Nay, Our Phil, we need to be represented."

"What about Ramsay MacDonald?" Leach interrupted. "That's a name we keep hearing."

"He's *Scottish*," said Snowden very slowly, making it sound as if that might be a crime. "But not like Hardie. He's been down in London for a long time" – he said this as if it merely compounded the initial offence. "In the last two years he has moved from the Liberals to the Fabians, then to the SDF and now to us. Who knows where he might be going next? When he stood for Southampton he only got a few dozen votes: not even the Constituency party supported him."

"What does he look like?" asked the red-haired girl.

"He is very tall," said Snowden, judiciously, "with broad shoulders and a narrow waist. He always wears tweeds, even in town. He climbs mountains and claims to read poetry in Latin and Greek. He gives himself aristocratic airs but he's more like a head waiter: the sort that smiles and bows and then spits in your soup."

"And does he have a nice moustache?" asked the blonde.

"It's big, black and bushy, even better than Hyndman's." He favoured her with her with a yet more beautiful smile. "I'm jealous, of course. But don't think that I am prejudiced – I really do not trust him. I fear that we are still awaiting our champion. Perhaps Tom Maguire, had he lived, could have been the man."

"Did you know Tom?" asked Fred.

"I met him only once" – the smile contracted to a grin – "He declined to take my photograph for fear that my face would crack his camera lens."

Now, as if on cue, The Labour Church Committee arrived, accompanied by their photographer. The protesting girls were swept aside as he set up a group picture with Snowden at its centre. Fred was left to smoke his pipe in peace.

Maguire's death last winter had been attributed to a chill caught while addressing an outdoor meeting, but he had been already in decline. He was drinking heavily and complaining how much the movement had changed, speaking as if recent events had taken place twenty years ago. In a terrible blizzard his comrades had broken down the door to discover his fully-clothed body on a mattress on the bare floor. There had been no food or fuel in the house but in his hand was a newly-purchased book, still wrapped in brown paper – Stevenson's latest novel, *Catriona*.

Hundreds had attended the funeral: the despairing poor and their families, for whom he had so tirelessly worked. The full ILP Executive Committee was also there, with Hardie delivering a muffled eulogy from behind a large white handkerchief – he either feared contagion or was hiding his blushes. The Executive had hated Tom, even depriving him of work by hiring inferior and more expensive photographers from non-union firms to record the great occasions of the ILP. Now that the coffin lid was nailed safely down, however, he had been transformed into a paragon of virtue, a universal favourite plucked by cruel fate just as he was about to blossom into full leadership. Poor Tom could never have figured on Carlyle's roll of Truly Great Men: he had not been re-nowned for his hygiene, smelling distinctively of developing fluid and bath-tub gin. Was it too much to ask that a man be remembered for who he was and what he had done? Maguire would have just thrown back his head and laughed at the absurdity of it all but that was no consolation to Fred, devoid as he was of any sense of humour.

The camera seemed to have survived its encounter with Snowden's physiognomy and now the crowd were giving him three rousing cheers. "I am speaking in Halifax tomorrow morning," he said, as the last hurrah faded. "And Keighley is a long way in the wrong direction. Instead of packing me back to Queer Street, is there any kindly comrade who could accommodate me for the night?"

The girls were whispering urgently in Willie's ear. "We've got a spare bedroom," he said at last, "And we can put the hens in with the cows and pigs." Fred had only once visited the family mansion, overlooking the wooded side of Lister Park. There had been thick carpets, French paintings and original Morris wall-hangings. There were even some servants, although their supposed masters and mistresses had appeared to be waiting on them.

☙

Victor and Mikey had finished the last of their food. The cottage loaf they had stolen from the workhouse had been supplemented by some apples scrumped from an untended orchard. Whenever Victor spat pips and core into his hand, Mikey's rough tongue would immediately lick them off. The boy would eat anything: when they passed the remains of a fire he would crunch the charred sticks like sugar candy.

Hanging on the wall at Sunday School had been a painting of a beggar-boy looking up with shining eyes at an ascending or descending Madonna. Victor had stared at it until the new preacher – crying, "Blatant Popery!" – had pulled it down, shattering the glass. Mikey's face – whether he was contemplating an apple, an angel or nothing at all – wore the same ecstatic expression. Furthermore, it was as if those worn and tattered rags had been designed to show off his chest and limbs: even grime and snot seemed to have been applied by an expert hand. Victor knew that he himself was looking ridiculous: good clothes gone to rags could not compete with rags that could never have been anything else. Evidently there was a point where ugliness became beauty, pain became pleasure, idiocy became visionary, and rags were a la mode.

The fog was now thick and grey, reflecting his mood as he dragged himself along, step by step, merely to get back to somewhere that he had no desire to be. Why hadn't he stowed away on another ship or struck out for London? Perhaps he didn't really want to run away at all?

As they climbed again, he could see the line of Mikey's cock. Snail-like aboard the *Ardendee*, it had now swollen into an ever-present erection, at which its owner absently scratched. Every half-hour they would stop and try to rub some warmth into each other's hands and feet. Then their mouths would lock while their bodies bucked and strained together. Mikey's lips had that familiar salty taste but, unlike the sailors, his tongue did not hide behind his teeth. Rolling a little way back down the slope, they felt to be forcing their way right through each other then, turning, forcing their way back again. Although Mikey was shivering he gave off remarkable heat. His skin seemed faintly luminous and his eyes grew wider and brighter, with the squint even more pronounced.

How could such things be anything other than good? Victor reminded himself that - beyond his and Mikey's bodies - out there in the world, all was very different. Sinfulness was their word for innocence, vice for virtue, and they punished, without mercy, acts that were as natural as the sun, moon and stars. Once he thought you could simply reverse everything - God and the Devil swapping halo and horns - but now he suspected that apparent opposites were inextricably bound up with one another. It was all just life.

Everybody knew that the world was all wrong. The only question was how far they dared to admit it. Perhaps each person thought that they were the only one to be in on the secret? They were all outcasts, quite unaware that there was nowhere for them to be cast out from. It was as if they were all terrified of not being terrified, as if fear was something they needed, like air. Now he understood that teachers and classmates, policemen and priests, so-called mother and so-called father had all known the truth. He had seen it in their eyes: the terror that he might suddenly blurt something out. Once the words were spoken everything would be different: like the opening of Pandora's box, except that this time all the woes of the world would go flying back in.

Perhaps, instead of running away, he should now stand his ground? If it *was* his destiny to speak, then the message would have to be delivered at the right time, in the right place. If you missed your moment you would never get another chance. He was sure that there was a formula or spell that would cause the world to explode ... and then, when the smoke had cleared, all the fragments would have recombined in natural, rightful forms. Those words were inside him, lodged at the back of his throat but he had not yet managed to cough them out.

He kept remembering the *Ardendee*. It was as if he had let the sailors down, even though most of them had sealed their fates long before he was born. If only he could have told them that the sins of the flesh were no sins at all, that all such things can be done in a completely different spirit! He imagined the *Ardendee* now, as a ghost ship, floating in nothingness, unwelcome in Heaven or Hell. Suppose that when he finally spoke his fateful words a great wind might spring up to blow them back home? He imagined the port blocked by the ragged sails of all those exiled, self-accursed mariners returning at last.

Victor knew that he could not do this alone: he needed a platform. He had heard of formerly secret revolutionary gangs that were now powerful enough to come into the open. Their leader, Hardie, bore a promising resemblance to the Western outlaw, Sam Bass. Apparently he was demanding, with admirable cheek, higher wages for working shorter hours. Victor's so-called father would rant and rave, as if he was the Duke of Birkenhead himself, that the army should shoot them all. It was the old who were the real enemy: people who had never been young or had succeeded in extinguishing all feeling, in forgetting everything that they had ever known. His sole worry was that, at thirteen, his own powers might already be on the wane.

He realized now that he had been talking aloud, his voice no longer shrill but resonant and deep. He had been making a speech – to an idiot and a sheep.

Why should workers work while bosses bossed? Why were the rich, wanting for nothing, more rapacious than the poor? Surely their well-nourished sons would be better suited to manual labour? – A team of public schoolboys would have dug your trench while Irish navvies were still spitting on their hands. And the daughters looked so bored and wan that scrubbing and scouring would surely come as a relief. The beggars should be living in the palaces because their rags would not keep them warm, while the Lords would sleep perfectly well in the gutter, wrapped in their ermine cloaks.

There was a low growling sound: Mikey had begun to snore. The sheep, which had grown increasingly agitated during Victor's performance, stamped a foreleg, rolled her eyes, then bolted down the slope. These were not the responses he had anticipated: changing the world might prove harder than he thought.

He rubbed his eyes: the mist was lifting. Looking back, he saw that they had been traversing a ridge with a sheer drop on the other side. So, without his realizing it, it *had* been an heroic enterprise, after all! Up ahead reared the great spur of the summit: something was gleaming, like a sword thrust deep into a white stone. When they reached it, however, it was merely a triangulation point.

Now the skies had cleared: the last fading cloud resembled a passing dragon. They could see the sheep, like a distant white ball bouncing across the emerald green foothills. Wales was revealed to be a beautiful place: you had to see it from above, as Attilio might say. If the people they had met had known the true nature of their setting, surely they would not have been so cruel?

No-one could climb a mountain by mistake: they had never really been lost at all. But Victor still felt – cairns and column notwithstanding – that he was the first ever to look upon this sight . . . or, at least, that nobody had ever seen it in quite this way before.

Two small hands were gripping his arm.

"Pushific Oshun," said little Mikey.

"Yes," said Victor. The sea was a dazzling silver mirror. "This is where it starts."

THE WARDROBE (1906)

As A GOOD Yorkshireman, Snowden had always hated Lancashire. As a good Socialist he knew that he should rise above such local prejudices but his eyes, ears and nose were telling him a different tale. There were equally poor and dirty parts of Yorkshire, of course, but their desolation had an almost peaceful air whereas over here everyone – even the addled, the crippled and the old – was in a tearing hurry. Trams passed in a blur and horses galloped without the whip, as if all Manchester was running away from something even worse than itself. It was almost as bad as London, except that everyone was tight-lipped. Perhaps they were afraid of contagion: as Fred would say, you could almost see the germs swarming in the air.

He did not like the looks he was getting: so many Red Rose men were murderers and thieves. A couple of roughs were half-shadowing him, wondering if his bulging bag might contain rent monies rather than thirty copies of *The Future Of Socialism* and a flask of tea. They would not know who he was: they probably thought that the ILP was a brewery and that a chairman was a person who – in the absence of furniture – could be used to sit on.

If only Ethel were with him! Man was supposed to aid and succour woman but in his wife's case the reverse was true. On first sight she had inspired in him an awe that had only deepened on further acquaintance. Even Shaw had been impressed. "In three months half a dozen such women would make an end of law in England. She's Lady Cicely from *Captain Brassbound* in the very flesh!" He seemed to be under the impression that life itself kept plagiarising his work.

When they had first met at Laycock's they had hardly spoken but thereafter she would usually be sitting in the front row of his meetings. He thought she was shy but once she had broken her silence she had not stopped talking. Love was her constant theme, but she did not seem to mean what most people understood by the word. The redeeming and transforming power of Universal Love: it was like Christianity crossed with Socialism but with God and all the more banal aspects taken out. Love: her wide mouth would savour the word, stretching it out to twice its usual length so that it rhymed with 'curve'. He was surprised to learn that she had a growing reputation as a Temperance speaker. Ethel's conversion rate – her mentor, Dr Aked, had confided – was quite unprecedented.

After a few months she had gone down on one knee, a manoeuvre that he himself could not have managed. "Let us combine our lambencies," she had proposed, "to further advance the inevitable victory of Universal Love." He had consented with alacrity: however had it come about that the movement's best-looking lass was allying herself to its most ill-favoured man? He had wondered whether she might be included with the party chairmanship: perhaps, at the end of his term, he would have to cede her to Ramsay MacDonald? Shaw had compared them to Salome and John The Baptist – "with the outcome likely to be the same" – but in fact they were blissfully happy. On some days Philip hardly used his sticks at all. True, his mother would not speak to Ethel or even acknowledge her existence but this only added to his delight. How wonderful to be the object of contention!

When they were apart he thought about her all the time. Sometimes he would forget where he was and what he was supposed to be doing: his eyes would slip out of focus and then Ethel would appear. Not as in a vision but as if she had magically taken on the form of a tree or a streetlamp or a passing cloud, which would reaffirm the absolute fact of her existence before reverting to their familiar roles. Presumably this was another manifestation of the power of Universal Love.

He passed along Fawn Street: a plaque announced that on this spot the last deer in Ancoats had been shot. The buildings were grey and hazy, like a half-erased pencil drawing. The deep puddles in the buckling pavement, swirling blue, yellow and green were the only sources of colour. The shapes they reflected bore no relation to his surroundings, as if they were portals to another, equally unappealing world. Engels had identified this district as the lowest circle of Hell: he had not exaggerated 'the measureless filth and stench', although Philip was sure that Our Fred would have been able to calibrate it all too precisely. It came as no surprise to find that Victor Grayson was living on the worst street in the worst part of this very worst of cities.

"Victor is a most remarkable young man," the Principal of The Manchester Unitarian College of Theology had written, "with a strong vocation for The Ministry. He has pronounced spiritual gifts and a rare ability to inspire trust and affection in all conditions of people. Unfortunately, he is in mortal danger of not only ruining his own life but also of damaging many others in the process."

It appeared that during the previous summer's unemployment riots, Grayson had been seen leading the mob and fighting with policemen. Neglecting his work, he had formed a Socialist Society for his fellow-students. There had been "well-founded rumours of women, drinking and even worse". What could be worse than drink and women? Philip wondered. Perhaps the boy wouldn't shine his shoes or wet-comb his hair? "He is a great admirer of yours," the letter had concluded, "And would most probably heed any advice that you might give him." It appeared that putting sinners back on the straight and narrow was all part of being Chairman of the ILP but Philip was slightly piqued at this latest evidence of just how respectable he was now considered to be.

Grayson's tenement was the most dilapidated of all. The wall was soft and sticky: Philip had not realized that stone could actually rot.

By the evidence of his nose the inhabitants subsisted on cabbage and glue. The stairs were cobwebbed and filthy and he did not like to touch the banisters: on each landing he glimpsed a small dark animal darting ahead. Holes in the roof revealed the clouds floating serenely on.

It was, of course, the last room on the top floor. At least there was a door – or rather half of one, hanging from its top hinge. A light knock almost brought it down so Philip ducked underneath, pulling aside a rough blanket that had been pinned across.

The room was surprisingly large and hexagonal, like a chapter house. The narrow windows had been papered over, with flickering candle-stubs the only source of light. There seemed to be no bed but ash-coloured blankets and pillows covered the floor. A three-legged stool was the only seat. Books were everywhere – open and face down, like a flock of settling birds. What kind of man would read fifty books at once? In the far corner was a pile of boots topped off by a large ladies' shoe. Snowden's stick prodded a flat, shiny object: it was a violin but with only two strings and a slice of mouldy jam and bread adhering to its soundboard.

A dark wardrobe loomed in the shadows: however had it got up those stairs? Its full-length mirror was scratched and fogged as if worn out by reflecting too much. Philip saw his own figure begin to slide, then slowly disappear. The door creaked open and a pale young man, immaculate in white wing-collar and dark suit, stepped into the room.

"I was looking for something," said Victor Grayson, "But then I couldn't remember what." His handshake was firm enough but with a slight twist, as if he was trying a lock. "If I had any sugar and milk we could have some tea – if I had any tea. But there's plenty to drink." He gestured at a half-filled bucket in which a number of dark bottles were bobbing about.

"I wasn't expecting you." The accent was curiously neutral with the hint of an American twang.

"It's two o'clock," said Philip, "I'm exactly on time."

"I'm afraid my friends are usually late – so late that you might as well call them early." He picked up a large silk cushion with the initials 'VG' embroidered on a red and bleeding heart. "From an over-enthusiastic admirer." Grayson rolled his eyes.

Snowden placed it on the stool and sat down carefully. He picked up the nearest book – Volume VII of Gibbon's *Decline And Fall*.

"A sad disappointment," said Grayson, "I thought it would be full of pictures." Before it was removed Philip saw that the margins were crammed with notes. He took out his silver cigarette case with its engraved motto, 'PER AMOR UNIVERSALIS': Ethel's image flashed across the metal as he offered it to Grayson. As the younger man's head bowed the candle flame shot up to meet his cigarette. Leaning back, he inhaled loudly, only to collapse in a coughing fit. Philip took great pleasure in such moments.

"They're a bit rough until you get used to them. Gold-Tipped Egyptians, sixpence a packet, my only vice."

"Oh, I do hope not." Grayson spluttered. He took a second, more judicious drag. "I feel sick" – the cough had turned to laughter – "Where can I get some of these?"

☙

Fred had been a Councillor for thirteen years but he had never got used to the Town Hall. He was sure that the frontage's thirty-five life sized stone kings all frowned whenever he came into view. He wanted to turn away but an invisible hand would always give a firm push between his shoulder blades. Once again the dark entrance swallowed him: it would be many hours before, with a raging headache, he would slip out the back way, into the safety of Toad Lane.

As usual, he paused and took three deep breaths under the city's illuminated coat of arms. Its crest was made up of John of Gaunt's hunting horn, the severed head of the fabled Cliffe Woods boar and a curiously spotted sheep, hanging limply in a weighing sling, over the words 'LABOR OMNIA VINCIT'. It was as if their enemies' own motto was announcing their impending defeat. "Labor doesn't mean Labour," – the Lord Mayor said, "It means bloody hard graft – something you lot know nothing about."

The corridors were crammed: evidently the new pictures had arrived. Since an art gallery had opened in the shadow of Lister's Mill, everyone was arguing about whether Dicksee or Draper was our greatest painter. The latest acquisitions fell into three categories: underdressed young women from antiquity, horses pulling carts through Suffolk mud and 'views' like *The Bay of Naples* or *The Tivoli Falls*. Now the macebearer came stamping through the crowd, holding the weapon as if about to take a bite out of its orb. The mayor was seldom in evidence but the symbol of his office required regular exercise, like a dog. By falling in behind, Fred forged through to the empty debating chamber. He was on time, as always, but no-one else was in any hurry.

The smell of carbolic and wax polish tickled his sinuses. The great domed room was oppressively clean: he felt sorry for the dust, floating in the air like a cloud of aphids, never allowed to settle. In the grain of the oak panelling he could discern the grimacing faces of the souls of murdered trees. Above all, he disliked the carpet, that glaring, triumphant purple. Arnold Evans, the city's medical officer, said that it was so the bloodstains wouldn't show. Arnold was currently suspended for drunkenness, locked up in Menston asylum to dry out. With what he had to see and smell every day, who could blame him for needing an anaesthetic? He claimed that alcohol killed all germs: if it wasn't for our livers we would all be immortal.

First there would be the Finance Group, followed by The Board of Poor Law Guardians; then it would be Sanitation, Housing and Education, then Finance and Education once again. Fred was the only man who sat on every committee. The carpet's pile was so thick and soft that you sank into it like sphagnum moss. He would feel his toes wriggling with treacherous pleasure and so he sat with his feet awkwardly tucked up behind the legs of his chair. A few Labour Councillors had entered, taking up their position further along the row: Joe Hayhurst, from the dyeworkers, gave him a grudging nod. The Trade Unions considered the ILP flighty and unsound, as if being paid by the bosses was more validating than being financed by the voluntary contributions of workers like yourself.

Fred was aware that some of his colleagues were envious of what they called his 'career', but he had never thought of personal ends: work just presented itself to be done. No-one directly accused him of ambition but he was often told how lucky he had been. Had luck made him chairman of the Sanitation Committee in the middle of the worst smallpox epidemic since 1880, after the incumbent had himself succumbed to the disease? He would be more than happy to resign his posts if competent candidates emerged. Recently, he had put himself up for re-election, even though as an alderman he was exempted for a full six years. "Cunning old Fred," they said. "Put your own head on the block and nobody will dare to cut it off." No-one would accept that he really believed in accountability, that any mandate should be endorsed as regularly as possible.

"You've outgrown this place," they would say. "You've served your apprenticeship: it'll be parliament next." At the last General election Fred had only failed by forty-one votes and was surprised at how relieved he felt. Next time he would be a shoo-in but he did not want to go to London. He had attended the recent International Socialist Conference where Bebel and Malatesta's debate – 'Social Democracy or Anarchism?' – had ended in a riot. Afterwards, from the opposite bank of the Thames, he had surveyed the House of Commons. It had brought to mind some monstrous saurian that had rolled on to its back and was now sunning its scaly belly while the realization of its own extinction slowly progressed towards its brain. Then, for hours, he had walked the streets. There was something unfathomable about the place. Down a Soho alleyway he had observed a swell in full evening dress and a ragged beggar chatting away to one another, laughing as they urinated against a wall. Fred had felt curiously excluded: neither of these men, he suspected, would have found anything to say to him.

"You can't skulk in Laycock's forever," Snowden was always saying. "Whether you like it or not, it's London for you. We have to keep moving forward or we die: that's the way life is."

Now most of the Councillors had drifted in, a full quarter of an hour after the proper starting time. It was like being back at school but without any teachers: these men acted as if there could never have been anything that they needed to learn.

Surprisingly, the Conservatives were the easiest to work with: unfailingly polite and accommodating, although their suggested compromises were always full of snags and catches. Some even supported Fred's proposals but only when there was no chance of their being passed. When voting became tight they would, with apparently sincere expressions of regret, revert to their traditional position. Everything they did was calculated to undermine the Liberals. Even though Campbell-Bannerman had just become prime minister, many Tories believed that their historic adversaries were doomed and that, in a few years' time, Labour – currently with only three MPs – would have succeeded them as the main opposition.

The Liberals themselves harboured no such fears: their hostility to socialism remained implacable. If the movement had followed the Fabian path, then victory would have taken a thousand years: permeation might work with limestone but not with granite. Briggs Priestley, Fred's old adversary, was now mayor. His political philosophy was simple: Thanks to God and Free Trade, every man, woman and child had got, was getting and would always get their just desserts. As Hayhurst said, it was a terrible thought that it could be anyone's just dessert to have to be Briggs Priestley. Now 'B. P.' left most of the talking to E. J. Smith who, sitting across the Chamber, was already tossing his blonde mane and shaking his fist at nothing in particular. As a staunch defender of the inalienable rights of the freeborn Englishman, E. J. had been provoked beyond endurance by

Fred's School-Feeding Bill, offering to fight the children of Bradford – 'one at a time or all at once' – for their entitlement to a plate of bubble-and-squeak. His interminable rants were accompanied by a sustained growling from Hayhurst.

"One of these days I'm going to deck that bouncy great bugger."

"Nay, Joe," Fred would say, "You'll never be mayor if you do."

"But wouldn't it be worth it?" Joe sighed.

Last winter the trade depression and freezing temperatures had caused great suffering, with the public provisions and the Cinderella clubs quite unable to cope. Most schools closed: it was impossible to teach under such conditions. For the neediest children the Poor Law Guardians provided a daily meal of a bun, a banana and a glass of milk. When Dr Evans analyzed the milk he discovered that it had been heavily adulterated with water. The Guardians' chairman had then announced that the liquid was not supplied as milk but as 'a beverage'.

'Bun, banana and beverage': when Fred heard the wild laughter that followed his words he knew that he had his enemies by the scruff of the neck. Once they realized how ridiculous it sounded, all resistance had crumbled: last November Bradford had become the first council in the country to assume responsibility for school meals.

Perhaps there were worse things than being ridiculous: the opposition had regrouped. Today Smith and his surrogates would be harrying the children's dinners through every sub-committee. Soon they would be able to muster enough votes in full council to reverse the policy but Fred had learned to be calm about such things. In 1899 he had miserably failed to pass the Longlands conversion but only two years later he had stood and watched it all come crashing down. The occupants had been rehoused in splendid new tenements on the other side of the city but they had not been happy. "We're North-facing folk," they complained, "Not South." They'd lost their sense of community: some even claimed to miss the privy middens.

Nevertheless, the city was changing. As well as school meals and council houses there were public swimming baths, health clinics, maternity hospitals, even nurseries for disabled children. Yet Fred still felt dissatisfied. It wasn't that there was still so much left to do, more a feeling that nothing had really happened at all – as if Longlands were hiding somewhere, waiting to return. Perhaps there were memories that could never be erased. What if they were to build a new city out of bricks of gold, only for the disgrace of the past to somehow persist? Whenever Fred walked through the former slums a phantom smell would assail his nostrils.

And when he lay awake, as he so often did, in the coldest and darkest hours of the night, he could still hear the cries of the night-soil men.

❧

Grayson lit another cigarette from the stub of the previous one: he had certainly taken to the Egyptians. He was describing last night's performance on St Peter's Fields by Buffalo Bill's Wild West Show. It made a nice change, Snowden thought, to just sit back and listen. The cowboys had been on bicycles and the redskins had been taught to juggle. There had been a bearded Venus and a human ostrich who waltzed together and Nouma Hawer, billed as the World's Greatest Midget.

"Shouldn't it have been the world's smallest midget – unless, of course, a midget's eminence is measured by something other than size?" Grayson blew a perfect smoke-ring, an art that Snowden had never mastered.

"They'd painted another horse to look like Charlie but it could hardly dance and when it reared it almost toppled over. At the end Bill himself was drawn round in a gilded carriage, too old or sick even to lift his hand to wave. It's a shame when your heroes let you down: you wonder if there was ever anything there to begin with."

Philip realized that he really did not want to be a disappointment to this boy.

"Do you know why I'm here?"

"You've come to tell me to behave myself. For some reason the seminary doesn't want to expel me and they think that I might listen to you," Grayson smiled, then blew a smile-shaped ring. "Perhaps they're right. I must have heard you speak a dozen times but I've never dared approach you. For weeks afterwards the words would be running through my head like music but then when I read the pamphlet of *The Christ That Is To Be* I realized I'd been unconsciously creating my own, different version: that's how influence works. And I've read all your 'Robin Redbreast' pieces. My favourite is the one about the four distinguished men of Keighley given silver caskets and illuminated addresses with the money being found by cutting the night-soil men's wages. 'And so let us pray' – he had Philip's tone off pat – 'that no other Keighleians will ever distinguish themselves in the future' . . . And on my wall I had the caricature that made you look like Doc Holiday, under the caption, 'Down with Socialism, Atheism and Anarchy!', after you'd got seven thousand votes in Blackburn."

"They tell me you have unusual gifts – perhaps even a genuine religious vocation. Such a thing is rare indeed. Unlike intelligence or beauty, charm or force of will, it cannot be turned to other ends. Despite my reputation, I do not really believe that if Christ and his disciples returned tomorrow it would be to sit on the National Executive of the ILP. The great churches are now mere institutions, like the banks: the mystical element will always lie beyond them. Normal standards do not apply in the transcendental realms. A Chancellor could be introducing a great redistributive budget but that would be of lesser significance than you – in some obscurer place – changing all of life with a few words, a gesture or a look. How must it feel to be God's instrument on earth, accomplishing things that even you yourself are not able to fully understand? If you even suspect that you have such a capacity you must not deny it. You would never forgive yourself if you were to compromise this gift."

Grayson took his seventh Egyptian. "You speak as if you yourself were once in this position."

There had indeed been a curious incident when Philip was thirteen. Ickornshaw Chapel had hosted a revival week: there had been no hiding place from the influx of preachers. One by one, his closest pals had been converted – until, on the final evening, Philip had felt himself rise to approach the penitential seat. At that moment a heavy hand had fallen on his shoulder, forcing him back down into his place. He wondered why his father had intervened: did he not think that his son was worthy to be called? Walking home, he had plucked up the courage to ask him. "I never laid a hand on thee," came the quiet voice out of the darkness, followed by a snuffling noise that was either suppressed laughter or a passing hedgehog.

"No," said Philip finally, "I have never been in your position." Grayson smiled as if he knew very well what had not been said and drew the cork from the next bottle. He was obviously not a serious drinker for no-one could have looked less like Horner and his crew. Philip offered his own flask: "May I recommend . . . weak tea with a dash of lemon?"

"I fear that I will never be a Good Templar."

Now Philip could catch not only the Scouse but also something lilting – Welsh, perhaps, or Irish? What *was* curious was the way Grayson would slur the first and last words of a sentence while enunciating fully and clearly in between. It was if he were fading away then returning, fading then returning. Perhaps it was the candlelight but the face kept changing – the eye-sockets deepening, shadows flickering under the sharp cheekbones. The skin grew paler but the lips remained unnaturally red.

Philip cleared his throat: "There have been, I believe, some difficulties with women." He hoped this would not initiate some unfortunate confidences, having once seen Blatchford and Hyndman unbuttoning their flies to compare notes.

"Ah, you must mean Miss Panton Ham and her friends. They were such nice ladies and little things seemed to mean so much to them."

"Is Miss Panton Ham the College Matron?"

"Yes. Isn't it a wonderful name? – 'As pants the ham for cooling streams when heated in the chase'. And she looks as she sounds – pink and white, a bit wobbly, breathless with honest enthusiasm. We had some good fun and I'm sorry that she is being made to suffer on account of it. She had no thoughts of marriage before The Committee put its oar in."

There had been rumours that Grayson's proclivities might be of a different order but obviously no-one could be both a ladykiller and a sentimentalist of the Whitman type. Philip himself had been accused of being puritanical and immoral, naive and corrupt, reckless and cowardly, all at the same time.

On the flaking wall hung a dusty print which Philip now recognized as Lord Leighton's *Hero And Leander* from Manchester Art Gallery. When he had been in training for The Excise he had dropped in to see it every day, highly amused that Hero was the name of the statuesque female whose huge soulful eyes he had years later recognized in Ethel's. Hero was the heroine. In the predella a tiny pale, naked male figure was lying on the rocks – Leander, drowned in the Hellespont.

"I don't think she'll be throwing herself in after him." Grayson had followed his gaze, "She's worn out the poor little chap. Sometimes I know how he feels. Perhaps we shouldn't be too sorry for the Panton Hams of this world."

"Why on earth do you get yourself entangled with such people when you don't even care about them?"

"I suppose I'm just curious by nature," Victor inhaled deeply, "Even when I know exactly what is going to happen. Besides, they can get nasty if you don't reciprocate. Trouble only gets worse when you try to avoid it: better to get it over with as quickly as possible."

He seemed to be trying to blow smoke rings down his nose. A faint scratching came from the direction of the wardrobe.

"Do you have a cat?"

"I don't think so. It's probably the pigeons roosting under the slates."

Philip wondered if the wardrobe might be the secret entrance to an opium den, like in the penny dreadfuls. How he wished that Ethel were here to shed some light on all this! For a man in his condition physical intimacy was not easy. Rare surges of virility could not be long-sustained but Ethel was fortunately able to achieve full satisfaction by vibrating against various sharp points of his anatomy while crooning into his ear her litany of Universal Love.

"I believe I once had the pleasure of hearing your wife speak in Liverpool" - Truly, the man *was* a mind-reader! - "She kept saying that drink was the Devil in solution" - Grayson took another comically furtive gulp - "At the end all the topers marched forward to sign the pledge, while all the Templars and Rechabites reeled into the pub next door. She is a most remarkable woman: you must be very proud."

❧

All Fred's childhood memories - happy or sad - were pervaded by the smell of excrement. The privy middens had been situated to the rear of the terrace, with one ashpit serving four households, although in the adjacent street they were shared by twice as many. The fours looked down on the eights whose only consolation was that some poor devils were sixteens or even thirty-twos. The stench served as a calendar: Christmas was the worst, when the consequences of the richer festive food hung frozen on the air.

Waste collections were irregular and always in the darkest hours between three and four in the morning. The contractors employed 'night-soil men' to crawl through the ashpit's narrow wooden doors then shovel the refuse into the backyards and from there on to the filthy tumbrils. The sounds of their arrival seemed to issue from the midden itself, as if the earth was spewing them up. They seemed to be under orders to make as much noise as possible, whistling and breaking into snatches of tuneless song or yelling encouragement as their silent terriers hunted down the squeaking rats. When Fred finally summoned up the courage to peep out he saw that they were huge and shapeless, wrapped in lengths of tarred cloth roped at the elbows and knees. Under the wide shovel hats their faces seemed to glitter like polished metal or glass.

Once he had seen a pair belabouring each other with their shovels while their colleagues, helpless with laughter, leaned against the wall. It was hard to see the joke: some had died of asphyxiation while others were said to have been blown apart when thrusting their lanterns into particularly gassy corners. Honey-pot men, drain sniffers, turd-stranglers: they had many names. "What has four legs, a wheel and flies?" – "A honey-pot man with his barrow". Fred still did not get it: surely they must have had arms? He would wrap his head in the blanket and hum loudly to himself but nothing worked. It was as if the smell would enter the bedroom and stand there, looking down at him.

After they had gone the knocker-up would come to summon his father and the others to the mill. It was a stooped old woman carrying a polished white stick or bone: she did not strike the doors but rubbed it against them to create a curious buzzing sound. She was regarded with great respect, as if she was a herald for the sun itself.

And then the cleaning-up would begin: first, the cobbles were swilled down. How slowly the tap used to run! It would take ten minutes for the drips to fill a bucket. And how heavy those buckets were! They dragged on his shoulders and bit red lines into his palms. Then came the scrubbing. He would always remember his mother down on her knees, as if prostrating herself before an altar or a throne. In a synchronized line, their bottoms rising and falling together, it looked as if the women were literally having their noses rubbed in it. Fred thought that he could hear faint laughter, as if hidden spectators were enjoying the humiliation.

The People were not responsible for the conditions in which they lived. You couldn't even blame the ones who ignored basic hygiene, as if to show they didn't care. Some would leave large cloacal handprints on the frames of the sheds: although Mrs Jowett scrubbed them off, they were replaced within the week. His dad claimed that the Lord Mayor was the culprit, that he'd seen him sneaking round the middens, in his cocked hat, robes and chain.

Who *were* the night-soil men? Where did they come from? What crimes had they committed to deserve their fate? His mother would not answer and his father just consoled himself that there were worse things than working at the mill. Young Fred had grown morbidly aware of his own digestive system, eating and drinking as little as possible, resisting his bladder and bowels until the pain became too intense. In the summer, if the moon was out, he would walk to the little copse on All Saints Road where he could bury his dung deep in the soughing grass. Why did the evacuations of humans smell so much worse than those of animals? He asked his parents if he could camp out in Heaton Woods but they only laughed. Fred was sure that he could feel the germs crawling up his nose. Before his elder sisters had died, according to his mother, the wind had blown across a smell like burning treacle.

'F. E.' was still speaking: the usual words in the usual order. As he grew more agitated he would jump into the air, as if the carpet were a circus trampoline. Fred had heard that the women who so assiduously cleaned this chamber were the wives of the night-soil men. It was hard to imagine what they might be like. Perhaps one morning they would have deposited their husbands' gatherings in Smith's place? Not even the plushest fabric would hide that stain.

Jim Sharp and now Snowden would twit him about his sanitary obsessions but who could be unmoved by such horrors? If you could not forget them you could only be obsessed. If you were to keep silent then you yourself might explode: the words would force their way out of you, like Joan of Arc's voices. And why shouldn't the saints or the angels or even God Himself wax indignant over the privy-middens of Bradford?

Wherever he was, he still dreamed of the smell. In London, he had stayed at Hyndman's 'little place', which made the Leach mansion look like a hovel: the notorious revolutionary was a shrewd player on the stock market. But even in Mayfair, swallowed up by that lavender-scented goose-down bed, he had still awakened at ten to four, gagging on the usual stink. Even with three pillows over his head he had heard the scratching and scrapings, the wooden wheels rattling over the cobbles. Snowden had given him a green baize notebook: apparently his best ideas came during sleep and he had trained himself to write them down. And so Fred's first entry had been, 'I know that I am not dreaming'.

Last month, after a particularly gruelling Finance Committee meeting, Hayhurst had coaxed him into the Cock and Bottle for 'a quiet drink'. It had been pandemonium, of course, except in the snug where, as if conducting a séance, a dozen men were sitting silently around the table. Although Fred had never seen their faces he recognized them at once. The night-soil men had grown fatter in retirement or perhaps merely added more layers of insulation. Their glasses were wedged between their gauntleted hands. The only smell was from their tobacco smoke: like heather being burnt off after the grouse season. Apparently the barmaid would not go near them: the empties were stacked up on the table to form a pyramid of glass. When one of them waddled through to the toilet a silence fell and even the fistic Hayhurst had shrunk away.

From across the corridor Fred watched them. After a while, all the heads slowly turned to look back at him. They knew who he was: the man who had cost them their living. Those unblinking, unreadable stares reminded him of a dog fox with a chicken in its mouth that he had once encountered by a farm gate. The creature had not moved: then, as now, Fred had muttered an apology and gone on his way.

"Education is about the spirit!" Smith was yelling. "About the soul! About all that is greatest in the Anglo-Saxon race! A school should be a temple not a barnyard, a fount of wisdom not a feeding trough!"

"Education on an empty stomach," Fred replied, "Is a waste of money." He had long since learned that when you combined the words 'waste' and 'money' the councillors sat up and listened. Jim Sharp had once observed that, as good Christians, you only needed to remind them that the cross and the nails had been uneconomical uses of wood and iron.

⁂

"You have only to *look* at my father and mother," Grayson was saying, "To know that they could never have been my parents. My so-called father deserted from the army, then worked as a docker until a crane crushed his foot, but we had a decent home with books and clothes and food on the table. When I was eight I became tongue-tied: so many things were running through my head that they got all tangled up and nothing would come out of my mouth. They took me to the doctors in Manchester and Leeds, then to a specialist in London: where did the money come from? On the last Sunday of every month my father would limp out of the house and not return until after dark, drunk, with his pockets stuffed with notes and coins. He was either robbing church collection boxes or picking up a mysterious stipend. I was the youngest child by ten years: my so-called mother would have been forty-seven when she bore me. My six brothers are all simpletons. I can only have been born on the wrong side of the blanket, the disowned son of a mighty father."

Snowden was always amused at how many people in the movement claimed to be of noble stock. MacDonald was not really the bastard child of a washerwoman: no, his father had been a Marquis, passing through Lossiemouth. Even Keir Hardie would hint that the blood of William Wallace was running through his veins. Perhaps those aristocrats who were beginning to espouse Socialism would be discovering match-girls and night-soil men perching in their family trees?

"There must be something wrong with me: I've always been content to be plain Philip Snowden of Cowling. Nor do I feel at all reincarnated. So many comrades – especially the Keighley ones – will recall in detail a whole series of previous existences-and always as celebrated historical figures – Cromwell or Cleopatra, Napoleon or Michelangelo. Some had even been fictional characters – Falstaff, Ruy Blas or Pantagruel. My wife once introduced me to three sisters who had all somehow contrived to be Helen of Troy."

"I don't think I'm Napoleon," said Victor, "Cleopatra, perhaps . . . But although I have no religious vocation I am sure that I have a destiny to fulfil. When I don't know what to do, the way always presents itself. When money is short an unexpected cheque arrives. After I was sacked from the factory, Reverend Haigh took me up and got me into college. His reference said I was 'a safe man of the highest moral standards', but then The Rev had unusual notions of safety and morality. And now the great figures of the day come knocking on my door. I'm beginning to suspect that this might be due to something other than my personal charm or a surplus of Christian charity. For example, I'm wondering just who sent you."

"No-one sent me. Dr Aked, your principal, is merely a mutual acquaintance."

"Not *too* mutual, I hope," Grayson sucked in his lips in a curious way, "But perhaps someone told him to approach you. We don't always know when we've been sent."

The interview was not going as Philip had anticipated. It was as if he himself was under interrogation, revealing more and more, while this apparently guileless young man became increasingly enigmatic. Nevertheless, it was a not unpleasant experience: he felt curiously at ease, as if this might have been *his* room, not Grayson's.

"The ILP is my main problem." Those long fingers were picking at the seal of the next packet of cigarettes. "Even though you are its chairman I still cannot bring myself to join."

"I've little love for it myself," said Snowden, "Too many prima donnas, too many impractical men. Hardie's great days are behind him: he's indecisive and forgetful and takes offence at the slightest thing. But someone has to hold the ground between Hyndman's sansculottes and organized labour, especially now that the Representation Committee is drawing the unions further in. We need their money and their numbers but there's a danger that they might take us over. All they care about is the next tanner on the wages: they would not have understood a word of our conversation. They're against anyone who might rock the boat, even if it's by getting them a shilling rather than their blessed tanner. They'll have no foreign policy but John Bull jingoism; they don't care about education or housing or health – except for individual injury compensations. I fear that MacDonald may be our Frankenstein, with the LRC his monster."

"Ramsay Mac came to one of my meetings." said Grayson. "I knew he was important even before they told me who he was. He laughed all through my speech, especially when I was being particularly serious. Afterwards, he shook my hand and winked: 'A canny rant, young man, a canny rant'." The impersonation was so exact that it was as if Philip's arch enemy had suddenly materialized in the room.

Could MacDonald have been behind all this? Had Philip been 'sent' in order to set two potential rivals at each other's throats? It was just the kind of thing that the man would do.

For the last ten minutes Philip had been trying to conceal an inexplicable and embarrassing erection. He had laid his tea-flask across his lap but its heat was only making things worse. He had tried to summon up detumescent images – the pudding faces of the LRC, Hardie's bird's nest beard – but nothing worked.

"I've heard tell of your rhetorical skills," he said, "How you can get your message across."

"Kill!" Grayson rolled his eyes and clawed at the air. "Loot and burn! Burn and loot! Kill! Kill! Kill!" He laughed. It's my variation on 'Come to Jesus' – I call it 'Go to the Devil'. Crude but effective: I'm developing my own style."

"Speaking came naturally to me," said Philip, "When I first stood up in Keighley Liberal Club I felt as if the platform was my home. I didn't realize that I was gripping the lectern, pointing my finger or smiling in a certain way. I was mortified when people told me but then I realized that knowing what you are doing does not make it false."

"However do you get your eyes to change colour? Blue, green, black or as red as burning coals! I've been working on it myself." "It's probably what they call mass suggestion. If people come expecting glowing eyes then that's what they're going to see. But we must never become cynical about public speaking: it's the only way to capture hearts and minds, to make people believe that The New Jerusalem is just around the corner. I shall miss proselytizing: I'm well aware that parliamentary debate will be no substitute . . . should I be fortunate enough to be elected, of course."

"But you know that's a certainty" – Grayson tapped him on the knee, "After the secret deal."

"What secret deal might that be?"

"The one you have done with the Liberals. You pull out and give them a clear run in the target seats and they do the same where LRC candidates have a better chance. Of course, being the chairman of the ILP, you wouldn't know about it but here in the shebeens of Ancoats we talk of little else."

Snowden had reached his accommodation only last week. Secrecy had been taken to ludicrous extremes: when he had met the Blackburn Liberals, at an out of the way inn, their faces had been concealed by broad-brimmed hats and mufflers with one peeping over an obviously false beard.

"I went down to London recently," he said. "John Burns showed me The Tower, The Abbey and Buckingham Palace. The Royal Coach came down The Mall, everybody cheered, and for the first time I had doubts. What chance did we have against such power, pageantry and tradition? Then he took me to the House of Commons. The debating chamber was almost empty: there was dust everywhere, the coloured windows were filthy and even the Speaker's wig looked moth-eaten. But the bars were full. You couldn't tell a Liberal from a Tory: they all looked grey and sick, crooning over their little whiskey-sodas. Then I knew that everything was going to be all right, that a score of honest and determined men would revolutionize the place. Perhaps one day you will be joining me there."

"If I ever do walk through those gates" – Grayson struck a match to light up the last of the Egyptians – "I will be carrying a flaming torch in my hand."

⁂

The school-feeding provisions were doomed: Fred had watched as, one by one, his majority had disappeared. Previously reliable allies were leaning back to study the ceiling, putting their abstaining expressions on. Some of his colleagues were grinning, not averse to seeing him taken down a peg or two. They were developing the mannerisms of their opponents – the slumped shoulders, the heavy-lidded glare, a tendency to laugh together for no discernible reason. He had asked Phil if he himself had begun to look like an alderman. "No, a cabinet minister," came the reply, which was hardly reassuring.

Smith was still smashing away at the crumbling wall of the Liberal rebels' resolve. It was not so much persuasion as coercion, an almost physical threat. Whenever he jumped off the carpet his neck muscles flexed, like a centre-half heading away a muddied football. The increasing brutality of the tirade indicated that he was becoming aware of the absurdity of his own position. He brandished his fists but by the look in his eyes he was in danger of bursting into tears. When they started flailing about they were done for: soon he would be calling everyone 'Comrade' and singing 'The Red Flag'. Fred's life was spent trying to convert people but when he succeeded he could not help feeling an even deeper contempt for them than for those like Briggs Priestley who seemed to have been fashioned out of stone.

Smith's motion was carried by four votes. Even though Fred had long been anticipating this he still felt sick. Victory deferred was even worse than outright defeat: how many months of unnecessary suffering would the children have to undergo before Smith's change of heart communicated itself first to his brain then to his larynx?

Now the councillors had returned to their pictures, celebrating the bequest of a huge canvas entitled *The Intellect And Valour Of Great Britain*. Gladstone and Palmerston were depicted approving a plan for the shelling of Cronstadt while Dickens and Tennyson posed awkwardly with a lenticular stereoscope and Thackeray and Dr Livingstone admired Sir William Armstrong's new cannon. The painting might even have had a mildly subversive intention, for in front of the fifty frock-coated worthies there lay a cocker spaniel, rolling its eyes in apparent despair. To a chorus of anticipatory jeers Fred rose again to his feet. "I will vote no money for the purchase of pictures. I will vote no money for any frivolous or decorative purpose until the needs of the children have been met."

❧

"It is all much more complicated than you imagine," said Snowden. Grayson's attitudes were a curious mixture of dewy-eyed idealism and shocking cynicism.

"On the contrary, the closer I look the simpler it seems. I subscribe to Mesmer's maxim, 'One health, one disease, one remedy'."

"But you're not a hypnotist or a fortune-telling quack. Politics has its own peculiar laws: first and foremost is that everything takes time." Glancing at his watch he realized that he had been here for fully five hours when he was to be speaking in Mytholmroyd at six o'clock. Now Grayson had vanished into the gloom and when he looked back at his watch he could no longer make out its face. All the candles had burnt out. Five hours! Perhaps the young man really did have mesmeric powers?

"I've failed in my mission, haven't I?" Snowden groped for his stick.

"No, you've succeeded in stiffening my resolve. If you want to persuade someone to give up politics, a politician is the worst person to send."

Pulling at the door, Grayson only succeeded in parting it from its final hinge. "Passing through Wales, as a little boy, I climbed Mount Snowdon by mistake. In a few years they'll be changing that 'o' to an 'e', whereas my own commemorative mountain will have to be completely renamed."

"I hope I haven't been a disappointment to you." said Snowden.

"On the contrary, you have exceeded all my expectations," Grayson violently pitched the redundant door down the stairwell, "Unlike The World's Greatest Midget."

Outside everything appeared somehow different. The traffic had slowed to a crawl and the pavement seemed to have been smoothed out. A couple of workmen touched their caps without apparent sarcasm: perhaps even Lancastrians were people too? When the tram to Exchange Station arrived the queue moved aside to let him board and a young woman rose to offer her seat.

"Thank you, miss," he smiled and handed her a pamphlet, "But your need is greater than mine."

Her face was so careworn that she blushed grey rather than red.

It had been an interesting afternoon. What strange thoughts and memories had come into his head: he had completely forgotten that moment in the chapel. Grayson was unusual, all right, someone you might not want on your side but then, not against you either. He certainly seemed an unlikely priest – unless he was to start his own religion. He would tell the authorities that the lad could be trusted to follow his own sense of destiny wherever it might lead him.

Philip's erection had finally wilted: his blood was coursing round his body while the air rushed into and out of his lungs. It was as if he was embarking on a dangerous adventure to an exotic and far-off place, rather than about to lecture to the Calderdale Workmen's Guild. The mill-girl was now holding *The Future of Socialism* upside down in front of her face. The hands were scraped raw with the knucklebones poking through. Fred Jowett would have wept to see them.

How mysterious this crowded tram now seemed: all these individual lives converging to sway together in silent communion. That old man with a goitre who, despite their steady progress, was being pitched about as if by a force nine gale – how sad it was that he would never see him again, never know his story or even his name. The mill-girl still hid her face but now her hands were rose-white and flawless . . . and he saw shining there on the finger of Ethel Annakin Snowden his own plain gold wedding band.

❧

After shaking Snowden's hand at the front door, Victor went backwards up the stairs, two at a time: he had been training himself in case such a skill might one day come in useful. Back in his own room he was deeply touched to discover the fresh packet of Egyptians left on the windowsill. He was going to try to make them last, so he collected all the stubs from the floor and crumbled the remaining tobacco into the bowl of a churchwarden pipe. Pulling back the curtain he watched Snowden board his tram, then reached across and with the long curved stem rapped three times on the wardrobe door. "You can come out now, Harry my dear," he said, "I only hope you haven't been tossing yourself off in there."

CHAPTER FOUR

GRAYSON WEATHER (1907)

IN SLAITHWAITE MARKET-SQUARE a crowd was gathering. One by one the people emerged, peering around as if astonished that so many others just happened to be there. Should one of their bosses happen upon them attending the wrong party's rally, they would claim that they were merely in search of lower-priced potatoes.

Such lunchtime speeches were a waste of time, Fred reflected, except to demonstrate a candidate's capacity for hard work. There were mostly old women, mothers nursing babies, a squadron of invalids in bath chairs and a gang of surly children who had apparently broken out of school. There was no sense of anticipation: the only sound was of water running down the cloughs. The sky had cleared but a fierce wind still blew facefuls of rain back down the valley. The locals knew when to duck but the incomers – party functionaries and gentlemen of the press – already resembled drowning rats.

With heavy emphasis the villagers pronounced their home as 'Slawt': Colne Valley was not a welcoming place. It had a vertiginous feel, as if the ground had been crumpled and folded only a few hours ago and now house, church and mill were sliding towards the river. A great shelf of moorland, Standedge, filled the end of the dale, blocking any escape to Sheffield or Manchester.

It was a long, sprawling constituency of three villages and a dozen smaller hamlets. Cotton manufacture predominated in the west, woollens and worsted in the east. With six hundred hands, Slaithwaite Spinning Company was the largest single employer. The farms along the ridges were tenanted from the Earl of Dartmouth. There were three score churches – one to every five public houses which, Fred suspected, was the divinely-ordained balance between virtue and vice. There was little serious poverty: trade had been strong for years, most of the mills remained un-unionised. Relatively prosperous, isolated and close-knit, its inhabitants surly but deferential, it was not obvious Labour territory. Its few activists, however, had been busy and resourceful. They had included the first ILP county councillor – the Marsden blacksmith, George Gartside – although the seat had reverted on his death. George had been loved for his good humour and cricketing prowess, not for his politics. On the other hand, one of the mill owners, France Littlewood, had recently joined the party – although mainly so that he could conduct the Honley Socialist Mixed Voice Choir.

The rain set in but no-one left. For these two weeks they were suddenly important, with the eyes of the country upon them. In nearby Huddersfield, every hotel was full. All the energies of the great parties were concentrated on their little patch of earth. Folk that usually ignored them now listened to their obscurest grudge and grievance but when the next general election was called, in a couple of years time, Colne Valley would have ceased to matter once again.

Fred was pleased that here, at least, MacDonald's pact with the Liberals was being flouted. You had to admire the bloody-mindedness of the local party, insisting on a three-way fight that they could not win. The National Executive had refused to accept their candidate – an unelectable extremist and not even a local man.

Now he saw a familiar figure crossing the square. Even with only one stick, Snowden was unmistakable. Some of the crowd were glaring, perhaps because he was MP for Blackburn, only two valleys away but on the wrong side of the border. How could a Yorkshireman represent a Red Rose town? And since the election he had become a favourite target of the press. The cartoonists had noticed a resemblance to Dr Nikola, an evil genius in the penny dreadfuls: he was always depicted in a long cloak with a black cat on his shoulder and a smoking bomb in each clawed hand. Philip had been deeply hurt: he would stare at his long delicate fingers, muttering "Nowt wrong with them, is there?" In contrast Jowett, MP for Bradford West, had made but one appearance in caricatural form – as a mongrel dog in eye-glasses, gnawing at The Royal Mace.

"If Snowden doesn't want to be notorious," MacDonald had said, "Then he shouldn't wear that damned hat." A thin-brimmed billycock, surely a size too small, fashioned from shiny reddish cloth, it resembled a tea-pot with handle and spout removed. It was a gift from Ethel: Shaw suggested that it served to conduct the invisible rays of Universal Love.

"Na' then, our Fred," said Snowden warily.

"Na' then, our Phil."

The vernacular seemed the appropriate way for two members of the House of Commons to greet one another. They were part of 'The Labour Earthquake' of twenty-nine MPs: what would people call it when the party had a majority?

"Did you know that Hardie and MacDonald have vetoed the candidate?"

"Of course," Philip put on his sweetest smile, "Isn't that why we're here?"

"Only three months ago, in the council elections, we were beaten out of sight: it truly is a hopeless cause."

"Perhaps," said Snowden, "But by-elections are funny affairs. Folk stop and listen rather than walking on: there is at least stealthy progress to be made. And they say that the young man is doing pretty well."

"He's twenty minutes late," Fred huffed, "For his own meeting."

"It's called making an entrance: I used to do it myself."

Just as Fred was about to demur, an enormous motor car slid silently into the square. The soft canopy was down and the bodywork gleamed: Fred's best guess at its colour was plum with a reddish-purple glow. Not a single raindrop had dared to land on its windscreen or bonnet. A few feeble jeers were drowned out by the wind. Instead of picking up speed, the vehicle drew to a halt. A door opened and a polished black brogue appeared, waggling provocatively. Some urchins threw handfuls of pebbles, all of which missed.

"Stop it, you fools," someone shouted, "It's the bloody candidate!"

At this, the passenger jumped out on to the cobbles. He was tall, pale and slim, wearing a well-cut morning suit, grey with thin silver stripes, over a white wing-collared shirt and a royal blue ribbon tie. His thick fair hair, heavily oiled, was swept straight back: in the centre of his chin was a deep cleft, like the imprint of a thumb. In his right hand he carried a rosewood walking stick with a silver top the size of a fist. Fred found it hard to believe that this man had, until recently, been studying for the priesthood.

The last stone, thrown by the smallest of the boys, struck Grayson on the shoulder but he did not even flinch. The familiar figure of Briggs, the local agent, came pushing through the crowd. Fred could never have imagined such an expression on that florid slab of a face – Briggs was, unmistakably, *smiling*. He took Grayson's arm and they moved towards the speaker's platform, passing the stone-thrower who, when his friends fled, had remained rooted to the spot. The candidate's arm stretched out and ruffled his hair.

"I think the car must belong to The Countess of Warwick," Snowden was licking his lips: unlike Dr Nikola's, his tongue was not forked. "Apparently Hyndman has" – he paused – "*converted* her to our cause."

The platform was an unpainted house door, precariously balanced on three hogsheads. Springing up, Grayson went into a curious hip-swivelling dance before handing to the little boy his extravagant cane. Then he interlaced his fingers and loudly cracked his knuckles.

"Good morning Slaithwaite." The voice was low and conversational but still carried beyond the edges of the crowd. There was a loud gasp, for he had pronounced it as 'Slow-wit'.

"Or should I say good afternoon? I'm sorry to be late but I was getting my hair cut."

Thrusting his fingers into his mouth he gave three piercing whistles like a train entering a tunnel. Those who had been skulking now stepped out of the ginnels and tapsters in filthy aprons appeared in the doorway of The Devonshire Arms.

"Do you like my new hairstyle, ladies?" Grayson brushed imaginary dust from his sleeves and tilted back his head. A shiver seemed to pass down his spine: he shook one foot then the other, like a cat flicking water off its paws. "A bit too short, perhaps, but it kept getting in my eyes. I don't know about you, ladies, but I always like to see *exactly* what I am doing."

Everyone seemed to find this funny. He presented his left profile, then his right.

"Have you noticed how all the chimneys in this valley are different sizes?" He gave an exaggerated wink, "Well, ladies, they do say that variety is the spice of life." He buckled at the knees, clutching at his heart.

The place was in uproar. Fred had never known an audience to react like this. Grayson effortlessly dominated the scene. Housewives ignored the stalls, tradesmen's boys forgot their errands and a drayman stopped his wagon, adjusting the straps so that his horses could also see and hear. No-one noticed that, directly above, a swarm of sparrows was mobbing a hen-harrier until Grayson pointed it out to illustrate how the humble many could combine to overthrow the mighty few.

The man had a curiously flickering smile, revealing teeth even less socialistic than Bernard Shaw's. How could he have been brought up in the slums of Liverpool? And his eyes were even stranger: they never blinked and seemed to change colour - green, then blue, then almost black. His right hand gestured extravagantly, while the flat of the other rested on the head of the stone-throwing boy who still clutched the stick, its silver fist pressed under his chin.

For a while the speech took a more conventional form. Unemployment was to be reduced, canals and railways nationalized, and an eight hour day, universal education and free school meals introduced. The tone, however, was ironic, as if Grayson was paying lip service to these things. In contrast, he spoke of women's suffrage with more surely passion than any man should, whereas housing and sanitation were never mentioned at all.

The crowd had more than doubled since he began. His remarks were increasingly directed to a knot of bonneted mill-girls who had scrambled on to the back of the drayman's cart. Their pale upturned faces seemed to blur and merge together like frogspawn. Three large clergymen had worked their way to the front. Fred thought that they were about to remonstrate but it was apparent that they heartily approved. The tallest and thinnest, with a huge wedge-shaped head, applauded loudest of all, turning his burning eyes on his fellows until their enthusiasm matched his own.

Now Grayson was distorting his face to imitate the features of his Tory and Liberal opponents. It seemed that these unfortunates walked oddly and had poor taste in clothes. 'Never trust a rich man who won't spend his money on a decent pair of shoes': he raised his left foot to allow an obliging shaft of sunlight to strike the gleaming toe.

It was a relief when a heckler started up. Such men were recruited by the established parties for beer money, although most would have done it for free. They were local 'characters' who would abuse referees and umpires, tender advice to folk who hadn't asked for it, insist on cheering up anyone who looked depressed or taking down a peg or two anyone who didn't. If a 'character' was particularly strong-lunged and persistent he could, in time, ascend to the stature of 'wag'.

"I'm not going to quote Scripture to you," said Grayson.

"Because you don't know any."

"How about this? 'The sound of the fool reacheth even to the ends of the earth'."

At this the sun came fully out and Snowden peeled off his fingerless gloves.

"I nearly became a priest, you know, but I didn't like the uniform or the hours. I ask you, ladies, what is a man without his Sunday morning" – that wink again – "Lie-in?"

"God save the King!" yelled the heckler unexpectedly.

"I've nothing against His Majesty. In fact, I'll be happy to buy him a drink the next time he's passing through Slaithwaite . . . before we put him in those comfy-looking stocks."

The crowd surged forward, breaking like waves against the improvised platform, but the little boy stood his ground, clutching the stick, staring fiercely back into their faces.

"Some say that I'm too young. Well, I'm already older than Chatterton and Keats were when they died. How old was David when he smote Goliath? And at my age Buffalo Bill had already killed seventy-three Indians. Well," – he assumed an American drawl – "I'm aiming to take my first two scalps right here in Colne Valley: your would-be representatives, Bright and Wheler – although by the look of them someone has got there already."

"You're no working man." The heckler tried again. "Where are the hooves on your hands?"

Grayson stared hard into his palm as if it might be a magic mirror in which the future would appear. Then he breathed on his fingernails and polished them on his lapels.

"Have you any hooves on your hands?" The man's own hands, punching at the air, appeared to be made of badly-fired brick.

Sadly, Grayson shook his head. "No, my friend. There are no hooves on my hands." Two long lines appeared at the corners of his mouth then deepened. "But it is clear to everyone that you, at least, have hooves on the brain."

As the crowed brayed, Fred wondered whether this man might not have hooves on his feet. Perhaps under those surely too-tight trousers there was a forked and lashing tail.

After a relatively orthodox peroration the speech ended in an abrupt and curious fashion.

"And after all these things have been achieved" – the tone was now subdued – "Then will come the greatest challenge . . . The emancipation of the human body."

Then he jumped backwards, out of sight, leaving the door rocking. For a good twenty seconds, the crowd stared numbly at the empty space and then there was an explosion of sound, as if from two thousand not two hundred throats. Fred was sure that he could hear the horses stamping and the birds singing. The tall priest pointedly clapped his bony hands before Fred's face but he kept his own resolutely at his sides.

"Have you ever seen anything like that?" Snowden almost chortled.

"No" – Fred firmly pushed the priest aside – "I can honestly say that I have not."

Grayson was coming towards them. As he passed people touched him on the shoulder, but lightly, so that he would not feel it.

"Very dapper, Victor," said Snowden, "I see that you've literally stolen the enemies' clothes. Allow me to introduce Fred Jowett of Bradford."

"I've long been an admirer of yours" – Grayson's handshake was insidiously soft – "Bun, banana and beverage! That's the stuff to give the troops!" Fred's eyes were refusing to bring his features into proper focus.

"Did you enjoy that? A good crowd always takes you to unexpected places. It wasn't my best but you have to get acquainted first. What I usually do is just chunter away and then suddenly sound the last trump: it really knocks their socks off. But you've got to be careful: I don't want to kill anyone. When I get to Westminster, though, I'll let them have it full blast."

He lit Snowden's proffered cigarette and took a great pull, hissing as he drew it down to the pit of his stomach. When he exhaled no smoke emerged. Fred felt as if he had never seen anyone really smoking until now.

"Do you actually think you're going to win?" His own voice sounded ugly, as if clotted with disgust.

"Well, Bright and Wheler are a couple of mutton-heads. When anyone asks a question their agents have to feed them the response, slowly, one word at a time. Everyone I meet has promised their support" – the smoke suddenly emerged from his mouth in one great grey ring – "But perhaps they don't want to disillusion me. Never wake a sleep-walker: Vote Grayson – that will be my slogan."

The clergymen were now leading the crowd in a distinctly secular rendition of 'The Red Flag'.

"How good it is to have God on our side," Grayson stubbed out his cigarette. "That's the curate of Thongsbridge, which is not even in this constituency. As Blatchford might say, he's six foot of socialist and six inches . . . of parson." Fred knew without looking that he was winking again.

"If you'll excuse me, gentlemen, I've got to track down old hooves-on-the-hands. I want him at all my meetings: a good heckler is a pearl beyond price!"

They watched him go. It was hard to tell whether the crowd was swallowing him up or he was swallowing them.

"It's true that voters don't like it when their sitting member deserts them for The Lords," said Snowden. "But even if the Liberal vote collapses, the Tories will still turn out. Nevertheless, Grayson is quite remarkable: he may even be the man this party has been waiting for."

Fred felt that he himself had indeed been waiting for Grayson but with dread rather than anticipation. Here at last was the real enemy – more dangerous than any mill-owner or aristocrat. For the first time in his life he actually hated someone. Had all that work served only to provide a platform for simpering demagogues to take over the movement for their own ends? What was worst was that he had not the least notion of what Grayson's ends might be.

"Don't fret, our Fred," said Phil, "He's just setting the old words to a new tune, as you and I did."

"Will you be speaking for him?"

"I'm not sure." Snowden scowled. "The local executive have refused to stump up my five bob expenses. You know that I don't care about money but it's a point of principle. If folk pay nowt they think you're worth nowt."

"One thing I don't understand," said Fred, "Is why Grayson concentrated on the women when they don't even have the vote."

"No," Snowden pulled down the brim of his notorious hat. "But their sons and husbands do."

❧

Hating Ramsay MacDonald was a solitary and exhausting pastime. In a party riven with tensions and rivalries he alone commanded universal respect. Even those he had worsted took it in good part. "You've got to hand it to him," they would say, licking their wounds. Snowden knew what he would like to hand MacDonald – one of Dr Nikola's fizzing bombs.

Tall and leonine, he was considered to be the best-looking man in the movement. He seldom smiled, spoke in a low Scots burr and favoured stiff tweeds, even in the warmest weather. He resembled not so much the illegitimate son of a washerwoman as some platonic ideal of a country squire. All the ladies, except for Ethel, were thrilled by his elaborate courtesy. "He flirts by not flirting," she said, "But I can feel his thoughts crawling across my skin." MacDonald had a distinctive smell – like fresh wood shavings – but Ethel knew where he had bought his cologne and how much he had paid for it.

His sheer competence and capacity for hard graft could not be denied. Away from politics he would repair to the Scottish mountains over which he would cover vast distances at incredible speed, striding without a second glance past golden eagles and the

Monarch of the Glen. He liked to go out in bad weather when no-one else stirred: on rare sunny days he would stay indoors and read. Joseph Conrad was said to be his favourite author: strange tales for a strange man.

Philip could hardly bear to look at him. In repose he was undeniably handsome but when he moved everything went horribly wrong. The way his arms and legs pumped when he was merely crossing the room! And those long earlobes, pinkish under fine white fur - Philip was sure that he could hear them flapping to and fro. And wasn't the mouth weak under the shadow of that splendid moustache? If you positioned yourself to his left, then ducked low and squinted, the face resembled one of the gargoyles on Wells Cathedral. When Philip was in the same room - even in the great chamber of the House - he would feel his chest tighten, as if the man was somehow depriving him of air.

In recent months party business had brought them together so often that Philip seemed to be spending more time with him than with Ethel. So here he was again at MacDonald's house in Lincoln Inn Fields, in the small back parlour that served as an office for the LRC. When Mrs Mac, spectrally pale and silent, had admitted Philip he had glimpsed, hanging in the hall, a hat just like his own, on which so much of her husband's sarcasm had been expended. Perhaps its effect would be different when stuck on that noble head?

As usual, MacDonald was sitting with the light behind him, although even if Snowden could have seen his expression he would not have been able to read it. Whenever he entered this room he felt as if he had been summoned and when he left he felt as if he was being dismissed. He hated having to call him 'Mac': the diminutive stuck in his throat like a fishbone - pronouncing it as 'Muck' gave him some relief. MacDonald, in his turn, addressed him as 'Snudden', snorted down that long nose as if it were a method of clearing phlegm.

"This Colne Valley affair goes from bad to worse," Mac began. "The candidate is acting as a magnet for the disaffected and mentally disturbed. Pernicious pamphlets such as *this* are circulating through the movement." He handed it to Snowden: the paper was grainy and coarse and the badly-set letters could only be read with difficulty.

WHI I AM ANARKIST

1. Bekase I am nobody but myself and nobody is me.
2. Bekase I believe in nuthin but voluntary taxashun and pa-ing nothink for alkinhole.
3. Bekase I have the inklinashun to marrie and kannot and bekase the other secks don't like me I am in faver of the State abolishing marridge. I am an ibsinite out and out.
4. Bekase I am not in faver of the State. The State cannot understand me even though it tryd. The Socialists thinks the State can but it kan't.

"I don't really think it's Grayson's style." Said Philip at last.

"Of course it isn't." Mac crossed his legs. "I wrote it myself."

"I wasn't aware that anarchists can't spell," said Philip, "And the few that I have met – although annoying in some respects – seemed to be reasonably popular with the ladies."

"It's just my little joke, Snowden" – Mac's sinuses rattled – "But one with a serious purpose. We must always keep a curb on envy and spite, however understandable such feelings may be."

Every time he opened his mouth he became more sanctimonious. Why was Philip the only person to realize this? At this moment, without knocking, MacDonald's two youngest children – radiant, curly-haired creatures – came running in. They dived under the table, then emerged, carrying between them a large sleeping tabby cat. Philip often wondered whether the man had hired himself this family for appearances' sake.

If the hatred had been mutual it would have been easier to bear but, as far as he could tell, MacDonald felt indifferent towards him.

It was, however, an indifference of such intensity that it rocked you like a physical force. They had never confronted one another: their relations were conducted with almost oriental politeness. How many times had Philip said that petty antagonisms must not get in the way of the cause? But when that head turned towards him, jaw set at a disgustingly indomitable angle, all such resolutions went out of the window.

"None of this should have happened." Mac had finished his cocoa. "We should have consulted the constituency party earlier. We should have made suggestions, not given orders. We should have told them to select Grayson for the General Election instead. I myself take full responsibility for all these mistakes."

Snowden was not fooled by this. The man really did believe that it was everybody else's fault but that only his own shoulders were broad enough to bear the weight of failure.

"Glasier is set against Grayson because he has always fancied the seat for himself. Hardie keeps relenting and then, for no apparent reason, opposes him even more fiercely than before." His voice quavered. "Over my dead body!" Mac's powers of mimicry were celebrated, although when he launched into his extensive repertoire of Grand Duchesses it didn't seem quite so funny anymore.

"I have been in correspondence with the young man," MacDonald picked up a sheet of cream vellum, "Seeking to discover what his intentions are. 'A change has got to come and nothing will be lost by precipitating it'" – his impersonation of Grayson was as good as Grayson's impersonation of him. "He seems to feel that the links between the main party and the unions should be severed. Perhaps when you see him you could say that I am far from unsympathetic to this view. Given a free hand I will send the unions to the Devil, along with the Liberals. But there is no reason why in the meantime we should not use their money and organisation. When the Liberals are dished we can make the unions reapply for affiliation on very different terms. I am sure you understand,

Comrade Snowden" – he *could* pronounce the name properly when he wished! – "Why I am loath to commit such sentiments to paper."

"You don't always know when you've been sent," Grayson had said. Now, beyond the ostensible message, Philip had the uneasy feeling that MacDonald had implanted some other purpose in his mind and that he would be leaving, all unawares, to do his master's will.

The Grayson business grew stranger by the day. Last night, Snowden had attended a banquet at the Lyceum Club with Ethel, representing the International Women's Association. Apart from a charity auction of modernist daubs and weirdly-angled sculptures, it had been a pleasant evening. He had been discussing the Moroccan crisis with Shaw and Lord Haldane: the respect with which his own remarks had been received indicated just how far the movement had come. What *did* surprise him, however, was just how well-informed everyone had been on the progress of the Colne Valley by-election. Even Mrs Keppel, current mistress of the King, had displayed a deep understanding of the shades of opinion in Golcar, Slaithwaite and Diggle

"I'm beginning to think that Grayson might win." he said.

"Was there ever any doubt about it?" MacDonald leaned back in his chair and stretched, the shadows of his fingers brushing the ceiling. "Soon the question may not be whether we are endorsing Grayson but whether Grayson is endorsing us."

❧

"Wheels will turn and a grey sun will burn
And bright will be dim and a victor will win."

For the last thirty years an old woman in Marsden had been repeating this gnomic but hitherto obscure couplet. Since witch-burning ceased it appeared that every village had its own

Mother Shipton. Victor had been taken to see her: the addled old soul could have been mumbling anything at all.

She had been right, though: the Liberal Philip Bright, son of the legendary free-trader, and Granville Wheler, a Protectionist Conservative were proving to be ideal opponents. They were obsessed with proposed changes in the Licensing Laws. One was for, the other against, although their agents, Sherwell and Ruddock, had to keep reminding them which was which. A verse circulated, composed by Briggs and Grayson, then arranged by Littlewood, to be sung by the Honley Choir in versions fast and slow.

> "Sherwell had a little lamb
> Its name was Philip Bright
> And every day would Sherwell cram
> What Philip must recite!
> To echo Sherwell everywhere
> Was Philip's nightly rule
> It made electors laugh and stare
> To see Poor Phil at school."

Poor Phil and the stuttering Wheler were both wall-eyed and scanty-haired with a curiously famished look. They resembled newspaper caricatures of Socialist fanatics while Grayson looked like the establishment candidate. The more he was advised to dress simply the more dandified he became.

"I'll wear rags or go naked but never will I be drab. My clothes tell our people that anything is possible. Our opponents cannot duck the real issues by drawing attention to supposed deficiencies in my manners and dress."

"That's what we're doing," crowed Briggs, "Now the boot's on the other foot."

The Conservatives had responded to the threat by painting their headquarters in stripes of red, white and blue and putting in an order for an enormous union jack flag. "They will be needing one large enough to cover the whole bloody constituency," Briggs said. This project was ill-fated: looms mysteriously broke down, then the reds and blues ran together until everything turned purple and they had to start again. Then the mill-girls struck, refusing to work through their lunchtimes and demanding double time for the extra hours.

How Victor loved the broad leather belts of the mill-girls! Every day they seemed to circle their already narrow waists one notch tighter. Each part of the constituency had its characteristic female type. In Slaithwaite, chubby blondes boldly brushed against you but got very hoity-toity if you responded too quickly. The tall brunettes of Marsden would stare into your eyes: he did not fully understand the dialect that streamed from the corners of their mouths but the import was clear enough. In Golcar there were pale redheads with heavily muscled arms who winked all the time. The unmarried girls would indicate their availability by carrying empty wicker baskets on their arms but he strongly suspected that most of the others wanted their baskets filling as well.

But Victor had forsworn the pleasures of the flesh and also signed the pledge for the duration of the campaign. On the second day, after he had failed to return from a visit to Manchester, a Colne Valley posse had stormed into The Horned Lamb at midnight to frog-march him out. However had they found him? They must have known more than he thought. His subsequent abstention had required no effort of will. Even when the weather improved he took no more than the occasional sip of water. "It's a shame you don't drink," people would say. The only way a working man could express affection was by offering to stand him a pint.

He often felt aroused but his erections were independent of any object or stimulus. Evidently what his first mentor, The Reverend Aked, had always said was true, "The virile member points upwards to Heaven, Victor, not downwards to Hell. Think of it as God's fingerpost, exhorting you to rise not fall."

Wherever he went he could feel Thongsbridge's fanatical eyes burning into him. Now The Reverend Swann had resigned as Marsden's Congregational Minister to also work full time for Socialism. Victor felt that such men were labouring under some misapprehension but nothing he said or did could deter them. He suspected that they had not been converted by Ruskin or Marx but by the art of an Ancoats Tailor: it was the cut of his trousers that had done the trick.

After a while he could leave his listeners to continue on their own. This slackening of tension only generated an even greater heat. He was practising a new science for which no textbooks existed. Cicero and Quintilian had hardly scratched the surface: *words* were only the starting point. There was no doubt that chance and nature actively helped him. When the sun was required to dim itself, obliging clouds would bundle across the sky. If he needed a dog, one would bark. After a duel with a rooster at Netherton Cross he had incorporated a crowing section into his addresses. Journalists had speculated whether this was some secret revolutionary code. Now, whenever he mentioned the names of his opponents the crowd would whistle Grieg's 'In the Hall of the Mountain King'. His instincts were unerring: everything he tried came off . . . And so he was borne along by the current until at last, twenty hours later, he would find himself washed up at the side of his bed – a creaking four-poster in Littlewood's guest room. And then, without even unlacing his shoes, still fully dressed, he would topple forward to sink blissfully into deep and dreamless sleep.

※

Colne Valley now held a horrible fascination for Fred. He came to campaign, of course, but also to follow the bewildering course of events. Why ever had the people cast off their habitual suspicion of outsiders for a man with such extreme views and outlandish manners?

"He's not from round here," shouted one heckler. "He's not even Yorkshire – he's bloody Scouse!"

"Shut up, you fool," said an even louder voice. "Our Victor comes from everywhere!"

It was as if they had known him all his life: a feckless but much loved youngest son. Dark rumours had circulated since the arrival of The Duchess of Warwick's secretary – a tall and slim young woman always at the candidate's side – but even these did him little harm. "There's nowt wrong with a young lad liking a bit of fun," said one old woman, a girlish blush spreading across her stony features. It was as if the by-election had made them believe that they were more exciting than they could ever have imagined. Perhaps every hamlet in Britain would soon be as incendiary as Moscow, Paris or Berlin?

From dawn until long after dark the man ranged the constituency. He seemed to be everywhere at once. One reporter had seen him above Netherley at exactly the same time that another had heard him speak on Scapegoat Hill, six miles away. Everyone had their own tale to tell about him. Perhaps he was really twins or even triplets? He thrived on confrontation: when a Honley butcher had berated him, waving his cleaver, he had merely nodded with such a droll expression of mock terror that the man had finally burst out laughing and presented him with a prime cut of beef which the Duchess' secretary passed on to the poorest family she could find.

Even without official endorsement the campaign did not lack outside support. Although Snowden and Clynes were the only other ILP figures to attend there were also the Pankhursts and Annie Kenney from the Suffragettes, Gavan Duffy and his wild Irishmen, Blatchford and the *Clarion* Group, Hyndman and the SDF. Sometimes Fred encountered Kathleen Conway, still wearing the green velour dress which had once so excited Jim Sharp. Her appeal was lost on him: those protruding eyes were strangely disturbing. She had recently married Bruce Glasier who was apparently Grayson's chief enemy on the NEC. "I'll campaign for

Satan himself," she laughed, "If he runs on the Socialist ticket."

National interest was growing. The People were all too happy to accommodate newspapermen in search of local colour. How Fred wished that they would not demean themselves in this way! Everyone claimed to be the eldest or youngest of seventeen children, their dialect thickening until they could no longer understand even each other. When the man from *The Times* requested a bill of fare at The Devonshire Arms he was offered a choice of worm-pie or a skilleted haunch of weasel. Some folk were said to have seen the barghest, a spectral hound as large as a shire horse with saucer eyes and a high-pitched yap, even though the creature had never been known to leave its cave in Trollers' Gill, forty miles away. It always appeared at by-elections, they claimed, although this was the first that Colne Valley had ever held. The campaign had coincided with a remarkable heat wave which nobody seemed to think was a coincidence. The tar on the roads melted, the earth crumbled, heather and gorse caught fire. Everyone's skins were burnt red or brown, it was even hotter at night than by day. 'Grayson weather', they were calling it.

One afternoon, as Fred was marching up the hill to Marsden station, Grayson's car came rolling in the opposite direction. The gleaming door swung open, a woman's voice called his name and before he knew what was happening he found himself inside. It was like entering a hothouse: Grayson, Briggs and the secretary were all doused in exotic and contending scents. Even so, Fred was sure that he could catch a different, fouler smell beneath. The green leather seat felt sticky to his touch: he hoped that those door handles were not solid silver. The car by-passed the main street, picked up speed and headed towards the fells. Only now did he register that the woman's tiny hands were gripping the wheel. He considered jumping out but they were travelling at a tremendous rate, at least thirty miles an hour. "Isn't this every Socialist's secret dream," enquired Grayson, "to be kidnapped by a beautiful woman in a big shiny car?"

She certainly knew how to drive, taking some corners flat out but then, by some sixth sense, slowing down just before a straying lamb or collapsed stone wall appeared. Even so, Briggs kept his hands over his eyes. "She's also my bodyguard," said Grayson, "Thongsbridge is getting more and more demonstrative. If necessary, I have instructed her to throw herself between us."

The man had twisted the mirror and was combing his hair.

"Why do you always wear blue ties?" Fred asked. "Why not red?"

"Because a red tie is *your* trademark. Besides, it's a bit too obvious: the sort of thing everyone would expect me to do."

He continued to prattle away – rubbish with some sort of double meaning. Fred succeeded in blocking most of it out.

"I'm glad we've had the chance of this little chat." Grayson concluded without apparent irony as the car left the track and careered across the fields, stopping at last by a large rock shaped like the back of a whale.

"My voice would be gone by now," Grayson swigged from a large dark bottle, "If it wasn't for Owbridge's Lung Tonic. It tastes vile but I reckon it has a hefty opium base." He climbed up on the whale's back. "Where is my audience?" The nearby farm appeared to be derelict and there was no sign of movement along the lanes below. There were only a few newly-shorn sheep, over by the wall, trying to fold themselves into a bare two feet of shade.

"Let's get back to civilisation." Despite his deerstalker Briggs looked utterly incongruous in a field.

"I am here to speak," said Grayson, "And speak I shall. At any moment a hundred lusty farm-boys gagging for Socialism will be breasting yonder hill." He cleared his throat and smoothed down his hair.

"Ewes, rams and lambs of Crosland Moor! On this very spot, on 28th April 1812, a century ago, a group of Luddites ambushed and killed William Horsfall, a mill-owner and Justice of the Peace, although notions of Justice or Peace meant nothing to such as he . . . The men were tried and subsequently hanged . . . But how bountifully the heather has grown since the oppressor's blood soaked into your good Yorkshire earth! And soon new blooms will be seen springing up from the blood of those forty thousand Horsfalls who are still leeching off the body of this suffering land."

The sheep – a curious local hybrid with long noses and spindly shanks – struggled to their feet and began to trot towards the speaker.

"I can see that Comrade Jowett is not amused," cried Grayson. "But if St Francis could address the birds, then I can do no less for your good selves. And besides, I know that you are no ordinary sheep, but those invoked by Engels and Marx, so long awaited by radicals everywhere. I immediately recognized you as the dictator sheep of the proletariat."

Fred turned on his heel. Instead of heading back down the valley he made for the skyline: he had to get away. After a few yards he was bathed in sweat. The angles of these slopes were subtly different from his familiar Dales. Striding too short or too long he would stumble every few steps. Small, slithery pebbles gave way to soft mosses that tugged at the soles of his shoes. This was the first time in ages that he had been in real countryside but it was not having its usual restorative effect. He could sense the hill's indifference, as if Nature herself had forgotten him. Evidently this was another price that you paid for being in politics.

He did not stop until he had reached the summit. Far below the car flashed silver in the sunlight. Grayson was still addressing the sheep: the congregation was swelling, with white dots moving down the fellside to join the rest of the flock. A grotesque shadow came sweeping across the lower fields: for a moment he took it for the spectral dog but it was only the Curate of Thongsbridge on a bicycle far too small for him.

Fred glared at a solitary skylark, held in suspension by its wild song and desperately beating wings. Even it was reminding him of

Grayson. If he tacked along the ridge he would come straight down on to the station platform and make good his escape. He would not be returning to Colne Valley: the whole place had gone mad or worse. He wondered whether it might vanish with a clap of thunder on polling day, leaving only a whiff of brimstone behind.

⁂

Even though nobody would notice, Victor was now changing his tie half a dozen times a day. He was also exploring the possibilities of hats: the white wide-brimmed Stetson seemed to go down best. The more dressy he became the more they liked it. The more extreme his speeches the louder they cheered. Now his audiences included mill-owners, wildly applauding the news of their own demise.

"We must break the rule of the rich and take our destinies into our own hands! The other classes have had their day, it is our turn now!"

"Is that why you're driving round in their cars?" enquired Hooves-On-Hands.

"Yes, and it is they who are chauffeuring me. If the blessed thing breaks down it won't be me crawling under the bonnet – at least, not in these trousers."

Even on these cloudless days there was always a wind, like the hot breath of a dragon. It had obviously taken exception to Victor's hat. He had borrowed the secretary's pins but this was a battle he was never going to win. Away it went at last, taking with it a tuft of hair, finally descending, after five or six giddy revolutions, to land athwart the head of Ernest Marklew. He was a funny little man with ribboned eyeglasses and a widow's peak, one of many such who silently tagged along behind. Now he stood as if petrified, eyes rolling in his crimson face, while Victor straightened the brim then pulled it down. The hat half-swallowed the head: its band rested on that long straight nose; mouth and chin were lost in the shadow. "There," said Victor, "it looks much better on you." The effect was more like a helmet: perhaps he could cut eye-holes in it?

"Keep it, Comrade Marklew. The hat has made its choice."

From that moment Marklew no longer merely stood and stared. Cursing loudly - and with surprising invention - he pursued his wind-borne Stetson around the constituency. The thing even blew away during indoor meetings but he would never abandon it. They said he even slept in it: "No, *inside* it," said Victor.

Despite the Owbridge's his vocal cords were shredded. He still chain-smoked, though, for without a cigarette his voice vanished altogether. Fortunately, Snowden and his Egyptians were often on hand, although Jowett had vanished from the scene. Why did the man dislike him so much? Such antipathy often masked a guilty physical attraction but he doubted that this was the reason. Try as he might he could not visualize Our Fred in any sexual context. Even if you took his cock in your mouth he would doubtless continue droning on about infant mortality or Tippler closets. He was generally considered to be the most boring man in the movement.

"Victor Grayson . . . Victor Grayson . . . Victor Grayson." Things were getting out of hand. It was as if every mouth could only form these four syllables.

"De-da-da-dum" - like Big Ben sounding a quarter past the hour. Only twelve years ago not even Tom Mann had been able to get these people off their knees but now they were talking as if Grayson had arrived in Wells' *Time Machine* from some wonderful and impending future. Fred thought they were bewitched but Philip did not take it so seriously. They applauded the bloodiest passages, true, but they were laughing as they did so. It was all a bit of fun. Even unregenerate Liberals and Tories admired him: once he had sowed his political wild oats he would doubtless be moving on to their own parties. "That young man will be anything he wants to be," said the Liberal agent. Apparently Grayson had helped to write a speech for poor doomed Philip Bright, culminating in a savage attack on himself.

Philip had expected the campaign to run out of steam but it never did. Every time he took the train from Huddersfield he could tell how much more the established parties' vote had crumbled. Marsden, Slaithwaite and Golcar were evenly split between red, yellow and blue favours: some contrary households sported all three at once. Hornby and Delph were solid red and Milnsbridge's blue was beginning to fade. He and Briggs had advised Grayson to concentrate on the main centres but he always refused. "I haven't found Cinderella yet," he said, "And bear in mind that every lane I walk down will retain my traces." What on earth was that supposed to mean? He kept hammering away at solidly Liberal Diggle because he liked the name so much: "I will be Master of Diggle ere I die!"

When Philip himself spoke, with those two token half-crowns merrily jingling in his trouser pocket, he made a point of never mentioning Grayson's name.

"Why don't you talk about Victor?" they shouted.

"Because he never talks about me. Your candidate only names the people he attacks and that is a good principle to follow. We would all like to pay each other compliments but there is too much else to do. The time for mutual back-slapping will be when our struggle is finally over."

His crowds were unusually subdued and the applause, when it came, could only be described as polite. Some folk even drifted away while 'Come to Jesus' was still in full spate. Unlike Lord Haldane, they evinced no interest in the Moroccan Crisis. "Bugger the Moroccians!" shouted Hooves-on-Hands. "And bugger the Blackburnians as well." It was as if Philip's constituency was a thousand miles away, not sixteen. Once he had lived for public speaking but now he took little pleasure in it. Even so, he could still make converts: his practised eye told him that during his twenty-six speeches the expressions on the faces of a hundred and fifty-three people had changed.

Although there had been no trouble during the campaign more and more policemen were patrolling the area between Marsden Station and the Conservative Club. They had an increasingly surly air and some were swigging openly from bottles of beer.

"Why are you here?" he asked a tall sergeant.

"Just in case."

"In case of what?"

"Civil disorder," the man tapped the handle of his truncheon, "We've got The Riot Act all ready to read."

As the train pulled out Philip lit his last Egyptian: that damned boy had smoked the rest. He squinted out of the window. No, it wasn't merely the rays of the setting sun: thirty-six hours before polling day, Diggle was turning red.

༄

"Bright (Liberal): Three thousand four hundred and ninety-five," announced the returning officer, framed in the none-too-impressive entrance of Slaithwaite Town Hall. "Grayson (Socialist): Three thousand six hundred and forty-eight. Wheler (Conservative): Thirty-three thousand two hundred and twenty-four."

This was indeed a remarkable result for there were only twelve thousand registered voters in the whole constituency. It was only at the third attempt that the correct figures were read.

"I hereby declare that the aforesaid Victor Grayson is returned as the elected representative for the Colne Valley."

The mill-girls had finally produced their flag: not a union jack but an enormous scarlet sheet. Taking off their matching headscarves they fluttered them in concert, having obviously been practising for this moment. Bright and Wheler were pointedly not congratulating Grayson so he insisted on kissing them on both cheeks. His mascot - he could never remember the little boy's name - handed back the silver-topped stick, gave an impressively formal bow and disappeared into the wildly-cheering crowd.

"The first scalp for Custer!" Victor's ruined voice was lost in the roar. Hands grasped his wrists and ankles and he was hoisted, chaired down the main street, then deposited on the familiar rocking door opposite The Dartmouth Arms.

"I am simply a bullet, fired by the Colne Valley workers against the established order" – it was the merest croak, but it carried perfectly well in the sudden silence. "This epoch-making victory has been won for pure revolutionary Socialism. We have not trimmed to get a half-hearted vote. We have proclaimed our Socialism on every platform. I have been returned through the work, devotion, love and idealism of the people of Colne Valley and, being returned, I shall feel that my duty is to be the old men and women's member, the starving child's member."

"You have voted, you have worked for Socialism. You have voted, you have worked for the means of life to be the property of a whole class, instead of a few small classes. We stand for equality, human equality, sexual equality" – his voice felt as if it was shattering like glass – "for the abolition" – it had gone but he managed to find a final whisper – "for the abolition of sex-ties."

Taking this as their cue, The Honley Socialist Mixed Voice Choir tore into 'England Arise'. Marklew went scuttling after his hat, which was making for the canal again. The crowd plucked Victor up once more and bore him, lying on their upturned palms, into the pub. He reached out to touch the ceiling. There could surely be no better moment than this: it was as if he was attending his own wake.

"Well now, my Honourable Gentleman," said Christine the barmaid, "Will it be milk or Owbridge's?"

"I'll have a pint of dark porter," Victor's voice had miraculously returned to normal. "And a treble whiskey."

"One thing I don't understand," Marklew panted, "Is why you, of all people, would want to do away with neck-ties."

"And how on earth are we going to abolish sex?" Thongsbridge gabbled into his other ear. "Whatever will we be putting in its place?"

"Irish, if you've got it," Victor called down the bar. "And if you're out of worms and weasels I'll have a chunk of that Wensleydale – no, dammit, give me the whole bloody cheese!"

CHAPTER FIVE

NAMED (1908)

RATHER TO HIS surprise Snowden was warming to his new life. From their roomy top-floor flat in Barons Court to the House was a mere six stops on the District Line. His comrades complained about how unfriendly London was, compared to the North, but he felt very much at home. In Manchester|or Leeds it was always perfectly apparent who was who and what was what, whereas here you would pass, in the short walk to the tube station, half a dozen people for who there was no accounting at all. Philip did not want to know the truth about the horribly scarred man who only sat out on his balcony on rainy days or the veiled and freakishly tall woman who every morning took her dogs – Pomeranians walking on their hind legs – around Hammersmith Cemetery. No, he was happy to speculate and dream.

Only when you were actually there did Parliament start to make sense. You even began to admire your opponents. The Conservative leader Balfour, for example – with his irony, his pauses, his lethal left eyebrow – was the best speaker in The House. With an astonishing repertoire of sniffing and throat-clearings he was the Paganini of the respiratory tract. He, in his turn, always turned up to hear Philip: according to Lloyd George he was struck by the resemblance to Watts' notorious Cardinal Manning portrait – 'a foretaste of Hell'.

Even as a new member in a small party, with the government enjoying a large majority, it was remarkable how much influence you could exert. His private chats with Churchill and Lloyd George had been revelatory: not only were these ostensibly flamboyant characters firm believers in sound economics but they also recognized that radical social reforms were inevitable. Paying off the National Debt, introducing means-tested old age pensions, shifting from indirect taxation to direct: all these things, they agreed, were merely common sense. Change was no longer the issue, only the speed of it. Lloyd George spoke of twenty years, Churchill a hundred, while he himself thought that two parliamentary terms would suffice. In contrast, Jowett talked of a few months and Grayson of weeks or days or even hours.

If only Fred would understand that raising all those parliamentary questions was counter-productive! And that labelling Lloyd George a profiteer for raising the Plimsoll Line was merely vulgar abuse. Even worse, he had developed another of his curious obsessions, about a secret treaty between the King and the Tsar by which Russia would gain Balkan territories for supporting the Anglo-French alliance in any German war. It was unclear how Fred – of all people – could have come by this information unless the plenipotentiaries have closed the deal over tea and buns at Laycock's. Now everyone groaned whenever he got to his feet. Sir Edward Grey, the Foreign Secretary, no longer deigned to reply. And there had been more serious consequences: the King had banned Labour MPs from his annual garden party. Poor Ethel had been terribly disappointed. By some oversight, Fred himself had been the only one to receive an invitation but he, of course, did not attend.

There was no need to treat the other parties as if they were your sworn enemies. This was politics, not war. John Burns, once the firebrand leader of the London Dockers, was now the Liberals' President Of The Board Of Trade but this did not mean the end of their friendship. Fred's provocations were counter-productive, for if you flattered JB he would do whatever you asked.

Burns had not been Philip's only old acquaintance in the Commons. On his first day he had encountered, in the lavatory, his old adversary from Salisbury Plain, Sir Walter Long, now Shadow Treasury Secretary and considered to be Balfour's most likely successor. He looked exactly the same, which made Philip all too aware of how much he himself had changed.

"My dear fellow," Long extended a well-lathered hand, "I'm sure that we have met before."

"I'm Snowden. From Yorkshire." He squared his shoulders. "Labour spokesman for Financial Affairs."

"Ah," Long was evidently none the wiser. "Jolly good."

Philip had wanted to say, "You nearly shot me twenty years ago," but he had always kept that memory to himself, not even telling Ethel or Fred.

After that their paths kept crossing, Sir Walter always hailing him with great enthusiasm. Last week he had seen him in Kensington Gardens, arm-in-arm with a rather affected young man, presumably his son. Long had been asking about Victor Grayson. "I may need to reassess my political orientations for he resembles Lyssipus' bust of Alexander the Great. Mind you, I'm not sure that one would find his licence to be altogether in order." Philip had thought it best not to respond to this.

Nevertheless, Grayson had not as yet been an asset to the party. His maiden speech had been a disappointment. The government had voted £50,000 to Lord Cromer for his services as Commissioner for Finances in Egypt: there was much to be said against this decision but Grayson had resorted to the feeblest raillery interspersed with feverish visionary passages. "The working classes, harried and hurried by the problem of living, are gazing with bleared eyes upon the perplexing medley and down again at their chains with a dawning glint of a new hope." Stuff that had served so well in Colne Valley was now jejune. "The upper classes, driven to desperate ennui by the daily round of insincerity, morbidly yearn for new gauds and excitements. Their brains atrophy, while their souls are merely salts to keep their bodies from putrefaction." He kept winking at the government front bench, as if on the point of enquiring whether The Prime Minister approved of his new haircut. You had to smile at the horror-struck expression on Campbell-Bannerman's face. Grayson had finished him off: the poor old boy was dead within the fortnight.

Grayson had been sponsored by Snowden and Clynes. "Hurray for the red flag!" shouted Will Thorne and even some Liberals and Tories had cheered as the young man was led to the Speaker's chair. Afterwards there had been a reception at which Hardie and Glasier made it clear that they were prepared to wipe the slate clean. They would pay his salary even though he had refused to sign the articles of the party. But then MacDonald and Snowden had attended a rally at which the new member had harangued a huge and cheering crowd. "There's going to be trouble. I tell you that when the House resumes its sittings there's going to be something done or you'll be losing your member."

"The boy certainly knows how to get them going," was MacDonald's only response. He obviously did not take such threats seriously but it had been impossible to ignore Grayson's subsequent reaction to the Belfast Docks dispute, where the strikers had pelted the army with cobblestones and broken bottles. "If our people have no shrapnel," he had written, "At least they have broken bottles." When the press and the party leadership condemned his words he had immediately travelled to Ireland to repeat on site his endorsement of the rioting.

Grayson seldom appeared in the chamber but he could often be seen in the bar. He made a point of drinking with the most unregenerate Tories, embracing their gauds and excitements with no obvious signs of morbidity. Head back, feet well apart – he had the unmistakeable drinker's stance, like the denizens of The Grinning Rat. He was also a familiar figure in those Fleet Street pubs frequented by Blatchford's *Clarion* gang and Hyndman's SDF. He was sharing a flat on Stockwell Park Road with the Union organiser, Sam Hobson. It had been hoped that the stolid and goodhearted Sam might act as a calming influence but within a week the place had become a magnet to the demi-monde. "I don't know where they all come from," grumbled Sam. "Theosophists, vegetarians, suffragettes and Edward Carpenter types, so-called artists and so-called models, even Lascars and Chinamen. There's been no sign of Victor for a week but I just can't get rid of them."

&

In the short walk from his room to the great gilt doors of Parliament, Fred had emptied his pockets. 'Never pass a beggar': following that principle in London was a strain on his meagre resources. Trade was in decline and this evening he would be meeting a protest delegation who had marched all the way from Manchester, but the King's speech, opening the new session, had made no reference to unemployment. There were to be Licensing, Education and Pensions Bills in which Fred placed little hope. The Liberals had shown no interest in reform until their recent by-election defeats. These already feeble measures would be further adulterated or even thrown out by The Lords.

The sense of his own helplessness was almost unbearable. Although he felt permanently exhausted he was hardly sleeping at all.

Even a weekend back home had not restored him. On Saturday he had not joined the ILP ramble from Ogden to Tong, visiting instead a wool-sorter in the final stages of anthrax: for every death he would table a separate Parliamentary Question. Then he had searched in vain for that burst drain in Wibsey. He must have walked further over pavements than his comrades had over grass and heather but the effect was not the same. Although she had always grumbled about the mud, Emily missed such outings even more than he. She could never manage the stiles and would instead crawl, with Fred behind her, through the narrow sheep gates that were now called 'Jowett Holes' by one and all.

Then his Sunday morning constituency surgery had extended well into the evening. Emily insisted on giving every visitor a cup of tea and two biscuits, even though most of them had never learned to wipe their feet or use an ashtray. As she skivvied away, every-one agreed that there was nowhere as welcoming as 10, Grantham Terrace. There were widows with hungry children and victimized mill-hands, a few poor deluded souls and many who were merely lonely. One old lad had fallen asleep by the fire. It had been three hours before he stretched, yawned and finally voiced his problem: "Do you know anything about dogs, Fred? Our Bessie keeps whining and her doings have gone all crumbly and white."

There had hardly been time to say goodbye to Emily before he left for the overnight London train. As he was picking up his suit-case she brushed the nape of his homburg before placing it firmly on his head. Then she had softly pinched the bulb of his nose while he made a doleful honking sound. As he opened the front door he had felt her palm pressing between his shoulder blades. He turned left into the alley: this was not a short cut but he could not bear to feel her eyes on him all the way down the street.

"Na' then, Our Fred."

How reassuring it was to see that familiar smile! How typical of Snowden to have waited outside so that they could go in together!

"Na' then, Our Phil."

Fred felt himself, as always, to be malevolently observed: these marble statues approved of him even less than the stone monarchs of Bradford Town Hall. The chamber was always flooded with radiant light that made his eyes swim: somehow it contrived to feel cavernous and claustrophobic at the same time. They reached the Labour benches and Fred took his usual place at the end of the row. He let one foot stray into the gangway, as if poised for flight.

Now the murmuring voices changed in volume and tone and he saw that Victor Grayson had entered the chamber. Although he seldom showed his face everyone knew who he was. Snowden gave a little grin, Hardie's black eyes narrowed and MacDonald's hand shot up to his moustache, as if an attempt might be made to steal it.

Fred had last seen him at the Huddersfield Conference. On the second day, Grayson had been slated to take the chair but he never turned up. Afterwards Fred had observed him in the nearby International Bazaar, sitting on a Turkish divan, puffing on a hookah pipe, contemplating the quarter-size log cabin that was the centrepiece of the North American exhibition.

"Greetings, Comrade Jowett." On his rare appearances, the wretched man insisted on squeezing in next to him and then fidgeting: fortunately he never stayed long. He wore a Tyrolean hat pulled down over his eyes: it was covered in white hairs, as if a cat had been sleeping on it. A green shirt clashed with the pale grey suit and he was actually wearing a red tie – and not merely red but scarlet, like blood flowing from a wound. He still smelt of that choking perfume: after some enquiries Fred had established that it might have been gardenias.

Business began with the referring of The Licensing Bill to its committee stage. While scarlet-faced Tories rose to assert the free-born Englishman's right to drink as much and as often as he chose, Fred became aware that Grayson was trembling violently. He turned but the face was obscured by the hat brim and left hand. Each finger sported a gold ring and a tiny wristwatch – surely a woman's? – hung off the surprisingly slender wrist. Now a cadaverous Liberal was defending the closure of a quarter of the country's pubs and the restriction of opening hours on Sundays and during election campaigns. Snowden had endorsed this – saying that a sober electorate would halve the Conservative vote – but Fred took little interest. He had not touched alcohol for four years but still resisted Phil's suggestions that he should sign the Temperance Pledge. It wasn't that he had given up drinking, merely that he never felt like it any more.

At last the minister slumped back into his place. Grayson's vibrating became so uncontrollable that it lifted him out of his seat. He seemed to hang in the air for a second before deciding to return to earth rather than bursting up through the chamber's vaulted roof.

"I wish to move an adjournment of this House." Grayson spoke in a calm and even tone. "So that it can deal with the unemployment question."

There was dead silence as Mr Speaker rose. He was a nonde-script man whose name Fred could never remember: perhaps it really was Speaker?

"I must inform the Honourable Member" – he coughed rather than spoke, "That such a motion cannot be taken at this moment on this particular day. If he would care to join me in the Whips' office, perhaps with a more senior colleague, I shall be happy to explain the relevant precedents and procedures." The voice had taken on a curiously eager tone, as if concerned that the young man should not feel slighted.

"I wish to move the adjournment of this House," Victor repeat-ed, gesturing with his hand, as if pulling aside cobwebs clinging to his face. "People are starving in the streets."

"Then why don't they go indoors?" Fred was sure that he rec-ognized Burns' voice.

Now the uproar began: the counter-cries of "order" and "sit down" merged into a chant as if all these men had done this many times before.

"The Honourable Gentleman must resume his seat." The Speaker almost pleaded.

"And remove that awful hat!" came a high-pitched shriek. Like a naughty schoolboy Grayson snatched it off and crushed it in his hands, but still he remained on his feet.

"I refuse to sit down unless you give me a proper explanation." His voice had never quite recovered from the by-election: you could hear the air rattling in his throat, as if speaking involved consider-able effort and pain.

"I must apologize," he continued, "For waking this House from its post-lunch slumbers . . ." The rest of this – something about overcooked mutton – was drowned out by the ensuing roar. The Speaker beckoned to the sergeant-at-arms who snoozed perpetually at the back of the chamber. Down he came, mas-sively dignified in his grey dundreary whiskers and, with two pudgy fingers, tapped his victim on the shoulder. Although

Grayson continued to speak he had stepped out into the gangway.

"I am willing to leave the House because I feel degraded to be in a country that will not consider the unemployed. I have a mandate to ask for legislation at this moment" – the roaring swelled again but he shouted over it – "Oh yes, you well-fed human beings can say 'order' but the unemployed have been goaded into disorder. I refuse absolutely to be bullied into silence."

He took a few steps, then turned and shouted, "You are traitors!" The pupils of his eyes were like black pinpricks. "Traitors to your class!" Fred felt the spittle hitting his face. One last time Grayson made that cobweb-clawing motion and then pushed his way out. The effect was somewhat diminished when his head came back round the corner at a curious height and angle, scanned the chamber and withdrew. He was obviously hoping that some of his comrades might follow him.

"It's an interesting tactic," Snowden had remained impassive throughout. "A bit crude but it worked for Plimsoll and Parnell. On the other hand, sailors and even the Irish are a good deal more popular than the poor. Also, it's a trick that you can only use once."

"He called us traitors," said Fred, "Traitors to our class."

"I thought he was looking at the government."

"What class could the Liberals ever be traitors to?"

"We are all traitors," said Snowden, "simply by being here. And it's a bitter lesson for a young fellow to realize that everything he has been saying up to this point has been childish and absurd. No wonder his stomach heaves and he has to vomit it all out. What we have just heard was Victor's farewell to his youth. A sadder and a wiser man he'll rise tomorrow morn."

Fred took out his handkerchief and dabbed at his nose: the smell of gardenias was overpowering.

"Bach," said H. M. Hyndman, raising the silver flute to his lips. "Sonata in C Minor." He blew a single ear-splitting note and smiled. "I may not be the best flautist in England but certes I am the loudest."

The moment that Victor had walked into The Cheshire Cheese his eyes had met those of the red-headed boy at the bar. He had not looked at him again and the boy continued his joshing with *The Clarion*'s typesetters but both knew that they would be leaving together.

The main saloon was full of revolutionary socialists while the public bar was held by poets so radical that their work could not be written down. The place had a literary reputation: Hyndman insisted on sitting under the portrait of Dr Johnson. The sound of his flute cut through the hubbub: everyone's movements were following the rhythms of the music – without realizing, the whole pub was dancing to his tune. On his table were two rows of tiny glasses, liqueurs of every colour of the spectrum, to be downed first with the left-hand, then with the right. You had to slam each glass down hard, as if it were your last drink before you faced the firing squad.

Victor was still assimilating the afternoon's events. He was not sure exactly why he had defied the Speaker. The tension had risen in his throat and he had to do something to let it out. He had hoped that it would be like the end of *Alice in Wonderland* when she says "You're nothing but a pack of cards" and the whole court disappears. The ranks of Hons and Right Hons, however, seemed to be multiplying: when he looked up, even the ceiling was composed of yelling, distorted faces. Thin lips split open to reveal rows of sharp yellow fangs. How many teeth, he had wondered, did Parliament contain? 628 × 32 was not a sum you could do in your head. And then you'd have to knock off twenty or so for Hardie's gappy set. It was a wonder that Victor's righteous indignation had not dissolved into helpless laughter.

The music stopped. Hyndman wiped his flute with a soft

yellow cloth then replaced it in the velvet-lined case. The police kept searching it for explosives: "Beware, gentlemen," he would say, "Herein lies a yet more deadly weapon."

His Majesty Hyndman, as Shaw had dubbed this immaculately frock-coated figure, had been part of the movement for three decades but was still regarded with general suspicion. Ex-Eton, ex-Cambridge, he was said to have become a Socialist when he failed to gain his cricket 'Blue'. Having travelled the world as a correspondent for *The Pall Mall Gazette*, he became intimate with Marx, Morris and Henry George, plundering their ideas – without attribution – for his best seller, *England For All*. He founded the SDF, funding it by his stock market speculations, supplemented by considerable winnings at billiards, backgammon and whist. He had recently returned to politics after spending two years in the Yukon and the West Indies to replenish his fortune. In the last election he had been narrowly defeated in Burnley: he would have won if he had not affronted local pride by comparing the place – unfavourably – with 'The most hideous Hell of Dante'. He was a notorious drinker and womaniser, always ready with his fists: the more people warned Victor off him the fonder of him he became.

"I would have done exactly the same, Victor," Hyndman was saying, "Although not in that hat. It's as well that I wasn't elected, for two Gullivers at once would have been too much for the poor little chaps. The Labour MPs are like burglars in a country house who, instead of stealing the silver, become fascinated by the plumbing, running the taps and flushing the lavatories until an awakened butler calls the police."

"And what are *you* doing exactly?" growled one of the printers. The red-haired boy had once again bested him at arm wrestling.

"I am waiting," said Hyndman.

"Waiting for what?"

"For when the SDF are twenty thousand strong. And then we will march."

"March where, exactly?"

"Why, I'll march them up to the top of the hill," sang Hyndman and everyone along the bar joined in with the rest, "Then I'll march them down again!"

After the landlord had called time, Grayson, Hyndman and the boy moved down to the drinking dens along The Embankment. HMH had an encyclopaedic knowledge of such places: when Victor returned on his own he could never find them. Whenever the boy tried to tell him his name he would clap a hand over his mouth: it was so much more exciting that way.

Everyone they encountered wanted to shake Victor's hand. With each drink the conversation became more scintillating: the laughter of the Gods boomed and echoed through those low-ceilinged rooms. How revealing it was, Hyndman observed, that, of the movement's prominent teetotallers, Hardie and Glasier looked as if they were toping brass polish while Snowden must surely bathe in absinthe. This prompted Victor to embark on his celebrated impressions. Snowden was Baron Snowed-up, Hardie Little-Miss-Canvas-Shoes, Henderson Arthur-Headless-Horseman. The Glasiers became the Glasshouses, their coat of arms a pair of knitting needles rampant on a field of lumpy porridge. Then there was a scabrous scene between 'Flora' MacDonald and Bonnie Prince Hardie in a Skye-bound rowing boat, where they are finally joined in three-way congress by the Loch Ness Monster; followed by an even more extreme fantasy entitled "Baron Snowed-up Explores the Passages of Joy". This culminated with poor Snowden, exhausted and bewildered by Ethel's acrobatic demands, having recourse to his walking sticks. Fred Jowett had been most difficult but Grayson had finally worked out a finger-show, projecting candle-lit shadows on a bare white wall. "BUN!" – the thumb and forefinger described a round 'o' – "BANANA!" – a stiff right ring-finger approached the first shape – "BEVERAGE!" – the finger entered the hole then reamed it vigorously, accompanied by loud slurpings and moans. "Mmm," Victor concluded, in a grinding Yorkshire accent, "How the littl 'uns do love it!" Then, with some difficulty, they worked out Victor's sum: The Mother of Parliaments could boast about twenty thousand teeth: "All of them rotten," said Hyndman, "All needing to be pulled."

The red-haired boy and Victor reached Stockwell just as the dawn was breaking. Sam Hobson was in the kitchen, grimly burning bacon. "Thank God you're back," he said, "The place has been swarming with Chinamen. And last night a bloody big burglar disguised as a priest was trying to jemmy open the windows. What do these people want? Do you owe them money or are they all in love with you?"

"They all want one thing," said Victor, as the boy began to nibble at Sam's left ear, "To be noticed."

"And what on earth were *you* playing at yesterday in the House?" Sam remained impervious to his new friend's attentions.

"Oh," Victor yawned, "I just wanted to be noticed."

⁂

"Such a protest as I made I felt to be needed at the present moment. I am ashamed – yes, literally ashamed – that the Labour members sat silently and backbonelessly while I was expelled for doing what they are conscientiously obliged to do. This will not be the end of it."

"I don't think backbonelessly is a proper word," was MacDonald's only response, "It makes us sound like a row of kipper fillets."

The newspapers were full of Grayson. Jowett suspected that the reporters had been given prior notice for they had all been on hand to interview him.

"I intend to organize an agitation of the unemployed throughout the kingdom ... the political game is played out ... we need something unconstitutional to agitate the ponderous brains of modern legislators."

Fred thrust the newspaper under the bench. They had given

Grayson every chance and this was how he had repaid them. Philip would never have admitted it, but he was deeply hurt.

The Licensing Bill had entered its final stage. As they emerged from the division lobby after yet another meaningless vote, Fred saw that Grayson was sitting by the gangway. With a charming smile he stood to let them pass. He was more soberly dressed in a dark suit, white shirt and purple ribbon tie. The green hat was not in evidence but Fred doubted that this was a sign of contrition. The rings and the tiny wristwatch had gone but Fred noticed that his left ear was now curiously red with its lobe caked in blood. He had evidently neglected to shave: the surprisingly dark stubble gave him a feral look.

"Before you procede any further, Mr Chairman" - today Grayson was not trembling at all. "Thousands of people are dying in the streets" - he looked around challengingly but this time Burns remained silent - "And I refuse to allow the House to carry on a moment longer while I am in it." The familiar cries of outrage and derision began. "I will not give order in a Chamber that starves the people wholesale. I have a mandate" - he shouted into the mounting bedlam - "I have the most enormous mandate!" He abruptly doubled over, as if he had been punched in the solar plexus. Surely the man could not be laughing?

"Will the Honourable Member allow me to explain?" - The Chairman had picked up Grayson's clawing gesture. "Does he understand that the House is in Committee and that the Committee can only deal with what the House instructs it to deal with?" He was showing not the least sign of anger or impatience. "The Honourable Member can only move when the business is reported to the House."

"Yes, sir, I understand." Grayson's feet were moving in a shuffling dance. "But the point I want to make is ". . . Whatever it might have been was lost in the roar. Grayson looked calmly round the Chamber then his lips twisted into a horrible leer. The head gave a little toss, the hips swivelled and he winked broadly at the

Liberal benches, like a streetwalker acknowledging a whistling gang of navvies.

"Does the Honourable Gentleman refuse to obey The Chair?"

Grayson ran a hand through his hair: "Quite so."

"Then I must name the Honourable Member and the sitting will be suspended and the Speaker sent for."

A distinct West Country burr was apparent in these final words.

"You may name me," Grayson shouted, "But you cannot shame me."

This drew some appreciative cheers but he pressed on regardless. "It is all very well to laugh. Members always adopt that attitude towards serious matters. I intend to obstruct the business of this House if it refuses to deal with the unemployment question."

Laughter turned to jeers. "Worse will be heard here before long, I assure you."

But nothing could be heard now. Grayson remained standing while the Chairman mouthed beseechingly at him. There was a flurry along the Liberal benches and Horatio Bottomley, MP for South Hackney, emerged. He crossed the floor, fists raised with aggressive intent, but then slowed and waddled on with distinct trepidation. He whispered something to Grayson who did not react, then backed away with presumably ironic bowings of his head. Fred saw that all his colleagues were also up on their feet, shouting. He and Snowden were the only ones still seated: he hoped that this would not be interpreted as a gesture of support for Grayson but he could not bring himself to join in.

After a while the Speaker entered the Chamber, followed by the Prime Minister. They were flushed and panting, as if they had run all the way down Whitehall. Complete silence fell, as when ragging schoolboys suddenly become aware of the presence of their Headmaster.

"I move that Mr . . ." Balfour paused and blinked, "Grayson . . . be suspended forthwith from the service of this House."

There was a great yell of "Aye!" but also a few "Noes" from the Conservative benches.

"What do the Labour Members say?" Grayson turned and cupped his ear to the ensuing silence. "As I was saying, I leave this House with the greatest pleasure" – The shouting began again – "No man who loves his kind could stay here another minute."

"The Honourable Member is not entitled to address this House after he has been suspended." The Speaker almost sang these words, like a priest reading the responses,

"I leave this House feeling that I gain in dignity by doing so." He turned one last time to the Labour benches. "I hope other Members will leave it too, for it is a House of Murderers."

From the Labour benches there came a frenzied booing – almost bellowing – the main source of which, to Fred's surprise, was Snowden. Even after Grayson had left the Chamber, this time without a backward glance, Phil continued to shout "Acting! Acting! Hypocritical acting!"

మ⅊

They had seen each other in Hyde Park, approaching from opposite ends of the Broad Walk. They could have avoided meeting but neither would step away from his path. Twirling his silver-topped cane, Grayson walked faster than anyone else: heads turned as he passed, just as they did for Philip, but for different reasons.

"Isn't this rather early for you, Comrade Grayson?"

"I'm afraid I haven't been to bed. I don't have time to sleep, these days."

Three giggling nursemaids vacated a nearby bench and, by unspoken agreement, they sank onto it.

"How I miss those refreshing naps in the House." Victor stretched out his legs, crossing the ankles. "And all those funny old men droning on about nothing."

"What did you expect them to do? Sing? Juggle? Fire pistols in the air? It's not the music hall: your little turn only wasted everybody's time and stored up serious trouble for yourself."

"For a whole month you did nothing but debate that absurd Licensing Bill. And when it got to the Lords, they threw it out, as you knew they would. You are wasting your own time: you don't need any help from me."

"Surely you now regret some of the things you said?"

"Yes: I should not have used the phrase, "House of Murderers": House of Cannibals – that would have been better."

It was unfortunate that this morning Ethel was away addressing the Lewisham Ladies Temperance League. She would have given Grayson a piece of her mind! "That nasty little nancy boy": she held her nose whenever his name was mentioned.

Philip opened his newspaper. "MacDonald says here that the movement is turning after the sons and daughters of Anarchy".

"I don't think I'm acquainted with them but they sound as if they might be fun." Grayson tipped his hat to another smiling young woman. "I wonder why smashing something evil should be considered destructive. MacDonald claims to be opposed to injustice but God forbid that anyone should try to do anything about it. As far as I can see when the party finally ascends to power – sometime next century – nothing will really change except that the poor will somehow feel better about being cold and hungry because their rulers once experienced such privations themselves."

Despite the sunshine, a mist was rising from the Round Pond. The crowds had a hectic air, as if suspecting that this might be the last fine day of the year.

"That is all very well," Snowden flicked his paper, "But why on earth did you refuse to share the platform with Hardie at Holborn Town Hall?"

"His suit clashed with mine. It was rusty brown with interesting yellow stains, while I was in silver-grey and samite. The audience would have lynched us both."

A large unclipped black poodle bounded up and licked Grayson's face. He just laughed, tickling its matted ears while its owner tried to drag it off. "Bad doggie!"

It was surely the same young woman who had passed, quite dogless, in the opposite direction, a few minutes before. Could she have borrowed the animal in order to effect an introduction? Now she was giving Grayson her card so that any cleaning bills necessitated by those muddy paws could be sent to her address. It was all very elegantly done. Philip wondered if, down on Rotten Row, a man was hiring out dogs trained especially for this purpose.

Grayson had become a celebrity. One of the society periodicals had even run a photographic sequence of a typical day in his life – mowing the lawn, pruning the roses, playing the piano, practising his golf swing and so on. While undertaking these disparate and unlikely activities he remained in immaculate morning dress. He was similarly prominent as a journalist in the radical press, although his writings were either trite or incomprehensible. Why didn't he just talk naturally and get someone to write it down? Nevertheless, according to Blatchford, his name on a paper's cover trebled its sales. He was now political editor of Orage's *New Age* as well as *The Clarion*.

At last the young lady drifted reluctantly away: the previously uncontrollable dog now had a dignified and satisfied air.

"What's all this stuff about hanging people from lamp-posts?" Philip enquired.

"That speech has been exaggerated and misquoted."

"Are you implying, sir," said Philip in his iciest tone, "That the *Daily Mail* cannot be trusted?"

After a brief silence they burst out laughing.

"But it is a serious matter," said Philip, "Your support will soon be ebbing away."

"I have received thousands of letters of congratulation." From his pocket Grayson produced a crumpled telegram, "'To Young Lochinvar – may your lance always remain sharp and true.' That's from Bernard Shaw. Did you hear about H. G. Wells? He said that he wouldn't trust me with a horse and Shaw replied" – he became Shaw – "'But why ever would you be wanting to trust him with a horse?'"

"I mean support where it really matters. Mr Shaw's opinions do not carry much weight in Colne Valley. You must never take your constituency for granted. I have heard that they are not happy with your attendance record and that France Littlewood may resign in protest over your antics."

"This is grievous news indeed," said Victor, "I hope he'll be taking his bloody choir with him."

"He'll be taking more than the choir. You'll be losing at least three hundred votes to the Liberals."

"And what about your famous hundred and fifty-three? I suppose you'll be deconverting them now?"

Snowden decided to ignore this. "The Colne Valley Liberals have already got a strong candidate in place: a local man, Leach, a non-conformist minister."

"I know him," Victor uncrossed his legs. "He's even madder than Thongsbridge. I don't mean independent-minded or unpredictable. I mean he's mad in the sense of being mad."

Snowden sighed. "I fear you will have to form your own party."

"That's what everyone is telling me to do."

"I suppose it will be called the National Grayson Party?"

"No, I was thinking of The Victors."

"I did hear that some local ILPs have been tabling motions calling for a unified Socialist party. How much support do you think that might have?"

"As of yesterday, two hundred and forty-six branches," said Grayson, "And tomorrow, who knows?"

Not only the ladies acknowledged Grayson but also some respectable-looking elderly gentlemen and a number of young men who seemingly had nothing better to do than shuffle dispiritedly back and forth. Wasn't that the son of Sir Walter Long?

"I have to say, Comrade Snowden, that you have rather disappointed me with all your nonsense about my dinners."

It had been MacDonald who had informed Philip that Grayson, having picked up his quarterly parliamentary allowance, immediately blued it all on a huge dinner in the Members' Dining Room, the extravagance of which had scandalized even the waiters. "It is Grayson himself that is the true enemy of the unemployed," Mac said. "And yet he calls us traitors and murderers. You were his mentor, Philip" – it was the first time he had ever used Snowden's Christian name – "So it will look better coming from you. Who knows, the lad may even thank you for it one day." When the allegations were investigated, however, no record of this orgy remained, no scandalized waiters could be found – only that on a different date Grayson and two companions had shared a one-and-sixpenny bottle of wine. Philip had been hauled up before the Privileges And Standards Committee to receive an official rebuke. He would not be trusting MacDonald again.

"You don't have to make things up, you know," Grayson patted him on the knee, "There's plenty of true stuff you can use. Would you like me to dish you some dirt?"

"What I don't understand is why you went to all the trouble of getting yourself elected only to get yourself thrown out."

"Try to imagine what might have happened if we had all defied the speaker. And kept on defying him, individually and collectively, day after day."

"We would have all ended up in clink," said Philip.

"And what if all subsequent by-elections returned more Labour members with bigger majorities who all did the same thing?"

"Talkest thou to me of ifs?" Snowden levered himself to his feet.

Grayson's face lit up. "Thou art a traitor!" he finished the quotation, "Off with his head! – *Richard III*, Act Three!"

Philip turned away without further words. That bench had

stiffened him up and now, try as he might, he could not help hunching forward, while his limp insisted on manifesting itself in its most grotesque form.

"I'll see you in Portsmouth," Grayson called after him. That was where the next Labour Party Conference would be held. God alone knew what fresh mischief the man was brewing up.

The filthy slush was working its way up Jowett's trouser legs. Why did they all have to trek down to Portsmouth in mid-January? And then, before the Spring arrived, the ILP's own conference would be up there in Edinburgh, at the opposite end of the country. The most sensible thing would be to measure the map from North to South, then East to West, taking the point where the lines intersected as the permanent site of every major gathering in the movement's calendar. The fact that this happened to be Bradford was, of course, quite incidental.

Opposite the hall there stood the unmistakeable figure of Victor Grayson, resplendent in an ankle-length Melton overcoat. To Fred's horror he was talking to what appeared to be two night-soil men. As he drew closer he saw to his relief that the sinister bulky figures were only motorists in driving gloves and leather jackets, with goggles and scarves around their faces. An empty car, its engine still vibrating, was slewed across the road. Now Grayson, presumably in jest, was trying to drag the men into the conference. Slipping on the ice, they fell, rolling all over each other while a third wrapped figure threw back his head and blew a loud *halloo* on a hunting horn. It was a typical piece of ostentation that did not bode well for the day ahead.

Since his suspension Grayson had toured the land, drawing huge crowds wherever he spoke, as if fighting an election that had not yet been called. His hearers reported that he was more brilliant than ever, although they remained curiously hazy about what he had actually said. It was hard to tell how far his support extended and how organized it might be. The National Executive seemed to fear that he would be storming the conference at the head of an army of theosophists, vegetarians and bottle-throwing Irish dockers, augmented by nonagenarian chartists, bushy-bearded Whitmanites and a maenad throng of soubrettes and suffragettes. Fred wondered whether the Colne Valley sheep would be attending as well.

On the opening day, however, Grayson had not turned up at all, missing the key debate on unemployment. "Presumably he has solved this problem but neglected to inform the rest of us," Snowden observed. On the second day he had put in a brief appearance just after lunch. Lounging elegantly against one of the pillars he had smoked two gold-tipped cigarettes and then left without speaking. He was obviously biding his time until the final day when any damage he might inflict could not be repaired.

Inside the hall Fred saw Hyndman strolling around with an insufferably superior air. It was a mystery just how this man was always able to obtain the necessary accreditation. The ship-workers' delegates made rude noises as he passed, so he turned and walked right into the middle of them. "I don't like to disabuse you, Comrades," he said pleasantly, "But in the entire history of humanity no slave class has ever managed to emancipate itself." Then he went on his way, chuckling, while they were still trying to think of a reply. Hardie believed that Hyndman was the Devil incarnate: Fred was increasingly inclined to agree.

Proceedings began but Grayson still did not appear. Up on the platform Hardie's eyes flickered between his well-chewed watch and the door: he feared Grayson even more than Hyndman. Snowden kept scribbling in a small black notebook a mass of figures and letters, bewilderingly linked with arrows and serrated lines: these, he claimed, represented all possible permutations of the conference votes. "When you get right down to it," he would say, "Every aspect of life can be reduced to an equation."

At lunchtime the rumours were flying. Grayson was said to

have gone off with some men in a car but no-one knew who they were or where they might have gone. Hyndman was claiming that he had been kidnapped.

"The only person who could kidnap Grayson," said Snowden, "Is Grayson himself."

For Fred all this was not a matter for levity: The man was poisoning the movement, setting comrade against comrade. His own latest *Clarion* piece had – for the first time – been devoted to a single individual rather than the wider issues.

"Grayson has abused men whose judgement he had never consulted," it had concluded, "Men are now described as traitors who undertook the task of founding a socialist movement at a time when the chilly frost of universal indifference was far harder to bear than the violent alternations between the excitement of hostility and the enthusiasm of fellowship in which Grayson now lives and moves." When he delivered his copy, however, he had found Grayson himself sitting in the office with Blatchford, a bottle of whiskey on the table between them. They had been perfectly affable but when he was leaving there had sounded a great roar of laughter which had almost blown him down those steep and narrow stairs. He had been sure that they would not print it but it duly appeared, uncut, in the next edition, followed by an open letter of reply from Blatchford himself. "Oh Fred, old friend, less politics and more purpose! Think less of mere elections and more of the unhappy and the poor! There's no harm in the lad – a little wild, perhaps, but that will mend." Fred kept imagining the two men finishing off the whiskey as they wrote this together.

Composite followed composite and references back were referenced back but there was still no sign of Grayson. The platform party gradually relaxed but then grew curiously angry: it was almost as if they were disappointed that the ceiling had not fallen in.

"He's been playing with us," said MacDonald, after they had sung 'Auld Lang Syne'. He's waiting for Edinburgh."

"Here we could have used standing orders to limit his speaking time," Philip agreed, "And we could rely on the Unions to vote him down. Here he could only wound, not kill."

"How our enemies will be laughing at us." wailed Hardie.

Fred was not so sure. Hyndman, his face like thunder, appeared to be on the point of belabouring with his flute case the entire miners' delegation.

Outside the hall, as Fred struggled into his coat, there came a blare of horns and wild shouts and the gleaming car slid out of the darkness. The driver's head poked out to vomit copiously on to the kerb while Grayson stepped down from the passenger seat. His coat now shone with a bizarre radiance, garlanded with elaborately plaited grasses and wild flowers.

"I hope I haven't missed anything too exciting, Comrade Jowett," Grayson looked and sounded completely sober, "Allow me to introduce my new friends. Captain Frederick Jane, Lieutenant 'Matabele' Smith and Ogmore 'One Round' Roberts, the noted pugilist. We have been discussing the Bosnian Question, the German naval threat and the decline of English ale all of which, they inform me, can be attributed to a great Jewish conspiracy. They were out for blood, waving pistols and uttering the most delicious threats until I persuaded them that we were all on the same side. I told them that Hyndman was the best cover point that Sussex ever had and that you, Fred, are third in line to the Hungarian throne."

The car jerked abruptly away with the sound of breaking glass as Jane and One-Round took the opportunity of jettisoning their dead marines in the direction of the cowering delegates.

"I've been naughty, I know," Grayson smirked, "But if there's one thing better than being whisked away in a fast car by a beautiful woman it's in one full of big rough men with guns. And as you can see" – he pirouetted – "In the dell behind that estimable hostelry, The Crown and Mitre, we managed to locate a bank of indecently early primroses."

From down the road there came a great rending crash. 'Matabele'

Smith – surely deliberately – had driven his car halfway up the trunk of a passing oak.

⁂

"Where is he, then? Where is the little bugger? We couldn't find him in London: we've got to come up to Scotland just to talk to our own MP." The Colne Valley delegation were not happy. "That Briggs does all his constituency work and even answers his letters. The Liberals have published his parliamentary record: he only voted in five per cent of the divisions. Finally we got a scribbled postcard saying that he considered it dishonourable to work up a fraudulent attendance rate like all the other Hon Mems do . . . You've got to laugh." They were not laughing – "He thinks a vice becomes a virtue if you own up to it." Snowden recognised some of his converts in their ranks. They deserved better than this! Happy though he was with Blackburn, how good it would be if a nice solid Yorkshire seat – aye, Colne Valley – was to present itself!

For the last few months the ILP executive had been preparing for Edinburgh. "This time," Hardie grimly observed, "There'll be no beer and primroses and drives in wee cars." Snowden's charts filled every page of his notebook: he had started using different coloured inks. Nothing had been left to chance: every delegate had been individually cajoled, threatened or squared. Nevertheless, he kept scanning the hall through a small brass telescope that pressed ever deeper into his eye socket. He had spent last night polishing it up: each delegation collectively flinched when it flashed in their direction.

MacDonald, as Chairman, made the opening speech. "How do we expect socialism to come about? A sudden change through force is quite unthinkable. We must above all be PRACTICAL – No romantic illusions can be allowed to stand in our path."

As if on cue, Grayson finally entered the hall. MacDonald

paused and glared, but he was not in the least abashed, tip-toeing down the aisle, one finger to his lips, before planting himself among the Colne Valley group.

"I see this party becoming a dominant power in the land," MacDonald continued, "By means of coalitions. We shall unite with section after section, not in a compromising spirit, which I hate, but in the beautifully natural way which in human experience comes of love."

Snowden's telescope was still trained on the conference floor. Grayson was whispering behind his hand: all around him were rocking with mirth. It had not taken long for him to talk them round again.

"Socialism will win . . . For it is served by men and women who employ in its service not merely their lips but their hands and hearts." As MacDonald sat down Colne Valley applauded with exaggerated gusto. Grayson had evidently been teaching them how to whistle – piercingly – with two fingers in one's mouth.

Every subsequent motion was slanted against the Graysonites and every vote came within two or three of Philip's predictions. A resolution confirming the ILP's association with the Labour Party was carried by 378 to 8. Then another that the ILP should not run candidates independently of it went through by 244 to 146. Outside it was growing darker: someone turned on the lights but soon they too began to dim. It had been drizzling all week but now it sounded as if a troop of horsemen were galloping along the roof.

Then came the key resolution: that no salaries should be paid to ILP MPs who, for so-called reasons of conscience, refused to sign the Labour Party Constitution, thus reneging on MacDonald's promises of last year. This was also passed by 332 to 64.

Grayson, deathly pale, rose from his seat. Today there would be no flirtatiousness. "You can keep your salary and you can keep your movement" – surely that venomous tone was an approximation of Philip himself? – "I would rather belong to a party of one – that had to beg its bread to preach the gospel – than sit in the House of

Commons as a puppet." The eyes flashed and in the silence – even the rain had stopped – Philip could hear the bones of the hand cracking as it made a fist. "Fortunately I am not a weakling or an enfeebled old man. I can, thank God, still earn my own living!"

You had to admire him: at least he had the courage of his own convictions, whatever they might be. But these words had a very different effect on Hardie who seemed to be about to leap off the platform.

"Weak? Weak?" he screamed, "The only weak man among us is our poor friend here."

Philip realized that the trembling finger was pointing at himself. The voice modulated into a sort of throbbing croon. "Our poor lame friend . . . Our poor poor crippled friend."

Many delegates began booing. Philip felt Fred's hand on his shoulder.

"That's a bit insensitive, Our Phil."

"I don't care on my own account" – he shrugged the hand away – "Can't you hear the Conference? That senile dolt has just swung them back to Grayson. Just watch how the lad exploits it."

It was at the last possible moment, on the final day, that Grayson stood up once more to move a reference back to the NAC report on his now notorious refusal to share a platform with Hardie. The decision had been that he would not be allowed to speak at any future meetings or rallies. As he was clearing his throat and looking benignly around, the sun at last came out, so brightly that there was an audible gasp as the delegates shielded their eyes. "Grayson weather," Philip sighed.

"How wonderful it has been to visit at last the land of Flora MacDonald and Bonnie Prince Hardie!" The man waited for the laughter to subside, then took a long deep breath. "Ah, Scottish air!" he exhaled, "If only you could bottle it! Still, a ten year old malt will do just as well. My only complaint is that no-one has yet taken me for a drive in the countryside and that Edinburgh's primroses do not appear to be in bloom. Perhaps they will not bloom again until we have grasped the nettle" – cocking his head, he assumed Hardie's voice – "or should I say *thistle?* – of our true destiny.

"Over the last few days I have been the enemy, the outcast, the scapegoat of the movement. Which is strange, because I have agreed with almost every word spoken from the platform. I would have been proud to have made Comrade MacDonald's speech: like him, I believe that our politics should develop in the beautiful natural ways of love – although there is perhaps something to be said for one or two of the unnatural ways as well. But although I go along with what the NAC *say*, I sometimes have problems with what they then proceed to do – or, rather, *not* do.

"But thank God I am not weak!" He yelled over the applause, swinging a fist that narrowly missed his own nose. "I have to admit that I spoke in haste and anger the other day. Because we all of us have our weaknesses. Mine is impatience – and over-enthusiasm, by which I can get quite, quite carried away," he twirled with a dancer's elegance. "Our greatest strengths become our greatest weaknesses: zeal consumes itself in its own flames while even the wisest strategist can temporize himself into impotence and inertia.

"It has often been said this week that we must carry the people with us, heart and soul, but this is surely impossible without open and fearless debate. Without the transforming heat of a bloody good row however will our separate tendencies melt and run together to finally combine? We must accept that even our most violent contentions can still be born of love. Surely we can disagree without descending to personal abuse? Why, I myself have been accused of loose-living" – he rolled his eyes and clasped his hands, as if at prayer – "When everyone knows that I am a nonpareil of temperance and self-denial." This occasioned the loudest cheer of the whole conference: Snowden was scribbling madly at his charts.

"Comrades, we must affirm the right of everyone here to be wrong, to behave foolishly, to be, as my friends on the NAC call me, 'a wretched nuisance'. It must never be forgotten that we are all of us striving towards a common goal. And that my weaknesses and your weaknesses, the weaknesses of the movement and of humanity as a whole can only be overcome and transformed by the collective exercising of tolerance, humour and good fellowship."

"The right to be wrong," Snowden groaned, before the applause crashed in. "Dear God!"

The motion was carried by 217 to 194. The Conference had supported Grayson against its own executive. Everyone was still laughing, seemingly unaware of the significance of the result. Fred watched as the heads of Hardie, Snowden, MacDonald and Glasier pressed together as if about to burst into close harmony song. Then Mac announced that he and his colleagues were resigning forthwith from the NAC. Someone from the floor immediately proposed a vote of confidence in them which was passed with only ten dissenters, Grayson not among them. But even as this was being announced, the four were leaving the platform. Hardie first, his chin jutting so high that he appeared to be studying the ceiling, while the top of Glasier's chalky, hairless head kept butting him between the shoulder blades. Next came Philip, his flailing sticks toppling the now empty chairs, and finally MacDonald, like an angry god on some pagan frieze looking for a lion to take by the throat.

Down on the floor, by a majority of 140, they had just withdrawn their support for Grayson and reinstated the offending paragraphs in the NAC report, but their Council did not return. Now Grayson was leading the Colne Valley delegation in singing, "Will Ye No Come Back Again?" . . . But Hardie, Snowden, MacDonald and Glasier had already left the building.

⁂

"I am an Independent Socialist Candidate. I have no friends or supporters in The House. My only allegiance is to my own conscience and constituents."

Victor had not wanted to stand for Colne Valley at the General Election. He had told the local party that he was too ill and disillusioned with Parliament but they had somehow discovered that he was planning to oppose John Burns in Battersea. Even this did not put them off: he had been shamed into going through with it.

The eight months since Edinburgh had been an anti-climax. Hardie and the rest still controlled the ILP, with poor old Jowett as its nominal chairman. The New Party had made little progress. Victor's speeches were still loudly applauded and he received sack-fulls of supportive mail but no-one had organized even so much as a day conference. Hyndman was still sulking about his Portsmouth non-appearance and Blatchford's daughters, he suspected, had been telling tales. The whispering campaign, however, was curiously un-focussed. He was said to have slept with people he had never met, to be smoking opium, to be betting on horses by means of a pin, to be in the pay of the Tories. Perhaps it was considered un-comradely to discredit people through things that they had actually done?

Colne Valley was very different this time. The January snows precluded open-air meetings and although the Labour Clubs and Mechanics' Institutes were always packed, there was something anti-climactic about it all. Audiences laughed or cheered a few seconds too early or too late and when Victor paused, they would applaud – but weakly, as if afraid of silence. Many of the old faces were missing. All the clergy had reverted to the Liberals. Hooves-On-Hands had died, with his funeral having the biggest turnout in Slaithwaite's history, and so too had Mother Shipton, whose final prophecy had been that the world would end in four years' time. And the little boy who had so proudly carried Victor's cane had apparently run off for longer and longer periods until last spring he had vanished altogether. In comparison with '07, this campaign was professionally done: every vacant space was plastered with posters of the candidate, in chiaroscuro, sitting on what appeared to be a throne, fixing passers-by with a level but enigmatic gaze. There were five hundred volunteers and a whole fleet of cars which regularly needed to be dug out of snowdrifts, and a newly-formed Socialist brass band to battle – apocalyptically – with France Littlewood's choir. Nevertheless, even the women and children seemed apathetic and the sheep, wintering on the lower slopes, seldom looked up from their feed. Victor had wondered, only half in jest, whether their problem might be too much organisation and too much money.

"Unfortunately, this election is not about us," Briggs had concluded, "It's being fought over Protectionism and Lloyd George's budget and Labour, whatever MacDonald might pretend, is incidental to these things. To make further progress we need either a major crisis or a long period of prosperity. For now, the Liberals have stolen our clothes: 'The undeserving rich against the undeserving poor' – I hear that Snowden is trying as usual to take credit for that line."

Boyd Carpenter, the Conservative candidate, was nearly as bone-headed as Wheler, but Leach, as Snowden had predicted, was a marked improvement on Bright. In what could only be described as a hysterical monotone he drove home his three or four basic points and managed to keep in check his personal eccentricities, except for a couple of days when he insisted on only walking backwards. Victor's name never sullied his lips: he referred to him as 'The Socialist Candidate' . . . "The Socialist Candidate who addresses his communications from a luxury hotel" – Victor had taken the top floor of The Queens' in Huddersfield . . . "The Socialist Candidate who never misses a meal" – Leach himself had never been seen to eat or drink . . . "The Socialist Candidate who scorns ordinary means of locomotion" – walking backwards, presumably.

The Liberals adopted a cartoon from *The Huddersfield Examiner* as their poster. It depicted Victor as a sansculotte in a Phrygian cap bearing the motto 'SELF', beating with broken bottles on a drum, at the head of a baying and subhuman mob; Boyd Carpenter, in rugger togs, stood under the banner 'FREE PEERS FREE BEERS', while Leach, attended by John Bull himself, struck an heroic pose and called for 'SOUND PROGRESS! . . . CHEAP FOOD! . . . BURDENS ACCORDING TO ABILITY!'

"I am deeply offended," Victor announced. "I would *never* roll up my sleeves in public. Nor do I play the drums or wear any hat with a brim less than three inches wide." He had determined not to drink in the constituency but back at The Queens, two miles outside its boundaries, he and the Blatchford sisters would prop up the bar far into the night. Tory and Liberal agents bought the drinks, which must have been the largest item on their election expenses. It was rumoured that he was engaged to both girls at the same time but neither was really serious, merely determined that her sister should not have him. With increasing weariness he concentrated his attentions first on one, then the other.

Things livened up a little when Thongsbridge returned. Once again he followed Victor everywhere, but now he was shouting "Judas! Sodomite! Antichrist!" He was almost as good as Hooves-On-Hands. "I remember how much you used to like my summer trousers," Victor would say, "It's a shame that you don't care for the winter pair."

On the day of the declaration Victor was disappointed to see that there was a new returning officer but fortunately the man proceeded to stutter and scramble the result in the proper fashion. They finally settled on –

Dr, Charles Leach(Lib) 4,741
A. Boyd Carpenter(Con) 3,750
Victor Grayson(Socialist) 3,149

A crowd of Liberals swept Leach up to carry him shoulder-high to a grand ham-and-eggs reception in The Temperance Hall. The tails of his old-fashioned coat flapped in the breeze, while his spindly legs and enormous feet dangled horribly down. He resembled a guy on its way to the bonfire: some people were just not meant to be chaired. Victor's own supporters, if only for the pleasure of out-shouting their rivals, insisted on his making a concessionary speech outside The Duke of Devonshire.

"The day is coming when Socialism, the hope of the world,

the future religion of humanity, will have wiped Liberalism and Toryism from the face of the earth." He noticed that many Liberals and Conservatives had stayed to listen and were applauding with the rest. "Stick to your flag! Don't let the colours be stained – stick to the gospel that first inspired your heart and you will live to rejoice in a victory that none can gainsay."

"Three thousand isn't bad, Victor," Briggs drained his second pint. "Especially as you've never really acted like an MP at all. You're a great lad but you're no politician. In fact I don't really know what you are. Hey, Christine," he shouted down the bar, "Give the Dishonourable Member another piece of cheese."

"We should abolish general elections," said Victor, "And have five by-elections every week so that a government could lose even a large majority within a year or so. Weak candidates would be ruthlessly exposed, every vote would matter and public accountability would no longer be just another empty phrase. Everything would seem possible, everyone would be full of life and hope, just like it was three years ago."

"Never mind," Briggs handed him a scroll of paper, "This will cheer you up." Victor unrolled it to reveal a crude but vividly drawn poster of a bristling bantam cock with Snowden's head stuck on the end of its neck. 'PHILIP FOR BLACKBURN!' read the heading and underneath:

> "Wey sed, eawr gam' cock cud feight!
> Hesn'd he done? Well, vooate o' reight!"

"Well, he's got The Dialect Society's vote," someone said when the rather forced mirth had subsided.

"And the cockfighters'."

"But not, I think, the cocksuckers'," said Victor.

At this moment the door opened and an enormous goose entered the pub. Only after a few seconds of stupefaction did it become apparent that what had seemed to be the creature's beak was the distinctively wide brim of a Stetson hat. It could only be Ernest Marklew, exquisitely feathered by fresh and glistening white flakes.

"Oooh! Is it snowing again?" asked Christine.

"No," said the goose, as if genuinely surprised by the question. It raised one white wing and shook it. "At least, I don't think so."

Tears swam in Victor's eyes as he raised his glass to the room: he was really going to miss Colne Valley.

CHAPTER SIX

BROKEN BOTTLES (1911)

"NEW YORK," Jim Sharp's letter began, "Is a funny place
. . ." But *was* it New York? Fred was sure of the 'N' and
the 'K' but the rest of it was swimming before his eyes. And was
it even 'a funny place'? Philip had spelt it out as 'Near dark in a
burning palace'. Jim appeared to have written each character at
different times, with different nibs and inks. His these's, that's and
those's were impeccable – except that the T's were sometimes dotted
rather than crossed – but the rest was impenetrable. Commas and
full stops were scattered at random; jagged parentheses yawned
open then never closed; battalions of question and exclamation
marks marched to and fro; words were underlined, sometimes even
twice – but the matter at hand remained obscure.

Was Jim doing well or digging a well? Or was he doing well at
digging wells? Apparently he had been having trouble with books
or boots – or was it beers? He had been looking for God – or was
it gold? There was a long sequence of letters and numbers that
might have been map references but the ones and sevens, twos and
threes and fives and sixes were interchangeable. This was the fourth
letter in twenty years and, as always, Jim had neglected to include
his address.

Fred still missed him – and in a curiously physical way. Every day
he would find his head turning left at a certain angle, expecting to
find Jim there in his proper place. He recalled how his friend would
growl so fiercely from the corner of his mouth while his eyes shone
with delight and the way he would press his prominent ears against

the side of his head whenever there were ladies present. Most of all, though, Fred missed those impossibly bandy legs of which their owner had been so ashamed. Perhaps he was out west, riding the range where nobody would notice – at least not until he got off his horse? Jim had been the most lovable of men but there was no reassuring him. Fred often wondered what he could have said in order to make him stay. Even now, he had the curious feeling that Jim was waiting for him to do something so that he could at last come home. It was as if even his bill to feed poor children during school holidays had all been about Jim – even though his friend had no children, as far as he knew, and was as far away as you could possibly get.

The fate of that bill still rankled. As he had resumed his seat, applause – that rarest of sounds – had issued from all parts of the House. Even the topers had applauded as he passed the bars. Everyone praised his rhetorical techniques: as if those thousands of hungry children had been merely heart-rending inventions, like characters out of Dickens. Even Lloyd George had congratulated him – how clammy that handshake had been! – before going off to re-table commons business so that the measure would not get its second reading, thus avoiding the embarrassment of voting it down. During his speech, Fred had deployed a large chart which showed how the weight of Bradford's children increased in term time only to fall during holidays. Now, whenever 'L. G.' spoke, he would unfurl with a flourish ever larger and more elaborate diagrams and graphs. The corridors buzzed with talk of the Welsh Wizard's brilliant new trick: Fred's own little chart and his speech and his bill were all forgotten.

"I've never got used to the place, laddie," Hardie often said, "And God help you if you ever do."

It had certainly left its mark on him: although he had at last stood down as leader he still haunted the chamber, shouting incoherently and shaking his fists. A couple of Llanelli strikers had been shot dead by the army: he seemed to feel that Asquith had personally pulled the trigger. The Speaker regularly suspended him:

it was like Grayson all over again except that, with his wild eyes and ragged clothes, Hardie actually *looked* like a fanatic.

If Snowden had felt mortified at being passed over as party leader for Henderson he was doubly so after poor Uncle Arthur had been rapidly supplanted by MacDonald. When the new leader supported the Government's Unemployment and Health Insurance Act, Philip and Fred had voted against. Fred had objected to the meagre provision being based upon contributions, while Phil had merely wanted to give Mac a bloody nose. At the recent Merthyr Conference, the so-called 'Bradford Resolution' had been passed, mandating MPs to vote according to their consciences, irrespective of the leadership's position. During the debate Snowden had revealed that MacDonald and the NEC had regularly made secret deals with the Liberals. He also contrived to give the impression that he himself had not been involved. "I suppose they must have discussed it whenever he went to the toilet," suggested Willie Leach.

Fred began to read Jim's letter again. For some reason he had not shown it to Emily but carried it around in his inside pocket. Every time he took it out he hoped that the words might have somehow recombined themselves into legibility. He had even tried holding it up to the mirror but to no avail. Philip was equally fascinated, even though he had never known Jim. He was set on its decipherment: in an office on Little Smith Street, so Lloyd George had told him, there sat a man who could crack any code. "There are ways, if you have the right connections," he said, "Be it New York or Novaya Zemblya, any man that is still above the earth can be found." But Fred did not think that Jim would take kindly to being 'found' – especially not through the offices of Lloyd George.

Lately he had wondered whether Jim – with his fondness for direct action – might not be tempted back by the growing industrial unrest. Dock strikes in Belfast and railway strikes in Newcastle were succeeded by lockouts in Lancashire and Scotland, culminating in those terrible clashes in South Wales. Rather than being about pay and conditions they were said to be ideologically motivated, applications of Syndicalism, a French doctrine which rejected the parliamentary route for confrontation in and around the workplace. Every violent act was a burning brand thrown on to the gathering conflagration that would sear and purify the world. Two veteran activists, Tom Mann and Ben Tillett, had returned from Australia to start a journal called 'The Industrial Syndicalist'. "The wombats and wallabies must have turned their brains," said Snowden, "But when you've got the peers and the Ulster Unionists behaving like anarchists, who can blame the workers for joining in as well?" Philip had actually read Sorel, the movement's philosopher, and been surprisingly impressed. "But he's a *poet*, Fred. All those rhapsodies of violence are metaphors for states of mind, or even states of the soul: these fools take everything literally."

Syndicalists were suddenly everywhere, especially around the newly-formed Central Labour College. Nervous, thin and pale, they were presumably relying on someone else to do the actual fighting. Jim would like the sound of it all right but his mind would change if he actually saw them.

Fred could not rid himself of the feeling that Grayson was somehow behind all this. He had suitably polluted the atmosphere: his *Clarion* columns grew more incendiary by the week and at the bottom of the page there was always an application form to join the new British Socialist Party. At least when he had been nominally a Labour MP they had been able to keep an eye on him. Heaven only knew where he was or what he might be doing. Fred had a vision of the man sitting in the Café Royal, laughing and raising his glass, while another Ton-y-Pandy miner was throwing himself upon the army sabres.

He had last seen Grayson two months ago on King's Cross Station. Before boarding the Friday night homebound train he had as usual gone into the Refreshment Room. While the waitress was filling his flask with tea he had heard the all-too-familiar laughter. Grayson and Blatchford: he knew that they were to address a rally in Leeds tomorrow morning. How he dreaded a night in their company!

They would always produce bottles of brandy and a greasy deck of cards. Fortunately they were oblivious to his presence and for once they did not have glasses in their hands. Instead they were engaged in throwing finger shadows against the window blinds behind them. Fred had stolen away: only when he was safely seated in an empty compartment did he realize that he had forgotten his flask.

As the train pulled out he had observed, with relief and indignation, that flickering across the diner's illuminated screen was a lop-eared rabbit, locked in combat with an enraged cockerel. Grayson's youth was some excuse but Blatchford must be at least sixty years old! Next day, up north, there had been much speculation about their non-appearance: the Police, it was said, had stopped the train at Grantham and dragged them off. When Fred had returned on Monday morning to retrieve his flask he had been almost disappointed not to find them still there, conjuring increasingly extravagant shapes upon those greasy and fly-blown blinds.

Jim's letter had been written on cheap paper that was already beginning to flake. The last page bore a blossoming stain like dried blood and a few sharp grains of sparkling dust were lodged in the corners of the envelope. Fred had sniffed and licked at them but they were quite without smell or taste. How strangely life turned out! There were nearly two thousand names in his address books – good comrades, most of them – but the new people he met every day never filled the gaps left by those who had died or drifted away. Perhaps it was true – as Philip had suggested – that if Grayson were to vanish Fred would miss him as much as Jim or Tom Maguire? Philip himself, of course, was utterly unsentimental about such things.

"But don't you miss the old days, Phil?"

"Nay," Snowden would reply, "I can remember them well enough."

❧

Victor could swear that this girl's tongue kept changing shape.

Sometimes it seemed impossible that one mouth could contain its length but at others he would search for it in vain. It would throb until their saliva bubbled and boiled or wrapped itself, like an adhesive dressing, around his own. One moment it would be lapping at his anus like a kitten at a bowl of milk, then dart up inside him like an eel. At least it wasn't forked and – no matter how much she smoked and drank – it was always a nice healthy pink in the morning.

Ruth was slim, without being in the least boyish. Her breasts were small, flat and almost square with long and raw-looking nipples that remained permanently erect. Her shoulders, upper arms and thighs were heavy with muscle: she attributed this to her childhood swimming at Lytham St Annes. Crowds of gentlemen had gathered to watch: "And I thought they were just admiring my French crawl." Her green eyes seldom blinked and when they did those long eyelashes batted away for a full minute, as if once started the mechanism had to run itself down.

Her hair was honey blonde but darkening at the roots and her bush was thick, prickly and black. It looked artificial but surely a merkin would have come unglued by now? Sometimes by the fire he could glimpse in it autumnal yellows and reds. Her weight and its distribution seemed to change: one moment the flesh was soft and yielding, at the next she was all bone. She would float above you like a mountain mist and then come down like an avalanche. What was the name of that hollow behind the knee where the tiny blue veins converge? When he touched it in a certain way she would thrash about, as if burning or drowning. Whatever her body was doing, however – even at the moment of climax – her expression would remain non-committal, as if she was waiting for an omnibus which, she suspected, might be full when it finally arrived.

She would hop about like a flea, the skin across her back rippling like windblown sand. Was it possible to learn to do something like that? Her limbs would contort into seemingly impossible shapes, and then relax so that the pose became graceful, perfectly natural.

"After you've sat for Orpen," she said, "You can do pretty much anything."

Nothing Victor said or did could shock her. It would have been pleasant to have seen her, if only momentarily, hesitant or non-plussed. There was, of course, no way of disgusting her, unless you were to offer her a nice cup of tea. "Hell's teeth!" she would hiss, loudly grinding her own, "What kind of girl do you take me for?"

They had met in Mayfair at a fund-raiser for the *New Age*. A. R. Orage, its editor, had appointed him as his deputy, a token position to boost the circulation. Victor's own name for it was the 'No Wage': when he did write something it was the devil's own job to get paid. That afternoon the usual crowd had been in attendance. A group of men with enormous moustaches, who were always locked in earnest conversation: Victor had taken them for Nietzscheans, arguing just how dead God really was, but, eavesdropping, he had discovered that their sole topic was the maintenance and grooming of their facial hair. Sydney and Beatrice Webb stood under a chandelier regarding everyone with undisguised disapproval. There were a few pop-eyed men and women who had something to do with Gurdjieff; a little knot of printers, their ink-stained hands circulating whisky flasks at lightning speed; and a couple of suffragette acquaintances from his Manchester days who were now, for reasons he could not recall, pointedly ignoring him. He resisted the impulse to waggle his tongue at them, vaguely recalling that they practised ju-jitsu.

Just as he was about to leave, a thrilling contralto voice had stilled the room.

"Do ye hear the children weeping, o my brothers?"

Turning, he perceived a tall, slim young woman wearing a large and edible-looking hat. She was standing on a round backed chair, one foot raised precariously but elegantly behind her.

. . . "Ere the sorrows come with years?"

He made his way over to Orage. Whenever the man saw him he would puff out his cheeks and fan his brow as if close proximity was too hot for mere mortals to bear. His nickname for Victor was The Infant Dionysus.

"Who is she, Outrage?"

"Ruth Norreys, the actress. I believe she is" - Orage rolled his eyes - "The toast of the town." This was his favourite phrase. Victor wondered whether there was anyone left in London to do the actual toasting - perhaps they toasted each other in rotation, like the *Clarion* mob?

> "'It is good when it happens', say the children!
> 'That we die before our time!'"

The full red lips trilled, then boomed. Her back's sinuous movements were evidently distracting her audience from the children's regrettable plight. The words could be seen travelling up her spine. That raised silver slipper had slid to dangle precariously off her big toe. Victor realized that he was smiling like an idiot - at the sheer unlikeliness of encountering such a creature here or, indeed, anywhere.

> "But the child's sob curseth deeper in the silence
> Than the strong man in his wrath!"

At the end of the recitation she did not step down but launched herself forward to land without the slightest stagger in front of Victor. Her eyes were level with his own: indeed, the two of them seemed to be perfectly aligned, for her left knee-cap pressed against his right.

"You seem to be enjoying yourself," she said in a reduced voice, as the applause subsided.

"It was one of the funniest things I've ever heard."

"Most people seem to find Mrs Browning profoundly moving," her forefinger flicked the scarlet volume, "But perhaps Daddy is right: you should treat tragedy as comedy and vice versa."

"Is your father an actor?"

"No," she turned away. "He's a bank manager, in Bolton."

Another shudder passed down her body, pausing awhile at the hips, presumably to indicate her disinclination to return to that most dreadful of towns. Only now did the familiar perfume, rich and sweet, hit the back of his throat. Gardenia: it was the first time he had smelt it on a woman.

Everyone in the room – even the moustaches – turned to follow her progress. Her arms remained at her sides, elbows out, and the outlines of her flexing shoulder blades were clearly defined. At the top of the columnar neck the small cat-like head was absolutely still. She appeared to be moving briskly but it felt like an age before she gained the door. What on earth must they have made of her in Bolton?

'Actress' was a broad term in London but it turned out that Miss Norreys really was appearing in *The Merchant of Venice* at the Criterion Theatre. That evening's performance was sold out but Victor had once memorably encountered the stage manager and so found himself in a splendid box, crammed in between two large, well-powdered and rather too welcoming ladies.

When Ruth finally appeared in the Second Act he had not recognized her. In a waxy blue-black wig she seemed to have gained a couple of stone since the afternoon. She was playing Jessica, the moneylender's daughter. There had been an audible intake of breath as she extracted from between her breasts a secret letter to be delivered to her lover, followed by an even louder groan at the way her fingers curled around its scroll. The poor servant had blushed and stammered and, exiting, tripped over his own feet, getting a laugh for what Victor was sure had been a quite unintentional bit of business.

> "O Lorenzo
> If thou keep thy promise, I shall end this strife,
> Become a Christian and thy loving wife."

184

As she had spoken these words she had turned to look directly at Victor's box.

Jessica then exited only to return almost immediately, ready for elopement, disguised as a boy. The two ladies were scandalized to find that Lorenzo was apparently also dallying with this winsome, if slightly top-heavy, youth. When she produced her father's box of ducats the audience gasped again: how could this metamorphosis have been affected in so short a time?

After Ruth had left the stage Victor grew increasingly restive. He had never seen the play before. Shylock was the best actor: the others seemed to be persecuting him for his very excellence. Portia, unconvincingly disguised as Bellario, weaved about the stage, stooping to retrieve the absurd little cap that kept falling off her piled up and greying curls. Her voice was clear enough at the beginning of her speeches but gradually broke down into incomprehensible burr and buzz. The quality of mercy obviously did not extend to Jews: that pound of flesh was the sort of trick that Lloyd George might pull. "If I were Shylock," the smaller of Victor's ladies whispered, "I'd cut out that merchant's heart, bung it on those scales and let 'em argue about it afterwards."

Ruth did not return until the opening of the final act, in a peculiar scene in which Lorenzo maundered on about the nature of music. Poor Jessica had only one line - "I am never merry when I hear sweet music" - a hint her lover refused to take. Victor's eyes remained fixed on her: by her breathing and the way her shoulders rose and fell and the little flickering around her mouth, it appeared that she was brought to a climax by the speech's rhythms and cadences, even though they were spoken by an oafish lump whose lungs wheezed at the end of every line. "And his affections dark as Erebus" - at these words her eyes closed, her head tilted right back and the male half of the audience moaned again.

Jessica had no more lines. She stood and watched as primary and secondary lovers acted out an elaborate routine about purloined rings before at last falling clumsily into each others' arms. What am I doing with these people? – her expression said – Why ever did I leave my father? Will I ever see any of these ducats again? To Victor, her silence dominated the final scene but his was not perhaps an impartial view.

After the curtain calls, having with difficulty detached himself from his two new friends, he made his way to the stage door. Ruth, dressed from head to toe in russet velvet, was already waiting there.

"You were the best thing in it," he said, "Apart from Shylock."

"You should have been here last night," she took his arm, "I was understudying Portia. She only appears at weekends and she's pie-eyed even then. I have a different interpretation of the role: sober and without a cleft palate. She hates me, the great fat thing: we're only on stage together for five minutes but she insisted on padding me out."

They crossed Haymarket and went into a pub. Shylock was already there, still in full costume, arguing with the landlord. "Poor fellow," Ruth whispered, "He has to drink to get into the part and then drink to get out of it again." Victor ordered a third double whiskey and placed it on the bar.

"Such injustices cannot stand," he said, "The Day of Judgement draweth nigh."

"I wish I could believe that," sighed Shylock, "But not even in Paradise, I fear, will we actors be allowed to run up a decent slate."

Ruth chain-smoked Turkish Ovals right down to their tips. She noisily sucked in the smoke but when she exhaled, equally dramatically, almost nothing came back out. Everyone in the place knew her – or at least, they all smiled or waved. Victor was aware that even the few women – slatternly demi-monde types – had eyes for her and not for himself. He felt rather – upstaged, did they call it?

Norreys was only her stage name: she was really Ruth Nightingale. Victor, recalling that handkerchief he found on top of Snowdon, was relieved that it still began with an 'N'.

"Do you have your initials embroidered on your handkerchiefs?"

"What a sinister question!" laughed Ruth, "I'm afraid not."

"Have you ever been up Mount Snowdon?"

"I'm afraid I don't understand these euphemisms. If you want to know something why don't you just ask me?"

"Nightingale is a perfect name for an actress: why did you change it?"

"Too obvious: everyone would be expecting me to sing."

Ruth was well-informed about the Labour party, especially MacDonald. "My God, what a man! Anyone would want to have him." She pinched Victor's inner thigh. "Wouldn't you?"

"Tombstone teeth," said Victor, "Pigeon chest, scratchy-looking moustache. Not my type."

"Some people are everyone's type," said Ruth, "All-powerful but weighed down by nameless sorrows. He'd be perfect as Wotan."

Victor was not surprised to find that she was a fervent Wagnerite. In fashionable circles this served as a sort of code. Whenever a woman spoke of *The Ring* you knew that you were in for an interesting night.

"Hardie and Snowden will do for Mime and Alberich," Ruth continued, "And you'll be Siegfried, of course. Don't worry, you kill the dragon and rescue the girl but then your sworn blood brother stabs you in the back with a dirty great spear."

"That'll be Hyndman," said Victor. He fought his way to the bar and ordered another round, watching while Ruth kindly but firmly brushed off her motley suitors.

"She's a poor actress but a true Bohemian," said Shylock, tilting his whiskey in her direction, "Utterly amoral but a grand, grand girl."

When Victor returned she drained her glass and slammed it down on the zinc-topped table so that it shattered, then picked up her coat. "I think we should go somewhere," she said, "And do something." On the way out he bought Shylock a last drink and handed the landlord a sheaf of BSP application forms.

Ruth had a man's – no, a boy's – attitude to matters of the flesh.

She reminded him of Little Mikey: true, he had been a drooling imbecile but otherwise the differences were not even skin deep. Their bodies had the same faint phosphorescence and they regarded him with that unwavering and unfathomable stare. She was utterly natural – or unnatural – in giving immediate expression to her physical instincts. A grand, grand girl: there was no teasing, mock outrage or token resistance – she gave as good as she got without negotiations. And she was never acting, she was always Ruth: perhaps actors purged themselves of pretence and illusion on stage?

She was quite perfect: so why did he feel such pity for her? She was utterly fearless and free: so why did he feel that he had to protect her? Sometimes a restless tenderness would constrict his chest until his head swam and he began to choke. Then he would wrap his hands round her neck and squeeze: he was sure he could feel a vestigial adam's apple. Her face would darken alarmingly, the eyes rolled like a doll's and the stiff tongue poked out of the mouth. He wanted to twist the head clean off, if only to screw it back on again but then the throat itself would break his grip, as Ruth could no longer hold back the waves of laughter that came pulsing up from the pit of her stomach. He was, he supposed, the physically stronger, but once she herself had gained a hold – especially when those swimmer's legs scissored round his neck – he knew that he would have been unable to free himself.

When he had told her of his relationship with Harry Dawson she had merely grinned. "His ears are different shapes" – her fingers ran across the photograph as if trying to read it like Braille – "Have you been chewing on them?"

"It doesn't do him justice," said Victor. "His eyes, the turn of his head, his walk – they're what make him so attractive."

"I can imagine." Ruth yawned and stretched. "Why don't you ask him to join us one of these nights?"

"I'm afraid Harry is none too keen on the ladies. Although he is the gentlest of souls, I once saw him deck a drunken barmaid who kissed him on the lips. And then he sobbed for the rest of the evening."

"That was probably for your benefit. Most of my pansy friends love me to touch them. Perhaps Harry is secretly a het?"

"An ill-designed affair with too many protuberances: that's his definition of woman. All that pulpy flesh, all those nasty fluids sloshing about: he thinks you belong in the ocean with the jellyfish and squid."

Ruth's hands ran across her flat belly and thighs. "He's got no room to talk: he's quite the little barrel himself."

"I suspect he was referring to your reproductive capacities. 'I know that I could never have come crawling out of one of those sacks of offal', he always says, 'I know that I must have fallen - very slowly and elegantly - from a bright and distant star'."

"I know the feeling," said Ruth. "Because I don't think of myself as being a woman." She leant over, unbuttoned his flies and took out his already stiffened cock. "And come to that" - her head slowly descended - "I don't think of you as being a man."

One of the priests that Victor had known used to say that making love was just the means of clearing the mind for the conversation - on the nature of the Trinity or the Four Last Things - that would take up the rest of the night. But Victor had always disagreed: sex itself was the deepest communication.

"Politics and love have nothing to do with each other, thank God," Blatchford once said to him, apologising for the rabid Toryism of his latest admirer.

"Everything is political," Victor replied, "Even love."

"No. Everything, including politics, is all about love," Ruth had interrupted, "And I don't mean love in the Ethel Snowden sense. I mean fucking."

Blatchford had blushed scarlet, then leaned over to stammer - in a weirdly pitched whisper - into Victor's ear. "Please remind your little friend that there are ladies present." Ruth, however, had been the only woman there.

Her own political position was elusive. It could best be characterized as being the precise opposite of whoever she happened to be with at the time. She would passionately argue in favour of free trade or protectionism, while presumably not giving a damn either way. If she walked in on someone else's argument she would never take a middle course but effect an outrageous synthesis of the furthest possible extremes. As a result she was sometimes accused of anarchism.

"I have yet to meet an anarchist," she would say in her best dowager tone, "Who knew how to fuck."

Once they joined a *Clarion* walking party for a weekend on the Lake District. Up in the mountains Ruth had kept breaking away from the group, taking the most direct and perilous routes. Victor had to restrain her from following Coleridge's celebrated ledge-jumping descent of Broad Stand, telling her that it could only be done by night and under the influence of Black Drop opium. One evening, coming down Sour Milk Gill, she had discovered a deep and perfectly oval rock pool. After supper they had re-ascended, stripped off, dived in and – with some difficulty – made love in the shockingly cold water. They had still been shivering at breakfast when they were informed that a vote had been taken and – on account of their inappropriate behaviour – they were to be expelled from the *Clarion* Ramblers' Club.

"Which of you limp-pricks went to the trouble of following us?" Ruth enquired. "Shouldn't Socialists – of all people – have better things to do?"

There was only one drawback about Ruth. Since they met, Victor's senses of taste and smell had been markedly impaired. He would still lift the lid of the coffee pot and sniff long and deep, then pile his plate with charred rashers of smoked bacon but he had to admit that he felt only a fading memory of former pleasures. Still, it seemed a very small price to pay.

❧

Philip's mother had rallied but she would never be going home again. This had been her fifth fall of the year – and those were only the ones she had told anyone about. Ethel had taken command, of course, sending up a Harley Street specialist to confirm the nature and number of broken bones, and then personally vetting every nursing home in the vicinity. Mrs Snowden would be spending her final years with kindly nuns in leafy genteel Harrogate. Ethel could not have been more assiduous but she still refused to visit the patient. "That woman is one of the deadliest enemies of love," she said, "I may be many things but I am not a hypocrite." The two of them had not spoken in five years. The last time the Snowdens had visited, Mother's Yorkshire dialect became so impenetrable that even Phil himself had no idea what she was talking about. Since then he would arrange for a car to take her to the Station Hotel in Leeds to join him for high tea whenever he was passing through.

"Eeh, our Phil," she quavered on their last meeting, "I'd have liked to see thee properly wed before I go."

It evidently suited them to dislike each other. Besides, according to Ethel, hate was just another aspect of Universal Love. But if Hate were really Love, didn't it follow that Love might really be Hate? He would never get the hang of Universal Love: one moment it was everywhere, the next nowhere – in everything then in nothing. It was quite impossible to pin down, rather like Victor Grayson.

The family home of the last forty years needed to be cleared out but this was one task that Ethel flatly refused to undertake. She would not even accompany Philip although she had arranged for one of her cousins to pick him up at Keighley station.

Leaving the man parked by the church, Philip walked along the main street. The few locals merely turned away as he passed: no-one even whispered 'scurvy gouger'. He paused outside The Grinning Rat wondering if his uncle might be inside: the place appeared to be derelict but then it always had. Nothing had changed. Surely someone should have replaced that ruined field gate by now? Unless it was another gate, warped and bent to the same angle by cows, sheep and the prevailing wind? And surely the ragged cockerel in the farmyard could not be the same one that had crowed and strutted through his childhood? But it did have that distinctive limp and knowing eye. How long did these things live? He was sure that it had recognized him: it had opened its beak and then closed it again. It gave him an uneasy feeling but a cockerel was only a cockerel, after all.

Three hulking brutes were lounging by the roadside: the land-lord's men, waiting to clear the house.

"Are you keeping owt?" the biggest asked, without taking the clay pipe out of his mouth

"I don't think so," replied Philip, "But I'll be stopping here for a while."

The man spat and turned away. Philip's left stick reached out and tapped him on the shoulder. "Do you have some objection to that?"

The eyes widened. "No, no." Being Dr Nikola brought you certain advantages. "Take your time, sir, take your time."

The old key turned slowly in the rusty lock and he was greeted by the familiar stale, dry, curiously hot smell – just like – as Ethel had observed on a recent visit to Regents Park – that which ema-nated from the Lions' Enclosure. All the upstairs furniture was in the hall to greet him: he had to crawl between the dresser's legs to reach the front room.

He could not remember ever having been alone in the house of his parents. Only the couch remained, so stretched and flattened out that it would no longer fit through door or window. Now it appeared that many of the sounds that had been characteristic of his mother's presence – those creaks and shuffling and that particularly martyred sigh – had to be reattributed to the building itself. Surely it was too early for her to be haunting it? Or perhaps it was his father: now that she was gone, Philip had the feeling that he might somehow be coming back.

But what had happened to Dad's books? The shelves were gone: a few religious tracts had been screwed up and tossed into the hearth.

Where were all those annotated works of history and politics, the well-thumbed Longfellow and Whittier? His brothers and sisters could have had no use for them. All that remained, wedged under the sofa's broken leg, was a slightly mildewed Collected Poems of A. C. Swinburne which he slipped into his pocket.

What, he wondered, would the father make of the son? Philip suspected that he would be proud, although he would not of course have admitted it. If anything, he might have chided him for not fully embracing his scarifying reputation. "To be liked is easy," he would say, "To be respected is all very well . . . but to be feared is best of all."

MacDonald did not take that view. Last week he had tackled Philip about it.

"We realize that for much of the time you must be in pain and for that you have all our sympathy" – since becoming leader he had started speaking of himself in the first-person plural – "But such bitterness and gall is ill-becoming to our spokesman on economic affairs."

"I hit hard," he had replied, "but I fight fair. And righteous indignation is not the same as bitterness."

"It might make you feel better," said Mac, "but we must present ourselves as a moderate and responsible party, ready to govern."

Perhaps accidentally, he had hit on the truth. As Philip watched his opponents pose and preen at the dispatch box his spine would seem as if it was about to snap but when he rose to let them have it, hot and strong, the pain magically disappeared. After his closing speech in the last budget debate he had been free of pain for a full three weeks.

From outside there came the sound of splintering wood. The three men had begun breaking up the worm-riddled sideboard. By their vigour, they were imagining it to be him. Autumn leaves blew around them but the branches of the poplar did not stir. Half way up its tarry trunk was a red and blue poster. GRAYSON SPEAKS! – it screamed, as if he might have been an oracle or a talking horse.

Below the words was a particularly irritating photograph of the man, smirking under the brim of a natty flat-topped hat, clutching his silver-topped cane as if it was a sceptre. He looked as if he was preparing to have the last laugh.

Lately Philip had even wondered whether he should remain in politics. Ethel was earning six times as much as himself: he was pleased for her, of course, but this was surely not a healthy state of affairs. She herself had resigned from the ILP to concentrate on women's suffrage only to be mortified by the tactics employed by what she called 'the weird sisters'. When she had organized a mass rally in the Albert Hall with Lloyd George as main speaker it had ended in a riot. "I had rather my nerves had been flayed through all eternity," she said, "than that our distinguished guest should have suffered such discourtesy." Lloyd George, of course, had been quite unperturbed. When they started throwing coins at him he had caught every one, then winked and put the money in his pocket. L-G and Universal Love now seemed to have become synonymous: Ethel kept saying that he had "a mystical destiny to fulfil". Philip had no idea what this might mean.

Grayson was speaking this very evening at Keighley Drill Hall. Philip had not seen him in almost a year but it was evident that the movement was far from freeing itself from his influence. Most of the latest *Clarion* had been given over to his article, 'The Time Has Come!': it had read more like a huckster's sales patter – for Owbridge's Lung Tonic, perhaps? – than a political manifesto. Nevertheless, Philip had been reminded of those religious sects who would announce the end of the world every two months or so: one of these days they might even be right.

Only last week he had been out on the Commons terrace talking to the Reverend Leach from Colne Valley about France Littlewood, who had almost died of influenza, when he became aware that little balls of spittle were spurting like hailstones from the corners of the man's mouth. Then Leach had fallen over after attempting to remove his trousers without first unlacing his shoes. Before the attendants carried him away he had begun to sing, in a high and sweet voice, words from a language that no-one could identify. "Grayson's revenge," said Sir Walter Long. "It is most unwise to twit the Great God Pan." Poor Leach had apparently not stopped singing since.

Jowett believed that Victor had been behind that summer's wave of strikes but Philip doubted that he had the organizing capacity. With the Lords' Die-hards throwing out the budget and the Loyalist Volunteers drilling in Ulster it was his opinion that the strikers had merely succumbed to the general mood. And there had been the weather: when the sun shines every working man becomes a revolutionary. It had not been Syndicalism so much as heatstroke and over-salted beer. Two days of rain had been enough to break those strikes.

With difficulty he knelt on the couch then thrust a hand down behind the cushion, deep into its intestines. "Always have a good rummage down the backs of things," Dad would say. "You never know what you might find." Philip was sure that it was he who had deposited those regular farthings there. But today there was no treasure, only an ancient handkerchief, crusted and shrivelled so that is resembled some exotic flower, an unmistakable relic from the almost forgotten years of his illness. It was unlikely that his mother could have overlooked it and surely even more so that she had left it for sentimental reasons. As he put it to his nostrils he had the strangest notion: perhaps he had never really quit his couch and the last twenty years had all been a dream? Perhaps Phil the cripple had somehow contrived to engender and send forth a second self to rise to the highest places in the land? Had he really been here all the time, nice and warm and safe, railing at the life he had lost? He could see that his own twisted shape was still indented in that faded fabric.

Out in the hall, the furniture had now cut off his escape so he turned into the scullery, where he paused to bend at the knees and squint one final time through the tiny window. A flaw in the glass made everything swim, as if the heather, grass and stone of the fell-side had been swept up in a great tidal wave. "The time has come!" he laughed aloud, even though this illusion still retained its power to cause the hairs on his forearms to rise.

He burst out of the back door to see the landlord's men trying to light a fire.

"What on earth are you doing?" he yelled, "That sideboard was a priceless antique!"

They stood there blinking at him, like scolded children on the verge of tears.

"Thank you for your patience, gentlemen" - he tossed each of them a shilling which they caught with a nonchalance worthy of Lloyd George. "We won't be keeping anything."

❧

"Na' then, Our Fred."

"Na then, Our Phil."

"I were just passing."

"I were just passing an' all." Fred slid his glasses back up his nose.

"I'm not going in, of course."

"No, I'm not going in, neither."

Snowden cocked his head, Jowett followed suit. Linking arms, they ascended the steps of Keighley Drill Hall, where a huge white bed sheet announced GRAYSON SPEAKS! in letters of blood.

"How much is it?" Fred enquired.

"Get yourselves in", growled the man on the door.

"Nay", said Phil. "It can't be much good if it's free."

"'Tis free to the likes of thee." He resembled one of the Sugden brothers but surely they had been dead these seven years.

In the hall everyone was standing, shoulder to shoulder, as if out on the terraces at Lawkholme Lane. What had happened to all the chairs? Philip had not realized how low the ceiling was: the tip of his cane could almost touch it. He had spoken here many times and it had always seemed to be of regulation height: perhaps they had lowered it especially for Grayson? As in the local hostelries, sawdust was liberally strewn over the bare boards: the walls appeared to be glistening with condensation. There was an overpowering reek of gin and beer.

The crowd was silent but he could hear it breathing in concert, like an enormous panting dog. It took a conscious effort not to fall into the rhythm. Nobody acknowledged them but their neighbours gradually shuffled away, leaving them in a square of empty space. To Snowden's right was a tall man reading a newspaper called *The Spiritual Telegraph*. Keighley had always been the haunt of occultists: Philip had considered them harmless but Ethel insisted that they got up to all manner of mischief out there on the astral plane. In front of Fred an even taller man kept muttering and slapping his own face but the three landlord's men next to him were paying no attention. Philip could tell that his three bob had already been drunk. The few decent working men in the room were looking apprehensive.

"At least the pubs will be empty tonight," Phil hissed into Fred's ear, "To say nothing of the cemeteries and madhouses."

The stage was bare except for a table bearing a carafe of brownish liquid but no glass. Time passed, but their satanic neighbour remained on the same page: 'PSYCHIC DISRUPTIONS EXPECTED' ran the headline. The crowd grew restive: first they hummed like a hive of bees, then began a curious stamping dance, dropping first one shoulder then the other, faster and faster, like a locomotive gaining momentum. Someone gave a piercing double whistle to complete the effect.

No announcements had been made: the speaker was now forty minutes late.

"There's a difference between making an entrance," said Fred, "And wasting everybody's time."

The audience were beginning to explore the sonic possibilities of a train packed with bees when, suddenly, Grayson was there. He had not entered from the wings but somehow materialized at the far wall with his back to them. He turned and put a finger to his lips and then, with the exaggerated care of a drunk returning from an all-night carouse, he tip-toed forward. As always, he was immaculately dressed: his cuff-links and tie-pin shot silver rays out into the darkness. Nevertheless, Philip thought that the man's neck had thickened and the upper torso was stiff: could he be wearing a corset?

Grayson picked up the carafe and sniffed it suspiciously, then pulled a face and replaced it on the table.

"Good ale!" He made a quaffing motion. "The true and proper drink of Englishmen!" – The audience erupted in shouts and cheers. "Borrow was right. He is not deserving of the name of Englishman who speaketh against Good Ale!" Philip observed that the occult-ist's features had reconfigured themselves in beatific form.

"It has been said that I drink too much," he continued when the noise had subsided a little.

"No! No!" came the response.

"And I realize that this puts me at a disadvantage here in Keighley where folk are too respectable to touch even a drop – unless they have the toothache or Mafeking or some such place has been relieved."

At this there was a horrible collective chuckle.

"Well, I *do* drink," continued Grayson, "I don't want to but I must. It is my duty as a revolutionary Socialist. I get letters from all over the world – yesterday even one from Shanghai" – he pulled his eyes into narrow slits – "Please to drink more, Comlade Glayson, we are lunning out of bockles to blake."

At the side of the stage a convenient Chinaman now submitted, with admirable good grace, to being tossed into the air.

"Ah, broken bottles, the artillery of the working class. Champagne bottles are the best – especially the Montrechat – they really fly when you put the corks back in . . . It's often said that those broken bottles have destroyed my career – or at least my chance of leading the Labour Party – but I'm not so sure" – he staggered sideways alarmingly – "I seem to be careering about as much as ever."

It was utter gibberish, of course, but Philip had to admit that it rattled on as seductively as ever.

"Now I want to talk about the great Lloyd George and his Labour Exchanges. You walk into a building where a man you've never seen before tells you who you are and what you're going to do. If you get a job he takes the credit but if you don't – well, it's all your own fault. Everyone laughs at you when you walk in and then laughs twice as loud when you come back out again . . . And yet this curious measure has been supported by Comrade MacDonald (loud booing), Comrade Snowden (more booing) and Comrade Jowett (virtual silence). "Hark" – Grayson cupped his ear – "I think I can hear Phil and Fred booing themselves. But they would no doubt protest that compromise is unavoidable and that the time to boo or cheer will be a hundred years from now. But how many Methusalehs are here tonight? . . . And how hard is it really – changing the world? They told Alexander the Great that Asia could only be conquered by untying the fiendish Gordian knot but when he saw that it was just a piece of string he took his sword" – Grayson slowly drew his finger across his throat – "And he cut it."

"Anyroad" – he tucked his thumbs under his waistcoat and stuck out his chest – "Back to those Labour Exchanges . . . On mature reflection I've decided that I'm all for them. In fact, I think we should have a universal exchange of labour . . . so Mr Churchill, for example, can come and dig the new drains up Haworth Road while you can all go and loaf about in Blenheim Palace. You'll need retraining, though. Take it from me" – he yawned and stretched – "Loafing is a highly skilled job."

He had developed some new mannerisms. The flirtatious, bantering tone had grown more aggressive. The voice was deeper, putting heavy stress on seemingly innocuous words. He stood at a slight backwards tilt as if leaning against an invisible support. The left hand would periodically form a fist and raise itself in front of his face, then he would stare at it bemusedly until it broke and the fingers fluttered down to smooth the lapels of his jacket. Such a gesture must have been considered and rehearsed but Philip had no idea what it signified. Glancing at Fred he was startled by his distinctly malevolent expression, as if the occultist was working some stealthy interchange of souls.

"Years ago," Grayson continued, "The great Richard Wagner pointed to a rioting crowd and said 'Out of the emancipation of that mob shall come the perfection of all art, science and religion'" – He scanned the hall. "And now I see it, ladies and gentlemen, written plainly on your good honest faces."

Fred's eyes were admittedly none too good but even when he squinted the crowd only looked more degraded. Keighley was the filthiest town in the West Riding. Improving its sanitation was almost impossible: you would have to raze the place and start again. And its inhabitants seemed to take a perverse pride in squalor. "Has it ever occurred to you," Jim Sharp had gently enquired, "That those folk have spent years getting things just the way they like them?"

"Do you think they enjoy watching their own children die before their time?" he had retorted but his friend had only smiled.

The heat in the hall was almost unbearable. The air was thick with flies: Fred was reminded of that huge bluebottle that had plagued the inaugural ILP conference and how Jim had joked, 'I see The Lord of the Flies has turned up: do you think he's for us or agin?' – and how he himself had shivered even though he knew that it was only a fly and that The Devil did not exist.

Right under the stage, gazing up in adoration, Fred could see a group of night-soil men, fully wrapped as if ready for their shift. The audience were giving them even more room than Philip and himself.

"How pleasant it has been this summer," Grayson continued, "to watch the working men of this country finally getting up off their knees. But now I hear that Ben Tillet has told his dockers to pray that God will strike Lord Davenport dead. This is a truly shocking statement from which all responsible politicians must disassociate themselves. Comrades, we must shoulder our responsibilities and relieve the over-taxed deity from this offensive task. In the name of humanity we must shoot the old bugger ourselves."

"Forty-eight seconds," said Snowden, having timed the subsequent applause.

"We must procure guns and ammunition. The workers will form a corps of destructive apaches and sabotage the industrial machine. They will dress in red and gold and carry wiggly oriental daggers with small brass canons which they can drag along behind them."

He paused and looked expectantly round the audience. "Behind them," he repeated with heavier emphasis. A planted questioner was obviously missing his cue. "Come on, man," said Grayson, capping his view, until - to cheers - a red-faced man appeared from the side entrance.

"But aren't you supposed to be anti-union?"

"I'm glad you asked that question. I am against trade unions until they go on strike. They are bovine wage-serfs until they down tools, when they are immediately transformed into heroic revolutionaries. I remain concerned that their demands are so petty: thruppence on the weekly rate! Or - when they're feeling frisky - a whole bloomin' tanner! They say they're hitting the bosses where it hurts - in the pocket - when they should be aiming" - his hands dropped to his groin - "a little lower. No, I'll start believing in them when they strike for public parks and picture galleries, demanding not buns, bananas and beverages but free ale and champagne in every canteen, voting for days at the races and nights at the opera and for the erection in Trafalgar Square - in Lord Nelson's place - of a sixty foot Keir Hardie, naked except for his watch and a strategically-placed teapot. I'll start believing in the unions when they start behaving irresponsibly, develop a sense of humour and demand the impossible three times a day."

Philip was scribbling in his small black notebook a jumble of letters and numbers, little squares and cubes: he was calculating Grayson's effect. But what kind of symbols and sums could represent these snarls, yelps and grunts? – Or the smell? Fred felt that he was standing in a rising pool of foul liquid with someone pressing hard into his back but when he turned no-one was there. The night-soil men kept pitching themselves forwards, raised hands grasping at the air: that drumming sound could only be their skulls striking the apron of the stage. Did Grayson know what he was doing? When their anger and resentment finally broke loose there would be no controlling it. Bullets or bayonets, *Times* editorials or motions in the House: nothing would make any difference. He was reminded of old woodcuts of Wat Tyler or Jack Cade: violence would not be their means but their ends. They would punch and kick and stamp until nothing was left and then they would throw stones at the sun and moon. Sometimes Fred feared that when Socialism did attain the summit he and Philip would turn round in triumph only to discover that – massed there behind them – The People were not The People anymore.

Grayson had now reached the end of a long discursive passage which, Fred guessed, had been composed of double entendres. 'Come to Jesus!' – Grayson's features pinched and whitened in an uncanny likeness to Snowden's. 'Or go to The Devil – if you haven't already.' With a brilliantly white handkerchief he mopped his brow. "I'm an Old Testament man myself: it's much more fun – nothing but wars, plagues and begettings. Nobody bothers with good and evil – it's all about sin." With a conjuror's flourish he refolded the handkerchief and replaced it in his top pocket.

"Thus saith The Lord God: Remove the diadem and take off the crown: this shall not be the same: exalt him that is low and abase him that is high" – His voice rose to a mighty shout – "I will overturn, overturn, overturn it: and it shall be no more, until he comes whose right it is; and I will give it to him." He raised one arm to point at the roof. "The sword, the sword, the sword is drawn. For the slaughter it is furbished, to consume because of the glittering.

Whiles they see vanity unto thee, whiles they divine a lie unto thee, to bring thee upon the necks of them that are slain, of the wicked, whose day is come, when their inquiry shall have an end."

In the ensuing silence Fred saw that Snowden's fingers were counting down from ten.

"Ezekiel 21," Grayson tittered, "Verses 26 to 29. No, I don't know why I've quoted it either." He turned and began to walk slowly into the wings. "It's just that I have a feeling that an awful lot of people" – his feet made no sound on the boards – "are in for" – his voice lowered with each step – "a very . . . nasty . . . shock . . . indeed." He stopped by the door and turned on the audience one final blissful smile. "Except, of course, for thee and me."

Now they stared in silence at the empty stage. Fred noticed that the carafe on the table, although untouched by Grayson, now seemed to be empty. When the sound did come it had a tangible physical force, like a gale: Fred set his feet wide apart and ducked his head. There were four distinct elements: a deep baying like hounds on the scent; a sort of warbling scream; thunderous volleys of stamping feet; and a curious metallic jangling that set his teeth on edge. Some folk had produced bunches of keys and were shaking them above their heads. It was almost unbearable but mercifully short-lived. The audience abruptly stopped, just as they had started, together. No-one, it seemed, wanted to stay and discuss what they had heard: they flowed rapidly through the narrow exits.

"And now they're off to burn the Town Hall," said Fred.

"That's what they'll be thinking." Phil was still scribbling away. "But when they hit the air they'll be wanting a pick-me-up in The Cavendish. Then they'll need a quick one in The Volunteers and The Rodney. Then they'll have to call in at The Albert, then at The Boltmakers, where at closing time they'll decide to leave the insurrection until the morning. But when they wake up, of course, all they'll have is a hangover."

Fred saw that the night-soil men had also lingered. One held a great rusty metal ring like a gaoler's, which had broken, strewing across the floor keys of all shapes and sizes. They were crawling on all fours, groping as if they were blind. Why did they have so many keys? What doors would they open? What places did these men have access to?

"Ezekiel, Whitman and Wagner," Philip flicked his notebook. "What kind of authorities are those?" At the end of his impenetrable workings he wrote and underlined a final figure. "Thirty-one: high, but nowhere near danger level. Much of the energy was dissipated when someone opened that window at the back . . . and, as usual, he couldn't resist playing the giddy goat."

Now, swigging from a silver hip-flask, the man of the moment had reappeared on stage.

"Still here, dear ladies?" he called and jumped down. "Did you enjoy that? I could see you gathering up your skirts, fearful of your virtue. Those hombres *can* get a little rough at times."

"I was born round here," said Snowden, "Keighley holds no terrors for me."

Grayson's smile was uncharacteristically thin. "They would have torn you to pieces if I'd given the word."

"What was it you were pleading for in Edinburgh?" Snowden clicked his long fingers. "Oh yes, tolerance, good humour and love."

"Different horses for different courses but it all comes down to the same thing in the end. You ladies didn't take me seriously, did you?"

"So," the fingers clicked again, "You didn't actually *mean* any of it?"

"It depends on what you mean by 'mean' . . . 'Frivolity is the higher seriousness', as Shaw likes to say."

Fred watched the night-soil men bumping into each other, snarling like dogs. Three more figures emerged from the shadows. Two women and a boy: there was something ghastly about their silent progress. Their eyes, large and unnaturally bright, were fixed on Grayson.

"Why didn't you talk about this new party of yours?" Snowden asked.

"For some reason it keeps slipping my mind."

"I thought it was going to turn the world upside down."

"Oh, it'll do that all right," Grayson sighed. "Although it had better be before the end of next week because I'm getting married then."

"Congratulations, although I must admit to being surprised."

"It was all your wife's fault. When Ruth read her book on Universal Love she informed me that there could be no escape, this side of the grave."

If people stayed still for long enough Fred could really get them into focus. The two women's lips were an identical shade of scarlet, their cheeks rosy, their eyes ringed blue-black. He had never understood why pretty women should feel the need to paint their faces. The brunette was turning in tight circles, while the blonde first tapped, then almost stamped her dainty foot. The pelts of unidentifiable animals hung round their necks.

"One thing I don't understand," Philip was saying, "If you're against the party and parliament and the unions and even the Syndicalists, who is there left to support you?"

"Just people," Grayson winked at Fred, "Not *The* People, just individual men and women who want a better, freer life."

"People like yourself, perhaps – and you're even less representative than those poor devils tonight. They're all you've got and you can't rely on them. When the cavalry come clattering into the square you'll find your mob army has reverted to its constituent parts. Just individual men and women, all with urgent business elsewhere."

"What you call the mob I call the multitude. And you do not lose your individual identity in a multitude, you find it."

"To be inside and outside something at the same time," Snowden said sweetly, "is a political, philosophical and anatomical impossibility. But then you can convince a suggestible audience of anything.

You can Graysonize them for an hour or two – and it's all very entertaining but it signifies nothing at all."

What relationship, Fred wondered, did the boy have to the two women? There were no obvious physical resemblances: his legs were short but the arms hung apparently uselessly down to the knees. The right side of his face was red raw, as if someone had tried to scrub away a bad attack of acne. Perhaps his sisters had brought him in the hope that a touch of the orator's hand might cure his afflictions of body and mind? Such illusions were not uncommon: in the early days of the movement semi-magical powers had been attributed to Keir Hardie – even, in some of the Irish areas, and much to his embarrassment, to Fred himself.

"You're a bit too *artistic* for this game," Philip was taunting Grayson, "I think you should start your own religion instead."

"I might just do that: I hear the theosophists are getting tired of Mrs Besant." Grayson turned away: from left and right the women pressed their bodies against his ribs. "I suppose you wouldn't care to join us for a convivial evening. No? Well, thanks for coming: I'll be seeing you soon – if not on the benches then on the barricades."

Fred watched them go. The strange boy led the way, half-limping, half-skipping: perhaps the Grayson cure was already taking effect? The night-soil men were leaving by the other door: their keys all accounted for, they were presumably off to put them in the appropriate locks.

"Why didn't you say something?" asked Philip.

"It would have been a waste of breath. None of that had anything to do with politics: it was all about himself."

"That's true, of course, but be fair, Fred, politics *is* all about ourselves. You, me, Grayson: we are who we are but the nature of our times has allocated us a political identity."

"I consider myself to be of no importance," said Fred. "All that matters is The Cause."

"Have it your own way, Our Fred." Philip took his arm and gave it an affectionate squeeze. "But surely what you're really saying is 'I *am* the cause'?"

As they were leaving, Fred felt something under his foot. Kneeling down, he closed his fingers on a tiny key. Almost weightless but finely-wrought, with sharp and elaborate teeth, it seemed to be made of gold rather than brass. Perhaps it might open a jewel case or the fetters of some fairy princess? The night-soil men had returned and resumed their crawling around but Fred slipped the key into his wallet. He did not like to think of it resting there between those filthy fingers.

CHAPTER SEVEN

THE BEST PLACE ON
EARTH (1913)

. . . And so Buffalo Bill had turned out to be just another flawed vessel: no better than the next man and possibly even worse.

The guide who had shown them the little town of Cody had taken considerable pleasure in revealing his feet of clay. Bill hadn't killed all *that* many people – and none in gunfights and never with a knife. He would pick them off with his rifle from a safe distance. Most of the great tales had been the inventions of his ghost writers. He had slaughtered the buffalo at the behest of the Goddard Brothers Meat Packing Company. "Nor is he descended from King Milesius, the Celtic ruler of Spain," the man informed them, "He's just another Galway guttersnipe like meself." And as for the 'first scalp for Custer' yarn – well, how much gumption did it take to maul a redskin's corpse? Bill was nothing but a fantasist, a womaniser, a mean and violent drunk. Ruth's elbow dug into her husband's ribs: "So you've been following in your hero's footsteps without even knowing it". A three week voyage across the Atlantic and a two thousand mile trek west: a long way to come just to be disillusioned.

They had been away from England for eight months since Victor's health had broken down. At the wedding the happy couple's friends – especially their former lovers – had been remarkably munificent and so their 'working honeymoon' had become a headlong carouse. They had hardly slept until their pockets were empty. It had been as if all that money had somehow infected them. Victor's lungs had seized up and Ruth alternated between laughing and sobbing fits without, she said, feeling in the least disturbed. Their best man, the impresario Arthur Rose, had organized a series of benefit concerts: they went to Italy but the Sirocco made Victor even worse. Now they had to convalesce from convalescence. The doctors recommended a sea cruise and change of air and so they found themselves in New York, inhabiting a freezing wooden bungalow out on Long Island. They had tried to economize but failed: the closer they were to disaster the more recklessly they spent. When her parents' allowance arrived they had not paid the rent or medical bills but bought themselves new clothes and two railway tickets to Wyoming.

The Cody guide had looked more like Bill than Bill himself. Perhaps that was why he hated his employer so much. Last year The Great Wild West Show had at last been declared bankrupt and Bill, ageing and sick, was reduced to touring with the Sells-Floto Circus. "He sent us this": The guide produced a postcard of Niagara Falls.

"Boys," it read in a shaky hand, "I'm in Hell. Nothing but yapping dogs, skinny women and elephants." The man's thumbnail flicked the card. "Serves him right," he said

Cody had built the town with his own money. Ruth and Victor stayed the night in the Hotel Irma – named after his youngest daughter. They were the only guests: the surly staff seemed to be holding them responsible for the absence of everybody else. The place was both ridiculously opulent and hideously cheap. A huge painting on the landing showed Bill atop a white, foam-flecked steed, about to bolt out of the frame, brandishing his rifle, half-turning to urge his comrades on, although there appeared to be, ominously, nothing but empty Prairie behind him. The hotel's famous cherry wood bar had been unfortunately closed for repairs after a group of Bill's girlfriends had fallen out over orders of precedence and smashed all the furniture and mirrors. "Now it's only the ladies who uphold the good old frontier traditions," observed their guide.

It was curious, Victor reflected, how, despite these revelations, Bill seemed all the more loveable. Hadn't he been more heroic in *trying* to be something rather than actually being it? Even as a child Victor had suspected that the Wild West Show might not have been an altogether accurate recreation of America but what blitheness and innocent gaiety there had been in all those stabbings, shootings and scalpings! It was life as it should be lived: such a spectacle could never have been created out of cynicism and greed. Recent photographs revealed that Bill, even in his sixties, had retained his beauty. Any real dishonesty would have shown on his face – in the eyes, if nowhere else. When you thought about it, Bill's failure had been more meritorious than any conceivable success.

Nevertheless, they almost felt relieved to be back in New York: on 49th Street sitting in the corner of their favourite – or, as Ruth put it, least unfavourite – bar. Their regular table was the one that did not fall over. As usual Ruth had entered by hitching up her skirt and kicking the swing doors open while giving what she fondly imagined to be a rebel yell. Nobody minded, for she had charmed them all, but Victor knew better than to follow her example.

"What we could do," she was saying, "Is start up a Socialist Wild West Show. Arthur Rose will write the songs and provide the dancers and soubrettes."

"We'll have Syndicalist war-parties, riding in circles, whooping and hollering, scalping each other or even themselves. Hyndman trick-shooting in his Mendoza outfit. Snowden and Jowett as Doc Holiday and Wyat Earp – gunfight at the Temperance Hotel! And old kiss-me Hardie would make the dinkiest buffalo: I could chase him round the ring then lasso and hog-tie him."

"I see you're going to be Bill," said Ruth, "So I'll be Annie Oakley, the peerless lady wing-shot."

"But you can't shoot."

"Oh yes I can. Bows and arrows as well. Papa taught me."

Victor sighed. "And I'm not sure I'd like to ride a horse."

"I'd pay folding money to watch you try."

The place was filling up. People did not seem to enter but rather to materialize gradually out of the yellow fog around the bar. A heavily bearded man, drinking steadily but without obvious pleasure was watching them from under his shaggy eyebrows. The creases of his shiny black-brown coat were crusted yellow, giving the impression that he was being clutched by skeletal fingers.

"Or we could brew up Socialism, bottle it and sell it by the quart," Ruth suggested, "You rub half of it into your scalp for a full head of red hair. And if that should fail, you can drink the rest."

Victor kept forgetting to be careful about laughing. When his guard was down the cough would seize hold of his throat and lungs. His mouth filled with bitter-tasting corded slime which, before he could spit, slid down his gullet, setting him hacking like a maddened watchdog. He couldn't breathe in England or Italy or France: he couldn't even breathe in the New World. Everywhere was either too hot or too cold, too wet or too dry. American rain was black and sticky and American dust was so sharp and all-pervasive that he could hear it crunching between his teeth. He was drinking more than ever: alcohol brought temporary relief but the next morning he would feel even worse than before. The cough eased and his eyes came back into focus: he took down great sobbing draughts of booze and air.

"It's not just Harry Dawson who is on the wrong planet," said Ruth.

Now the bearded man approached, dragging behind him a large and evidently heavy sack. His other paw clutched a jug full of white liquid which he placed on their table.

"It's good to hear a familiar accent," he said in a high-pitched voice. "You're from Liverpool and your good lady is, I fancy, a Bolton lass."

"That's very impressive." Victor reluctantly removed his feet from the third chair.

"Not really." Some problem with the man's legs made sitting down a complicated operation. "I saw your pictures in the paper. How's the lecture tour going?"

"It's more of a holiday, really. A sort of honeymoon, in fact."

"A honeymoon? And you're spending it here?" The man leant forward to draw his jug under the table's rim. The top of his head was covered with scabs. "It must be Kismet running into you today on the twentieth anniversary."

"The twentieth anniversary of what?"

"And you call yourselves Socialists! The founding of The Independent Labour Party, of course!"

"I don't call myself a Socialist," said Ruth, "I call myself an actress."

"And I'm afraid I now belong to the S.O.B. party." Victor watched in fascination as the jug reappeared. Its contents were now dark green. A saffron-coloured forefinger agitated its surface and with a fizzing sound and a tarry smell it turned the deepest black.

"What's that you're drinking?"

"Milk," said the man, with what might have been a smile. "I was there, you know, at the first meeting. With Hardie, Blatchford, Aveling and the rest. Tell me, how's Fred Jowett getting on?"

"He looked well enough when I last saw him," said Victor, "Although he didn't have much to say for himself."

"That doesn't sound like Fred. I hear he's in Parliament now," the man broke into broad Yorkshire. "That call'oil will suit him reet enough. What about Tom Maguire?"

"I don't recognize the name."

"He'll be dead, I suppose," he sighed, "He was never strong. I'd have thought he'd have been canonized by now."

"How long have you been away?"

"Nineteen years. I nearly came back when all those strikes started up but by the time I made it to New York they'd stopped again."

"It was naught but a passing fancy," Victor half-sang, "Like a music hall song that everyone whistles for a couple of weeks."

"What about the synecdochists or whatever you call them?"

"They all seemed to vanish one morning."

"Probably police spies," said the man, "There's a lot of them about."

"Why ever would you want to cross the ocean just to go on strike?" He flinched, for Ruth was using her Portia voice. "Why don't you start a revolution right here?"

"America is much too big," he mumbled into his jug, "And nothing stays still long enough to become a target. By the time you've got yourself up to oppose something it's already ancient history."

He was quite unable to meet Ruth's gaze. Sometimes the head would swivel in her direction but then the eyes would roll back or close.

"How old do you think I am?" He asked Victor.

"Sixty?"

He groaned. "Wrong by fifteen years."

"Beards always age a man," said Ruth, "I can't imagine why anyone would go to all the bother of growing one."

"It's shaving that's the bother," said Victor, although he himself needed only the lightest scrape every other day.

"I've got something for you." The man upended his sack: by the lumps and bumps Victor expected a shower of boots but instead it was books, all identically bound in pale blue with golden letters on the spine. They looked as if they had been carried around for some considerable time.

"My masterpiece. *Heaton: Best Place on Earth.*"

"Some friends of mine went to school there," said Ruth, "They didn't think much of it."

"Not 'Eton', Heaton!" The man exploded the 'H'. "From the Anglo-Saxon, 'Heah', high and 'tun', farmstead. It's a district of Bradford."

"I spoke there once, in the Village Hall," said Victor, "Good turnout but a stodgy crowd."

"And you never guessed that the finest wooded valley in the country lay a mere stone's throw from that very spot?"

"No," said Victor, "I never did."

Ruth examined the title page: "What do the initials A. B. stand for?"

"A Bradfordian, of course."

"Why didn't you put your name on it?"

"There's some folk I wouldn't care to know about it."

"It looks long for a poem," said Victor.

"Yes, it's all in there. I had to take a few liberties, of course. The bit where the warriors of Heaton fight off the mammoth riders of Chellow Dene – well, I imagined that, or rather I dreamt it. And I moved one of the Civil War battles from the bottom to the top of the hill. But there's plenty of comedy, too – like when the Bentley brothers storm the Constable's pinfold to rescue their prize pig. And there's tragedy: The Harrying of the North, when the Normans tried to wipe everyone out. "Ilbert de Lacy hath it," says the Domesday Book, "and it is waste." He took another swig from the still bubbling jug: "Vasta est."

"It hasn't changed much," said Victor.

Ruth hopped up onto her chair, stuck two fingers in her mouth, and whistled. Victor had spent many hours teaching her the art until she was even louder and shriller than himself.

> "Thy beauties, Heaton, have ne'er been sung
> By stranger-bard or native poet's tongue:
> So may my humble muse beg thee
> To pardon my presumption, if I fail
> In th'attempt thy virtues to rehearse
> In rustic strains of this untutored verse."

Some of the men at the bar had frozen with glasses half-way

to their lips: one who had just taken a great swig of beer was not swallowing it. The stillness was so exaggerated that it was as if they were having their picture taken.

> "Many a time I have seen me
> The panting hart in shady dell
> While Lister's mighty chimney
> Upholds the firmament itself."

In Heaton, evidently, the poet had been loved by beautiful women and even the shyest of woodland animals would come unbidden to his call. It was hard to see why he had ever left the place.

> "Succour for the weak and strength for the frail
> Caressed by the breezes and swept by the gale."

It seemed as if the audience would gladly sit there for the full two hundred stanzas but Ruth licked her forefinger and flicked on to the end.

> "When pleasures cloy and gilded palaces pale
> When tyrants wax and good men fail
> Hie yourselves to Heaton Vale!"

"They loved it," said Victor.

"They're not applauding my words. They're applauding" – he paused and blushed – even his hands turned red – "Her performance."

"Nonsense" – Ruth resumed her seat – "Cheers and yells are for the performer: good solid clapping is for the work itself. They'll all be at the pier head tomorrow morning: Heaton can prepare itself for an invasion of Irish and Swedish longshoremen."

"Better than the Normans," said the man.

"Here's a little something of my own." Victor presented him with a much thinner volume.

"People's Penny Pamphlets No.3" – he peered at the cover – "*God's Country: The Emigration Humbug* . . . Do you know, I haven't had a decent humbug these twenty years. They're what I've missed the most – those stripy lumps that get bigger and harder the more you suck them."

"Yes," said Ruth, "I know the ones you mean."

The expressionless barman brought over another round, on the house. This time the man openly took out a thin vial and carefully added a few drops. "This is the last one" – he lapped at it like a cat – "If I really get started I don't stop for days. I'm leaving tomorrow morning: heading west into the mountains, courtesy of Herbert Hoover."

"There's gold in them thar hills," said Ruth.

"I'm not looking for gold. I go in for a more general sort of prospecting. They call me a drifter but I've always had a purpose: every step takes me closer to the prize. Mind you, I've lost count of the number of times that I've arrived somewhere a week or so too late. I wouldn't say I was unlucky but the other day I unpeeled a banana and there was nothing inside it."

"How awful," said Ruth.

"That was a joke," he growled, "I don't even like bananas. Anyroad, I could have lived well enough off other folk's leavings but where would the satisfaction be in that? All I want to do is to *find* something. I don't care what it is: I just want them to say 'there's that man who staked everything on a single throw and won'."

"I see why you're still a Socialist," said Victor.

"I think I know how it's going to be. I used to feel that I had plenty of time so the disappointments only whetted my appetite but lately my resolution has begun to flag. The things I say sound stupid to my own ears, as well as everyone else's. I suspect that the very moment I lose hope I will find what I'm looking for. I'll raise my pick above my head and as it's coming down I'll say – 'Well, that's me done' – and then I'll be drowning in oil and water or buried under an avalanche of silver and gold."

"That's an optimistic view of Fate," said Ruth.

"Is it?" The man almost looked at her. "Suppose that once you've lost hope you can never get it back again? What happens if you're given what you want when you no longer believe in it? There's got to be a catch or it wouldn't be life, would it?" He drained his milk, then cinched his sack and rose unsteadily to his feet.

"I don't think I like this country," said Victor.

"New York isn't America," said the man. "In fact, America isn't America either. You've only got as far as the USA - just another spot on the map, a place like any other. Whereas America takes a bit of finding because - as a friend of mine used to say - 'America is here'" - he tapped himself twice on the chest and turned away - "or it is nowhere."

"I wonder how well he knew Goethe," Ruth said as they watched him go. "I've always liked bandy legs on a man: I feel like turning him upside down and pulling them until he snaps like a wishbone."

"It was like meeting The Ancient Mariner. I'm sadder all right but none the wiser. What was in his little bottle that turned the milk so black?"

"Laudanum, I think. He smelt like my maiden aunts."

"God, I hope I don't end up like that!"

"No," said Ruth, "You've already found what you were looking for. Now all you have to do is to use it properly." She squeezed the inside of his thigh. "Did you notice that he didn't look at me once?"

"But he really wanted to." Victor put an arm round her shoulders. "And he did keep trying, poor devil."

"He made me feel ashamed of myself, somehow" - she did not appear particularly ashamed - "Why didn't he tell us his name?"

"Why didn't we ask him?" said Victor.

~

"The Prime Minister expressed great sympathy for the Bill standing in my name. But he could find no room for it this session. And yet he could find room to indemnify Sir Stuart Samuel against the payment of possible fines for voting as a member of the House of Commons after his firm had accepted a government contract."

Jowett sniffed, dipped his pen into the well and plodded on.

"Sir Stuart is enormously rich and, to say the least, precedence might have been given to a Bill to feed children who otherwise will go short of food as against a Bill to relieve a rich man from penalties for offences which have been proved against him."

Fred wanted to scream. Cramps stabbed at his abdomen and chest: it was physically painful to maintain the tone necessary for the *Bradford Pioneer* – judicious, more-in-sorrow-than-in-anger, with the sarcasm measured out grain by grain. He kept remembering Prime Minister Asquith's kindly smile as he had doomed The Holiday Feeding Act. Apart from indemnifying the vicious and sanctimonious Samuel, time had also been found for Bills on horse-breeding, plume-wearing and the diseases of bees. If only he had sufficient power of language to flay such absurdities! Tom Maguire and Jim Sharp were the best cursers he had known but they were long gone. Grayson could have done it but he would have digressed from starving children to the advantages of pleated trousers and the right temperature to serve champagne

The House of Commons grew madder by the day. The Kaiser was building battleships and drilling his new army regiments. Even in Bradford people knew that he must be preparing for dangerous colonial adventures, if not all-out war: some of the mill owners in Little Germany had already anglicised their names. No-one in The House, however, evinced the least concern. Even Liberal members who shared his fears would groan whenever he tried to raise the matter. "Get back to your sewers, Jowett," they shouted, "You nasty little man."

Even back home he felt restless. This morning he had received two letters from Snowden, both hysterical in tone, one inveighing against MacDonald, the other against Lloyd George. Although still nominally their spokesman on financial affairs he was seen less and less frequently on the opposition benches. Now, judging by the stamps, he had embarked with Ethel on a foreign tour.

Grayson, however, had returned. Fred's heart had sunk when he saw the papers: he had hoped that the man would stay in America forever. A photograph showed the couple disembarking, with Mrs Grayson apparently biting her husband's ear. She did not look as if she would be a stabilizing influence.

"The best thing about New York," the main quote ran, "Was the sight of the ship that was to carry us away from it. When I left England it was said that I had been drinking lager beer, that I had the capacity of an ancient Falstaff, that I'd been smoking wild Woodbines. It was even said that I was not properly married but when I counted my money I discovered that the ceremony had cost me two pounds, fourteen shillings and sevenpence-ha'penny – and I certainly ought to be married for such an amount. But now I am back, refreshed and ready for a national speaking tour that will reunite the radical Socialist elements of this realm."

He had not changed: if anything he sounded even more frivolous than before. What new havoc might a refreshed and readied Grayson be about to wreak? Fred often recalled that terrible night in Keighley: there seemed to be an ominous significance to his choice of opening venue for the comeback – this evening at St George's Hall, Bradford. Fred had not been invited and he certainly would not be stumping up his sixpence –the man was getting ten times Snowden's rate!

For the rest of the evening he was quite unable to return to his article. When the clock struck eight he wondered if Grayson would be on time or tarrying in the wings to whip the audience into a frenzy of anticipation. He tried to tackle his outstanding correspondence but the interchangeable and so often indecipherable tales of injustice and misfortune swam before his eyes. At

Christmas Emily had given him a little magnifying glass but its effect had gradually faded. Nor could he face the broadsheets and pamphlets: he sometimes took a guilty pleasure in these, for even the movement's best orators wrote in prose as stilted as his own. It was strange how you could see where other folk were going wrong and then make the same mistakes yourself. The stack of unread books was now as tall as Emily: in the hope that he might review or endorse them people sent him the strangest things.

Someone had evidently written a volume of verse all about Heaton. Fred had always found poetry – even Morris or Whitman – deeply depressing. He assumed this was its desired effect. "Thank God for art." MacDonald, a great reader, had once observed. "If it wasn't for Art we would probably all expire from the sheer joy of existence."

He snapped the volume shut. There was no time for the woods and hills: he had done his best to forget them. Even on the train he would keep his head buried in his papers, eyes averted from even the briefest flash of green. If he were to feel even for a moment the soft ground yielding under his feet he feared that he would lose the strength to carry on.

The Town Hall clock struck eleven. Fred went into the yard and lit his pipe. It was unusually quiet for a Saturday night. There was no sound of post-Grayson singing or gunfire, no red glow of riot in the sky: all the stars appeared to be in their usual alignment. After a while this silence became oppressive: he realized that he was humming to himself. A stealthy movement caught his eye: a small dark animal had slipped over the back step of Number 14 – a cat – no, a rat, by its smell. When he went back inside the perpetual drip of the kitchen tap had ceased: even the stairs no longer creaked. There was no sound from the children's room and when he sat on the edge of his bed Emily did not seem to be breathing: he gently shook her awake to reassure himself that everything was still all right.

At breakfast the next morning he could see his constituents

already gathering for the weekend consultation. They had a distinctly woebegone air: it began to rain, so Emily opened the door half an hour early. They were not interested in The Holiday Feeding Act or the threat of war: all they wanted to talk about was Victor Grayson.

St. George's Hall had been packed, with another fifteen hundred turned away. Grayson had turned up all right – in fact he had been fully two hours early – but had rapidly become too drunk to take the stage. When Arthur Gardiner went on as substitute the crowd had booed him off; when Jim Larkin, one of the best-loved figures in the movement, had followed someone threw a ladies' shoe that hit him on the head.

"I saw Victor fall," one man said, "He sort of floated down like an autumn leaf. He was still smiling even though his lights had gone out. His wife was there – a bonny lass but a bit fast-looking. Half-cut herself, I reckon: she kept shouting something about Heaton and showing her teeth like a horse."

"He wasn't singing or anything," said another. "He just sat there with his face glowing like a saint's. I had the strangest feeling that there was a point to all this, as if he was trying to express something he couldn't put into words. I left the meeting determined to get drunk myself but I just couldn't manage it. The more I had the more sober I felt. It was the vilest feeling and now I haven't even got a hangover to take my mind off things."

"They've done summat to him," everyone kept saying and their tone and expression implied that Fred himself might have been part of this obscure conspiracy. Only one man accused him directly by reading out one of his own *Clarion* articles. "'The gift of platform oratory is a dangerous one . . . if his skill is employed in setting not class against class but men of the same class against their kith and kin, it were better if he had no such skill . . . I have met many such and beyond merely a personal following of their own they have left nothing but bickering and animosity' – Now that's not very nice, is it, Fred?"

"I did not mention anyone by name," he replied, "So it is revealing that you have made such a connection."

Willie Leach, the last man in, was probably the most inconsolable. "It was a horrible sight," he finally said, dabbing his eyes with his scarlet handkerchief then blowing his nose. "We've got to do something to save him from himself."

"We've been doing nothing but try to help him for the last six years," said Fred. "I was in Colne Valley every single day in defiance of the NEC's directive. Snowden and I sponsored his entry into The House. I sat right next to him, ready to advise and explain, but even then he smelled of drink. We spent long railway journeys together but all he wanted to do was to play cards. When he was forming his own party Philip and I went to Keighley to try one last time to talk some sense into him. What else do you think we should have done?"

"Nay, Fred," said Willie, "I'm sure you did your best."

He did not sound particularly convinced: Fred had to admit that he had not quite convinced himself either. Could he have been wrong about Grayson? From the first he had seen him as nothing but a threat, even speculating whether he might not be an unusually cunning police infiltrator, but there was no doubting the affection in which he was held, even among otherwise grudging and moralistic comrades. Out in Colne Valley they were steadfastly refusing to endorse any other parliamentary candidate even though Grayson had not entered his name. At the last NEC meeting MacDonald had suddenly grabbed Fred's arm and hissed – apropos of nothing – "Whyever did we abandon Grayson to that rackety Bohemian crew?" But he had made no answer and Mac had said no more.

Willie looked as if he was about to start crying again.

"Here, take this," Fred handed him the poetry book, "It's more your line than mine."

"Heaton!" Leach read, "Albion's lofty crown where mighty eagles sore! Typical Heatonite!" – he laughed – "Three hundred feet of elevation and they think they're on Mount Olympus. Even when they're lying in the gutter they still manage to look down on everyone else!"

Only after Leach had left did Fred recall that the man was himself Heaton born and bred.

⁂

Every time the Graysons moved they thought they had found the lowest and filthiest flat in London but the next one always contrived to be even worse. Theobold Street was even closer to the centre of Hell than Southwell Park Road.

The wardrobe had shattered in transit, as if struck by lightning, so all their beautiful clothes were hanging from nails banged into the russet-streaked walls. It was like being surrounded by gibbeted boys and girls whose flesh and bones had rotted away. Victor's stained but trusty mattress was now wafer thin and twice its original dimensions. The room was otherwise unfurnished, apart from a bottle of whiskey, two glasses and a soda siphon balanced on an upturned packing case. "Whether we move on to mansion, castle or palace," said Ruth, "This box will always be our dining table."

Although they had managed to stave off bankruptcy, the receiving order's repayment terms had been merciless. Victor's engagements were infrequent and when he did speak with something of his old fire the audience would look disappointed, as if cheated of suitably outrageous instances of his decline. As for the journalism, Blatchford would not stump up until the article had been delivered and fully edited. The 'No-wage', of course, did not pay even then. Lansley at *The Daily Herald* would have nothing to do with him: Victor's only appearances were in Will Dyson's unflattering cartoons. Their former friends and lovers were no longer so generous. Ruth's pregnancy had thrown them into a frenzy of prurience: it was as if procreation was in their case a monstrous crime against nature itself.

Victor had finished the last bottle. He drank brandy in public and whiskey in private. His consumption was the same as ever but the effects were very different. Intoxication – slurring of words and loss of balance – had hitherto been a short intermediate phase: after a couple more snorts, befuddlement would be succeeded by a wonderfully cold and lucid euphoria. He would drink himself beyond drunkenness to reach, as it were, a higher sobriety. Alcohol had been his fuel, his means of propulsion, but now it failed to push him through that stupefaction stage. It was as if he had been on a gleaming express train, passing from one great city to another, which had terminated, abruptly and inexplicably, at some benighted halt. And now he was reeling along a greasy platform with no deputations stepping forward to greet him, alone in the mocking silence and the dark.

The drinking had left his sexual powers unimpaired but he did not find this reassuring. He had begun to suspect that his cock was leading an independent existence. Even when he was unconscious it apparently ploughed doggedly on. It was shorter but thicker with a ruddy sheen, as if it had been wining and dining too well. Last night Ruth had drawn a nose and eyes above its pouting slit and topped it with a little tricorn hat folded out of paper. "Vive l'Empereur!" she had cried: it did look horribly convincing. Soon the thing would take over his speechifying: he would be wheeled into the rally on a bier, draped in a red flag with a hole cut into it. Muzzy with cognac and camphor he would dimly hear the crowd roaring as his right honourable member rose to orate. It would wax and he would wane so that, at the last, all that would remain of Victor Grayson would be a six-foot talking cock, spouting nonsense.

Ruth herself was growing ever more demanding. "Until you're married you're just an amateur," she said, "But afterwards it's a full-time job." She had taken to consulting a French edition of *The Perfumed Garden* and De Sade's *Justine*, the flyleaf of which had been inscribed 'Ex Libris A. C. Swinburne' in a hand suspiciously resembling her own.

"If you insist on ticking everything off," he complained, "You'll have us fucking till Doomsday."

"That's the idea," her fingers went walking up his thigh, "So that when the world ends we won't even notice."

Her latest initiative had involved him learning to suck himself off: at last, almost snapping his spine, he had managed to just brush the glans with the tip of his tongue. Hitherto, dallying with the ladies had given his arsehole a welcome rest: most could not be persuaded to insert so much as a fingertip. Ruth, in contrast, was so fascinated that she sometimes seemed to be trying to climb inside. She liked to sodomise him with a well-greased plastic figurine of The Virgin Mary, the arms of which she had considerately filed off for the purpose. "There's only one place for this," she would say, "And that's the best place on earth." Victor had supposed this to be yet another revolt against her upbringing but once when they were passing Westminster Cathedral her father had shaken his fist. Perhaps he was merely outraged by its stripy pink tower?

It was fairly certain that the Mother of Christ had been responsible for Victor's rectal tear. It was the worst of places to be injured: internal, comical and shameful, painful and almost impossible to heal. You can rest an arm or a leg or pretty much any other part of your body, but you can never refrain from defecation. It twinged and throbbed like the devil but Ruth remained unsympathetic, discovering in his viscous ointments and rubber sitz baths sources of uncontrollable hilarity. Worse, she had decided to interpret his groans and protestations as signs of encouragement. "No, that *hurts!*" had merely prompted her to insert another finger. "No, I mean it *really* hurts!" only made her vigorously agitate her wrist. And then he had started laughing too and that had really really hurt.

"If it's a respectable front that you're after," Hyndman had said after the wedding, "I wouldn't have thought that the lovely Ruth was quite the ticket."

"Well," Victor replied, "You've got to be married to someone."

"No you haven't," snapped Hyndman.

"But you are, aren't you?"

"I would advise you, Comrade Grayson," His Majesty said slowly, with heavy emphasis, "Never again to mention your wife and mine in the same conversation." All the muscles in his face had clenched: one hand jerked up as if to slap, then fell limply back again. Victor was sure that only the absence of gloves had prevented the man from challenging him to a duel. He could picture the scene: dawn breaking over some misty copse on Hampstead Heath, Hyndman squinting down the barrel of an impossibly long pistol, Captain Jane and Matabele Wilson bustling about as seconds, and finally himself, falling with a ball lodged in his chest. By the time he had stopped giggling, HMH had swept out. Victor had never even seen his wife: she was said to be twenty years older than him and to never leave the house. They were always described as 'a devoted couple'.

Blatchford had been no better. He had claimed that since the wedding his daughters had been inconsolable.

"But they were never interested in me at all."

"You don't understand women, do you, Grayson?"

"Perhaps not the idiotic ones," he had replied, "But Ruth and I rub along well enough."

The day of their marriage had been peculiar in itself. Sunshine and rain alternated so rapidly as to create a flickering effect that caused his head to swim, so that he had to support himself on Ruth's arm. The wind had gusted from every direction at once but her elaborate coiffure remained undisturbed. He felt like a child again: what on earth, he wondered, could this big but rather jolly girl be wanting from him?

Their guests – all long since drunk – had kept bursting into snatches of highly inappropriate song and the best man, Arthur Rose, had been quite prostrate with emotion. He had slipped Ruth's ring on to his own little finger and had to be forced to relinquish it. It had all been predictably ridiculous: the registrar appeared on the point of bolting for his life . . . But when the vows were read everything changed. It was as if time itself had stopped. He was aware of being looked at by an unknown gaze that scanned and penetrated every part of himself. Perhaps they really were gathered together in the sight of God? He suspected that the deity neither approved nor disapproved but was, if anything, mightily amused.

". . . For better for worse, for richer for poorer, in sickness and in health, to love and to cherish, till death us do part."

He wondered if anyone else could hear his responses. His mouth and throat had locked so that the words merely vibrated, like purring or growling, in his stomach and chest.

"In the presence of God I make this vow."

Then they had kissed, in a surprisingly formal manner, and the future and the past had receded and the clock hands began to crawl onwards again. Outside on the steps they were pelted with ragged bouquets plundered from Ranelagh Gardens: there could not have been a single red flower left in South-West London.

God and marriage! How dull, how conventional he must secretly be! He wondered if he had only wanted to smash up the world in order to be able to lovingly return it, like a jigsaw puzzle, to just the way it was. Could it be that, beyond a certain point, the simplest things took on a forbidden glamour? Or, as he had suggested to Ruth, when you had grown tired of shocking everyone all you could do was to try to shock yourself. "Oh, my darling" – although she was always laughing she rarely smiled – "Have you only just realized that?"

Victor always fell in love with wherever they were living. He liked to pace around their room while Ruth was at the theatre: she was still understudying but at least her advanced state of pregnancy had relieved her of supplementary padding. He very much approved of the way that, whenever the door was opened, the ceiling's plaster would float down like snow, and how those patches of blue-green mould would move along the skirting-board or Ruth's empty dresses would whisper and rustle even without a draft. And if you trod on certain floorboards the bottles and glasses would, as if through some ghostly agency, go rattling along the box's top. Ruth had been wondering about rigging up a fake medium act. Increasingly infrequent visitors were horrified by what they found, which only made the couple prouder of the place.

He was sure that there was such a thing as success in failure. There was no doubting his own capabilities to gain and exercise political power: it would not be difficult to outmanoeuvre Hardie, MacDonald and even Snowden – their personal vanities and prejudices made them utterly predictable. He could become Leader of the party or Prime Minister or president or even some sort of king but what then? He suspected that each subsequent triumph could only further corrode the essential Victor Grayson. He would no longer be defined by his aspirations but by his achievements and these two could never be reconciled. At the Colne Valley by-election the striving and contending had been glorious but the resulting sense of anticlimax had been well-nigh unbearable. Once you knew that you could have something what was the point of taking it when you would only have to toil night and day to keep it? And even if you were the ruler of the whole wide world there would always be the danger that you would miss an even better opportunity if it came along. It would be like leaving a bar with a handsome stranger just as a truly beautiful one walked in.

Even now, people still took it upon themselves to inform him that the world was at his feet. He had received overtures from the Liberals and the Conservatives and even the Irish Home-Rulers. But didn't the keenest pleasure lie in spurning the prize, declining the laurels, leaving everyone struck dumb with incomprehension? It was they who were the deluded ones, for how many of the lays and legends of heroes had furnished happy endings? But all this, he had to admit, was beside the point: the truth was that his pride revolted at success in the same way that his stomach would vomit up a meal of rotten meat.

He observed that the bottle and glasses had begun agitating themselves even without his touching the board. Tonight, after the theatre, they would be joining Ruth's father for supper. She kept bringing the two of them together in order to watch them argue. In fact, they had liked one another on sight but tacitly agreed to spar around and strike attitudes so as not to disappoint her. When Pa Nightingale had last been in London Victor had informed him that he had determined to take to heart his celebrated advice and play the tragedy of life as if it were a comedy. "But tragedy and comedy only exist on the bloody stage!" the now truly exasperated man had bellowed. "Real life is a serious matter!"

⁂

After Ethel Annikin Snowden had finished speaking she dropped off to sleep but no-one cared to break the silence. She was, it appeared, the only woman on the train: perhaps American wives travelled separately, in the caboose? Ever since San Francisco the men had been openly staring at her: either all Americans were slack-jawed or it was, yet again, what Philip had begun to think of as The Ethel Effect.

As usual, what had begun as a conversation became a harangue and then her head had slowly turned to address the whole carriage. She was still almost literally beside herself about the war. What really rankled was that those kings and ministers had waited for her to be safely out of the country – nay, out of Europe – before embarking on their lethal silliness. "And surely they must have threatened Lloyd George at gunpoint or replaced him with a double? Unless, of course, that dear brave man has remained at his post in order to moderate the more bloodthirsty excesses?" Philip suspected that L-G would be relishing the whole thing.

She had also been betrayed by her suffragette sisters who had agreed to suspend all agitation for the duration of hostilities. In return the government had pardoned all their prisoners and bankrolled the Pankhursts for a nationwide morale-boosting tour. "They were happy enough digging up golf courses, slashing paintings or breaking hat-shop windows but at the first real challenge they fall into line." Her voice rose to a mellifluous shout: "We should be marching on the munitions factories, blocking the slipways with our own frail bodies, chaining ourselves" – here she had clutched wildly at her bosom – "to the mortars and the cannon mouths!"

At this, two of the craning heads had disappeared, their owners having presumably fainted. She had given a satisfied little nod, then let her head fall back on to her De Morgan travelling cushion and closed her eyes. The face flushed and the full lips pouted, as if angelic forms were already embracing her up there on the astral plane. Even though the train was running smoothly, its motion still contrived to rhythmically toss her up and down, to and fro.

"I wish I were like you," she often said, "And could sleep through anything" when in fact he slept poorly and she was always dropping off. "I wasn't asleep," she would protest, "I just rested my eyes for a moment." She disliked trains as much as Philip liked them. The vibrations were uniquely soothing to his spine: if only life could be lived entirely on trains! There was something magical about a really long journey: after a while you felt that the carriage remained stationary while endless vistas of plains, cities, clouds, rivers and mountains were set rolling past. "It's not like we are crossing a continent," Ethel had announced, "More as if the continent is crossing us." She certainly had her own perspective on things. In Alberta the Mayor had introduced her as "perhaps the most original lady thinker in the world": Philip had felt her stiffen – she had not appreciated that modifier, or the implication that she might have rivals elsewhere in the universe.

This had been her fourth tour of the United States. Her rotating subjects were 'Great Women I Have Known' – (delicately implying that their greatness had resided in knowing her) – 'Peeps At Parliament Through A Woman's Eyes' (on the wit and wisdom of Lloyd George). 'The Politics of Love' (Lloyd George's feminism) and, most popular of all, 'Great Temperance Heroines'. Philip suspected her of embroidering some of the more sensational tales – especially of the drunken brute who had supposedly chewed off the arm of his long-suffering wife. She had, of course, redeemed him in the end.

Now the men were stealing glances at Philip himself, in which envy and pity were curiously combined, rather as they might contemplate the lion-tamer at a circus. They were beginning to wonder whether there might be some prices not worth paying in order to have a beautiful woman at your side. Just look at what she'd done to that poor devil with his ravaged face and crutches! They wouldn't be venturing into her cage – no, not even with a whip and chair.

During this eight month tour – which had also taken in South Africa, Australasia and Canada – Philip had been thinking about his future. A new career of authorship and public speaking beckoned. Although Ethel's talks had been well-attended he had been the undoubted star of New Zealand's prohibition of alcohol campaign. And he thrived on the travelling, remaining unaffected rounding The Horn while even seasoned sailors were throwing up. Folk in the colonies regarded him not with fear or deference but with a sort of amused respect. And he had realized – after a lifetime of sheltering under hats – that the sun was not his enemy and that his leprous skin, given the slightest encouragement, became nut brown. He had watched lions on the Veldt, climbed Ayer's Rock, been made an honorary chief by alarmingly tattooed Maoris. His fiftieth birthday had been celebrated under the shadow of Table Mountain.

They had even visited Niagara. His father's bookmark postcards had not prepared Philip for the overwhelming reality: he had felt that either The Falls or himself had no right to be there. The scene resembled the end of the world: as if the waters would not stop until they had sluiced everything away. Ethel, of course, had not been impressed: she felt that it was merely showing off in a suspiciously masculine fashion. After she had returned to the hotel, he had stayed for another hour, shifting his weight from stick to stick, before realizing that although he had stood back from the edge he was still soaked to the skin. He had been stone deaf for days afterwards and even now he could still hear that pitiless roar.

From such distances England seemed increasingly unappealing. He often recalled that final mortifying conference clash with MacDonald after which every faction had regarded him with equal loathing. "Perhaps too little, Our Phil," Jowett had said, gently squeezing his shoulder, "And perhaps too late." He felt as if sentence had been passed: he was finished as a force in the Labour Party.

But now things had changed. In San Francisco letters from home – ninety-seven for him and one hundred and fifty-one for Ethel – had finally caught up with them. A cable revealed that Henderson was now party leader, MacDonald having resigned in protest at the outbreak of war. "No need for soon return – all over before you get back," Uncle Arthur had concluded, so Philip had immediately rung New York and booked a transatlantic stateroom, then half-carried a protesting Ethel on to the next Western Pacific train.

He was at a loss to understand MacDonald's tactics: it was, of course, impossible that he would be acting out of principle. With him out of the way, however, new possibilities opened up. Henderson could only ever be a stopgap, Glasier was a dying man and Grayson – according to Jowett's letter – had fled his creditors and joined his wife in a theatrical company bound for Australia. When Philip got home he would first consolidate his Northern power base – perhaps it was time to roll out the good old 'Come to Jesus' once again? – and then – holding his nose the while – take soundings among the Trade Unions.

There had been twelve pages from Fred, mainly about the second reading of The School Feeding Bill and MacDonald's courage in the face of a war-maddened press and public. When, at an emergency conference, Hardie had called for a General Strike he had been threatened with revolvers by his own comrades. "It is The People who will suffer," the letter concluded, "They will pay in millions of lives and in anguish and sorrow. Let us keep our minds calm, our hearts free from hate and one purpose always before us – to bring peace as soon as possible on a basis that will endure." Poor simple soul! It seemed apparent that, after initial skirmishing, the warring sides had settled into defensive positions prior to treaty negotiations. And as for that Schools Bill: Lloyd George's letter to Ethel had revealed that it had not been a result of Jowett's advocacy but a deal between the government and the NEC. Maintaining working-class support for the war had been the determining factor.

Like Ethel, Philip had never seriously entertained the possibility of a major European conflict. Why ever would the financiers and kings put at hazard everything that they had gained? "Out of sheer boredom," had been Fred's curious explanation. His friend's predictions had been surprisingly accurate but Philip felt that there had been an element of luck, like a blind archer firing arrows into the centre of a target. He folded the pages back into his briefcase, then screwed into a ball the telegram from Blackburn informing him that a hundred of his constituents were already D. or MIA. This message had obviously been garbled or transposed.

Now they had reached the highest point – the mining town of Leadville, under the jagged peaks of Mount Elbert. No-one got on, no-one got off; clouds of dust hung suspended in the air. The place looked derelict but Philip could feel the faint vibrations of those thousands of men toiling underground.

On the descent the train, perhaps exhausted by its long climb, gradually slowed to walking pace. The steam hissed, the brake groaned, the carriage began to judder then buck. Ethel awoke, eyes blazing and fists clenched: her communion with the seraphs had obviously been interrupted at a vital moment.

The mountainside had a freshly-gouged look, as if the great glaciers had only just departed. Up ahead Philip saw in the yellow-grey landscape a sudden flash of colour. Between the track and the dynamited cliffs stood a stunted tree with a pale blue trunk and long snowy tendrils streaming in the wind. Only when the thing straightened, stretched and shook itself did he recognize it as a seated human figure.

The train slid on for the last few yards and then stopped directly opposite. It was an elderly man, bearded like an Old Testament prophet. Clenched between his teeth was a reversible pipe, presumably to continue smoking should he find himself hanging upside down: the fronds around the mouth were tobacco brown. He had taken off his boots: the feet were blistered and swollen to unnatural size, with the toes seemingly fused together. The man's bright and darting eyes, however, betrayed no weariness. His legs were braced and his spine curved like a drawn bow. Philip was reminded of those swamis who, according to Ethel, spent their whole lives sitting in mystic contemplation when, had they wished, they could in a blink of an eye have flown anywhere in the world. The man was striking at a flint to start a fire in a hearth of small pebbles. Once the dried grass took, he fed the flame with pages from a blue-backed book. Similar volumes were strewn about in front of a fissure in the rock just wide enough to squeeze through. He ducked down to light his pipe, inhaled and exhaled then, catching Philip's eye, gave a broad wink.

The rest of the carriage had also noticed him. Although they were laughing they had apparently taken offence. "Get a shave, old timer!" one called. Another took money from his billfold, leaned across and waved it out of the window. Philip resisted the urge to sink his teeth into that hand. "He's trying to decide whether to eat his boots or his feet," sneered a man in a Grayson-ish hat. In fact, Philip could see next to the books a bloody pile of rat-sized animals: could they perhaps be gophers?

The train sighed and began to roll. Philip raised his hand in farewell and the man, after tossing another book on the fire, waved back. Philip sat down next to Ethel to watch him out of sight.

"What a curious fellow. Rather impressive, I thought. All alone in the middle of nowhere. I wonder what his story is."

"Not an edifying one, I shouldn't think," Ethel's eyes closed once more. "He had a toper's nose."

At a bend in the track the cliff became visible once more: the column of smoke was still rising but the man had disappeared. Now the train felt as if it were plummeting through space. Far below lay the flat and fertile plains of Kansas and Missouri. If only Philip could have stayed to share that gopher supper! Who could tell what they might have talked about under the stars before slipping into the fissured rock to sleep? Could this have been a prophet, a second Moses come down from the mountains with a new set of commandments, so terrible that he had decided to burn them before they could blast away the certainties of mankind? Philip had felt that he was looking into the eyes of a man with answers. Perhaps he might have explained this curious war or even what on earth Ramsay MacDonald was playing at?

CHAPTER EIGHT

WAR IS THE CURE (1917)

A T T H E U S U A L time Emily had awakened from her usual dream. She and Fred had been out on the moors, in mist and driving rain, lagging behind the rest of the walking party who were encouraging them with rousing choruses of "England Arise":

> "From yon fields and hills
> Hark! The answer swells:
> Arise, O England, for the day is here!"

She never recognized any of them – it was as if their features had been washed away. Eventually they reached a dry stone wall, unusually high and sheer: the others scrambled over but Emily, bedraggled and ashamed, had to duck down to the Jowett Hole. Sharp stones cut into her elbows and knees: she crawled and crawled but never emerged on the other side. The laughter of their companions was now mocking and cruel – and where was Fred? She could no longer feel him pushing gently from behind. The way grew darker and narrower until there was no going forward or back. Her huge paw-like hands began hopelessly to dig. Fortunately she knew that this could only be a dream: her aching joints no longer permitted her to gad about, especially not on all fours.

Without looking at the clock she knew that it was ten to four, when Fred would always wake with a loud cry – half shout, half sob. Even when he was away her own eyes would open out of sheer habit. He must be halfway to Petrograd by now, travelling with

MacDonald to the International Workers' Conference. The government had returned their passports, for Lloyd George was desperate to keep post-revolutionary Russia in the war. She imagined Fred out on the Baltic Sea, lying awake, listening to the night-soil men scraping at the hull.

According to Fred, the sounds – horses' hooves, creaking carts, laughter and foul oaths – persisted for a full two minutes after waking, while the smell lingered considerably longer. He would light a taper and go downstairs only to return half an hour later. "Cold out," he always said, even when it wasn't, and then sigh as she snuggled into his back. For the rest of the night his nose would continue its sniffing. How was it possible to be haunted by the ghost of a smell? When they moved from Telford Street it had seemed that his delusions had ceased: it had taken them a full month to cross the city and find him. Since then, even though the night-soil men had only appeared on Thursdays, Fred had begun to hear and smell them seven days a week and had become ever more obsessed with cleanliness. Dr Metcalfe would chaff him that copious internal applications of brandy were the best disinfectant, while Snowden observed that his old friend could out-sniff any gun dog. What was odd was that Fred's nose was on the small side whereas Keir Hardie had once told her that his own huge and hairy snout registered no odours whatsoever.

Her eyes were getting heavy. The bed did not want her to get up: it clung and pulled her back like a sphagnum bog. Might it not be for the best, the pillow whispered, if nobody in the world ever bestirred themselves again? The top blanket had been reversed so that its rough side was tickling her neck: she must have retrieved it from the floor without waking. As a child she had slept solidly for eight hours every night: according to her sisters she made no sound and never shifted her position – but when you were young you had nothing to worry about.

From the backyard there came a curious sound, like a poker raking ashes in a grate. Perhaps she was beginning to share Fred's hallucinations? Then someone coughed – or rather cleared their throat as if about to make an important announcement – but all that followed was a muffled thud and a curse. Where the middens had once stood there were treacherous undulations which even her own feet had never learned to negotiate. Could it be Little Emily's ex-fiance? Although he had broken with her because of the family's opposition to the war he was often discovered mooning about in the darkness. The poor lad was wasting his time: the Jowett girls slept even more soundly than their mother had done.

"Arise O England," Emily sang under her breath, swinging her legs out of bed. A faint grey light was seeping through the wooden shutters.

> "Come and swell the song
> Silent now so long – England is risen and the day is here."

There was nobody outside. It must have been one of the neighbours. They were often skulking about, icing up the Jowett's back steps in winter and urinating down their coal hole in summer – they presumably considered these to be patriotic acts. Half a dozen windows had been broken: 10, Grantham Terrace had to be boarded up every night – so far no-one had summoned up the courage to smash them by day. Nor had they yet resorted to fire, which was what she really feared.

Crippled soldiers had returned with tales not of heroism but of unimaginable hell. Now everyone seemed half-mad with confusion and grief. The destruction of the city's newly-formed 'Pals Regiment' had been the worst: on their first day at the front two – thirds of those fathers, brothers and sons had been killed or seriously injured. Now there were regular reports of the lost men reappearing in their usual haunts – running for trams or clocking on and off in the mills, mysteriously whole again. Although dead, they apparently had money in their pockets: they were seen in the food queues and in the pubs, drinking quietly at their usual tables.

They would not let go of Bradford and Bradford would not let go of them. Even Emily could have sworn that she had glimpsed the Watson boy back at his bedroom window opposite, stretching his long white arms and yawning in the sunlight. All of her nephews from Queensbury and Thornton were dead and her beloved cousin Eli, who had lied about his age, was now deaf and insane but none of these had affected her as much as the death of their tortoise.

It had been a gift from a sailor to mark Fred's persistent but unsuccessful opposition to the government's raising of The Plimsoll Line. The man had claimed that the little creature was already well over a hundred years old. They had christened it Nunquam, Blatchford's pen-name, which the children shortened to Nunc, thus pointedly converting the Latin 'never' into 'now'.

Fred maintained that its steady onwards tread embodied the spirit of Socialism. Nunc was supposed to be deaf but whenever political matters were under discussion his tiny head would move with comical solemnity from speaker to speaker. Snowden had told them that, for reasons that remained obscure, Achilles had once challenged a tortoise to a foot race. Having given his rival a sporting start he was never able to pass it because when he reached its starting point it had already crawled away and so on and on, with the tortoise maintaining its lead even though it dwindled to an immeasurably tiny fraction of a second. "Zeno's first paradox of motion," Philip had concluded, "I often feel that way about you, Fred." His tone indicated that this had not been a joke. How thrilled the children had been to find that, unlike the greatest hero in antiquity, they flew past their pet in a mere couple of strides! In summer Nunc lived outside in a roomy hutch which Councillor Hayhurst had made for him: he had learnt to raise the hasp to enter or leave and loved to roam at night. They joked that he was better than any watchdog: although he could not bark, being dumb, he had once taken a sharp nip at Ethel Snowden's ankle.

Nevertheless, Emily was sure that she had heard him die. On the night after Fred's departure there had sounded a sustained and high-pitched scream that had left her eardrums throbbing. She had not found the body until the next evening. On the wall at the end of the terrace was a saddle-shaped mound where the builders had mixed their cement, on which everything that was lost in the maze of streets - ribbon, glove or brooch - was left to be reclaimed by its rightful owners. It was here that what was left of Nunc had been deposited.

With a sharp blade or cutting tool the killers had managed to precisely quarter the shell - which, before or after death, had been scorched by fire and gnawed apparently by human teeth. The rest of him had been finely diced into cubes of grey and scarlet flesh, although there was no sign of that meekly inquisitive head. Little Emily and Little Ethel had buried him in a wooden pencil case among the parterres of Horton Park and then sung - or rather shouted - every last verse and chorus of 'The Red Flag'. Poor old Nunquam! At least the Pals had some idea of what they might have been fighting for. At least they had died at the hands of other creatures like themselves. Emily wondered how the mothers of Bradford would have felt if their sons had perished as an incidental result of a war between tortoises.

Fred insisted that The People were no longer quite themselves but she suspected that their true colours were at last showing through. Long before the war she had glimpsed dislike or even hatred in the eyes of his constituents - especially the most obligated. Did his courage and dedication only remind them of their own meanness and cowardice? Did he force them to face the uncomfortable reality of the situation? Or did they despise him for being fool enough to serve them, unable to see that they were not worth the effort?

Nevertheless, from other wards or even out of town, they came to him with their problems. After many illiterate recruits had signed away their parents' rights to allowances, it was Fred who had ensured that the Army Forms were altered and that back payments were made in full. Thanks to him, the pension to widowed mothers had been doubled to seven shillings a week. A soldier's pound note, sent home but lost in the post, had been refunded with two shillings interest. Fred always insisted that these 'little victories' were the ones that really mattered: if you put them all together over a period of time, they would eclipse the great political convulsions of the day. He had recently moved his office up to the newly-built attic: it was rumoured that this was to allow him to signal by flashlight to overflying Zeppelins. Now his petitioners could queue on the stairs rather than out in the yard: they kept apologizing for the wear and tear on her carpet – as if carpets were all she would care about.

Sometimes she wondered whether Fred's beloved People were properly human at all. Despite their weeping and wailing, war seemed to agree with them. Every morning she would watch old Mr Duffy marching down to the postbox, the military satchel strapped across his chest bulging with letters to his seven grandsons, serving in every branch of the British Expeditionary Force. There had been eleven of them at the start of the conflict. How spry he looked, his bright eyes scanning the heavens for hostile aeroplanes, his ears cocked for incoming shells! He no longer limped but held his walking stick in both hands, like a bayoneted rifle ready to thrust up into the belly of any passing Boche. And what a time the Active Services League were having, forcing white feathers on any man in civvies! Aldermen Fawcett and Johnson were organizing boycotts of suspect butchers – they considered that there was something unEnglish, even downright Hunnish, about pork. The mob still broke the windows of foreign-named shops – even though the Muller and Hoffmann boys had fallen with The Pals and Sargent Meekosha had been awarded a posthumous VC. Last Summer Low Moor munitions factory had exploded after a leak of pieric acid: thirty-eight died, most of them firemen. In response the mob attacked the row of cottages on Daisy Hill where the war refugees – the Belgiuminians, as they were locally known – had been rehoused. Anyone who was different – too tall or too short, markedly well-favoured or ugly – was in for it. Men even suffered for their elaborate facial hair: even though surely no German spy would cultivate a Kaiser Bill moustache? Lifelong cripples and the chronically sick were viewed as cunningly prescient malingerers. There was a deaf-mute on Manchester Road – a big soft lad, universally-liked, whose silent presence had now assumed a sinister aspect. Who could tell what unguarded words he might have jotted down and sent off to his German masters? They had taken away his beloved carrier pigeons: their feathers had been plucked, no doubt, by the harpies of the ASL.

Only last week five policemen had arrived with a warrant to search the house. No-one had told them what they were supposed to be looking for, so they had drunk a pot of tea and then left. Why couldn't folk understand that opposing the war was not the same as being pro-German? Articles and letters in the local press referred to Fred as 'Jewitt' – but why ever did they think that Jews would support the Kaiser? According to their friend Morel, the Germans were if possible even more anti-semitic than the Russians.

"She's a spy," a voice from the bread queue had hissed as Emily walked by. Turning on her heel she had stared into the woman's strangely unfocussed eyes. "Beg pardon?" "Shepherd's pie". The broad features had twisted into a horrible simper, "That's what I always say. You can't beat a nice Shepherd's pie." Emily had recognized her as one of those letter carriers who delivered the mail now that all the posties were at the front. Apparently it was not the blue uniform that was baggy but the woman herself. It was no wonder that Fred's letters – when they arrived at all – were dirtied and torn.

She looked in on the girls. There they lay, perfectly flat and straight, breathing almost inaudibly, the two dark heads on the pillow staring up at the ceiling. They had become accustomed to the sound of breaking glass, to being greeted by jeers or silence, to the sight of their beloved father coming home with blood on his face and egg and flour on his clothes.

Last year at Drummond Road School someone had thrown a fizzing explosive at him. It had turned out to be a bowling jack with a wicking fuse and 'BOMB' daubed on its side. He was dogged by Havelock Wilson, leader of the Seaman's Union, who had pledged himself to purge the Labour Movement of pacifists and traitors. At a hostile meeting in Swansea there had been a commotion in the audience: Wilson and his henchman Captain Tupper and a gang of toughs had come down on the Birmingham train. As they moved forward, however, they were set upon by local jingoes – if anyone was going to smash the faces of MacDonald and Jowett it was going to be them. The notorious Tupper wore a suit so tight that he could hardly walk but it didn't hinder him from throwing punches. Someone hit him with a chair but he hadn't even blinked, just plucked up his assailant by the throat and thrown him against the wall. As the battle raged, the platform party had left on exaggerated tiptoe by the side exit. Emily had not been in the least afraid but when you were lying in the darkness listening to people moving around outside your home, it was a very different matter.

These days, descending the stairs was as hard as climbing them. Halfway down she became aware that the sounds had begun again – more regular and purposeful, as if someone was slowly feeling their way across the yard. She was sure that she could hear a sniffing, like some horrible fairytale ogre – fee-fi-fo-fum – seeking out its prey. And it seemed that there was more than one of them because from the front yard that scraping sounded once more. She paused and the sounds ceased: they were listening to her listening. If she should cry out would it deter them or give the confirmation they were waiting for? Tentatively, she advanced her left foot and the shuffling began again. She moved the other and the scraping started up. When she stopped, they stopped.

If she had called for help no-one would have come. The Jowetts were increasingly isolated. Hardie was dead, Bruce Glasier seriously ill and the Snowdens seldom ventured out of London. Uncle Arthur Henderson was in the cabinet, keeping the unions in line, while the old *Clarion* crowd was even more pro-war: Blatchford and Hyndman, under an enormous union jack, had formed the

National Defence Committee. In Bradford, on the day that the King announced that he was embracing temperance for the duration, Willie Leach had taken to drink. "This'll show him," he muttered, loudly gargling his gin. But as people withdrew into the shadows, so others stepped forward to take their place: it was as if, by some natural law, the numbers and composition remained the same but with ever-diminishing levels of intimacy and trust. Fred was still in mourning for his old comrades, although many of them had not seemed particularly comradely at the time.

E. D. Morel was a recent addition. Although undoubtedly sincere and fearless - he had made his reputation by uncovering Belgian atrocities in The Congo - Emily never felt comfortable with him. Was he English or French or Belgian of even some kind of African? Roaming the world seeking dangerous causes to adopt, he seemed to belong everywhere and nowhere. Now he was in Pentonville Jail under the Defence of the Realm Act for sending a pamphlet to a famous pacifist novelist in neutral Switzerland. The brave ladies of the Bradford Humanity League were also at His Majesty's Pleasure, and Fenner Brockway, who had succeeded Hardie at *The Labour Leader*, was locked up in the Tower of London itself. His wife, Lilian, always carried a huge fan made up of all the white feathers that the ASL had given him. Councillor Hayhurst was their closest local friend, even though he was wildly patriotic. Although they had become councillors at the same time he had never really taken to Fred until the last three years when - in spite of the Jowetts' opposition to the war - his affection and respect had grown. Emily found him a reassuring presence: it was hard to imagine anyone daring to rummage around in his backyard.

There, there - there again! It wasn't her imagination or the house settling. Someone had gently but firmly closed the kitchen door. In a curious reflex, she had plucked down the thick black family bible. Replacing it, she looked around the sitting room for a more practical weapon. The poker in the fireplace presented itself but what a silly shape it was, ending in more of a crook than a point.

It would hardly do for poking, let alone hitting, and she feared that merely to poke an intruder might provoke him even more. And now her arm had locked and she could not lift the thing above shoulder level. When she stepped back into the narrow hall she could hear from the kitchen a hissing sound, like a fire catching, but there was no smell of smoke. Her knee pushed at the door and it swung slowly open – apparently knowing better than to give its customary squeak.

A small dark-clad figure was standing at the sink with its back to her, vigorously scrubbing its hands. She took a step forward: the poker grew even heavier in her hand but then, as if drawn by some magnetic force, pulled itself up towards the ceiling. Although she was sure that she had made no sound, the man slowly turned round. He was shockingly white-faced and his lathered hands hung limply in front of his chest. The poker was beginning its descent when the glitter of the fountain pens in the man's waistcoat pocket arrested it. She knew him now, even though he had taken off his glasses and was wearing an unfamiliar tartan muffler: Fred had unexpectedly returned.

"How long have you been here?" she asked.

"I just came in. I've been looking for Nunc: his cage is all smashed to bits."

"Was there anybody else outside?"

"I haven't seen a single soul between here and the station. It looks completely different at night. Do you know, I nearly turned into Ashgrove by mistake. Even our Street looked strange: I've never noticed that dogstooth pattern under the gutter – has it always been there?"

"I thought you'd be in Russia by now."

"It's a long story," said Fred, "That will keep until morning. But then I suppose it is the morning." He picked up his eye-glasses from the window sill, breathed on the lenses then began polishing them with the soft yellow cloth. "Well, we made it to Aberdeen all right but then who should turn up but Wilson and Tupper who ordered their members not to sail. So there we sat for two days waiting for the government to do something and when they didn't we caught the sleeper train back. MacDonald has gone on to London." He held his glasses up to the light. "Were you really going to hit me with that?" Emily realized that she was still brandishing the poker. As she laid it on the kitchen table a ripple of pain measured the length of her arm.

"They've done something to Nunquam, haven't they?"

"They probably thought he was some sort of land-mine or they held a mock-trial and executed him for not knowing the words to 'God Save The King'. You know what The People round here are like." Fred had caught his breath when she said 'The People' – only then did she realize the venom she had put into the words.

It was all very curious. Fred had been walking through a Bradford that wasn't Bradford anymore and then she, in the kitchen, had stared for fully ten seconds at a Fred who was no longer Fred. It was astonishing how things could suddenly go all to pieces and then abruptly come back together again, just as they had always been.

At last Fred was satisfied with his lenses. "Do you happen to know if Dr Metcalfe has examined those wool sorters in Tong?"

"Yes," said Emily, "He's absolutely certain that it's anthrax."

"That's good," Fred pinched the glasses back above the bulb of his nose. Now he was fully himself again. "We've really got the beggars this time."

᙮

"But my chief criticism of the present conflict," Snowden glared around the packed hall. "Is that recruitment began at the wrong end. As it was the old men who started it surely they should have been the first ones called upon to fight?" At this there were some titters: only Our Philip would dare to laugh at the war. "If we had taken nonagenarians and then worked our way down, with any luck no-one young with life still to live would have needed to be sacrificed."

Ethel joined in the applause. This was how she had first seen him: up on his crutches before an enraptured audience. He had made her think of a scarecrow in a field who, nourished by sun and rain, had astonishingly come to life. Although the eyes blazed and the fingers clawed the air, she could discern that beautiful green-gold aura pulsing steadily away and hear behind his words the booming descant of Love. And then he had paused, looked directly at her and smiled. That smile! That smile! Not even Lloyd George could match that smile! Sometimes she liked to close her eyes, clap her hands over her ears, empty her mind and count up to fifty, then look at him as if for the first time. And the magic always worked: even now, fifteen years later, she knew that she would still have got up and followed him.

She was seated halfway up the centre aisle: she was tired of being goggled at on platforms. Behind Philip, she could see that Kathleen St. John Conway Glasier's hat had been placed on her own designated chair, giving the impression that a delegate from the peacocks was in attendance. In the chairman's seat, Bruce Glasier, after yet another coughing fit, was spitting into a grubby hand-kerchief and then examining the result. When he had struggled to his feet to introduce the speakers the audience had risen as well. A standing ovation just for being ill! Perhaps he would drop dead as an encore? Now his eyes were rolling upwards as if they could already espy the place awaiting him on the Executive Committee of Paradise. Like so many Socialists, he was never happy unless he had something to complain about. And as for his wife, all she had ever wanted was to sacrifice her youth and beauty on the altar of something or other. What sort of people were these whose sole pleasure in life was to suffer? Especially as suffering itself was the merest illusion. As Goethe had written: 'No-one is ever ill unless they choose to be'. Philip had been given up as a hopeless cripple until one cold January morning he had risen from his bed by sheer force of will. And she herself as a little girl had mended her frac-tured arm overnight just by staring at it, without blinking, while ceaselessly whispering under her breath the magic word 'LOVE'.

Katharine St. John Conway Glasier! What a great mouthful of names for such a poor scrap of a thing! And how hoity-toity she got if you missed one out or scrambled them! Just because she was a curate's daughter and had been to Newnham! She was tall but droopy with unnaturally long arms and a head that came to a pronounced point which, together with her long straight nose, gave her the appearance of a soldier from the Bayeux tapestry. Curiously, the newspapers often linked her photograph with Ethel's, usually in heart-shaped frames, as 'The Belles of the Labour Movement'. "I am not of the Labour Movement," was Ethel's stock response, "And nor is my husband, although sometimes we and the Movement coincide."

It was strange to think that, many years ago, Katharine St. John Conway Glasier had turned down a marriage proposal from George Bernard Shaw. "I never felt he really *needed* me," had been her explanation. Ethel shuddered: neediness was bad enough but the need to be needed was beyond endurance. Some people had said such things about her and Philip – if they only knew!

"And we should extend the conscription of life to the conscription of wealth. This war should not be financed by loan but by taxation of the profits of the rich."

Even under Henderson's leadership, Philip remained the party's financial spokesman, being the only one with any understanding of economics. Whatever he said on a Monday, the Liberals would be parroting by the end of the week: ever since the 1911 Budget it was as if the nominal Chancellor was shadowing him. But that was typical of Lloyd George: part of his genius was knowing which ideas to steal. What a scamp he was! He had somehow persuaded poor Phil to sit on The Venereal Diseases Commission and then on the Liquor Control Board, while favouring with the plum jobs the most peculiar types. Hyndman, the self-styled revolutionary, was getting nice and fat chairing The Food Committee.

Philip had continued to speak out against conscription, taking up the cases of shellshock victims and conscientious objectors. Most of the so-called pacifists struck Ethel as markedly aggressive, looming and glowering like murderers, and among the shell-shocked the most terrifying symptoms turned out to be faked while the comically unconvincing were all-too genuine. Sir Walter Long - on Philip's suggestion - had sent an admonitory circular to local draft boards but the conscription of lunatics, epileptics and even men with missing limbs continued. The notorious tribunal in Market Bosworth had rejected every application but then - on the grounds of national interest - exempted the members of the local fox hunt. Although they often laughed about it all, she remained angry that he was wasting his time. Such things should be left to the Fred Jowetts of this world.

It was all a matter of perception. She had been talking to a soldier who had a shell explode right next to him but walked away unscathed. When informed that this was because he and the shell had contained equal and compatible amounts of love he had been positively rude: "My mates all got blown to bits". Why was it that most people had a positive aversion to enlightenment? She had often speculated whether it might be possible for a wounded man - if he was in the correct state of mind - to just think the bullet back out of his body and then heal up its bloody path. For those unfortunates who had been blown apart, she conceded, it would be more difficult. Perhaps they had, through their foolishness, already expelled every last atom of Love from their bodies and would have exploded even without the intervention of the shell?

Today's exordium had been long, even by Philip's standards, but his hearers remained rapt. This was the one power that Love had not bestowed upon her. Whenever she made a speech she knew that she was being looked at but not listened to. As Chairwoman of The Peace Crusade she must have addressed over half a million people but how many would remember a single word she had said? In contrast, everyone loved to parrot the Pankhursts' mindless slogans.

Ethel had recently broken with the suffragettes: feminism, it appeared, no longer had anything to do with femininity. Emmeline and Christabel were now hysterically pro-war: you had to admire the way that L-G had manipulated them. How well he understood the sex! Sometimes she wondered if she herself might not be a woman at all but the last of an older race – the seraphs, perhaps – or, more optimistically, the herald of an altogether new type.

There was a scuffling sound behind her followed by a curious howling, as if a dog had got into the hall. Then a perfectly bald man in a threadbare overcoat buttoned at the neck came stamping down the aisle. She could not tell what he was saying – he seemed to be some kind of Celt – but he was carrying a large square placard which read:

OUR SONS
ARE DYING
WHILE
SNOWDEN
SNEERS

The letters had been carefully blocked in black except for those of SNOWDEN which were in shivery scarlet like the cover of a penny dreadful. Philip had broken off his speech and was already down the steps, quite forgetting the canes on which he had made his entrance. He put one arm around the man's shoulders and began whispering urgently into his ear. Back on the platform, Glasier rose and tried to speak which only brought on another coughing fit. The audience applauded again: like children, they never tired of something they really liked. Ethel remained unconvinced: why ever would cancer of the bowel make one cough?

Philip virtually sprang back on stage. "Let me be clear," he said, "I consider this war to be a futile waste of human and material resources." With a downward movement of his palms he extinguished the resultant cheers. "But I think there has been nothing more magnificent in our history than the way in which, at the beginning of hostilities, the young manhood of this country responded to a mighty impulse and rose as one." The bald man had turned away and was standing as if to attention with tears pouring down his face.

How brilliantly Philip could improvise! Recently, in the House, when a young Conservative MP was denouncing conscientious objectors as cowards he had risen on a point of order. "In the light of these stirring words" - he had smiled his sweetest smile - "may I enquire why the Honourable Gentleman is not himself at the front?"

"That, sir," the wretched man had stuttered, "Is a matter for my own conscience." At the roars of laughter that followed he had blushed and run out of the chamber and had not as yet returned.

It was significant how little antagonism Phil had provoked, whereas MacDonald and Jowett were hated for saying similar things. In his own constituency, he had declined to endorse the mayor's recruiting campaign. "I'll support you when it's a matter of defending our shores," he had said, and afterwards every member of the Corporation had shaken his hand. They knew that he was no coward, that he was a man who fought his own daily war with pain. And his imperturbability amidst the madness made them feel somehow ashamed.

When men got tired of drinking and gambling, war was the only thing that could restore their jaded appetite. Sometimes she wondered if it was all an excuse to get away from their wives. They did not seem to realize, poor things, that wherever they went - on the battlefield, in the skies, even at the bottom of the ocean - Love was already there, waiting for them. And Love could not be blown up or drowned: even the wounds that opened up on their bodies were oracular mouths through which its sweet voice whispered its gentle but implacable reproofs. Perhaps they were bombarding Flanders merely to create nice flat playing fields and were teaching rugger and cricket to the Hun? They would all be smoking and drinking and sniggering at dirty stories - and there were bound to be the usual over-painted women simpering about, all that most men could cope with. But surely it was significant that Lloyd George should be, as Prime Minister, the man in charge of the whole thing? The deep and mysterious currents of Love were at work, selecting and purifying the race. Perhaps all those silly men would blow each other up - along with the Pankhursts and the simperers - and humanity could make a fresh start. She suspected that dear naughty old L-G would be all too willing to take on the burden of restoring the world's population to its optimum level.

A few weeks ago, he had dropped in on them after visiting Henderson, who lived at the other end of Woodstock Road. This had been embarrassing because Phil and Uncle Arthur were not on speaking terms. Ethel had been impressed to see that the gleaming official car was still parked down the street: L-G must have walked - or, more likely, trotted - the intervening fifty yards. He had been dancing on the doormat in an elaborate display of wiping his feet. "I like a house with an attic," he said, sniffing the air as if savouring some atticky smell.

He had ostensibly come to discuss the progress of the Liquor Bill but she could tell that he had an ulterior motive. Although his head inclined towards Phil he was watching her the whole time: he was one of those people who could look in several directions at once. During the next hour his minions kept running in and out with messages: he needed that constant sense of drama but she suspected that they also provided him with excuses to leave - she was flattered that he did not avail himself of them. "Not bad news, I hope," she had said after the third interruption. "All news is bad for someone, dear lady," he had replied with an almost imperceptible wink. The face was smooth and ruddy-cheeked like a child's - it was unthinkable that he was a year older than Philip! - but when he smiled the eyes vanished in a lattice work of tiny creases. His hair was silvering beautifully but it was far too long at the back, hanging lankly over his collar - if you hadn't known who he was you might almost have called him seedy. And that moustache! She was sure that he must be chewing and sucking on its ends! And those tufting eyebrows! How she would love to lick her fingertips and smooth them down and then snip away with her tiniest pair of scissors! And she would throw out that awful soft slouch hat: some heads were just screaming out for the biggest, shiniest and silkiest of toppers!

"You must visit us properly some time – dinner, perhaps," Philip had said and then been obviously disconcerted at the alacrity of L-G' acceptance. "A week today will be perfect but don't put yourselves out. It's talk I live off, not food. I want to know about MacDonald – I don't quite get this game he's playing . . ."

"There was nothing written on those pieces of paper," Philip growled after the PM had gone. "Unless it was in invisible ink." He remained quite impervious to all the liveliness that just bubbled out of this wonderful little fellow. All he would concede was that he was "the most devious man in the Liberal party – which is saying a great deal."

The important thing was for her to be alone with L-G. Philip took little persuasion to spend an extra night up north. He hankered after a Yorkshire constituency, perhaps Colne Valley – "I've won it once already, for Grayson, ten years ago." She had seen from L-G's eyes that he needed to speak to her: perhaps he was already planning a post-war political realignment – with the best of the Liberals and the Socialists forming a new alliance to sweep away the Tories forever. But it was more than that: she was utterly certain that he knew things – deep, eternal things – that even she had never guessed at.

She had been watching at the window for hours beforehand. Something told her that he would appreciate a veal cutlet but she was unsure about the raspberry compote. She kept craning her neck for the silent arrival of that great limousine, but then at half-past on the dot there had sounded the click of the front gate: He must have come from the opposite direction. She flew to the door before the knocker could descend and flung it open to reveal a dumpy female figure, wrapped as tightly as a parcel and with bright little button eyes. It was Margaret, L-G's wife and she was alone. Her husband sent his apologies, she explained, but there had been a sudden emergency at the Manpower Commission.

"I'm not in the least surprised," Ethel observed but the woman did not laugh. Although she maintained an unwavering close-lipped smile she seemed utterly devoid of a sense of humour. The subsequent hours had been painfully stilted: 'Maggie', as she had grimly insisted on being called, had expounded on her tribulations over re-organizing the VAD, whatever that might be. Ethel had the curious impression that Maggie was equally disappointed not to find herself alone with Philip. Everyone seemed to be labouring under misapprehensions: L-G, she suspected, was being naughty again!

"And now, from the East, warmer winds are blowing. And who is to say that a spring time of joy might not give place to a summer of peace for this whole suffering world?"

Phil was shifting into his 'Come-to-Jesus' mode. Sometimes she wondered whether he might not be an even better public speaker than L-G. He certainly had more range and variation: If L-G was like a great soloist – Schnabel, perhaps, or Paderewski – then her husband was an entire orchestra. Nobody could inspire an audience like him: he filled them full of energy and self-belief. But L-G was different: it was as if he went inside his hearers, one by one, found their deepest, secret place, then sort of squeezed it, half-playfully, half-threateningly, then exited again. Philip, for all his sarcasm, was unmistakably good whereas there was something a little dark about L-G. That half-contemptuous nickname – The Welsh Wizard – was merely a statement of fact. Perhaps there was another power, beyond even Love, into which he tapped?

"And now we can dare to dream that dank autumn and cruel winter will never return. For, mark my words, as sure as the sun sets, revolution will come to Britain."

In March, the Russian revolution had brought the movement together again. Suddenly everyone looked ten years younger: even

Glasier stopped coughing for a while and Snowden, Henderson and MacDonald were observed talking amicably for a full ten minutes. Philip had moved a resolution calling for peace negotiations and the setting up of workers' and soldiers' councils in Britain. Those who had jeered him in the Grayson years now elected him Chairman of the ILP. And she and he had been so enthused that they had taken premises in Soho to house The 1917 Club, as a focus for the new radicalism. Unfortunately, it acted as a magnet to disreputables such as Russell, Wells and Augustus John. She was sure that none of the so-called actresses and models who attended them had ever heard of Kerensky or Prince Lvov. Within a few weeks it had declined into just another low dive and the Snowdens had resigned, after the rest of the committee had applied for a drinks licence. There were always people who just had to spoil things for everybody else.

She had considered informing the PM of the situation but feared that he would go down there to see for himself. He was not to be trusted around women but by that twinkle in his eye you knew that he was mainly teasing. She was reminded of Rags, the dog she had as a child, although he had been a border terrier not a Welsh one. He used to roll in the muddiest puddles, push his nose into the dirtiest messes, chase birds and squirrels, then plonk himself down in front of you, scarlet tongue lolling out, stiff tail rhythmically beating the ground. Bad – but oh-so-adorable –doggy-woggy! Whenever she encountered L-G she was surprised not to see a white fluffy tale poking through the seat of his trousers. When Philip had mislaid one of his bedroom slippers she felt that L-G must have stolen it. He would be hiding behind the sofa making a growling noise and worrying it with his lovely yellow teeth. Bad dog! Just the thought of him made her hug herself with delight. And she was thinking of him all the time since he had telephoned her the other day. He had invited her to Churt, his country house, where they could have a nice long chat, for the secretaries and the message-runners and even Maggie would all be on their way to Chequers. An assignation with the Prime Minister! She felt like Trollope's Lady

Glencora, abut to do something rash. She had decided, after some thought, to tell Philip. "He obviously wants something and will be wheedling you to bring me round. Well, you can tell him that if it's another of his blessed committees, the answer is No." Dear Philip: the only man in the world he could ever have been jealous of was MacDonald. How silly even the best men were! Now, up on the platform he threw his arms wide and let his voice ring out like a hundred golden trumpets.

"Soon we will see beautiful rays of sunshine, throwing their radiance far beyond the black clouds. And we will see, far below, what we have hoped for, worked for and fought for – that universal peace among nations without distinction of race, colour or creed."

There was fully twenty seconds of silence before the audience began clapping. Many even whistled or cheered but up on the platform no-one moved. These days it was the practice not to applaud, perhaps for fear of looking smug. As the enthusiasm persisted, even began to swell again, the Glasiers sat back in their chairs, tilted their heads and in perfect unison nodded three times. This did not seem to signify approval, more as if their worst fears had just been confirmed.

⁂

All in all, Bolton was not the ideal place for a morning constitutional. You had to dodge the cracks and puddles in the pavement and the dark heaps of mud or shit but at least they were some distraction from the faces of the crowd. Why did every man Ruth passed feel the need to smirk or roll his eyes and mutter? When she was a little girl she had thought that it was because of her father but now it was hard to believe that all men from New York to New South Wales knew Papa too. Perhaps a bank manager's daughter – wherever you might roam – remained a bank manager's daughter.

The bolder ones would stop, then turn and fall into step behind her. They would follow for hours but seldom get up the courage to say or do anything. This morning she had acquired just two - one tall and thin, one fat. The former affected a black velvet jacket and ribbon tie which did not complement his long grey face, while the latter, despite his sandstone tweeds, resembled a master butcher. The bohemian's trousers were ridiculously baggy while the butcher's were correspondingly tight. In the shop windows she watched their reflection: they remained ten yards behind, seemingly quite unaware of each other.

She used to blame herself: was she giving off some sort of come-hither stink? After all, tomcats won't even sniff at queens until they've come on heat. But she soon realized that if a girl put even the tip of her nose outside her front door it was assumed that she could only be after one thing. And whatever you did - if you ignored them or put your tongue out, swore or even kicked them - they took it as an encouragement. These two had a pleading look in their eyes, contrasting horribly with their swaggering. They were so intent on Ruth that they never noticed a couple of middle-aged ladies trying to give them white feathers: undertaking and master butchering were probably reserved occupations.

One of the best things about being an actress was feeling those male eyes when you went on stage and knowing that soon they would be looking at you in a very different way. Art lifted them momentarily out of the slime: she was sure that for a few hours afterwards they would stop ogling women - or at least ogle them as Cleopatra, Beatrice or Lady Macbeth.

As with her first child, her pregnancy would not be showing until relatively late but nothing would put them off. "The little girl can watch," said the one-armed Major who kept bothering her on the voyage back from New Zealand. This morning she had left Elaine at home: the cloth doll and lop-eared teddy bear - dubbed Thesis and Antithesis by Victor - had been embarking on what promised to be another prolonged bout of infant dialectics. Anything was better than sitting in that doleful house with its pervasive smell of mutton and brass polish and its walls crammed with garish hunting prints and Dutch genre daubs of grotesque boors pissing into fireplaces. the House of a Successful Man: no wonder Victor was always extolling the virtues of failure! Silence was the rule: Ruth restricted herself to fifty well-chosen words a day. Last night when she went up to bed she still had eleven in hand. She was cheating, really, for she had kept up an incessant internal dialogue with either Victor, somewhere out on the Western Front, or the unborn child, lying coiled in her womb.

The drizzle had stopped. She would have liked to have taken a turn around Queens Park but it was safer to stick to the main thoroughfares. As a girl she had discovered that men liked to lurk in bushes. What they exposed had been wrinkled and flaccid apart from one chortling old gentleman whose genitalia were apparently composed of a single white and gleaming sac. And so she had burst out laughing at the sight of her piano teacher's engorgement, certain that the so-spiritual Edgar had been playing some sort of joke. Victor must have reacted in the same way when, as a six-year-old in church, he had looked up from his devotions to see the Reverend Father's cock arcing out of the shadows, giving off a mystical light.

"There'll be no bankers, backbiters or bailiffs out on the battlefield," Victor had said when he enlisted, which had brought to her mind the vision of lines of bowler-hatted men crawling through barbed wire and bursting shells with distraining orders clenched between their teeth. How thrilled he had been to see the great powers of this world succumbing to his own enthusiasm for dressing-up and make-believe! It was a shame that Buffalo Bill had died before he could take his rightful place at the head of the show.

"Why do you want to join up, Mr Grayson?" The Dunedin recruiting officer had asked.

Victor blew imaginary smoke off his forefinger. "I want to get a shot at those pesky injuns."

"I know just how you feel, mate, but India's on our side, along with the rest of the bloody colonies. Never mind, there's always Johnny Turk – he might be black and stinky enough for your purposes."

Ruth had gone through the motions of trying to dissuade him: "You've no idea of what you're getting yourself into."

"I never know what I'm getting myself into," he had replied, "But I've been speaking to some of the wounded. Half said it was like Hell, the others that it was even worse. Incompetent officers, utter confusion, blood and guts, mud and gas, shit and rats everywhere. They weren't only physically or mentally damaged but sort of morally obliterated. I don't want to be a hero – I just want to see if I've got enough common sense to be a coward."

Victor's decision had received a great deal of attention in the New Zealand press. His own employer, *The Maoriland Worker*, described him as a drunk, a lecher, a conman and a traitor to his class. "They're the sort of men," Victor said of his ex-comrades, "Who, while the Huns were assaulting their wives and crushing their babies' skulls, would be drafting a motion complaining that such conduct was not in keeping with the true spirit of internationalism."

"Surely you can't believe in this cause?" they asked.

"Of course not," Victor replied, "It's merely kings and bosses setting people at each other's throats in order to expand their spheres of influence. But the cause is incidental. It's war in general, the principle of war, that I support. To someone like me it feels like the natural order of things. So now I am no longer Victor Grayson" – he had given a smart salute with the wrong hand – "But merely a number. I am Private 45001 – but you can call me nought-nought-one."

From the moment he donned the uniform those physical symptoms that had so tormented him – catarrh, sinus headaches, vision going out of focus – had all disappeared. He had even given up drinking. Ruth had been reminded of one of her favourite Liszt stories. In the 1830 Paris revolution the nineteen year old composer, long since sunk into the darkest depression, had leapt out of bed to join the insurgents at the end of his street. "The cannons cured him," his mother had said. Victor, in his uniform, looked radiantly handsome if nothing like a soldier. As the regiments marched down to the dockside she had picked him out among thousands. He was out of step: or, rather, everyone else was. She knew how much he would be enjoying the physical sensations – those stamping feet, those shouted responses – and she saw that the fingers of her right hand were curled as if closing once again around the shaft of his cock.

Her two admirers were coming closer: Meat and Death – she could almost feel their breath on her neck. How tiresome it all was! If Victor wanted somewhere worse than Hell he should have hied himself to Bolton. Horrible tortures, lurid flames, hideous demons – all would have been a relief from this mixture of oppressiveness and insubstantiality, as if you were drifting away while being simultaneously dragged down. When people asked where she came from she would always reply: "Hall i' Th' Wood".

"Wherever is that?" To which she would carefully enunciate, in her best Ellen Terry tones, "Why, North of Back O' Th' Bank, of course."

Bolton lay in perpetual fog: Papa's mill owning chums would argue over whose chimney was tallest or pumping out the blackest smoke. London pea-soupers were romantic and picturesque – sometimes you couldn't even see your feet! – but here it was as if they were burning plague victims on a wet bonfire. Through the murk you could sometimes glimpse the outline of The Pennines but hills and dales had always nauseated her. She liked big cities and deserts: New Zealand had been too bloody green.

Dr Fenster had once again recommended a change of climate and the southern hemisphere was the only place they hadn't tried. If that failed, Victor said, it would have to be a different planet. They had left their rent and bills unpaid and down at the quayside, for the first time, there had been no-one to see them off. Ruth had joined the Alan Wilkie Company, taking Shakespeare to the antipodes, while Victor would lecture and write for the emerging socialist movement. Apparently he had a large following – thousands of signed photographs had already been shipped across. Wilkie had turned out to be a genius, an avant garde follower of Granville-Barker and Poel, but his wife and leading lady, Frediswyde Hunter-Watts, had taken against Ruth from the start. Although she was half her size, half her age and twice as talented, she was reduced to playing The Nurse to Wattsy's Juliet. Still, she had her moments: she was sure that the good citizens of Napier and Timu would never see a finer Perdita. And when she was Little Jenny in Shaw's *Major Barbara* and her Bill Walker had slapped her too hard, the outraged cattlemen of Bowral had stormed the stage and she had to beg them not to lynch the wretched man.

For a delicious moment she imagined the Bowral boys rampaging through Bolton, whips and ropes in hand, but the Germans were probably still her only realistic hope. Last summer a wandering Zeppelin had dropped its bombs but missed the Town Hall and the factories, destroying instead six slum houses on Clink Street. Why were random casualties always among the poor?

Ruth had seen a Zeppelin while out with Arthur Rose on her first night back in London. No-one was firing as, humming its little tune, it blithely floated above the Thames. It had looked somehow organic: as they watched, a ripple ran along the tight silk fabric and the seam under the belly appeared to pulse. "My God!" said Arthur, clutching her arm, "It reminds me of Victor!" If you wanted your faith in humanity restored you couldn't beat a night out with what Papa called 'Unspeakables of the Oscar Wilde sort'. Arthur suggested writing a musical revue about the war, with an orchestra of heavy ordnance and a chorus-line of amputees. 'Zeppelins Over Soho', it would be called and they improvised a title song.

"I'll always love you till the moon eats the sun

While there are Zeppelins over Soho you'll be the one."

But London had changed in the last three years. It was as if the narrow streets had shifted and realigned themselves at different angles. Why, she even mistook Duck Lane for Berwick Street!

"There's the club that those dreadful Snowdens have opened," said Arthur, "Best not venture, my dear. It's far too louche for little lambs such as we."

They ended up dancing downstairs at the 400 Club. The place was packed and the small band was playing a funny gargly jazz, as if they were all on The Titanic at the bottom of the sea. It was jolly enough until some drunken swells emptied a basket of ping-pong balls over the floor and then cut the lights. There were squeals and curses, the sound of breaking glass and heavy bodies falling to the ground, while someone kept impersonating the cry of a peacock. Arthur had led her out of an emergency exit to emerge on a starlit Oxford Street. "Now I know how those poor boys in the trenches must be feeling," he said, rubbing his knee. Their Zeppelin had gone but some chunks of masonry the size of human heads were lying in the middle of the road and bits of plaster came floating down from Selfridge's. "The stage is a wonderful life," said Arthur, as if reading her mind," but perhaps cruising about the skies bombing people might be even more jolly."

Dear Arthur! He wouldn't have lasted five minutes up north. The good folk of Bolton would not tolerate the slightest deviation from their brutish routine. When she was a young girl, boys used to throw mud at her: this meant that they liked you, the Bolton equivalent of sending flowers or penning a sonnet. Really, they might as well have been wearing animal skins. She half-expected to see the tiny head of a brontosaurus peeping round the Town Hall tower, which had been modelled, she was sure, after Papa's shining pate. The shrapnel had merely pitted its front: however could they have missed the bloody thing? There was nothing worse than neo-classicism: until her dying day she would be a Gothic gal. She and Victor often went to the House of Commons – the same attendants who used to throw him out now shook his hand – but they never bothered with the main chambers, just looked at the carvings and the glass. If she was carrying a boy she wanted to call him Augustus Wellby after Pugin but Victor was set on Winston Spencer. He had contracted the curious notion that he was Churchill's illegitimate half-brother but there was, thank God, not the least resemblance. Everyone needed to dream, however, and those who did not have the luck to be actors, artists or Zeppelin pilots had to make the best of things.

There were plenty of canaries hanging about: female munitions workers whose skins had been stained by the chemicals. They looked the better for it – at least yellow was a colour! – but they did not seem to approve of Ruth. Four years ago, she recalled, everyone had taken exception to her emerald stockings. 'Little-Miss-Piss-Down-Her-Legs!' – when they jeered at you in Bolton you had to be doing something right. She doubted that even one of them had ever heard of Ida Rubinstein. Now a face – closer to an ageless Chinese Mandarin than a young English girl – was thrust into hers. "Mata bloomin' Hari," it snarled. Of course! A young woman dressed in a pearl grey topcoat and matching drop-brim hat, strolling alone down Deansgate, oblivious to the importuning of Bolton's most eligible swains – what else could she be but a spy? The canary looked as if she had more to say but then Meat and Death came shouldering past and knocked her back into the gutter. The fat one now looked thinner while the thin one had thickened up: perhaps they would end up balancing out or exchanging shapes? If only Victor had been here: in half an hour he would have had their trousers off.

It was rare to find a man who really liked women. Most so-called ladies' men were so horribly needy: if a girl didn't open her legs they acted as if it was the end of the world, even if she was just another name to add to their list. Victor was no Don Juan or Casanova: he behaved as if women had some secret to vouchsafe, something far beyond sex. If rebuffed he merely bowed good naturedly and moved on. His attitude to men was even more casual: sex was merely an extension of shaking hands. That combination of insatiable curiosity and utter indifference made him irresistible. It meant that he stayed with her not out of habit or need but because day after day, minute after minute, he kept choosing to do so. And if they ever did part she was sure that it would be without recriminations or regrets.

She had assumed that he must be representative of Socialists but most of them were just like Papa's Masonic cronies - flabby and vulgar, always staring at her breasts - and the rest were obviously mad, though not in a romantic way. And their women were even worse: skeletal, pop-eyed fanatics or great galumphing things like Blatchford's daughters. It amused her how the comrades obviously considered Victor to be a baffling case when, in fact, he was perfectly consistent. All he ever did was to follow his instincts. Drinking, for example: he was not really an alcoholic but sometimes the next drink would insist on following the last and he would let it flow through him, like a culvert allowing some mighty river to pursue its course. He rarely gambled but when he did you could not prise the cards or dice out of his hands. Such a nature disabled him as a politician: unlike the Snowdens and MacDonalds he was quite incapable of apprehending where his own interests lay. The audiences didn't care, of course: they were thrilled when he turned up legless and even more when he didn't turn up at all. It was the same in her own world: solid professionals such as Betterton were merely admired while everyone had loved Burbage and Kean. For an actress, however, it was apparently only possible to win the acclamation of the general by being generally fucked.

She saw that she had unwittingly retraced her steps, for here was Town bloody Hall once more. On her sixteenth birthday Edgar had smuggled her inside to play the enormous Prince Albert organ. She had ground out a deafening version of 'A Fairy Went A-Marketing', the effect only enhanced by his own organ - which she now knew to be regulation issue - slapping on the keys.

> "Perhaps the self-same song that found a path
> Through the sad heart of Ruth when sick for home
> She stood in tears amid the alien corn."

This was pretty much how she felt, even though no-one, not even Victor, had ever seen her cry and there was no corn to be had in Bolton – not even for ready money. Nor could she find any cucumbers or radishes, for which she had developed a craving – for the smell, rather than the taste. All she had bought this morning had been a stack of embroidered patriotic postcards. The words of a poem – 'With Love To My Dear Boy' – nestled among a riot of flags, crowns and roses, while in the background a line of sepia soldiers were apparently marching down into their graves. In the centre of the composition two severed arms – one khaki, one bare – were intertwined. Judging by the number of bangles on the latter it could only belong to The Princess Salome herself. It was monstrous but, in its own way, a masterpiece of compression. At least it would give nought-nought-one a laugh.

She had no difficulty in understanding why he had joined up. If something dangerous was going on who would not want to be part of it? Who would willingly miss out on history being made, even if an incidental part of it was your own sweet self being blown to blazes? It wasn't heroism or self-sacrifice that made us human but curiosity. How relieved she had been when Victor passed the medical: as she had informed her baffled parents, she could not bear to think of him being safe. It was not bullets or bombs that might kill him but boredom. She would have enlisted herself but there was no front line fighting regiment for women. It was such a waste, after Papa had taught her how to shoot with rifle, pistol and bow. She had even considered disguising herself, like Sweet Polly Oliver in the old ballad who had pulled on a pair of trousers and marched off to join her lover at the wars. It would have been nice to be lying in the mud with Victor: she would not trust him with a gun though, for he was sure to start shooting in quite the wrong direction.

Turning on her heel, she passed straight between her startled pursuers and made off briskly back down the High Street. She would lose them the way she always did; men would never follow you into Madame Cathcart's. Sanctuary: the dress shop was for her what Notre Dame had been for Victor Hugo's gypsy dancer. With a smile and an explanatory jerk of her head she walked past the ladies at the counter and went out of the back door. If you knew your way around the maze of ginnels and cut-throughs you eventually emerged half a mile away.

The alleys were as filthy and rat-infested as ever. At least the privy middens had gone, although it seemed that the smell might linger for all eternity. But then, as Victor always said, there were worse things than shit. A gate that had always been open was now padlocked and she heard something tear as she vaulted over it. She imagined the baby chuckling at the situation: it was never too early to be warned about men and their ways. How long would those two benighted souls linger outside Cathcart's? Almost certainly they would come back tomorrow at the same time: she knew how their minds worked. Perhaps she would put on the same clothes and enter through the back door and leave by the front just to see the looks on their faces. She would have to buy something, though – if only a ribbon or a hat-pin or a pair of those ludicrously frilly white lace gloves.

꧁꧂

"Everything in Aberdeen stank of fish" – Fred was saying – "The hotel even more than the dockside. And wherever we went we were followed by Tupper's gang with a couple of plain-clothes policemen and a journalist from *John Bull*. But Mac just laughed at it all: he was speaking German just to annoy them – not proper German but made-up guttural noises."

"*John Bull* printed his birth certificate last week," said Councillor Hayhurst. "On the front page, so that the whole country would know about his bastardy." He cracked his knuckles. "I'd like five minutes alone with that Horatio Bottomley."

"They misunderstand his position," Fred continued. "I don't think he's anti-war at all but after they accused him he embraced it out of sheer cussedness. Well, on the second morning we were sitting at breakfast enjoying our fish porridge and fish tea and Mac was reading and chuckling – you wouldn't have thought that a book called *Heart of Darkness* would be so funny – but his eyes kept straying towards the outline of the Grampians. Then he stood up, wrapped some fish toast in his napkin and threw it and the book into his haversack. 'See you later, Comrade', he said and trotted out of the hotel. The pickets, the policemen and the reporter went after him, leaving just one poor lad, who looked a bit simple, to keep an eye on me.

"The sun came out but then at midday the wind got up and by three it was blowing a gale – sheets of horizontal rain went past the window, first one way then the other. My guard limped off home. At seven, just after they sounded the dinner gong, I heard a terrible bellowing noise. It was Mac, eyes blazing, soaked to the skin, steam rolling off his clothes: with all the pomade washed out, his hair hung right down over his face. He was chanting:

> "'Up and down, up and down
> I will lead them up and down
> I am feared in field and town,
> Goblin, lead them up and down'.

"– It's Shakespeare, I think."

"Puck, in *A Midsummer Night's Dream*," said Hayhurst. "I was in it once on a WEA Summer Course. At Ruskin Hall they still talk of my Bottom. MacDonald was there too but he wasn't Puck – he was Oberon, of course."

"He told me how he'd dragged them over fences and ditches, through marshes and bogs. 'Give 'em their due, they didn't give up. And the dumbkopf peelers never once took off their bowler hats.' Finally he had double-timed it up to the top of Morven and sat there waiting for them. Seeing the clouds coming in he had run along the ridge and, as the summit disappeared in mist, had slid down the scree on the other side, leaving his pursuers crag-fast. Then he had jog-trotted the twelve miles back, pausing only to take in an interesting church and to return a straying lamb to its mother. 'This rain has set in for the week' – I could hear him crunching the bones of his haddock – 'I wonder if they'll ever be seen again. Lord, what fools these mortals be!'"

"He's always had an air about him, right enough," said Hayhurst, "But it's true what Snowden says – he's too full of himself to be of any real use. If only everything in life was as simple as hiking up a hill." He spoke these last words slowly, dropping and adding aitches – "'iking hup ha 'ill" – with eye-rolling relish.

Hayhurst smelt of peppermint and tobacco but this was said to conceal a perpetual whiskey reek. Emily had never seen the least sign of inebriation in him but she had heard of folk who needed drink to maintain an appearance of sobriety. His face looked as if it might be sticky to the touch. When he was on the point of losing his temper the blood would rush to his cheeks and eye sockets so that he appeared to have donned a scarlet mask. He smoked Kendal Black Twist, the strongest tobacco in the world: how men loved to make such boasts! His short red tie had a tight and tiny knot: the ends were frayed as if, like a bull, he had snapped his tether. Emily was fascinated by his hands, still stained with red and blue dyes: folk said that he had administered so many beatings that the blood would never come off.

"Eh Missis," he said in a wheedling tone, "You wouldn't have a little drop of ale, would you?"

It had become a running joke between them. "This is not a temperance house" – Emily would tell him – "It's just that none of us are ever thirsty." Hayhurst groaned as she poured him another cup of tea.

She always dreaded moments when attention might be drawn to her hands, which were usually concealed beneath sleeves four inches too long. Crude, spatulate, studded with carbuncle and bone, they were more like paws or even fins. People thought they were the result of years of brutal toil but in fact she had never gone into the mill. Her father had been a successful dealer in shoddy and she had not left home until, at eighteen, she married Fred. She had never become reconciled to these hands: after all, they were the only parts of your own body that you were really aware of. How different her feet were! If only they had allowed her to tackle the piano with those long sensitive toes! She was certain that she was walking around with somebody else's hands. One night a witch had sneaked into the nursery and snipped them off then added insult to injury by stitching on these grotesque replacements. They still itched, especially in cold weather, and she could tell that they were as eager to be gone as she was to be rid of them. If only they could saw each other off! She would watch the beautiful ladies floating down Leeds Headrow, dreaming that one day there would be a shock of recognition and the respective hands would rip themselves free to wriggle across the pavement and be reunited with their rightful owners. Emily particularly coveted Ethel Snowden's, so delicate and tiny, ivory and mother-of-pearl, which seemed only just able to raise a tea-cup to those tremulous lips.

"The neighbours have just killed the children's tortoise." Fred had not enquired as to the exact circumstances of the death and she was not going to tell him.

Hayhurst ground his teeth. "Did you know that the Chinese used tortoises to tell the future? Poor old Nunc: those daft beggars probably thought he knew something they didn't – which isn't difficult because they don't even know they're born."

"The People are frightened and unhappy," Fred declined the proffered tobacco pouch. "They know in their hearts that the causes of the war have nothing to do with their own lives. They are merely called upon to do the fighting and dying. And they are only angry with me because I keep reminding them of this: if they didn't know I was right they wouldn't hate me – they would pity me and try to talk me round."

"I don't pity you," said Hayhurst, "But I am trying to talk you round. Who knows what may come from this war? Suppose the Tsar is only the first to fall? Didn't Marx say that force is the midwife of progress – or was it that progress is the midwife of force?" He flashed a couple of wicked-looking punches past Fred's nose. "I know you don't like it but there's good force as well as bad. It's fists not pacifists that will change this wicked world." He had picked up from the mantelpiece that little golden key that did not fit any lock and kept tossing it from one hand to the other.

Fred lit his pipe. "If only everything in life could be as simple as hitting people." With a mouthful of smoke he extinguished the taper.

Emily had to smile at the contrast between the two men. Although they were sitting in similar positions – legs crossed, one hand supporting the chin while the other wafted their words across the room – the effect was very different. Hayhurst was twice as bulky but his head was smaller and perfectly round. His neck kept jerking as if head-butting unseen adversaries: the shoulders rolled and the feet stamped – first the left then the right then both together. Fred did not move. It was obvious which was the stronger: only weak men needed to exert physical domination over others.

"I am not a pacifist," said Fred, "I am not hypothetically opposed to wars, only to this one."

"Eye-po-the-tickle! There are no hypothetical wars. No hypothetical guns firing hypothetical bullets. As far as I know Hypothetica hasn't even got an army. It's us – Great Britain – that's at war – you me and everybody else. That Kaiser's a bad lot, so let's get it over with and then, fully-armed and kitted out, move on to our real enemies – the Tories, the Liberals and the bosses. But even when we've had our revolution – no matter how socialistic things may get – we'll still be British or at least I bloody well hope so. You're right that our lads aren't fighting for the King or the flag but it's not all for nothing but for them to be able to decide their own future."

"Those who do come back and are still in one piece," said Fred.

"Many won't be coming back," agreed Hayhurst, "But those that do will have had their eyes well and truly opened. They'll be battle-hardened and properly fit, all ready to make a new world. And don't forget that we'll be able to call on an international proletarian army – The Red Army!" – His voice rose to a surprisingly reedy tenor – "England arise! The long, long night is o'er! Faint in the East behold the dawn appear!"

There was certainly something compelling about him. Emily's head had swivelled to follow the pointing finger and she had almost glimpsed an answering flash of scarlet in the sky. But surely the East was in the opposite direction, out beyond Bierley? Nevertheless, she felt, as always, a little breathless when he was around. In addition to the drinking he was said to be an indefatigable Don Juan, although no names were ever mentioned.

Whatever would it be like to be loved by such a man? She imagined him as an eagle, mercilessly descending on its prey. Although it was evident that many women might find this an alluring prospect Emily had a strong suspicion that when all the screaming and clawing was over, he might burst into tears or go into a sulk, like an overtired small boy. But all this was the purest speculation, for she had never known any man other than Fred.

She recalled how assiduously he had helped her through her pregnancies: to her surprise he had not been in the least squeamish and by the third had known as much as any midwife. His lovemaking had always been slow, gentle and considerate: whenever he got on top of her she was reminded of Nunquam patiently scaling his favourite hassock. She ran her fingers over the yellowing wallpaper. When she and Fred had decorated their parlour they had taken the repeated indented motif to be of fruit and flowers but now it called to mind dozens of candlesticks held aloft by skeletal arms. How they had enjoyed doing that work together! For the first and only time her hands had felt as if they really belonged to her. That wicked witch had obviously left her with a house painter's pair.

The Town Hall clock struck one. Hayhurst sighed, replaced the key on the mantelpiece and got to his feet. Emily feared for the ceiling: he seemed to have grown in the last few hours. "Chapel," he said, putting his hands together as if in prayer. Now she saw that a crowd had gathered by the front gate. News of Fred's return had evidently spread. They appeared to be remonstrating with Hayhurst's bike and then listening, heads judiciously cocked, as if the machine might be posing a strong counter-argument. "Bloody 'ell," Hayhurst put on his cycle clips, "Opposing this war is even more dangerous than fighting it. If you want a good scrap just call yourself a pacifist." Emily saw that the face had donned its scarlet mask.

"Boche swine!," someone shouted as Fred opened the front door but the jeering tailed off when they saw Hayhurst descending the steps. He stamped, as if crushing hard-shelled insects, then effortlessly vaulted the splintered gate.

"Listen 'ere," he said in a pleasant voice, "If it wasn't for Fred Jowett you'd all still be crawling around in your own filth like the pigs you are" – he sniffed loudly – "I always think there's something 'Unnish about pork."

A pale-eyed man in the front rank took a step forward and spat. He had aimed to miss but Hayhurst interposed his boot, so that a pearl of phlegm slid along the well-polished toe-cap.

"You're lucky that Comrade Jowett is a decent and forgiving man," Hayhurst continued, "But I am not, so I'm afraid I'm going to have to hit someone." Jumping sideways he struck the man in the face: it began as a punch but then the fingers fanned out into a slap that sent him reeling backwards, flattening Mrs Guthrie, an elderly woman who had been brandishing a large bible.

"I suppose you hit cripples an' all," said a ragged fellow with a badly deformed leg.

"No," said Hayhurst, "I kick away their crutches." This he did so expertly, with a sweet swing of the spat-on boot, that the padded wooden crutch sailed over the heads of the crowd. The other foot poked gently but firmly into the ribs of the fallen man.

"He's a war hero," a voice shrilled, but everybody knew what had really happened. Milky, as he was known, had been run over one Sunday morning – as he lay dead drunk in the gutter – by the corporation dairy cart. This had been one of Fred's earliest municipal reforms: Milky seemed to hold him personally responsible. He had kept his pride however: he drank away his compensation money in a single weekend and subsequently refused to accept his free weekly crate. He seemed to be managing well enough, however, for even without the crutch, he scrambled up and took to his heels.

"And I hit ladies an' all," Hayhurst said, "Although I always take my cap off first." As the rest of the crowd followed Milky's example, he sprang onto his saddle and, blowing the Jowetts an extravagant farewell kiss, set off in pursuit. They could hear him shouting all the way down Laisterdyke Lane.

⁂

"There has been nothing more magnificent in our history than the way our young manhood, in response to a moving impulse, rose as one at the beginning of the war."

How was it, Ethel wondered, that words which had seemed so magically apposite could fall flat a few hours later? Many of this morning's audience had also crossed the river from Wandsworth to Holborn but they were not in search of novelty: familiarity was the whole point. Philip's ringing phrases had obviously needed a sobbing man with a placard to make their full impact. She recalled how that horrible Grayson boy had planted his own hecklers so that his so-called ripostes could be well rehearsed. When she had congratulated Philip he had said that he had anticipated such an interruption: it was as if he could not admit to having surprised himself.

She had reluctantly rejoined the platform party: apparently her morning absence had given offence. Now hundreds of eyes were upon her: it felt as if tiny insects were crawling over her body. Surely that fat man on the third row couldn't be winking at her? Her face was burning: although Philip reassured her that her skin was invariably marmoreally cool to the touch, she sometimes feared that she was on the point of spontaneous combustion. You became accustomed to such apparent contradictions when you served the powers of Love. She must look horribly incongruous wedged in between the Glasiers, their bony elbows almost digging into her ribs. She fixed her eyes longingly on the exit: perhaps if she wished hard enough she could free her astral body and go floating out of the hall to plunge herself into the sunlight of Red Lion Square? She had long ceased to dream of Lancelot or Galahad but perhaps someone might still burst through the doors to save her? She had to admit that - even though she knew that he was attending a war conference in Paris - her eyes and heart were expecting Lloyd George to appear at any moment. Absurd - for she knew that he would not be watching the doors at the Hotel Crillon, that his mind would be focussed on Clemenceau and Foch, that for him she had ceased to exist. He would not be giving her the least thought until the allotted time came but then he would give her his full attention.

Ethel . . . how marvellous the silly name had sounded in that Welsh lilt. Better suited to a parlour maid in some dismal farce, it had blighted her youth until she realized that it must be a diminutive of Ethereal. And her maiden name had been even worse: Annakin - as if she was some incendiarist disciple of Prince Kropotkin! But now everything was as it should be: SNOWDEN! O, the perfect elevation of being named after a mountain! It was both threatening and reassuring at the same time: everyone else was freezing in a blizzard but she and Philip were nice and snug in their own little igloo. And it had two syllables - SNOW-DEN - as every good name should and it had two N's - her favourite letter - and she had lost that horrid K that used to stick like a fishbone in her throat.

Now the exit door was slowly swinging open and her whole body tensed but it wasn't L-G but - of all people - Ramsay MacDonald. Wasn't he supposed to be in Russia? His feet made no sound as he loped, like a scraggy wolf, down the aisle. From the knees down his trousers were caked with a greyish mud: whatever could he have been doing? The audience began clapping - even those at the front who could not yet have seen him - but Philip's voice effortlessly rose above it. MacDonald did not ascend the platform but instead slid into the usher's seat on the very first row.

There he sprawled, chin back, hands clasped behind his head. His long legs, wide apart and at full extension, tightened his trousers over the crotch. It was as if he was vaunting his own potency and health. The eyes met hers: they were empty, without the least spark of life, let alone Love. He was considered handsome but there was something repulsive about him. How could a grey-haired man's moustache have remained so black? He was evil - but only in the sense of utter negation: he wasn't human enough even to be bad. Evil and error were illusive products of our fictitious material existence. Most people were nothing more than phantoms, generated by the dreams or nightmares of others. That was why Grayson had disappeared: everyone had left off imagining him. If only Philip would accept that, if he tried hard enough, there was a very good chance that MacDonald would be wished away.

LOVE: she could not stop saying it. First the L, tongue flicking deliciously against the palate; then the mighty O, which she would draw out until her head began to swim; then the V, her teeth meeting with a click only to be forced apart by a final grunt - UH - like when you hit a shuttlecock with a little extra vim. She was sure that no-one had taught her the word: she had always known it.

"Love divine all loves excelling" - what a shock it had been to hear that being sung in a church! Before she could speak she had been aware of the currents of Love, ebbing and flowing in the darkness of the nursery. And she could hear them too, a wonderful music that made Gounod or Mendelssohn sound like mice squeaking and scratching in the wainscot.

It was amusing to see men snigger or flinch or blush at the word, as if it was a blasphemy too terrible or too delicious to be spoken. They confused Love with sex, poor things, just as they thought that beauty and good looks were the same. Surely no-one could miss the way most faces fell apart when they exhibited the least emotion?

Her husband's face, chalk white and fleshless, twitching with the effort of fighting his pain, then flashing into a smile: *that* was real beauty. Her own appearance, as she constantly reminded people, was quite beside the point: she was a hundred times more beautiful on the inside. Nevertheless, they still assumed that she must spend all her time titivating herself when in fact she had never sat for more than ten minutes in front of a mirror. She felt that it would have been vain not to have bothered, for half the women in the movement were trying to give that impression while manipulating the resulting disorder in elaborate, would-be picturesque ways. She was sure that Katharine St. John Conway Glasier was as fussy as any princess. How many hours had she practised that pose – leaning forward with head back to lengthen that already too-long neck, eyes brimming with tears, one delicate white arm half-extended towards the tragic figure of her husband? It was a tableau worthy of Flaxman, although even he would have struggled to represent those coughing fits.

She had referred the Glasiers to her friend, Lady Victoria Murray, the celebrated Christian Science healer. "You must forget all about your ulceration," Lady Vi had told the unfortunate man, "And try to believe that Love is health and think about only happy things – kindness, goodness and so on. And no bad thoughts: if you Love your cancer it will go away." Ethel had her doubts, however: if you Loved your cancer surely it would be even more unwilling to leave you? Love was all-powerful and universal but not un-discriminating. Admittedly, throwing off cancer would be more than a morning's work but Lady Vi should have started by doing something about his posture – got him to stand up straight, with shoulders back, rather than hunched over, as if watching the tumour moving under his clothes. Philip never acknowledged his own pain but sometimes his eyes would bulge and fill with blood and when she took his hand she would see that the fingernails had bitten deep into the palm. Sometimes she wondered whether such agonies were rites of passage for those whom Love loved the most.

She had heard that Lady Vi had got them down on their knees:

another mistake, for real prayer could only be done standing up or - preferably - while in brisk motion. Ethel had never been sure about God: why should Love go to the trouble of growing a long white beard? And it had to be said that Jesus, although doubtless well-intentioned, had been more of a hindrance than a help. The crucifixion, for example, was a serious lapse of taste: it was obvious that - nails and spear notwithstanding - he could not have been in the slightest discomfort. It had been a ridiculous charade, merely confirming the illusions of pain, ignorance and fear. By playing at being human he had merely deterred people from realizing The Divine in themselves.

"The violence of this war has merely uncovered in an inescapable and literal form the violence that was perpetrated during the so-called peace," said Philip. "Millions have fallen on the battlefields but a million millions have lived in needless ignorance and slavery and died before their time. War is capitalism with its smiling mask removed." MacDonald, Ethel noticed, had now crossed his legs. "Madness and cruelty assail us every day: we are never safe - not by our firesides nor in our dreams, nor even strolling on a sunny day in a leafy park."

None of his hearers would have understood this reference. Last month something had happened but they had taken pains to ensure that no word about it appeared in the press.

Ethel had been walking down Albemarle Street on her way to St. James' Park. To find herself with two free hours on a fine afternoon was the rarest of pleasures. Her legs were feeling particularly full of Love but that didn't make her go any faster - if anything, she slowed down to relish every step. There were said to be twenty-six bones in your foot but she was sure that she could feel twenty-eight. The street was deserted except for an elderly gentleman who emerged, twirling his cane from the portals of The Royal Institution. He was in morning dress but bare-headed which, even in the sunlight, seemed odd. The silver hair was en brosse and the suit seemed to shimmer and ripple like water held in suspension. She might almost have taken him for Lloyd George had it not been for his decidedly military air.

As they drew level he beamed and raised his cane in salute but then, with no change in his expression, his elbow bent to swing it hard across her face. By some unaccountable reflex her right arm partially parried the blow but the stick still caught nose and cheek. Although she staggered she did not fall but the man was flat on his back, arms and legs thrashing. It was as if she had attacked him. "I'm awfully sorry," she said, "Are you hurt?" She offered her hand but he rolled into the gutter, crawled on all fours for a few yards, then sprang up and bolted back inside The Royal Institution. He had forgotten his stick: picking it up, she saw that the wood had split below the handle.

She put her fingers to her brow: they came away bloody. More blood was dripping from somewhere on to the pavement but the large scarlet drops fortunately missed her clothes. She was sure that she had heard something snap in her face but she felt no pain, of course. Her vision was going in and out of focus but her legs, quite unaffected, moved serenely on.

Then, without warning, she found herself enveloped by a pinkish mist. She was unsure whether it had risen or descended upon her. Buildings, trees, sky -all were blotted out. She stopped walking, for the pavement had dropped away, but her legs were evidently redundant as she was now floating along. There was a soothing humming or buzzing in the air and a sweet dusty smell as if she had just peeled the tissue paper off a box of Turkish Delight. Her nose tickled but the sneeze would not come. She examined the broken cane: its silver knob had been engraved with Don Quixote charging the windmills. It was a lovely piece of work: you could even pick out Sancho and his donkey looking disapproving in the background. It was the kind of stick that a man would miss.

She could not have said whether she remained in this haze for seconds, minutes or hours, but when she found herself abruptly back in the sunlight again, she realized that she had been borne clear across Piccadilly – presumably passing incorporeally through the traffic – to be deposited outside the entrance to Green Park station. The pavement was packed but no-one seemed to be paying her any more attention than usual. Taking out her pocket mirror she discovered a faint red line across her left cheek but no damage to the nose or mouth. One curious thing: her pupils had dilated to black pinpricks. Then her feet blithely rattled down the stairs and onto the platform where an empty carriage was waiting just for her.

When she got back to Golders Green, the stick was no longer in her possession. She had no recollection of changing at Euston on to the Northern Line. The mark on her face had vanished but now her lips and tongue had swollen up so that when Philip came home she had difficulty making herself understood. He had insisted on calling the police even before the doctor came but when she tried to describe her assailant the only face that came into her head was L-G's. She described him anyway: the PM was sure to have an alibi. Only after the constables had gone did she realize that she had forgotten to mention the Don Quixote stick. Next morning her mouth was quite recovered but a black eye had risen on the wrong side of her face. Philip had insisted that she stay in bed and so it was that, in mid afternoon, she had been there to take L-G's unexpected but long-awaited call. Perhaps it had been delayed concussion but she was sure that through the static on the line he had been asking her to chair a Royal Commission on Love.

Mysterious mechanisms had been set in motion. No matter how much you served Love or how deeply you submerged yourself in it, you could never predict or control it. Despite Mrs Baker Eddy's efforts there was not, as yet, an exact science of Love. How silly Shaw's 'Life Force' was, with all that nonsense about Love being 'nature understanding itself'. Love had nothing to do with understanding and everything to do with feeling. And it felt as if you were swallowing the whole world while being swallowed by it as the same time.

It had to be admitted that there was more Love in Socialism

than Liberalism: it was as if Lloyd George had ingested the entire quota that had been allocated to his unfortunate party. In the main, however, politics seemed incidental to Love. Winston Churchill, for example, had positively vibrated with it when sitting on the Conservative benches but had lost it all after crossing the floor. And she recalled seeing some trade union delegates arriving at a pre-war Labour Conference. How big and vulgar they had been, reeking of beer, clucking and whistling at her as they passed! But as they had ascended the platform their heavy boots had sounded out a thrilling and unmistakable ralletando. Truly, Love's ways were unfathomable!

Love was everywhere but so was negation. Everywhere you looked you could see them fighting. On her arrival in this hall, for example, she had examined her allotted chair. Although its front legs were healthy enough, shiny and full of sap, the back pair was utterly inert. She had no hesitation in demanding a replacement, explaining her reasons in full. At last, Glasier had grudgingly agreed to swap: it was rather a disappointment that so far, despite his spasms, the thing had stubbornly held firm. Furniture was not the worst of it: Many poor souls were actually walking around in bodies that were part-alive and part-dead. Whatever must it feel like? Take Katharine St. John Conway Glasier, for example. Her right hand was accept-able down to the wrist but that arm was utterly lifeless and the left was equally bad, apart perhaps from the elbow. Ethel gave her bust the benefit of the doubt but those feet looked as if they had been cut out of a Rossetti painting and glued on. And those round, cornflower-blue eyes were all wrong, goggling blankly like a doll's.

"I see the children sharing with the old folks in a thousand joys which the loving care of the strong can confer: I see our modern towns swept away and in their place beautiful cities whose buildings reflect the pride of the community in their common life . . ."

Now he had the audience in the palm of his hand: she could see them reacting even before he spoke the words.

"I see a people healthy, happy, cultured, contented, whose wealth is life, full and free, whose ways are ways of pleasantness, whose flowery paths are paths of peace. Is this but a vision or is it a prophecy of a day that shall yet dawn on a world ransomed by love and sacrifice?"

"What is he like?" People - usually women - were always asking her. And then, after she had told them of Philip's courage, humanity and nobility of spirit, and quoted from Henley's 'Invictus', Swinburne's 'Mazzini' and Kipling's 'If', they would merely repeat the question. "No - what is he *like?*" What answers did they want? Some so-called intimate revelations, no doubt, at which they would tut-tut or commiserate. Most people were incapable of understanding even the simplest of things.

The room had darkened and there had been a sharp rattle of rain against the windows but now the sun had returned. Ethel could discern the figure of a man silhouetted behind the exit's frosted glass: a latecomer awaiting a suitable moment to enter unobtrusively - not everyone was as inconsiderate as MacDonald. As she watched, the blurred head cocked first to one side then the other in an unmistakable and characteristic way. The light behind him had taken on that pinkish glow - no longer mist but pale fire, those flames that did not burn, the flames of Universal Love. She knew that it couldn't be but it was, it was, it was! L-G! L-G! L-G!

⁂

So here she was again with dear old Emm and Pee. Although she mostly despised her parents there were times when all the childish love and trust came flooding back and she just had to go home. Such moments, Ruth had to admit, always seemed to coincide with when she was unwell or in worse financial straits than usual. After she had married Victor, Mama had ignored her letters and refused to come to the phone but no sooner had she fallen pregnant than she had heard on the stairs that familiar barking cough. Victor had sworn that he had not contacted the family: mothers evidently had a sixth sense about such things.

"That damned gravel still isn't loud enough." It had been Papa's constant complaint throughout her childhood. He seemed to expect their front drive to crackle and growl even when it lay quite undisturbed. She loved to recall his expression when, after her dancing lessons, he had watched her fluttering silently across it. But now, no matter how much she shuffled and kicked, it would hardly even whisper. Their house in Hall i' th' Wood seemed to become larger, darker and squarer by the year, but Papa was all-too-aware that it was not The Hall and nor was it i' th' Wood. He had always dreamed of buying Sam Crompton's old place, with its mullions, ogees and cusped St. Andrew's crosses, but Lord Lever had gifted it to the Council as a museum. Now any shiftless beggar could walk in for free, without even wiping his feet.

Discontent lay over the house like a thundercloud: she drove Papa wild by calling it Crotchet Castle. The butler had a cleft palate but she was sure that he was called something like Diggory Death's-Head. All the other servants seemed to be indentured mutes: even the stairs no longer squeaked and the tight-hinged doors would never slam again. Ruth constantly hammered away at the piano: the silence splintered but when she ceased it promptly froze over again. Emm and Pee were not speaking: they went stiff whenever they found themselves in the same room, sitting down to dinner as if hinged at the waist.

"There's nothing wrong," said Papa, "We talk right enough when you're not here."

"Whatever do you talk about?"

"About you, of course – where you are and what you might be doing."

She opened the front door and there was her daughter, standing on the threshold. Elaine did not look pleased to see her but nor did she look displeased: that expression never varied. She would not be following her mother on to the stage. She extended a formal hand which Ruth reluctantly shook: she did not take after Victor either. Ruth recalled his reaction to her birth. He had been away on one of his gambling bouts, returning in a foul check suit considerably too small for him. "Aha! It's a baby!" he had proclaimed triumphantly, as if there might be a prize for making the correct guess. But had Elaine ever really been a baby? Even now, was she a child at all? It was as if she had been sent as a living reproach to her parents' fecklessness, like Father Time in *Jude the Obscure* who kills his sisters and himself 'because we are too menny' – Elaine, though, could already spell better than that.

Motherhood was a role for which Ruth had been miscast. Whenever her daughter materialized she had to search her memory to recall just who this might be. This time she wanted a child that really *was* a child. Shouldn't infancy be angelic or demonic, a higher form of being? If it could live its childhood intensely enough perhaps she might even join it there? Asked whether she wanted a boy or a girl she would always reply 'Neither' which people chose to hear as 'either' – but what she really meant was 'both'. She felt as if no-one had given birth for a couple of thousand years.

The afternoon post was laid out on a silver salver. Ruth recognized the florid hand of Mrs Panton Ham. Now that Victor was in the trenches, his old amours seemed to have formed a committee to ensure her well-being. Panty was always sending food parcels: not, as yet, a flitch of bacon but homemade jams and pickles with a distinctly alcoholic kick. Underneath her ominously bulky envelope was a field postcard from somewhere in Europe.

I am quite well. ✗

I have been admitted into hospital
 { *sick* } *and am going on well.*
 { *wounded* } *and hope to be discharged soon.*

Signature only } Albert Victor Grayson

Date 27 June 1917

WtW85—P.P.948   8000m.   5-18.   C. & Co. Grange Mills, 8. W.

If they were fighting a war how did they find time to write or even to tick a box? There could at least have been splashes of mud or blood, a bullet hole or a burn.

"Look, it's from Daddy." Elaine winced and put a finger to her lips: she had taken to the moribund atmosphere like a duck to water. Clutching the card in both hands she held it up to the transom's light, turning it round and round before handing it back. She really was an odd little creature!

The card was of the cheapest paper: the print had already blurred. "I am quite well" was surely inappropriate. Other options were needed:

> I love you
> I am afraid
> I have caught the clap
> I am dead
> I am in Heaven/Hell

She wondered why he had signed his full name. Perhaps it was in protest over the censorship of his previous letters? She had discovered that other servicemen were not so closely monitored. Why ever had they let him join up if they were not going to trust him? Who did they think he was spying for? He had been provoking them, of course: "How I miss your (█████████████)" – well, presumably that wasn't "conversation". And "There's plenty of (█████████████) in the camp but (█████████████) is hard to find" might not refer to butter and margarine. Sometimes the words dotted about the page had formed themselves into a sort of poetry:

"You can't (█████████████████) fall asleep
(█████████████████████) when you're (███████████)
Singing (███████████████████████████████████)."
She wondered whether he might not be blacking out his own letters for dramatic effect.

"I'm feeling on top of the (███████████)": surely that could only have been 'world'? The Army were obviously concerned lest the Hun discover what planet they were on. Anything of a military, political or personal nature had been excised which left precious little to write about. Even the weather was off-limits: it might be possible to fix a regiment's position by references to sunshine or rain. The censors allowed neither abuse of the Germans nor sympathy for them: in fact, they didn't want them mentioned at all. The identity of the enemy was apparently a closely-guarded secret. What was there to hide? Everyone knew that the lines in Flanders had been static for the last two years but soldiers on leave - like the Alderton boys across the road - remained tight-lipped about the whole show.

"Most of your recent letters have been blocked out," she had written. "Best stick to exhorting me to keep the home fires burning or to wipe the tear, baby dear, from your eye-eee"; perhaps she had been censored in her turn? Victor's last letter had been completely black - like page 73 of *Tristram Shandy* after the death of Parson Yorick.

Elaine accompanied her across the hall but then turned and went upstairs. Ruth had to admit that her stumpy walk was all too reminiscent of Winston Churchill's. No-one else emerged: Emm would be in bed with one of her headaches, while Pee was out at the golf club, playing the nineteenth hole.

Ruth's piano almost filled the smaller sitting-room. She was always relieved to find it still there as if, like Dizzy the cat, it was an essentially wild animal that, for some reason, kept choosing to stay with them. Emm and Pee had been shocked when she had first picked out the wedding march from *Lohengrin*: they had not bought it to be played but as an ornament or symbol. When she was at her exercises a crowd would gather outside: they did not look like music-lovers, more as if they were thinking of burning down the house. She would breathe on the polished wood and then watch the vapour disappear before fishing out the tiny key that always hung between her breasts and unlocking and then - ever so slowly - lifting the lid. She was not a good pianist but she was determined to be able to play a few difficult pieces – even though she knew that when she managed to reproduce The Lugubrious Gondola with the notes all present and correct, it would still be – in any way that really mattered – all wrong.

Apparently Liszt had been inspired by the black-draped gondolas in Venice, bearing the dead down The Rialto. Only later had he realized that it had been a presentiment of his son-in-law Wagner's death. What Papa called 'morbid music' always cheered her up: if she wanted to be depressed she would play 'Boiled Beef And Carrots' or 'God Save The King'. Besides, when she closed her eyes, she did not visualize coffins but a large wooden cradle, rocking to and fro.

She could feel that the baby was enjoying the vibrations. For the last six months she had been aware of it watching and listening, in full knowledge of everything she said or did or even thought. 'The history of man for the nine months preceding his birth would be far more interesting and contain events of greater moment than any three-score and ten years that follow it': she had written these words in her commonplace book but could not recall who had said them. It was usually Goethe. She imagined the child not as some sloppy embryo, smugly curled in on itself, but already muscular and tough, like the ignudi of Michelangelo that Victor had smirked at in The Sistine Chapel. He himself had claimed to remember being in the womb: it was tedious, he said – like being stuck on a long railway journey with Fred Jowett, without a book, a bottle or a deck of cards. Nevertheless, she was sure that she was carrying no ordinary child. It was as if all the things that he had spouted on about – Peace, Liberty, Justice, Freedom – had ceased to be cloudy abstractions and were taking on physical form. There they were in her womb, readying themselves. If Victor was to be killed, she thought, it would be at the very moment that her waters broke: perhaps while he was breathing his last she would be giving birth to him once more.

There was a terrible rattling and rumbling: the piano shook as if coming apart under her hands. She had often wondered what Liszt's celebrated rubato might have sounded like. The 'Gondola' was a curious piece: its meaning lay in the physical sensation of playing it – she understood it through the pains in her wrists, the tightness of her shoulders, the knotting of her hamstrings. When the child was born, she was sure, it would be frowning while its tiny fingers formed an F minor chord.

It had, she suspected, been conceived that night in Dunedin when they had ended up in bed with a drunken, tubby but enthusiastic bar-maid. Victor had extinguished the lights – which was unusual because he liked to see what he was doing. The ensuing darkness had been particularly dark: the room had seemed to be full of other silent presences. She was sure that, at one point, a cock that was not Victor's had been inside her. Perhaps the bar-maid had been the real father? Her genitals had been regulation female but her cheeks had been curiously stubbled and could that have been an adam's apple bobbing away among all those chins?

It was curious how seldom they had encountered a man willing to go with both of them. Victor's boyfriends, of course, all retched at the very thought but why did the so-called hets have no curiosity? Had they never wondered what it was like to suck a cock? They seemed to define themselves by what they would not do rather than what they did, like the ever-narrowing sects of already narrow religions.

Most men changed when you got them into the bedroom – and usually for the worse. Their bodies could not lie and flatter like their tongues. Only Victor had not been a disappointment: he had changed, all right, but kept on changing, minute by minute. He had thousands of selves, but they were all Victor. He was usually an athletic and imaginative lover but sometimes he was shy and fumbling as if he had never been with a woman before. Perhaps a number of his selves were yet to lose their virginity? But he was always beautiful, his every movement suffused with a sort of humorous grace. He was even elegant when drunk: he did not usually care to dance but in his cups he would grasp her waist and at dizzying speed whirl her around the room. Staggering, vomiting and collapsing were enacted with economy and style, like some music hall novelty act. And he never hurt himself: she had seen him pitch down steep flights of stairs to land sickeningly on his head, only to spring up and stroll away without a hair out of place.

When they were alone, he loved to watch her brushing her hair with a hard-bristled silver-backed brush. He would position her naked on a chair with her other hand holding a cracked oval hand-mirror which she would slowly tilt until their eyes met in the glass. And then, watching each other, they would talk of apparently trivial things. Victor practised his impersonations - they had a growing tendency to run into each other - while she worried that her hair - long but unusually fine - might be beginning to fall out. He never blinked and her own eyelids would ache with the effort of keeping them open. Perhaps soon she might be left to face the world alone, pop-eyed and bald? Then his voice trailed off and his reflection disappeared: after a few seconds she would hear a tuneless whistling in her left ear, his warm breath seeming to pass through her head and out the other side. Then his open hands would move just above her breasts and throat, the displaced air fanning her sensitive skin. It felt as if he was all over her but they would not actually touch each other for another twenty minutes.

As a little girl she had spent hours with her legs apart, exploring with her fingers, straining her neck in vain attempts to see fully inside herself. But she had never paid any attention to her arse, apart from wiping it at appropriate times, until that first night with Victor. Now it was no longer merely a place of evacuation but a portal for new energies that coursed through her body. It seemed to fix her to the world, like the nail in the centre of a Catherine wheel. Edgar had accused her of thinking that the sun shone out of it: now she wondered whether that might not be literally true. The way most women of her acquaintance behaved, it appeared that she was the only one with any orifices at all. Victor said that during boring meetings he would amuse himself by imagining the platform party tearing each other's clothes off and slotting into some labyrinthine mass-orgy but she just couldn't manage it. Those Snowdens, for example: what on earth might they be doing?

Even above her playing she heard a faint sound from the hallway: not even Mama had been able to find a silent letter-box. Her legs almost gave way, as if she had been sitting there for days, but she still reached the wire cage before the elderly parlour maid. The last note was still hanging in the air as she stared in bewilderment at another half-dozen field postcards. They were identical to the last one: even the date was the same. Why had Victor, five days ago, felt the need to tell her, over and over again, that he was 'quite well'? Was he trying to convey that there was, on the contrary, something desperately wrong? And if so, what did he expect her, far away in Bolton, to do about it? She sniffed at the topmost card, then rubbed it over her lips. It felt cold and dry: although the edges were blunt, the surface was curiously roughened. Holding it up to the light she saw that it was dotted with tiny perforations. The others were the same, except that their patterns were different: could it be a code, some form of Braille? Each hole was underneath an individual letter. "H-O-P-E-T-O-D," it read. "HOPETOD"? Then it continued: "I-S-C-H-A". The whole of "DISCHARGED" had been pricked, except for its final 'D'. She read on to the end. "HOPE TO DISCHARGE IN YOU AT FIRST OPPORTUNITY".

She picked up the next:

"IN WIPERS SAFE AND WARM HOPE BOLTON'S NOT TOO LOUSY".

Oh you naughty, naughty nought-nought-one! Once you knew it the trick seemed fairly obvious but perhaps the volume of such cards precluded proper examination?

"WAR IS THE CURE I HAVE BEEN SICK AND NOW I AM BEING TRANSFORMED"

Victor had obviously appreciated the Liszt story. He wasn't musical but in his publicity photographs he was often seated at a grand piano or – even though he hated nature even more than she did – gardening in a fetching straw hat.

"NOTHING TO DO NO QUIM NO DREAM NO WANKS I AM IN THE BETTER PLACE NOT ETON".

That went without saying, of course: in New York, Heaton, Ypres – the best place on earth would always be wherever nought-nought-one happened to be.

Returning to the sitting room she picked up this morning's card.

"THOU HAST DOVE'S EYES".

That was from *The Song of Solomon*. Victor's biblical citations had served him well in the Labour movement: a truly bad man, they reasoned, would not be quoting from The Good Book.

She would have to reply in kind. She took up 'With Love to My Dear Boy' but its trite verses were not conducive. 'WIP MY ARSE' and 'COME INCIDE ME' were the best she could do. What she really wanted to say was 'Thy teeth are like a flock of sheep' – her favourite line in the 'Song' – but the letters were not there. What could you do without a 'k'? You couldn't have cock and you couldn't have fuck. You couldn't have spunk or spank or prick. No licking or kissing. No stockings or knickers or even socks. No Bakunin or Karl Marx. No Shakespeare or Keats. No walking, no talking. No Katharine St. John Conway Glasier, no Ethel Annekin Snowden. No killicks or kerseymeres or spondulicks. Everything she liked had a 'k' in it.

Fresh ammunition was needed. With three great springs she plucked down from the bookshelves *Hymns Ancient And Modern*, *The Collected Poems* of Mrs Hemans and – from the very highest – Papa's well-thumbed *Satyricon*.

※

Darkness was falling but the Jowetts had not yet turned on the lights. It was curious how your vision adjusted: Fred's face and hands were giving off a silvery phosphorescence. Emily's eyes opened wider and wider until they seemed to fill her whole face: she knew that if she so much as blinked then everything would be blotted out. They sat in silence. For the first time in two years there were no shutters on the windows: there was no longer any need. An hour after Hayhurst had left, a queue had formed outside but these were not people with the usual problems – they had come to apologize. Very few, however, could bring themselves to direct utterance: they hemmed and hawed, asked questions to which they already knew the answers, then shook Fred's hand and almost bowed themselves out. Mrs Guthrie had appeared: instead of her Bible she was holding up a large cake as if it was the crown for some royal coronation. After she had presented it with a deep curtsey they had difficulty restoring her to the vertical. A cake! With the scarcity of eggs that really meant something. Still hot from the oven, it was studded with angelica and cherries. Emily's eyes met Fred's: both knew that they would not be eating it.

In mid-afternoon there had sounded a series of crashes, as if the front door was being kicked down. A cairn of letters was blocking the hall. Many had been franked last year and clumsily resealed. Some were addressed to other local pacifists, with a whole bundle for Willie Leach in Manningham. Later Milky had called to reclaim his crutch. Emily had re-sewn its arm-rest: although he complained that she had used the wrong colour thread his heart wasn't in it. "Our Tibby's just had kits," he grumbled, "Three lovely calicos and a grey and white tom. Little Emily and Ethel can have first pick."

When she had gone down to the shops everyone had been smiling and waving. Such hectic gaiety made her wonder if the war might have ended. She was ushered to the counter where, with the broadest wink, the butcher threw in an extra twist of meat. And she had almost vomited for it had reminded her of what had been left of Nunc.

Now the aroma of the world's strongest tobacco had finally dispersed, leaving a faint tang not of whiskey or peppermint but, unmistakably, of human ordure. Fred's tilted nose continued its sniffing. Emily recalled that Hayhurst's father and grandfather were said to have been night-soil men. When he had assumed his council seat, the Tories had congratulated him on having crawled out from his privy middens.

"Why, so I did," Hayhurst had replied, "And so did you. And yet we're all still knee-deep in shit: that's politics, that's life. The world is a dunghill, haven't you realized that yet?"

Emily found the silence unsettling: it was as if there had previously been a ceaseless sussuration of plotting and gossip. She almost missed that sense of persecution. If only a big jolly brick would come bowling through the window! Evidently it was true that you could get used to anything – that even torture, regularly applied, became nice and comfy after a while. According to Morel, warders had to physically drag long-time prisoners out of jail when their sentences were up.

Now, if anything, the room seemed to be getting lighter. She had not noticed the gradual yellowing of the walls or how black the nicotine halo above Fred's chair had become. Every time he visited, their son, Fred Junior, offered to repaper it for them but she did not want things to change. "That should see us out," Fred said when they had finished doing it, all those years ago. She remembered that although there had been a heat wave, they had been unable to open the windows because all the sash cords had been painted over. After they had mixed the whiting, size and water and distempered the ceiling, the glass panes were thick with condensation and the fumes from the glue were choking them. They had shut the curtains and, virtually naked, completed their work. Then, sticky with sweat and paste, they had fallen on each other with unaccustomed passion. The bare floorboards had cruelly abraded her elbows and knees. Afterwards, she had gently touched his face: even her hands suddenly appeared beautiful. Then they must have dozed off because they had only just managed to unglue themselves and find their clothes before the children returned from school. "Job's a good 'un, Dad," Fred Junior had said, admiringly.

"What disturbs me," Fred was saying, "Is that it was all such an act. Hayhurst wasn't the least bit angry when he hit those people. He didn't even take his pipe out of his mouth. He was just demonstrating the power of the fist. Mind you, I think what really scares people are those flying aitches of his."

Emily was not so sure. She had a curious notion that The People had somehow willed Hayhurst to do it, that the man had just taken his cue. They knew that they had gone too far: it was as if they were standing, too afraid to move, on the edge of a crumbling cliff and had needed someone to do something that would jerk them back to safety once again.

Fred slowly raised his fist until it was pressing under his chin. "*This* is all they understand, all they really respect. Liberty, equality, fraternity – all fall to the ground like empty gloves without *this* inside them."

The fist looked ridiculous. If you had drawn on it a couple of narrowed eyes, a letterbox mouth and two further dots for nostrils, it would have been Hayhurst to the life. Emily must have blinked because everything suddenly went as black as pitch. Even the gaslight on the corner had apparently guttered out.

They sat once again in silence. She knew that Fred was crying over all the cruelty and injustice in this world. And she was crying too, because – even in the darkness – her hands were looking so very, very vile.

CHAPTER NINE

OOZOLEM FOOZLEM (1920)

A NAKED MAN was standing at the open window of a pent-house flat, watching the crowds on Bury Street below. This morning it had seemed as if the whole world had flooded down to St. James and now there they were, flooding back again. It was curious how since he had moved in he had never once seen anyone look up. His lights were always on and his curtains left undrawn. If only they knew what they were missing! He jutted his hips controposto and set his cock and balls swinging like a pendulum, then turning back inside, examined his reflection in the half-length mirror.

While he had slept the shrapnel in his right hip had shifted its alignment and that raw red patch like a target pinned over his heart was itching and weeping again. He clawed his fingers through his pomaded hair, transforming it to a crown of sticky quills, then clenched his face into a silent scream before slackening it and letting his tongue loll like a hanged man's. Then he watched as everything fell perfectly back into place again. There it was: the roguish yet solemn mask of Victor Grayson, perennial charmer. Dear, dear ladies! Sometimes he almost regretted that he had not been wounded in the face. Thank God that his gentlemen friends' attention was usually focussed lower down. "First, my dear, I look at the feet," Arthur Rose used to say. "And then decide whether to venture further up."

Victor began to examine his more recent injuries. The bruising on the chest and ribs had formed itself into the colours of the rainbow while a storm cloud appeared about to burst over his lower abdomen. Being beaten up by strangers – unexpectedly, briskly and efficiently – had been a new experience. Up until now he had only exchanged a few slaps and punches with friends. His shadow assailants had obviously known their trade, inflicting the maximum pain but with no lasting damage. They had favoured the kidneys: it had been a relief when he had stopped pissing blood. A black eye rather suited him: perhaps he should fetch out Ruth's old greasepaint and touch up the other one?

Georgian House was a very discreet establishment. Sometimes there were footsteps on the stairs but he had never seen any of the other tenants, even though there were fourteen doorbells in the hall. They obviously kept different hours to his. Leaning forward, he let the tip of his nose touch the glass to leave a blue smear: all flesh is grease, not grass. He knew that when he returned from the pleasures of his night the mark would have been removed and there would be fresh sheets on the bed and all the ashtrays would have been emptied and cleaned. Last week he had returned within half an hour with a new friend, only to find the work already done. When he questioned Mrs Porter, the manageress, about this nocturnal phenomenon she had merely smiled her Gioconda smile. Perhaps for five guineas a week one should expect no less? He had always liked fine living but now for him to feel really comfortable it would have been necessary to have put a few shells through the wall and fill the place with mud. If he turned his rooms into a trench would they lower the rent or raise it?

When he had got back from the war everything had seemed all wrong. Out in the mud he had never felt cleaner, surrounded by death he had never felt so safe. However much he might lather and scrub in his marble and porcelain bathroom he could never get his skin the way it had been in Passchendaele. Although they hadn't had a bath in weeks the soldiers' flesh had been as smooth as silk, with a glorious rippling shine. Profuse sweating had flushed out every pore but although their unchanged clothes would stiffen like cardboard the only odour was a pleasant one, the faintest tang of brine. Victor often though that although they were fully thirty miles inland he could hear the waves of the North Sea rolling in and out, but it was merely half a million men breathing together. More delicate noses than his would have been revolted by the battlefield stench but to him putrefaction and shit were the essential human smells, gentle reminders of our own mortality. And when the brigade was busy clearing itself of lice and fleas the singeing chest and pubic hair reminded him of old Snowy's wonderful Egyptian cigarettes. The only smell that had ever distressed him had been the perfume worn by the Countess of Warwick and her driver at the Colne Valley by-election: it had scorched the back of his throat but it had seemed ungrateful to mention it to them at the time.

"War is the cure": Ruth had said in one of her letters and she was right, as she had been right about so many things. Thank God he had been with the DINKS - The New Zealand Rifle Brigade - and not with any of the British regiments. As they had stamped raggedly but enthusiastically along the roads of Belgium it had been hard to tell the difference between officers and men. They had adopted as their anthem the chorus from *Il Trovatore* but with new words:

> "Oh my what bloody big chunks of beef!
> Oh my what bloody big chunks of beef!
> Oh my what bloody big chunks of beef!
> Bloody big chunks!
> Bloody big chunks!
> Bloody big chunks of beef!"

The longer and louder they sang it the funnier it became.

It was rumoured that Bill Hughes, Prime Minister of Australia, had warned General Haig that if he ordered even one ANZAC soldier to be shot for cowardice or desertion, then the troops would be removed from his command. Haig was known to consider that such executions were 'good for morale'. As the DINKS were waiting in quarters at Westhoff Farm while the brasshats ruminated over yet another Big Push, they had chafed under the unfamiliar discipline. In the mornings they would polish to a mirror shine their badges, buttons and boots then march up and down in the rain for hours, deafened by three full regimental bands, then go back, polish up and march out again. One morning a couple of the Aussies, whose view of rules and regulations was even dimmer than their own, sat in their vests with their hat-flaps hanging down watching the whole thing.

"Hey," one finally shouted over, "Are you boys enjoying this or what?"

"Of course we bloody aren't," came the reply.

That afternoon a good five hundred Australians had ringed the square. As soon as the marching began they produced bugles, kettles and kazoos or mess-tins and spoons and utterly drowned out the band. They even had a hideously discordant seven-piece banjo section. Unable to hear the RSM's shouted commands over this charivari, the serried ranks of men wavered, then clashed, then broke asunder. And despite all threats, imprecations or beseechings the Aussies kept up their relentless onslaught until the parade ground was empty. After that there had been no more parades – much to Victor's disappointment, for he had been secretly enjoying the whole thing. He actually *liked* being given orders, especially really stupid ones by the ugliest and most incompetent officers.

※

Although his flat was as full of reflecting surfaces as The Palace of Versailles, Victor still preferred to use the silver-backed hand mirror that had been his mother's. As a child he had imagined that it had once belonged to a beautiful but ill-starred princess who had been turned to ice or stone. But now he had determined that it must have been a love token from the scion of some noble house – although it was hard to imagine his baggy old mama ever having kindled even a spark of desire. She had never given the least confirmation of his suspicions – only staring blankly at him, like a horse in the rain – which made him all the more positive that they were correct. If he held the little mirror at a certain angle and then moved it at a certain speed he could sometimes glimpse shapes and bright colours that were not in the room. It was as if he was seeing the life that he should have had, the world that he should have been in. With fine tweezers he addressed his nose: the wells of his nostrils were becoming positively senescent. Expertly, he plucked out four white hairs – Blatchford, Hyndman, Snowden and MacDonald – the last of which was fully an inch long. Then his left hand gripped an invisible lapel while the right reached out as if to take a tiny pinch of air and turning towards an elaborately tasselled lamp he began, in his most orotund tones, to speechify.

"Ladies and Gentlemen . . . First of all we have – and I hope you ladies will pardon my French – the Chamois . . . Well, the shameless Chamois jumps from precipice to precipice and back to piss again!"

Every platoon had possessed someone who could do 'The Showman' monologue. Although there were many different versions his comrades agreed that, for delivery at least, Victor was the master. "You should be on the halls, nought-nought-one," they said and he had indeed considered it as a post-war career. Through Ruth, however, he had learnt that all these performers only had the one act and that what appeared so joyously spontaneous had been calculated to the last pratfall and double-take. Their audiences apparently liked them none the worse for this but imagine having to do 'The Showman' night after night for the rest of your life! At least Ruth had got to play different parts, but then he recalled the Shylock from *The Merchant of Venice* who had not been able to drink himself out of his character. He had recently encountered this man again: he was no longer Shylock but going under the unlikely name of Maundy Gregory. He had quit the stage and after four years engaged in clandestine operations for The War Office was now setting himself up as some sort of criminal mastermind. He was certainly well-heeled and had put on a great deal of weight.

⁂

Out in the trenches many of his fellows could have been called beautiful and he had become as familiar with their nakedness as he was with his own but he had never felt the least desire for any of them. Love and friendship had always been his twin summits but now a third – comradeship – soared above them both. How absurd it had been when those ILP drones called each other comrade!

"Good morning Comrade Glasier."

"Good morning Comrade Jowett."

Out here was true brotherhood. The manly hand smiting the shoulder – once ridiculed – now seemed to him to be the summit of human tenderness. He particularly savoured those times when they lounged about hunting their lice, sharing food and penning letters home. Part of his own popularity was attributable to his food parcels. Dear old Panty! Compared to her own vast pink healthiness the rest of the world must seem starveling and undernourished. "I am a happy man because I have one rissole and two slices of bacon in my valise!" he had written to Ruth in a letter that had been censored, presumably because the Adjutant had taken 'rissole' to be an obscenity. Those pin-pricked postcards had been a lark: he recalled the nigh-pathological smuttiness of her last replies. What an eye-opener that girl would have been for Professors Krafft-Ebing and Freud!

Victor had acquired a reputation for prudishness because he would not go with the whores. A couple of them kindly offered to take him on for free but he was enjoying his celibacy too much. It had to be admitted that he felt a little superior to his comrades: in uniform they could do some of the things that they had never dared to, whereas for him the war provided a break from daring rather too much.

"How many women have you had, Grayson?" The corporal once enquired.

"I don't know," he had replied, "I've never kept a count and besides, I don't think it's as many women as men."

They had all laughed and given him the raspberry until the only other Socialist in the unit had quietly informed them that this was perhaps not a joke.

Mud: for the first time Victor felt that his surroundings were in harmony with the contents of his own head. He would never forget carrying his full pack up to the front, when it had been impossible to find any footholds so you progressed by a sort of floundering roll. When they laid wooden duckboards the mud just swallowed them up. Sometime you could hear it burbling to itself like a simmering pot and at others there was a familiar slurping sound that made him look down, expecting to see someone's head bobbing rhythmically away at his groin. He had been trying to find a way of fucking the lovely glistening ooze: perhaps his comrades could tie him naked to a flagpole and then slowly lower him into no-man's land? What he really wanted was for the mud to rise up and compact itself to fuck him in the arse: it was hard to see how you might manage *that*. It could have been worse, though, for he had been rather concerned that he might feel an urge to fuck the dead. At night you could hear the cries of injured soldiers who had crawled into shell craters only to drown as the holes gradually filled with water. There was something soothing and bucolic about these sounds, like alpine goat-herds yodelling at each other across the peaks.

On the second morning, returning from taking water up the line, he saw his first corpse. He had been looking at the yellow, blue and scarlet thing for some time before had realized what it must be. Could it have been someone he knew? – the spleen did look awfully familiar. How momentous it was that an ordinary unexceptional Tommy, sitting there scratching his balls and listening to his stomach rumbling could have been transformed in the blink of an eye into something so beautiful! It was a bold, almost abstract composition, like one of Turner's sunsets: you could imagine *The Fighting Temeraire* being towed away into it. Then, further on, there had been another body, charred into a peculiar position, seated with both arms outstretched and fingers curled as if playing an invisible harp. He could almost hear the music: a swirling and saccharine swell that made his teeth ache.

There were rats running everywhere but you seldom saw a dead one. Any unbiased observer would have concluded that it was they who were winning the war. By night the lines were plagued by swooping bats and by day, whenever there was a lull in the firing, Victor had never heard birds singing so loudly. They had to get all their news and gossip in before the guns started up again. And you *never* saw a dead bird or bat: the bullets and shells apparently respected their neutrality.

"And now the leopard" – Victor switched off the lamp and pointed dramatically at the mantelpiece, where a curiously part-melted brass figurine of vaguely feline aspect was winking in the firelight.

"The leopard has one spot for every day of the year. 'What about leap year?', you ask. Well, chums, just lift his tail."

At least he had not lost his perspective back on Civvy Street. He might not have had a rissole in his valise but so long as he could don a freshly laundered white shirt and clip in those onyx cuff-links that Ruth had bought him in Dunedin, all was right with the world. And he still loved to take down his tie-racks, letting them stream behind him like the banners and gonfalons of a Saracen army before, breathing deeply, he buried his face in them. He was sure that he could identify, purely by smell, each individual colour. Then he would put on his little brass tie-pin marked 'A' for the ANZAC Brigade. Some veterans got riled by this, maintaining that only the survivors of the Gallipoli massacre had any right to wear it. And so, if asked, he always replied that it stood for Adulterer – even though these days he was a mere widower and had little to do with other men's wives. Having known a woman like Ruth rather spoiled you for anything else.

Women: he appeared to have given them up – all finished, napoo. He seemed to have been the only man in London who had lost his wife during the war, while millions of women were alone with little prospect of ever finding a mate. Even the pretty ones had a desperate air and the most unprepossessing of men – that runt H. G. Wells, for instance – could set himself up as a Don Juan. So for Victor – youngish, just about in one piece, and still reasonably famous or even infamous – it would be all too easy. Too easy to be worth bothering with. And you couldn't really talk to women about the war: while it was on they thought it was glorious and now they all said it had been Hell, reversing their positions only to compound their original errors. He still knew a few elderly and generous ladies who asked little beyond being squired with a few gallantries to theatre or opera then dinner. To make one of them smile or even laugh surely meant that your life had not been lived entirely in vain.

You knew where you were with men. Or rather you knew where you weren't. His new imperative appeared to be to fuck only people who had fought. The lovemaking was energetic and reckless but above all achingly sad. The other night he had brought back a sailor, still beautiful although missing most of one ear, the skin of whose lower back and buttocks had the appearance of Roquefort cheese. Victor was sure that he had felt a distinct magnetic pull as their flesh and their shrapnel came together. And there was the blinded major who said that he did not want his sight back: that if he was to be granted one wish it would be for a pair of arms that would be long enough to reach as far as the moon. Despite those empty eye-sockets Victor had an uneasy feeling that this man could see him perfectly clearly.

"Ah, now the *rhinoceros*, the richest animal in the world. To those familiar with the classics, the derivation of its name is interesting:

rhino, meaning money, *soreass*, meaning piles. There you have it, ladies and gentlemen, piles of money!"

❦

Jack Johnsons! Minenwefers! Whizzbangs! Woolly-bears! How wonderful were the names of the shells! And those vital salients – Hill 60 and Hill 40 – how mysterious they sounded until you saw that they were merely the heights in metres of two measly tumps that only partially relieved the universal flatness. At least they were something to deploy behind, an eminence from which to snipe. After a couple of days, however, they had assumed Himalayan proportions to his eyes. But how beautiful the lights were – what with the British Verys, the multi-coloured distress rockets, the slowly descending German parachute flares, the trenches were perpetually en fete. His favourites were the airburst shells, exploding in a magnesium flash to pepper the area with steel ball-bearings. One caromed off his tin hat, setting his head ringing with exactly the same note as the stroke of Big Ben. A firework display followed by a shower of presents: it was like some fabulous birthday party. Grotesquely-shaped chunks of metal lay about, parts of some blasted ordnance that no-one could identify. Everyone was thrilled by the tanks: although obviously lethal they inspired much mirth, especially when for no apparent reason they would suddenly topple over. There was something playful and jolly about them, like the armadillo that Ruth had seen on the edge of the Nevada Desert and so much wanted as a pet.

People kept telling Victor that he should have been there when they undermined Mesrines Ridge and blew it up with a million pounds of Amatol. They said that there was no smoke for hours afterwards, just blue flames and red flames, even green and brown flames, as if the earth itself were ablaze. That was supposed to end the stalemate but, instead of following it up, Haig had insisted on pitching camp. Then King George V had paid a 'Victory Visit' during which they had staged a ludicrous re-enactment of the engagement, while the Germans were regrouping and digging in new fortifications. And so the Big Push had become the Pig Bush, once again.

"If I am to be blown up, the more thoroughly it is done, the better" - this was Victor's favourite line from Shaw's *Major Barbara*. Back in New Zealand, Freddy Hunter-Watts - playing Sarah Undershaft - had delivered it perching on a huge shell. There had been a gasp from the men in the audience: as Ruth had observed, it was the shell you felt afraid for. And it was almost disappointing how the closer he came to the action the less fear he felt. And actually being under fire was rather delicious - like being told off after running away or being barracked in the House of Commons. And he had the same feeling: that the German guns, despite their apparent hostility, were in fact urging him to go on just as he was. How he wished that his so-called comrades were here so that he could take them up the line and say, "Here it is! *This* is what I was trying to tell you about!"

An observation balloon, sausage-shaped with attendant ballonets, like a silver sow with her piglets, floated serenely above. It was generally reckoned that its crew had landed a cushy number: the troops felt that they were being looked down on, snootily. When it *did* catch fire - sparking and combusting at terrifying speed - Victor knew that it was the most beautiful thing that anyone would ever see. It was as if the sensation of orgasm was manifesting itself physically in the sky. Victor had come without touching himself and he was pretty sure that many of his mates had done the same. They watched as the pilot jumped from his basket. The wind caught his opening 'chute and blew him back up into the flames. There had been a curious sound from the ranks: half-groan, half-cheer. Although you felt sorry for the poor devil, he had heightened the effect even more.

Victor had been given a bright yellow armband - not, as he thought, as an imputation of cowardice, but to indicate his status as part of the barbed wire clearing team. He was the cutter: it could have been worse, they could have given him that impossibly solid mallet or those lethal rolls of wire that you had to bowl along like the hoop of some monstrous child. The heavy wire-cutters were attached by a lanyard to his shoulder straps and then fastened into a webbing belt. He was also carrying, in the lower flaps of his greatcoat, a phial of iodine and a five-yard bandage with an enormous gauze pad in case they should happen upon any injured elephants. His colleagues were Jock the wire and Aron the mallet: their surnames – now redundant – were not dissimilar to the names of their allocated equipment. On their first night out Victor had been unable to shape the tangled wire into his own name while Jock managed to twist out a fairly long message in German. "It's something about arseholes," he said, "And they're not going to like it."

The darkness was very dark. The air was like black velvet rubbing against their skin. Sometimes Victor saw strange things – ghosts, perhaps, or hallucinations. At first he had put them down to random fog shapes or to a whiff from a residual pocket of mustard gas but on the third night the haze had parted and he had seen distinctly – out of his Liverpool childhood – those three old women who had lived around the corner. They had only ever left their houses for the services at St. Iggy's. The poor things had obviously taken a wrong turning.

When the brigade had finally moved up into the front line Victor became aware of a maddeningly insistent sound, like the dripping of a tap. A sniper's bullets were at regular intervals hitting the exact same spot on the parapet above. Even Annie Oakley, the peerless lady wing-shot, would have struggled to match such accuracy. It was like the Chinese water torture: sometimes the bullets and raindrops would set up complementary rhythms. Perhaps the idea was that you would grow so used to it that you would stand up, thinking the worst that could happen would be to get wet, only to have your head blown off.

There were other dangers than bombs and bullets. Gas gangrene, when the contaminated mud seeped into your cuts. Even more common was trench foot, caused by standing around in saturated socks and boots. He saw a man on a stretcher going down the line: his bare feet, hugely swollen, were the most beautiful cerulean blue, like the sky on the hottest day of summer. The man's expression had been perfectly self-possessed: indeed, even the seriously wounded made little or no acknowledgement of their pain. Aron the mallet, however, was always complaining about a wooden splinter down the back of his thumbnail. "It hurts like buggery," he insisted, to scornful laughter, "And you can die of it too, when it goes septic."

Sometimes, when people were tired of 'The Showman', Victor would give them a speech. 'The Radical', he called it, combining violent and increasingly incoherent rhetoric with a series of impersonations - Keir Hardie's Scottish stuttering, Ramsay Mac's leonine preening, Snowden's 'Come to Jesus' routine which ended with Victor falling to his knees, and even poor Jowett's 'bun, banana and beverage' peroration with its crude hand and finger gestures. Lloyd George would put in a guest appearance, his Welsh warbling modulating through Irish to German and finally resolving into the plaint of a cragfast sheep. "We will not rest until we have strangled the last king with the guts of the last priest" - that always brought the house down. They liked it even more than the shameless chamois and the oozolem foozlem bird but he suspected that they would have been just as tickled if he had delivered, perfectly straight, one of his own deathless gems of oratory.

One day, however, he had got around to the war itself. The apparent causes of the conflict, he informed them - those squabbles over colonies, trade, borders, spheres of influence - were entirely beside the point. They had served merely to nip away the veil that hid the truth, that war - rending, tearing, pitiless, insatiable - had been there all the time. Just as the spark in the baker's shop in Pudding Lane that started The Great Fire of London had revealed that everything is always on the point of bursting into flames. Those overcooked loaves had been incidental to that conflagration, just as the bankers, politicians and kings were to this. War was beautiful and perfect and an end in itself – like making love, it did not require a reason or excuse (audience cries of 'Hear Hear').

"War is the father of all things," Heraclitus had said, but Victor had begun to speculate whether it might not be their mother as well. ("What's he saying about his mum?" someone enquired). The great explosions that shook the land felt more like natural phenomena than anything man-made: the earth seemed to be going into regular convulsions. Was something hitherto unimaginable about to be born? Perhaps, like soldier ants, they were in the process of building an enormous nest (everyone applauded here because someone – not Victor – had farted loudly).

The front had become static and self-sustaining. If the war existed independently of its supposed causes then the battle now existed independently of the war. Victor was beginning to warm to his theme, even though he was, as usual, not sure whether he really believed any of it or not. This was war refined to its purest and most elemental form. There would be no more parades (cheers), no more prancing and dancing, no more plumes and waxed moustaches (more cheers), no death or glory charges, no strategies, no pincer movements, no flankings or outflankings. All we heroes had to do was to sit or lie around and then, when called for, go crawling through some mud.

Clausewitz ("Who's-iwitz? 'E's lost 'is wits!") defined war as "an act of violence intended to compel our opponent to fulfil our will." But whose will was being done here? Not ours, not theirs, but the will of the battle, the will of war itself. All this would never, ever end and the war, battle and front would become as fixed and familiar reference points as the moon and the stars and the sun?

At this, someone had thrown a boot at Victor: aimed to miss – just – it hit the sandbags behind his head and slid down. It was a German boot which they had kept as a souvenir. When they had found it the other day it had still had a German foot in it. It had obviously been blown some distance – there was no further trace of its former owner. There had been some debate about its provenance but it was surely too solid and meaty-looking to be anything other than Boche . . . Either the man had forgotten to put his socks on or the blast had sucked out the layer of wool between leather and flesh. Victor had been surprised by its weight: how was it that humanity contrived to walk around on such things? The foot had been removed and buried with full observances. Victor wished that he could have thought of something appropriate to say, like Hamlet over Yorick's skull. Poor devil – death had gobbled him up but jibbed at his right foot.

He knew that he had lost his audience but he struggled on. "Comrades, how wonderful it is to watch something being utterly destroyed. You should see the crowds in Manchester when a factory chimney has to come down. But no sooner is it gone than we realize how much we loved it, how we are already missing it, how its absence leaves an empty hole in the air and all we want is to see is our old friend back up again, the same as it was. That's why all our Utopias will never arrive: everything will be put back just the way it was before. The rich may be a little poorer, the poor richer, the church steeple higher or lower, the roads wider or straighter but nothing will ever really change. All a man can do with his life is to pick up the world and give it a good shaking then put it down again and go home."

At this there was a great shout of laughter: turning, he saw that Jock the Wire was standing behind him. He had retrieved the boot and, placing it over his groin, had begun to pump away at it.

"What the Hell are you doing?"

"Oh, pay me no heed, Cutter," Jock cackled, "I'm just fucking aboot."

⁂

It had taken twenty attempts to get his tie just right: things he used to do automatically he now had to think about. He turned away from the dresser but there he was on the other side of the room in the gold-framed mirror over the king sized bed.

"And now we have the Oozolem Foozlem Bird. This bird, ladies and gentlemen, once a year descends from his mountain fastness into the valleys below. He then stalks through the villages till he finds the fairest and most virtuous of the opposite sex. Then he fucks her, and finally eats her, thus avoiding for his unfortunate victim the shame and disgrace that would otherwise be her lot."

Ruth had died giving birth to their second child – Margot Eloise – who had also perished. No wonder the tiny creature had fought so fiercely against coming into the world, knowing that it was to be christened after those appalling Nightingale aunts. If they had called it Fanny or Molly, his own preferences, they would both probably have been alive today. Apparently Ruth had overtaxed herself in pregnancy: her mother complained that she could never get her to stop gadding about. The Nightingales had borne off the elder child and now he could hardly remember her name. Ethel? Emily? Eleanor? – Certainly something beginning with an 'E'. Ruth was buried in the Catholic section of Kensal Rise cemetery: Victor's name had not been included in the inscription on the white marble headstone. Last week, after a disappointing assignation in the vicinity, he had gone in search of the grave. It had been near a large yew, he recalled, but now the tree seemed to have gone. He had taken this as a sign: Ruth obviously did not want to be seen like this, reduced to grass and stone. Grass and stone couldn't gad about.

Now Victor could see that a star-shaped patch was spreading across his shirt front. Although it would not show under the waistcoat he would know all right. He had always dressed to impress himself, not other people. The liquid seeping from his wound was colourless but it stained yellow. He threw the shirt into the laundry basket: after a few minutes its collar was already grimy.

Sometimes Victor wondered if he might not have got himself a blighty wound on purpose. But then, although you could deliberately step into a sniper's line of fire or perhaps even, by some weird affinity, into that of the bullet itself, it was hard to see how anyone could deliberately step into flying shrapnel. He often thought of the two boys in the next trench who simultaneously shot each other in the left foot. How close had they been when they were doing it? Were their rifle barrels actually touching the flesh? Had they looked at their own foot or the other's? He liked to imagine that they had been staring deep into each other's eyes. For how long had they paused before pulling their triggers? He imagined them counting down to the moment – but how quickly and from what number? He even had the idea that they were singing but he could never quite catch the song.

⁂

The full offensive had been timed for 5.25 a.m. Why on earth hadn't they made it half past? Victor imagined the General Staff wrangling for weeks, consulting astrologers and haruspices, poring over chicken entrails and tarot cards in order to divine the most auspicious day and time.

Of the Second New Zealand Brigade, Victor's First Canterburys had taken the Green Line, while First and Second Otago took the Blue and Red. The rains came pissing down as they were starting out from Marsh Bottom: the word 'marsh' no longer did it justice and any bottom it might have possessed had long ago been sunk. Although every gun in the universe was firing they could still hear their officers' whistles setting them up and running. Victor discovered that he could hardly move at all, encumbered not only by the cutters but by his greatcoat, worn en banderole like a horse collar. He could only lean back and shuffle, legs wide apart, knees thrust forward, with his spine feeling as if it was about to crack. There was a distinct downward pressure on the top of his head, as if an invisible hand was trying to press him into the mud.

They were under light and sporadic fire and only a couple of men had been hit but to his left he could sense rather than see that Second Otago was being mown down by machine guns. Then they reached a thick patch of uncut wire: he and Jock and Aron, also with cutters, sprang at it and began snipping away. He had begun to love the twanging of cut wire: it felt as if the three of them were playing some elaborate piece of chamber music. "Just talk among yourselves, lads!" he shouted to the waiting troops but some were so impatient that they tried to leap it only to become entangled, kicking and cursing until they were cut free. Now they were running again with Victor in the van, moving in marsupial-like hops, taking off again before he could begin to sink. Downhill was easier: you just dug your heels in and slid. They could now see the two pill-boxes, perfectly positioned for enfilade: there were as yet no muzzle flashes – they were waiting for the optimum moment.

Then, even in the midst of the barrage, Victor heard, near and to his right a muffled but curiously distinctive explosion, like someone inflating and then bursting an empty paper bag, and he knew, in the split second before he was hit, that this had been *his* explosion, the one meant especially for him.

He seemed to be floating in mid-air for some considerable time: he saw his left boot go drifting past and was relieved to see that unlike poor Fritz's it was still attached to his leg. He had the distinct impression that there had been two explosions, not one, and that the second had occurred somewhere deep inside himself and that they had then rushed towards each other, to converge at his left hip. Surely this could not be what being shot was like? He did not feel to have been penetrated: there was nothing sexual about it at all.

When he finally came back down to earth the mud gave him such a great wet welcoming slap that all the breath went out of him. Then it began to rock him to and fro, like a ship at anchor: he wanted to sleep but feared that if he did he would be sucked down into that bottomless marsh forever.

His hands had begun to grope at his body. The cartridge clip in the breast pocket had gone and so had the pocket itself and he could see that a chunk of chest flesh had been neatly scooped out as if by a spoon. Judging by the patches of numbness and stickiness, he was wounded in the hip and lower back: oddly enough the apparently uninjured right side was the more painful. He had made no conscious effort to return to the vertical and certainly no-one had helped him but suddenly there he was, on his feet again.

He was surprised to find that his comrades were all still around him: he would have thought they would have been miles away by now. When they saw him, however, they looked horror-struck: perhaps his nose was gone or he had been scalped or even trepanned, with his brains bubbling out of his cranium?

"For Christ's sake, Grayson, take it to the dressing station!" They shied away as if he might be contagious.

On hands and knees he began to crawl back the way he had come. He could have walked but crawling seemed more appropriate to his new wounded status. It also seemed right to be retreating with his arse up in the air – although whether out of defiance or invitation he was not quite sure. It took him an hour to cover the quarter mile. Laughing was the main problem: someone felt to be tickling his ribs and there was a constant nagging at his funny bone. He kept stopping to recover himself: it was like when he and Ruth would laugh themselves into virtual insensibility over things that in retrospect never seemed in the least amusing. Perhaps it was out of a sense of relief at not being dead or because something that had always been about to happen finally had?

When he did reach the dressing station, however, it was no laughing matter. The wound dresser had been killed: horribly injured and mutilated men lay in piles, crossways, like logs. It was apparent that most had been brought here so that they could die in company. The next station, he was told, was fully two miles away, parallel with the lines, on the other side of a pale morass that appeared to be closer to quicksand than mud.

Now an Aussie with a stretcher-bearer's armband was helping him along: it was a while before he realized that the man was himself wounded, trailing one leg, and that whenever he tried to speak he was evidently gargling with blood. An artilleryman and his horse moved silently alongside them. Victor at first took them for ghosts, for they were utterly porridged with thick grey mud: there was something comical and edible-looking about them

"Let's get you on, mate," said the man, in a curiously cracked voice. He and the stretcher-bearer picked Victor up by his ankles and knees and put him on the horse's back. "'E's on the wrong way round!" said the artilleryman, so they plucked him down, reversed him, then stuck him back again. Victor didn't reckon that it made any difference whether he could see where he was going or where he had come from. The horse tilted its head and rolled back its eyes to get a look at him. It did not seem to like what it saw - he felt a shudder of distaste running right down its back. He looked around to thank the stretcher-bearer but the man had already vanished.

"Hold on to the mane. Both hands. Hold on tight." The man's accent was hard to place, some weird hybrid of Scots and Irish. "Do you know any songs that horses like?"

"The Red Flag?," suggested Victor, "England Awake?"

"Best just whistle," said the man, "but none of your parade ground stuff." He held the horse by a rope bridle: all the rest of its harness had gone.

Victor settled on Wagner. Much of what Ruth had liked seemed to him to be merely formless shouting but there were some damn good tunes. The *Tannhauser* overture went down well but when he thoughtlessly modulated into 'Colonel Bogey' the horse shied - too parade ground by far.

At first the animal seemed to glide over the mud without lifting its legs, as if it were a toy being pulled on runners across a polished nursery floor. The artilleryman kept muttering into its ear, his accent passing through German, then Italian, then something like Chinese. Victor was reminded of his own unstable Lloyd George impersonation - perhaps he would start bleating next? This was his first time on a horse. In New Zealand Ruth had often tried to get him in the saddle but he always declined, preferring to smoke his Abdullahs and watch her as she rode to the horizon and then came riding back again. Now he could understand the appeal, even though the throbbing and bouncing was better suited to the female anatomy than the male. Why hadn't he been out riding horses rather than chasing love and fame? He told himself that if he came through this alive he would go riding every day - even though he knew perfectly well that he would do no such thing. He had often dreamed of horses but when he awoke he had merely assumed that it was all to do with sex. And when you dream so frequently and vividly of something you can come to believe that it belongs solely to the realm of sleep.

Apart from the thousand shells bursting every minute and the ceaseless rattle of small arms fire, it was all rather peaceful until Victor made the mistake - perhaps coincidental - of starting to whistle Ride of the Valkyries. That did it: placid old dobbin was transformed in an instant. Making a great spread-eagled leap into the most treacherous looking pool, it began, like a mole, to wildly burrow into the mud. Surprisingly, the artilleryman's only reaction was to join in the whistling - and he really *could* whistle, utterly drowning out the whizzbangs, making Victor fear for his own eardrums. They plunged even deeper: the creature was apparently determined to delve into depths of which Marsh Bottom was merely the start. Then all was flurry and confusion: he could have sworn that the horse had rolled right over - not once but twice - without either man being crushed or losing their holds on bridle or mane.

"For God's sake keep whistling!" shouted the artilleryman. "He likes this one!" Now it was as if the mud had tired of this rough and senseless treatment - the horse shuddered at the impact as the deeper clay, rolling and knotting itself into a huge fist, punched it in the belly, sending it sailing clean out of the mire. At first Victor thought he'd been hit again: he was floating in that same giddy weightlessness but this had unmistakably real duration. Then the horse wildly bucked and kicked out with its back legs: Victor, losing his hold on the mane, was shot forward and found himself with his arms wrapped around the neck. Owing perhaps to its shell of crusted mud it felt cold but it was pulsating in an oddly sinister and slithery manner, as if he were embracing a boa constrictor. Now the two men's whistling had lost all semblance of a tune and had become an ear-splitting scream like the warning signal of a train as it enters a tunnel. And then suddenly, for no obvious reason, just as the rain stopped, Victor's steed slowed once more to its ruminative and measured plod.

Victor was almost disappointed to see the dressing-station: if he could just continue to ride he was sure that he would be healed of all his wounds. He dismounted unaided but his legs felt most peculiar. He feared that he might be doomed to be forever riding an invisible horse, like that poor rickety hobo that he and Ruth had run into in New York.

The horse whinnied: the first sound it had uttered. Victor patted its nose: it gave him another distinctly disapproving look.

"What's its name?" he asked.

"Charlie" – said the artilleryman – "After Chaplin."

Charlie! The same as Buffalo Bill's charger!

"What colour is he?" he asked.

"He used to be white." The man's teeth – what a beautiful yellow they were! – shone through the mud. And now Victor knew that if he were to scrape it away he would uncover the unmistakable features of Colonel William S. Cody – Greatest Of The Indian Fighters, Buck-Skinned Bayard Of The Old Frontier, Defence And Sucker Of Womanhood And Children.

The man went darting up the hill to return with a tin mug full of steaming black liquid which he thrust into Victor's hands. Victor's mouth opened but he could only stammer. The artilleryman reached out and softly laid a grey forefinger across his lips. "Put your thanks in your coffee, Maori," he said in a deep and thrilling Irish-American bass, "It's all in the game."

And so Victor had watched them go: the tall artilleryman and his horse had faded away into nothingness long before they reached the mist. When he sipped his scalding coffee he discovered that it had been liberally laced with rum.

☙

"The armoured armadillo! This is an extraordinary beast. When pursued by his foes, does he run away? No! Does he climb trees? No! He retreats and farts defiance at his nonplussed foes."

He was out of hospital within a few months, then discharged on medical grounds with a 30% disability pension. He never collected a penny of this: in Parliament he had supported doles, allowances and so forth but these would not do for Victor Grayson. He should have been paying the army for having dragged him out of the rut and set him on his feet again.

Even before his discharge he was speaking at pro-war rallies organized by The Seamen's leader, John Havelock Wilson. He had turned down a suggested threesome with Wilson and his sidekick, Captain Tupper, saying that he drew the line at practising necrophilia and bestiality simultaneously. Perhaps it was they who had arranged for him to be beaten up, although they had seemed to take it in good part at the time. Wilson was always encouraging him to target MacDonald – he had a peculiar grudge, something to do with a Scottish mountain – but Victor still retained a soft spot for him. He had settled on "When MacDonald and Snowden talk to you of 'Peace Peace Peace' they are doing the same work here that Trotsky and Lenin are doing in Russia" which, when you thought about it, could even be read as a compliment.

Many of his speeches focussed on what he called The New Bond that had been forged in the trenches between the aristocracy and the working class. He had been particularly impressed by the young subalterns he had seen and heard about when taking water up the line. "It's not that he's brave," one Cockney had said of his Captain, "Just that he's stark raving bonkers." but his tone made it clear that he valued this particular form of madness more highly than any courage. Victor's criterion for human worth was now a simple one: whether people did taxing and dangerous things that they were not obliged to do. The toffs could have left the hoi polloi to do the dying but no, there they were, elbowing their way through, keen as mustard to get up and at 'em, to be the first to go.

"I am a hard-shelled Socialist but I must confess that our peers and privates are fighting for something more elusive than beer and skittles. Some call it patriotism . . . religion . . . God . . . whatever it is, they are at present weaving out of the world's troubled skein, the warp and woof of a new era . . . 178 peers are fighting at the front . . . the war has taught us that henceforth there will be no classes, only grades. The gradation will be determined by ability and what the Germans really mean by KULTUR."

At such moments Victor would find himself ducking as if a boot - with or without a foot in it - might come flying out of the darkness.

Back in London he saw very few people from the old days. Apart from Gregory and Arthur Rose, all Ruth's theatrical cronies had disappeared. He still saw Hyndman, for they belonged to the same clubs, but the man was a shadow of his former self. He could no longer handle his drink and had developed a disconcertingly strabismic glare. All he talked about was The Great Jewish Conspiracy - although it was unclear what they were conspiring to do - and what he called 'spy waiters' in London's restaurants, warning Victor off virtually every decent place in town. He had also developed a fanatical admiration for the French premier, Clemenceau. "The Tiger's the man," he kept shouting, "The man to show those bloody Yids!"

Only last week Victor had run into that insufferable Bradford MP, Willie Leach. He was a dreadful gossip but he did have some great stories about Ethel Snowden's recent visit to Russia. Apparently, at one Kremlin reception, she had sailed up to Trotsky, who had just returned from supervising the massacre of the Kronstadt sailors. "You and I are in the same business, Comrade

Trotsky," she had boomed and when the man looked baffled, concluded even more loudly, "The business of LOVE!" Then, as The Bloody Commissar blanched and cowered, she had caught hold of his goatee and given it a playful tug. Poor old Snowy: why did the most practical of men always get involved with the scattiest women? Some natural law must be involved. Apparently Snowden, looking for a winnable Yorkshire seat, had been sniffing around Colne Valley. That would be the richest irony: no wonder there had been so many anguished letters begging him to stand again!

From the street below there came the sound of shouting and breaking glass which always lifted the hairs on the back of his neck. There was something both ominous and playful about it, as if fairies and elves were fighting with broken bottles. Or perhaps it was just the shellshock victims crashing about: he particularly liked the ones who seemed to be patting invisible dogs or moved like novice skaters on melting ice. He put on his jacket: he had just had half a dozen suits made, with the old-fashioned collars he favoured, all of them in trench-foot blue.

"I will now show you the camel. This particular animal eats mud, shits bricks and has a triangular arse-hole. Hence the pyramids."

Victor had only gone to bed with Maundy Gregory to find out what he was up to and he suspected that the man had acted from the very same motive. It was rumoured, he knew, that he himself was in the pay of the Russians, the Irish rebels or the New Zealand government. Gregory's body bore many scars but it was hard to tell how he had come by them. Most of his battles had probably been recreational and paid for by the hour in pounds, shillings and pence. He was incapable of graceful movement: obese was the word although he was not excessively fat. He wore expensive silk drawers which always felt slightly sticky to the touch: he would never take them off, so you had to sort of work around them.

Gregory liked to talk afterwards: he was most indiscreet. Once he had confirmed that Victor was not dangerous in one way he seemed quite unable to grasp that he might be dangerous from other points of view.

"I keep telling L-G to ennoble your Labour comrades - Lord Henderson or Viscount Snowden or Ramsay, Earl of Lossiemouth - but he says they'll never accept. They'd like to, right enough, but their grim acolytes would hound them to their graves." Gregory had even tried to suborn him: perhaps an OBE? Or how did Lord Grayson of Cockermouth sound? Or even the Baron of Crouch End? "I'd like to be King," said Victor, "if you could arrange that. I'd like to be the King so I could abdicate."

Gregory obviously saw himself as an epic and satanic figure, like Vautrin in Balzac's *Lost Illusions*. Such people often pretended that they were tragic demi-urges warring against God and Fate when in reality they were merely nasty petty crooks, the type you could find hanging about outside any Liverpool pub, just after closing time.

Victor had made a speech to a tiny BSP splinter group in Shadwell in which he had revealed that Lloyd George had bought himself a mansion and was busily making money by selling off honours before The National Government's Tory majority replaced him as Prime Minister. He had also alluded to "the sinister machinations of a monocled dandy with an office in Whitehall." News of these words had obviously been relayed to Gregory well ahead of the morning papers because he had called round later that night.

"To be dubbed a dandy by you, my dear, is really quite the compliment." He begged him to walk across his bare chest in heavy shoes which was how Victor, to his chagrin, became aware that his favourite brogues were distinctly down at heel. He was sure that Gregory could feel it - he was certainly giggling about something. "Well, my dearest, carry on the good work," he said blithely as he left after breakfast. It was hard to know what he meant by that. After discovering that twice the usual sum had been left on the hall table, Victor determined to press on further and faster.

He was also investigating whether the Irish insurgent, Roger Casement's homosexual diaries had been forgeries. It had to be admitted, though, that he was playing this game with Gregory mainly for the sheer fun of it. Who really cared that rich fools were paying through their noses for meaningless honorifics? 'Corruption is the most infallible symptom of constitutional liberty': yes, he rather agreed with Gibbon. And as for Casement, there was no bringing him back, for they'd already hanged him in Pentonville Jail.

His sources of income were various. He had discovered a talent for backgammon, alternating between frenzied attack and stifling negativity. He rarely lost but this had happened with other games until their novelty wore off. It was amazing just how cruel cards and dice could be when they suspected that you did not love them anymore. There were still the old ladies, of course, and his five regular gentlemen and sometimes significant sums mysteriously appeared in his deposit account. His last bank statement had come as a pleasant surprise.

If he had really desired riches he could have had them. Friends in the business world had sounded him out but he had informed them that his only possible relation to money was to spend it. After his war speeches there had even been talk of a Conservative seat but he had again demurred. When he was among reactionaries he advocated red-blooded Socialism and among Socialists he would unfurl the red white and blue. He couldn't stop himself: he was becoming ever more reckless with the passing years.

The Labour Party had been slaughtered in the post-war election, called by the National Government with the slogan 'Make Germany Pay'. Although his friend Edgar Whitely had put up a bonny fight the Liberals had retained Colne Valley. Victor had intended to speak in his support but something always came up. And now, God help us, the trade unions were setting themselves up as the vanguard of the working class. Victor had spoken against wartime strikes but now he disapproved even more. If the workers wanted something why didn't they fight for it rather than merely withhold their labour? At least the Irish boys had their bricks and broken bottles. How could *not* doing something ever be conceived of as a positive act? Now the Triple Alliance, the Red Clydesiders and the editors of The Daily Herald were threatening to call a General Strike in protest at President Wilson's line at The Peace Conference. It was hard to imagine the lads in the factories sacrificing their beer and 'baccy money over that! It was no coincidence that most of these self-styled leaders were Scots: as soon as you heard that accent you knew that everything was about to go belly up. And here was Victor himself, in limbo. His powers of persuasion were as potent as ever but to what use could he put them now? He remained a spellbinder but when he had his audience in the palm of his hand what should he tell them? Where the hell are we supposed to be marching to now?

It was time to go. There was all the difference in the world between merely leaving your home and Going Out. When he Went Out he felt like one of the Round Table Knights rattling over the drawbridge of Camelot and heading off into the countryside in search of chaste maidens, horrible ogres and The Holy Grail. One important thing: you should never Go Out in the daylight, although to Come Back in it was perfectly acceptable. Since the assault he had he had also begun to drag his left foot, pausing periodically to give a little gasp as if at constant pain nobly borne. When he and Snowden met again they could cross sticks and trade limp for limp.

He polished off the whiskey: although he had largely lost the taste for the stuff he still drank because he felt that it was the sort of thing that Victor Grayson should be doing. Anyone watching – through the keyhole, say – would be disappointed by anything less. He refilled the smaller pewter cigarette case: it had been engraved 'To VG from QL'. He was VG, of course, but who the hell had given it to him?

He looked outside again: the crowds had thinned but that dark taxi-cab was still parked on the corner. It had been there for at least an hour. There was every chance that it was waiting for him – but would it be with threatening or amatory intent? He decided to ignore it and walk to his favourite restaurant in Chandos Street. Tonight he would be drinking rather than eating. The food he had dreamed of in Belgium had tasted better in his imagination than anything he had subsequently ordered back home. Besides, Hyndman reckoned that the 'spy-waiters' were putting bromide in the sauces. Perhaps he could get dear old Panty to send another of her gargantuan food parcels? How nice it would be to know that once again he had two slices of bacon and a rissole in his valise!

In the long mirror that hung on the inside of the front door he watched himself advancing. It was a curious feeling: to be Going Out only to meet yourself Coming Back In. He put his hands on his hips and, after an almost imperceptible hesitation, the mirror self did the same.

"We now come to the whoo-hoo bird. He eats red pepper and flies backwards . . . Hence the trade winds."

Whatever did all these mirror-selves do when he left them behind at night? Did they come out to play or did they just glare suspiciously at one another? He pulled open the door and stepped into the silent hall, then turned to finish his routine.

"Now then, you small boys, get into the boats, because the elephant is about to piss."

CHAPTER TEN

RIMA (1924)

A ND SO, ONE winter's morning, the sun rose with a reluc-
tant air to reveal that a foundry man was Home Secretary
and a mill hand was Lord Privy Seal. There had been nothing like
it, according to *The Daily Mail*, since Caligula made a consul of
his horse. An engine-driver was Secretary For The Colonies and
a coalminer was Minister Of Health. It was like something out
of Aristophanes: soon there might be cabinets of frogs and birds.
A crippled excise man was Chancellor Of The Exchequer and a
starveling clerk, Prime Minister. And Fred Jowett, former whitening-licker and loom-overlooker, was now First Commissioner
Of Works, the steward of royal palaces, castles and manor houses,
forests, public parks and statues, and, indeed, the very bricks and
mortar of Parliament itself.

The gates of Buckingham Palace creaked open for this rag-tag
crew to receive, from their sovereign's own hands, the seals of office.
The Royal Equerry, Lord Stamfordham, had instructed them where
to obtain appropriate yet economical morning suits. "You would
be surprised, gentlemen, just how many princes and potentates,
nabobs and satraps are wearing – as they strut their stages – Moss
Bros seconds!" Nevertheless, their new clothes still contrived to
be either too baggy or too tight, with an irresistible attraction for
dirt and fluff. And only now did they realize the unacceptability of
their boots, as the scuffed toes came peeping out from under those
knife-edged creases.

"Looking ridiculous is all part of being taken seriously,"

MacDonald reassured them but he himself was immaculate, of course – as Shaw had said, he would have looked prime ministerial in deerskin and woad. Wheatley, to general consternation, had defiantly turned up in a bowler hat, rather than the regulation topper, but had then, at his swearing-in, gone down on both knees and insisted on kissing the King's hands. If he had not been dragged off, said Mac, he would have gone on to kiss considerably more. Afterwards, the Red Clydesider had claimed that he was only being ironic.

Ethel Snowden had accompanied her husband, the new Lord Chancellor. Apparently she had squeezed His Majesty's shoulder and whispered, "We are all kings and queens, ruling over our own lives." George V had bowed in grave and silent acknowledgement of this information. Jimmy Thomas, who followed them, had expressed disappointment that the Royal Seals had not been balancing beach-balls on their noses.

Jowett had the longest wait, being twentieth of the twenty on the list. Not permitted to read the departmental documents that he had already collected, he sat aimlessly crossing and uncrossing his legs. Having been stared down by every portrait in the corridor, he contemplated the battered felt hat on his lap. He had meant no offence, merely forgotten, but it had gone down even worse than Wheatley's bowler.

At last Mac and Stamfordham had called him forward. Emily had told him that he sometimes walked with his feet pointing outwards at ten to two, so he was concentrating on keeping those heels and toes nice and straight. When he did look up he had the impression that, high above, the great chandelier was keeping pace with him. The room itself, however, was surprisingly unimpressive: far from small but somehow poky, with alcoves at irregular intervals and mis-matched furniture distributed at random. A white cloth on the longest table displayed traces of an elaborate breakfast: coffee had been spilt, newspapers were crumpled up, ashtrays were overflowing and a silver tureen was still half-full of kedgeree. There was no throne to be seen – indeed, there were no chairs of any sort. Did these people eat standing up? Perhaps, in their world, everyone was always either on their feet or on their knees?

The King was leaning against the edge of a large desk, the top of which was considerably dustier than Emily would ever have permitted. He was not wearing a crown or robes but a dark suit, closer to blue than black, with a smear of ash on its right sleeve. He was tall but not as tall as his prime minister and he appeared to be slightly cross-eyed: on coins and stamps, of course, you only ever saw his profile. What was truly impressive, though, was that beard: it actually shone, with a pale auburn light.

"Mr Frederick Jowett, Your Majesty. First Minister of Works." Fred had never seen MacDonald looking so relaxed. It was as if he had just been confirmed in his lifelong belief that wherever he might find himself he would always be – in the truest sense – The King.

"You are the member for Barnsley, are you not?" The voice was surprisingly high-pitched.

"Bradford East, Your Majesty." Fred's throat had constricted so that the last word lost its 'sty'.

"My mistake," said the King, graciously. "Do pardon my ignorance but exactly where *is* Bradford – in relation to York, say, or Doncaster?"

"If you were to divide the country sideways and lengthways, Your Majesty, and then stick a pin where the two lines cross, that would be Bradford."

"I wasn't intending to divide my kingdom, Mr Jowett, or to stick pins in it, but I'll bear that in mind when I do."

The oath itself was mercifully brief. The seals were merely pieces of paper which you had to sign. It was rather like getting married in a registry office. The King's cigarette burnt slowly, even though he was puffing away: perhaps it was some special regal blend?

"Bradford is a long way from London, isn't it, Mr Jowett?" MacDonald and Stamfordham, with a conspiratorial air, had ducked into one of the alcoves.

"It is indeed, Your Majesty".

"And yet I understand that you return there every weekend. Do you not find such journeying a trial, especially in these winter months?"

"I do, rather," said Fred, "But there's nothing like peace at home, is there?"

The King's eyes came back into focus. "I beg your pardon?"

"Peace at home . . . Your Majesty," Fred added.

And then the man's face fell apart. Fred felt that it was somehow unnatural to see a laughing King. Surely there had been nothing untoward in what he had just said? He knew that he had not misspoken and that his 'Your Majesty' had been only a couple of seconds late. And his shoelaces were tied and all his fly-buttons fastened: MacDonald had made a point of checking when they arrived. It must be those brown brogues - but surely they could only provoke a wintry smile? Unless, of course, kings were easily amused: perhaps they spent their whole lives laughing?

"Tell me, Mr Jowett," - the mirth ceased abruptly - "Did you really mean those words that you spoke in Edinburgh last year?"

"Which words in particular, Your Majesty?"

"About the" - George V picked up a sheet of paper - "The swell mob and the senseless and wasteful displays at race meetings, royal levees, weddings and funerals." He flung out his arm dramatically. "For the Royal Homecoming it is roses all the way - but for the miner's wife trudging to the Guardians for relief, it is tears all the way."

Fred was still wondering how best to respond when he heard his own voice. It spoke without hesitation in a firm but curiously rueful tone.

"Yes, Your Majesty. I did and I do."

The King's face began to quiver again. "But might not your miner's wife pass a nice rose bush as she trudges" - he paused, then repeated it with even heavier emphasis - "Trudges to the

Guardians?" he dabbed his eyes, "And perhaps I might suggest to you that even kings can cry."

"Tears of laughter, perhaps, Your Majesty."

"Well, well," said the King, extending his hand, "As long as there's peace at home: on that at least all men can agree."

It was not a firm handshake. The fingers pressed against the inside of his wrist, as if testing the pulse. Only now did Fred realize that it was not merely the tobacco - the man himself smelt of nothing at all.

"Thank you, Mr Jowett." The King turned away.

"Thank you, Your Majesty."

Apparently no-one was going to see him out. The room seemed to have both expanded and contracted in the last few minutes: he nearly had to duck the chandelier, while the doors were a very long way off. He was worrying that he might make a wrong choice and step into a bedroom or closet when a door opened noiselessly before him. But just as he was crossing its threshold he heard the King's voice again.

"Ahdidanahdo!" It was run together into a single word. "Nay, nay! There's nowt like piss at 'ome, is there?" The laughter was mercifully cut off as a footman, stepping behind him, dropped the latch. Fred felt as if the hair on top of his head had risen and then burst into flames. Sweat poured down his cheeks, while his heart seemed to be trying to fight its way out of his chest. "Ahdidanahdo!" Although kings could no longer have you hung, drawn and quartered, they evidently still had their methods. He imagined a winter evening around a roaring log fire at Balmoral with all the little princes and princesses clamouring, "Go on, Daddy! Do that frightful Jowett one more time!" – "Ahdidanahdo!"

How peculiar it was that after almost sixty years on earth he could still be made to feel ashamed of who he was and where he had come from. But at least it had taken the King himself to do it. And there was definitely no strain of dialect in which 'peace' could come out as 'piss' and he had never used the word 'nowt' in his life, not even to Phil, and he was absolutely certain that he had not dropped that 'h'. What would the King have made of poor Hayhurst, dead in the Spanish 'flu epidemic? Or, more to the point, what would 'Ay'urst have made of the King? He would probably have - in his own favourite phrase - stuck one on him and then made his escape on a bicycle.

"His Majesty has been singing your praises," said MacDonald afterwards. "You made quite an impression. Ah, that fatal Yorkshire charm!" Then he had turned to Snowden. "And the man who can manage the purse-strings of this country can manage anything!" - he slapped him on the back with alarming force. "That's Trollope, you know. From *Can You Forgive Her?*" It was evident from Philip's blazing eyes and heightened pallor that forgiveness was the last thing on his mind.

❧

Ethel had stopped speaking to Philip after he had accepted the Chancellorship but then refused to move to 11, Downing Street. Such were their separate commitments, however, that it had been a week before he realized.

"We can't be living next door to MacDonald," he explained. "How could we ever relax knowing that he might be only a few inches away? He'll probably drill holes in the walls. Do you know what he said in Cabinet yesterday? - 'If only we could put the working-class to sleep and not wake them until we've arranged everything.' And do you know what I said? - 'If only we could do the same with you, Prime Minister.'"

Ethel clapped her hands, "And never awaken him again!"

"There's no point in moving from St. Ermine's, just when we've got it so cosy," Philip continued, "The Liberals could pull the plug on us at any moment. Minority administrations are lucky to last a year. And I'm happier working in The Treasury: I've got my office in Queen Anne's Throne Room - all rococo or ormulu or some such. I told my staff I wanted it painting over scarlet, with Trades Union banners instead of all those cherubs and flowers. You should have seen their faces before they realized I was joking! Anyway, it makes more sense for Clynes to be at Number Eleven because he'll be deputizing whenever that fool is gallivanting round Europe. How he thinks he can be PM and Foreign Secretary at the same time is beyond my comprehension. Surely no-one would have voted for him if they had known he was capable of such enormities?"

"I only wish you had asked me first," Ethel poured herself another cup of camomile tea. "For I would have put up with any amount of inconvenience for even a week at Number Eleven or a day – no, an hour – at Number Ten. Just so we could have looked at each other and said, 'Here we are'." She drained the cup and sighed. "Never mind, at least we have this little Eden, all of our very own."

With the proceeds of her American speaking tours and royalties from the best-selling "Through Bolshevik Russia," they had been able to buy outright Eden Lodge – ten rooms and an acre of land – in Tilford, Surrey. The door of each room bore the name of an American state. If we ever *do* move, Ethel would say, it will only be to take possession of the other forty. The one problem with Eden was that it was almost *too* idyllic: whenever Philip settled into his brown leather wing-chair – which had surely been moulded just for him – he never wanted to get up again. Sidney and Beatrice Webb lived nearby but they saw little of them. How dull one's comrades were away from politics but what fun one's supposed enemies – Lloyd George at Churt, Beaverbrook at Cherkeley Court - could be! The press was full of speculation about a new political alliance but the Snowdens' visits were purely social. Ethel was always popping over to Churt: she was trying to persuade L-G to sue Bernard Shaw for the thinly-disguised portrayal of him as Joyce Burge in *Back To Methusaleh.* She particularly objected to the line "I can see the future not only because, if I may say so in all humility, I have been gifted with a certain power of spiritual vision but because I have practised as a solicitor" – and also the stage direction "Enter

Burge, conveying an impression of shining like a church window". "Why is that supposed to be funny?" she kept asking, "He can't help glowing – that's just the way he's made." Fortunately, L-G found it as amusing as everyone else. "Sometimes I wonder," she complained, "whether he is quite worthy of his own glorious destiny."

Almost all Philip's time was spent at The Treasury. He even installed a folding bed behind a screen: despite dire warnings, the ghost of Queen Anne declined to appear. He had not known such mutual respect and unity of purpose since those early days with Fred. Warren Fisher, the Permanent Secretary, was solid as a rock and Willie Graham, the Scottish MP who he had requested for his Financial Secretary, had turned out even better than he had hoped. The man's command of his brief verged on the supernatural: his photographic memory did not explain how he could know statistics even before they were announced. Graham had no outside interests: when they took him to Lords he had rarely glanced up from his graphs and charts although whenever he did a wicket obligingly fell. "He looks like a thumb with a face drawn on it," was Ethel's verdict, "And a fairly grubby thumb at that." She did not approve of economics. "Love is the only currency that matters," she told Fisher, "The whole financial system would grind to a halt if Love was not there to lubricate its parts." Fisher had not even blinked. "Dear lady," he said.

Above all, she was suspicious of Montagu Norman, Chairman of the Bank of England. "His eyes never quite meet yours," she said, "I don't need to ask whether he is married." On the contrary, Norman's gaze was direct and his handshake firm: his appearance, manner and nature were in perfect harmony. You could read his mind simply by watching those bright eyes and mobile hands.

"He is so dreadfully over-groomed," said Ethel, "I'm surprised that he has any time left to run his bank. That beard didn't grow itself, you know."

"What about Lloyd George's moustache?" Philip unwisely retorted.

"A moustache adorns, a beard conceals," said Ethel, "And, besides," – her fingers made a snipping motion – "L-G knows that he must keep it ragged and untamed."

With his wide-brimmed hat and flowing cape, Norman might have stepped out of Van Dyke or Hals. He did not support himself on his silver-topped cane but held it at his side like a permanently-drawn sword, although it was impossible to imagine him ever entertaining a single aggressive thought. He always travelled incognito, as Professor Clarence Skinner, sometimes wearing a false beard over his own.

"We must get back on The Gold Standard as soon as possible," he said at their first meeting, then laughed. "I'm afraid I've got a bit of a bee in my bonnet about it." He took up his beautiful fedora and showed Philip its interior. A Barberini bee had been perfectly embroidered along the band. "She doesn't sting but you'll sometimes hear her buzzing, especially if Maynard Keynes is about."

The Gold Standard had fixed the level of sterling against other currencies on the basis of its value in gold. After a century of almost uninterrupted growth and stability, the country had been forced off by the outbreak of war. The Gold Standard! How thrilling those words sounded in Norman's reverberating tones! Philip imagined it as a glorious shining banner at the head of a host of mounted knights in armour. He could almost hear the thick gold leaf flapping in the wind as they lowered their lances and charged. Gold! In the Treasury's deepest vaults there lay great black coffers that would creak open to reveal countless yellow coins, gleaming in the darkness.

The recent Chamberlain Committee had recommended an immediate return but some deluded folk – not least MacDonald – were expressing doubts. According to Keynes and the Webbs and their Bloomsbury friends, national money management was the only way to achieve price stability. "It's vulgar to use one's knowledge of the markets to speculate as Keynes does," was all Norman would say, "Like backing your own horses: it's just not done." He understood politics as well as any politician, art as well as any artist, knew as much about wine as any sommelier and his racing tips – which Philip resolutely refused to take – were usually spot on. His Holland Park mansion was full of curious paintings – naked girls holding doves or lambs in strategic places – but the carpets were Persian, the dinner service Royal Doulton, the glasses Irish crystal. Although the brandy and wines were of the very finest, Philip stuck to carafes of water but even these were transformed by the addition of sliced lemons or limes. One evening they were seated in Norman's drawing room, having lit their cigars with an extended ritual the necessity of which Philip had not hitherto realized, when four burly men in evening dress, had silently entered. He had watched in bewilderment as they produced musical instruments from their cases, sat down and, at a sign from Norman, began to play.

Snowden had never heard anything like it. When the strings rose in crescendo they somehow created the illusion of trumpets and drums and agonised or ecstatic human or animal cries. It was becoming almost frightening until they suddenly converged on a noble and tender theme. It was as if a cool white hand was soothing his brow. He was fascinated by the very look of the instruments: it was as if the candlelight was melting the rich brown wood into molten yellows and reds. What a perfect accompaniment to an exposition of the terms of trade! Norman leaned forward and refilled their glasses. "The most important factor we must always bear in mind is" – a sudden wail from the viola drowned him out. The palms of his hands made a downwards damping movement and the musicians obediently retreated into near-inaudibility . . . "Profit margins. Seven per cent would be, if anything, on the cautious side."

"What *is* this music?" Snowden asked.

"Brahms," said Norman, patting his chest on what was surely the wrong side for the heart. "It's always Brahms with me!" His beautiful hands made a wild upwards gesture and the music burst forth once again.

Fred had not slept well. He had not been sleeping well since he had returned from Hungary three years before. After the end of the war there had been Communist or Socialist uprisings throughout Europe, all of which had failed. In Germany, the Spartacist Rosa Luxemburg - a Comrade of the ILP - had been arrested, beaten and drowned. "What a woman!" MacDonald had groaned, "What a waste!" - for all the world, Snowden said, as if a clumsy waiter had just upset the sweet trolley on its way to his table. In Hungary, Bela Kun's faction had taken power, only for reactionary forces under Admiral Horthy to stage a counter-coup. The so-called Red Terror had been followed by the White. There had been news agency reports of atrocities and reprisals: to reassure international opinion, the new administration had invited a Labour Party delegation, led by Jowett, to investigate.

In the prisons of Budapest there had been no bloodstained walls or piles of naked corpses, no sobbing or screaming, but the smell of murder, rape and torture was still hanging on the air. It was obvious that the delegates were there solely to have the wool pulled over their eyes. Healthy-looking prisoners, four to a cell, sat reading or playing cards, their smiles confirming the words of the interpreter. They had been well-treated and well-fed, no-one had laid as much as a finger on them: in fact, they were so happy they wanted never to leave. After a good lunch with the governor, however, the delegation had been led by mistake back along the same corridors to find that very different prisoners - ragged, blood-stained, foul-smelling - had been crammed fifty at a time into each cell. And some of their cheerful acquaintances of the morning now wore perfectly-fitting uniforms, promoted to the rank of guards.

Luckily, their hotel clerk was sympathetic: at night they would sneak out through the kitchens to discover the true state of affairs. It was evident that the Whites had indulged in an orgy of looting and violence, with their particular targets being Communists, Jews and good-looking young women. To save bullets they chose to bayonet most of their victims, often defecating and urinating on the corpses. They liked to pick up children by the feet, whirling them playfully for a while, before dashing out their brains against a wall.

Fred had become all too familiar with broken limbs, skins scorched black from electrical shocks and the marks left by various types of knout. One torturer would ponder long and hard – often consulting his victim – before making his choice of implement from a case of twenty-four. A white-haired man in an alleyway had unbuttoned his trousers to display his genitals, burned by cigarettes. Why were they interrogating you? Fred asked.

"They kept asking me the time," was the reply, "And because they had taken my watch I could only guess."

"Why did they let you go?"

"Because, finally, I guessed right."

They could tell that none of these people were lying to them. Nor had they been exaggerating: often their voices would tail off into silence – there were things that they could not talk about. Fred would never forget one woman's blank-eyed stare.

"They made her sons rape her," said the hotel clerk.

"How old were they?"

"Thirteen and ten."

The main torturers had introduced themselves by name to their victims. And they all had their distinctive methods. One, nick-named The Pianist, extracted alternate teeth to create a keyboard effect. Another, Paul Pronay, would burn or incise his own initials on the buttocks or chest: 'PP' – like an artist signing a canvas.

The British Legation was situated on top of Buda Hill, with even better views than The Royal Palace itself. Mr Hohler, the High Commissioner, had reacted to their findings with genuine moral outrage. "How dare you suggest that a Christian gentleman like Admiral Horthy could have had any part in such things?"

It was possible, he conceded, that after the fighting there might have been some individual instances of excessive zeal but full order had been restored within thirty-six hours. Many of the names on Fred's list were volunteer irregulars who had immediately returned to their far-flung villages. As to the specific allegations, most were obvious inventions. The man whose hands were supposedly cut off, for example, had in fact been born without them.

"He had been in the violin section of a symphony orchestra," said Fred.

"Then he probably cut his own hands off. This isn't England, Mr Jowett, some of these people are fanatics. And as to the so-called violations: all these women are notorious prostitutes and I ask you, gentlemen, how can a prostitute claim to have been raped?"

Nevertheless, Hohler had arranged an audience with Admiral Horthy himself. Fred had to admit that the man - who had just been appointed Regent - had a truly impressive presence. He sat in an elaborately carved high-backed chair, utterly motionless, while his attendant staff were shouting and throwing their arms around. The square head sat on the massive shoulders: the neck seemed to have retracted. Fred had never imagined that a single human chest could display so many medals and badges: rather than having been pinned or sewn on they appeared to have grown, like moss or mould, out of the blue serge itself.

The Regent then spoke for twenty minutes, fluently but without moving his lips or varying his tone, creating an eerie, almost orac ular effect. At last the translator stepped forward. "All the names you mention are not irregulars or peasants but decorated army officers. Many are on His Excellency's own General Staff. So there is, of course, no truth to any of these allegations but His Excellency would like to know just who the allegators are."

As the deputation was leaving, one of Horthy's retinue - a small man with a long neck and a pronounced adam's apple - approached, holding out his right hand. Fred, without thinking, shook it. The hand was surprisingly large and swollen, its knuckles red-raw and its middle two fingers had been taped together. The man stepped backwards, clicked his heels and bowed. "Paul Pronay," he said.

What struck Fred was that he had looked neither guilty nor defiant but complicitous, as if recognizing a kindred spirit.

The visit had all been for nothing: the press at home merely swallowed the official line, with Fred himself dismissed as a well-meaning dupe. At least they had managed to get some of the refugees to Vienna and then – in the case of the youngest orphans – on to Britain itself. But this was little consolation, for these children had already witnessed more than any human being could surely ever bear.

Jowett was not naive. From an early age he had observed human cruelty and meanness and known them for what they were. And he had even seen the darker side of The People – in the audience at Grayson's Keighley speech and the mobs that used to gather in the worst days of the war. But at least they had been driven by rage and fear, whereas what had happened in Hungary had been of such a gloating and calculated nature that it chilled the blood. And those apologists for the terror struck him as being, if anything, even worse than its perpetrators.

Time did not heal: the memories became more vivid and frequent. Now it was as if he had actually witnessed all those things that he had been told about. Sometimes, at the most banal moments – when he was having his tea, say – he was suddenly transported for a few seconds, to a torture chamber in central Budapest. He fell prey to dreadful fantasies in which he would batter away at the torturers' faces until his fists resembled those of Paul Pronay, or instruct a band of irregulars to perpetually rape Hohler and the legation staff, while politely apologising for their excessive zeal.

The horrors filled his dreams. In London he kept waking with a cry, drenched in sweat, to find on consulting the clock that a mere five minutes had passed. It had seemed better at home, lying next to Emily, until he discovered that he had been talking in his sleep in a language she did not recognize.

"Perhaps I was snoring," said Fred. He had only leaned three words of Hungarian but the accusers' voices were perpetually running through his head. Now he pretended to be asleep, waiting for Emily's breathing to deepen and slow before he allowed himself to slip into a fitful doze. He suspected, however, that she was doing exactly the same thing. He had not told her about Hungary, except to say that the people there had not had much to eat. The next time he went abroad - to Ireland, to investigate the excesses of the Black And Tans - he had discovered, on unpacking his unusually heavy suitcase, that she had filled it with cans of meat and condensed milk.

At least The Ministry left him little time to brood. His first official visit was to Chester Le Street in County Durham, where new coal seams had been opened to meet wartime demand. Thousands of temporary tin structures had been erected for the extra workers drawn from outside the area. Now, five years later, as production continued, they had remained, rusting and tilting, without sanitation. He had ordered their demolition and the immediate provision of decent housing and utilities. How wonderful it was - at last - to make things happen!

With all this to be done, it was surprising how much of his time was taken up by statues. He had not realized that there were so many - or how often they needed cleaning or how easily-damaged they were. He had authorized a new inscription for Frampton's Edith Cavell memorial outside the National Portrait Gallery - her own last words before she faced the German firing squad. 'PATRIOTISM IS NOT ENOUGH: I MUST HAVE NO HATRED AND BITTERNESS TOWARDS ANYONE'. "Cut those words deep," Fred had instructed the masons. She was depicted not as a goddess but as an ordinary woman standing alone before a sheer wall, head tilted in defiance but with a hint of forgiveness in those stony eyes and slightly-parted lips. Every day he contrived to visit it: when he ran his fingers over those words he could feel his own hatred and bitterness beginning to ease. Now he dreamt of statues - of torturers scourging white marble figures while gradually petrifying themselves.

Recently he had been approached by the committee set up after the death of W. H. Hudson, the writer and naturalist, to erect a memorial at the bird sanctuary in Hyde Park. They had commissioned the sculptor Jacob Epstein but his designs had been rejected by Fred's predecessor. Now the chairman, Cunninghame Graham – an old comrade – was applying again.

His civil servants had warned him about Epstein. "The BMA will never be forgiven for those frightful nudes on Agar Street . . . he's never heard of fig-leaves – although you'd need a fig-tree to preserve the modesty of that monster on Oscar Wilde's tomb. It's merely smut – ugly, aggressive smut, like a big stone fist crashing into your face. It's Assyrian – no, Babylonian . . . The wretched things wouldn't seem so bad in a museum but the idea of someone knocking them out here and now – in Bloomsbury, of all places – doesn't bear thinking about."

"Play it safe," Mac had instructed his ministers, "Before you say anything, think of how it would look on the front page of the *Daily Mail*." This newspaper always referred to Epstein as "the Jew sculptor". Fred recalled a cartoon in which a wild-eyed hooknosed madman, clutching an enormous electric drill, was advancing towards an apprehensive Venus de Milo. Epstein was said to keep a string of mistresses in his studios: sometimes his wife would shoot or stab one but no charges were ever brought. In artistic circles, the laws of the land –as well as accepted standards of morality – did not apply.

"Why can't we get Frampton to do something like the Edith Cavell statue?" Fred asked his permanent secretary.

"I believe Sir George did tender but his designs were rejected. Besides, in the royal parks, portrait representations of anyone other than the sovereign are forbidden."

"What about Peter Pan?"

"Master Pan is, as far as I am aware, a purely fictional creation."

Cunninghame Graham, with his broad-brimmed hat, cape and beard bore some resemblance to Philip's new friend, Montagu Norman. Although a small man, he had a reputation for physical courage and aggressiveness, being particularly celebrated for knocking out a number of policemen at the great Trafalgar Square riot of 1888: it had taken eight of them to finally subdue him. Even now, at seventy-one, he retained a bristling air, as if he was looking for the next head to punch.

Fred had always been suspicious of him. Although radical enough, he had been part of that raffish metropolitan crowd. Like his good friend Hyndman he professed a curious patriotism, describing himself as a soldier of the King and an enemy of the state. He mistook kicking up a fuss for serious politics. If there was a hopeless cause he would espouse it, if there was a fight going on he would join in on the losing side. In recent years he had become disillusioned with the Labour Party - presumably because of its very success - and was now an advocate of Scottish Nationalism.

Fred finished leafing through Epstein's drawings. Scribbled zigzags framing scowling female faces: he could make nothing of them. They were like something a child might do, in a very bad temper.

"Why do you insist on this particular site?" he asked Graham. "Why not somewhere less exposed - a private square, perhaps, or Epping Forest?"

"Because it is the very spot where the young Hudson spent his first night in London, having climbed over the railings after arriving penniless from Scotland." The man's accent became more pronounced. "Are you familiar with his work?"

"I'm afraid not," said Fred.

"This is where the subject of the statue, Rima, comes from." Graham handed him a large book bound in emerald and grey. "*Green Mansions* - not his best, but it's what he'll be remembered for. It goes deep - perhaps deeper then he intended."

"Why did you choose Mr Epstein? Someone wrote that they could not tell whether one statue was supposed to depict a human sacrifice or a birth."

"Both at the same time, probably," laughed Graham, "And a good deal besides. The point is, comrade, that the piece has to be angry and provocative in order to assert the persistence of wild nature – of Rima, that bright goddess in human form – right here in the heart of our so-called civilisation. Hudson died bitter and disillusioned: this will be his testament – his final warning but also, his revenge."

"I am afraid I cannot hold out much hope."

"I am sorry to hear that," said Graham equably, "Shaw is on our committee: he said that if *you* do not agree, then no-one ever will."

They shook hands: how delicate the man's fingers were! At least with Hayhurst the danger signals had been unmistakable.

"Nevertheless, I hope you can find time to read this book. If it interests you perhaps you might care to drop in on Epstein. He tells me he's developing some new ideas" – he winked – "Even more controversial ones."

Why, Fred wondered, would anyone want to build a monument to man's bitterness and disillusionment? He opened the book at random, to be confronted by a smiling bird. The bright eye on that cocked head seemed to pierce deep into his chest. "Collared Puff-Bird," read the caption: although the illustration was in black and white and cross-hatched grey, he knew that the creature must be brilliantly-coloured. He did not recognize the buds on the branch on which it sat.

The story was evidently set somewhere in South America. Each chapter was headed by a woodcut of an exotic animal or bird. Chapter Five had a line of yellow-winged sugar-birds, the next a pair of impossibly jolly toucans. There was a brown woolly monkey, then two long-crested hoatzins, a bell-bird followed by a rootling tapir – all of them, in their different ways, appeared to be laughing. Even the dullest one rejoiced in the name Superb Tanager and two black vultures, outlined against a scraped expanse of dazzling whiteness, looked majestic rather than threatening. And here at last was Rima herself but Fred could not see her face, for it was buried in the thick, stripy fur of a coati, which, like a cat, affectionately butted its head into her shoulder. What a lovely spiky tail it had! If only they could get a sculptor to simply reproduce that image . . .

but neither girl nor coati bore the slightest resemblance to George V or any member of his family.

That night he slept for a full seven hours. No-one was being tortured in his dreams. The statues were still there but now they were birds – stone birds flying around a dense tropical forest, their wings shifting with iridescent colours from beyond our spectrum.

☙

At the Treasury there was just one problem: whenever Snowden was speaking to his closest colleague the name always came out as "Grayson" by mistake. "Call me Willie," suggested Graham but, as Norman said, that would never do. What a ghastly notion: Victor Grayson, of all people, exercising control over financial affairs! He would probably take The Gold Standard for the name of a public house; the sinking fund would be well and truly sunk – it would all have to go on silk ties, chorus-girls and champagne.

Snowden had recently been contacted by Mrs Grayson. He was surprised that the man actually had a mother, especially this careworn but respectable old lady. Throughout their interview he half-expected her to tear off her hat and wig and coat to stand revealed as Victor himself, immaculate and infuriating as ever.

He had heard the rumours. Apparently Grayson had not been seen for fully three years. It was said that he had been drinking with friends in a London bar when a beautiful dark-haired woman appeared in the doorway and beckoned to him. Grayson put a coaster on top of his whisky and soda. "Don't any of you touch that," he said, "I'll be back in ten minutes." But he had never returned.

"I'd know if he was dead," said his mother, "I'd feel it. He's always loved to run away, to play hide and seek: he's waiting for someone to go and find him."

"I'm afraid he is not a child anymore, Madam." She reminded Philip of his own mother. Ethel believed that a woman with children was no longer properly human: she pronounced the word 'mother' as if it had to do with moths.

"He never was a child," said Mrs Grayson. "He was a baby for a long time and then, all of a sudden, he was a man."

What could he say? He had promised to help but there was little he could do. He had sometimes wondered how he would have felt if Grayson, returning from the war, had tried to re-enter politics. Compared to the new radicals, perhaps he might not seem half so bad.

The Red Clydesiders were the worst yet – always being thrown out of the chamber for abusing the Tories, who took great delight in provoking them. Their leader, James Maxton, was glowering and cadaverous, his lank black hair parted in the middle, like some mediaeval executioner: Philip himself looked positively winsome in comparison. The first time he saw Maxton he was sitting out on the Commons' terrace with his feet up – each boot almost as large as his head – drinking a glass of milk and reading a garish cowboy novel. He wore a lapel badge which read 'High Explosive: Handle With Care!' All the more galling was that he claimed to be a huge admirer of Philip and to have converted to Socialism solely on his account. What an asset a more reflective and sobered-up Grayson could have been! If only Graham had just a little of that vim and brio – and if only Victor could have had a little bit of Willie in him!

Most Chancellors could only dream of going into a budget – especially their first – with an unexpected surplus that would allow them to establish themselves as a giver rather than a grabber. But now, although it seemed too good to be true, there was no doubt that Grayson – no, Graham! – had been right about that £50 million. Taxes had risen while expenditure fell and the Sinking Fund was paying off the debts of war. The Sinking Fund! – Philip visualized it as a great and treacherous bog across which those doughty but heavily-armoured Knights of The Gold Standard must perforce wend their way.

Through talking with Norman, he had come to realize that his own economic philosophy was Gladstonian rather than Socialist. He stood for free trade, debt reduction, limiting public spending, direct taxation rather than indirect, a balanced budget and, of course, a speedy return to The Gold Standard. It was hard to see how any rational person could dissent from these aims. People like Keynes called for more public investment to reduce unemployment but how could you spend money that you didn't have? Any housewife would tell him that you cannot buy new things until you have paid for the old. Jowett advocated tax rises but income tax had already quadrupled since 1914. Putting sound finance above political dogma would reassure those who hesitated to support a redistributionist Labour party. Social justice would come in time but the electorate must be led towards it, step by step.

Snowden was certain that this period in power, however short-lived, would be the first of many. The party could rest secure in the knowledge that its bedrock support would enable it to fight off any Liberal revival. The industrial heart of the north would never be anything other than Labour. You could start at Sheffield, then drive through Penistone, then his own Colne Valley, then Huddersfield, Elland, Dewsbury, Halifax, Bradford, Keighley and beyond and never for one moment be out of a Labour constituency.

Nevertheless, Colne Valley was a funny place. After Philip's election had been announced in Slaithwaite Town Hall there had been the merest smattering of applause. Then he was driven to a celebration at Marsden Labour Institute. As the open-topped car passed through the crowd - most of which would have voted for him - not one head turned to cheer. He smiled and waved regardless but he might as well have been in a hearse. The King told him that when he and The Queen had visited in 1913 the streets had been almost deserted. "Nothing personal, Your Majesty," he had replied, "Up North we take pride in pretending to be unimpressed." He had thought it best not to mention the Grayson enthusiasms of 1907.

As they were entering Marsden, a dishevelled young man darted out of a ginnel, threw a stone that scraped the car bonnet and then fled. It was said that, as a child, he had been adopted by Grayson as a sort of mascot. "It were Victor's touch that turned his mind" – their tones did not imply any criticism.

When he finally entered the Institute, nicely packed with party workers, he had been greeted by a cackling crone who enquired, "What ha' yer done wi' our Victor?"

"Nay, love, I've 'et 'im all oop," he replied, then ducked away as a skeletal fist swung at his head. It was wiser not to joke about these things.

Grayson was still a tangible presence in the valley. Snowden understood the notion of charisma but how could its magic still be working fifteen years later when the charismatic individual had long since decamped? As far as he could tell – leaving aside the wilder local legends – the man had not set foot in the place since losing it in 1910. And in his short time as MP he had left all the constituency work to his agent, only turning up for gala days when there would be crowds and photographers and plenty to eat and drink. What kind of communal benevolence did not merely forgive this but accepted or even celebrated it? They seemed to feel that he was, in some mysterious way, still among them. "Our Victor": it made his skin crawl. The "our" closer to a gasp, "ah!" and then the tongues clicking on the "Vict" followed by a grunt of expelled air – "Uh!" It was very like the way Ethel pronounced "Love". He still felt, however, that his own relationship with his constituents ran deep. Although they had been charmed by Grayson he had never understood them. All that yelling and laughing and clutching at one another had been utterly out of character. Now they were themselves again – slow, silent and suspicious of the least expression of feeling. No-one – except perhaps some of the old pagan Gods – could live in a state of permanent intoxication. The occasional bright morning was still hailed as 'Grayson weather' but they were now living in a Snowden climate where you had to wrap up well and never forget your umbrella, where the sun itself was grey, filtered through clouds, and usually gone by midday.

Snowden had not been in the least nervous about presenting his budget. He had slept long and deep under Queen Anne's increasingly benevolent gaze and had risen without a trace of stiffness in his limbs. He did not need his sticks but still deployed them for effect: folk were disappointed if he wasn't limping. He was fully aware of the historical significance of the moment but his hands were not shaking, his mouth was not dry and his heartbeat was if anything slower than usual.

In the last few months he had become famous. The walls of Eden Lodge were now lined with newspaper caricatures of himself - no longer as the terrifying Dr Nikola but as the pugnacious Yorkshire battler, fists clenched, chin out, back ram-rod straight. His sticks were never shown: they drew him not as he looked but as he truly was. His favourites were one of Grayson - no, *Graham!* - and he as a cruet, twin bottles labelled 'Vinegar' and 'Oil', and another, after his war reparations speech, of himself arm-in-arm with John Bull, both of them resplendent in matching union jack waistcoats. There was no mistaking the affection in such portrayals, whereas MacDonald was always depicted as dishevelled and befuddled, as if he had just been ejected by a rapidly revolving door. Not as he looked, in fact, but as he truly was.

"The Housewives' Budget": he already knew what the press would call it. Duties on sugar, tea, cocoa, coffee, chicory and prunes were drastically reduced. "This, if I may say so, is the greatest step ever taken towards the cherished radical dream of a free breakfast table." Even Lloyd George and Asquith, he noticed, were joining in the Liberal cheers.

"Is that what Radicals dream of?" Norman had enquired when Snowden had read him the speech, to the muted accompaniment of the adagio from Brahms' Opus 8 Piano Trio - they liked it so much that they had the musicians repeat it for two hours. "Free breakfasts? I thought it was buns, bananas and firing squads."

Even the Conservatives had applauded when he repealed the McKenna Duties, a supposedly temporary wartime tax which had since been renewed every year. Free trade for the motor industry!

He had a momentary vision of those knights-at-arms driving a fleet of limousines – with little replicas of The Gold Standard fluttering on their gleaming bonnets. He repealed the Corporation Profits Tax (Cheers) and the Limited Companies Tax (More cheers), then reduced the Entertainment Tax, providing cheaper seats for theatres, cinemas and music halls.

"Now to the Capital Levy," he said, with slow and dreadful emphasis, "There will be" – he paused – "No change." There was a great sigh of relief and a single hollow groan – from Jowett, most likely. "Death duties" – he cracked his knuckles – "No change. But as for Income Tax " – another general intake of breath and an even longer pause – "No change," he almost trilled, letting his eyes twinkle roguishly from beneath his brows.

Afterwards, in the lobby, he was greeted with handshakes and congratulations – but almost entirely from Liberals and Tories. It was typical of MacDonald and the rest: they had agreed to everything in Cabinet but were now acting as if it had nothing to do with them. What *did* surprise him was that so many of the 'haves' had believed that this, the first 'have-nots" budget, would mean the end of them. Now they were overcome with gratitude.

Later, back in Holland Park, after a supper of jugged hare followed by summer fruits swimming in a delicious but suspiciously potent-smelling ichor, Norman revealed that most of his friends had been expecting to hear the sound of heavy boots crunching up their gravel drives, followed by rifle butts hammering at their doors. "It's what they would have done in your position, Chancellor," he said.

"My friend Jowett believes that just as the poor are expecting us to free them from poverty so the rich are, with equal eagerness, waiting for us to free them from their riches."

"Oh yes," Norman smiled and motioned the musicians to move at long last on to the allegro. "But only, I fear, in our deepest and most secret dreams."

The advantage of the Ministry of Works was that – unlike Snowden and Graham, who looked paler by the day – Fred was out of the office for much of the time. He liked to see what he was taking responsibility for. Last week, Gilbert Scott had shown him the dome of Sir John Soane's mausoleum, the inspiration for his public telephone box. "There are no new ideas," said Scott, "Just old ones in a different context." He had intended it to be painted silver but Fred felt that this would not be noticeable enough.

"Why not red, like the post boxes?"

"Or The People's Flag, Comrade Jowett?" the architect laughed.

When the Mayor of Bradford, Alderman Barraclough, had visited he had found Fred on the roof of Westminster Hall drinking tea with the slaters. The stone ceiling was in danger of coming down on the Honourable Members below. "It was riddled with cracks," the men were saying, "That's the problem with you chaps – you never think to look up. Don't trust a place until you've been up on its roof and down its drains."

"Does the dignity of your office mean nothing to you?" asked Barraclough. It was rumoured that when he rose in the night to relieve himself he would put on his mayoral robes and chain.

Fred had been investigating Hyde Park before giving permission for Hackney cabs to drive across it. Rather to his surprise, this had caused a furore: according to this morning's papers, the tumbrils and guillotine could only be a few days away. 'No hatred and bitterness towards anyone': he felt the words under his fingers as he met Nurse Cavell's unblinking stare. He had paused on the way to Epstein's studio: his civil servants were amazed that he walked everywhere, as if a vast trackless waste lay between Whitehall and Guildford Street, rather than a mile of Yorkshire sandstone pavement.

He was 127 pages into *Green Mansions*. It was the first novel he had ever read – unless *Hard Times* or *News From Nowhere* could be said to count. He had never seen the point: wasn't there already more than enough to learn about *this* world? Why create other realities – whether bafflingly different from or teasingly similar to our own – in which you could never draw a single breath, eat or sleep or affect in any way the events unfolding before you? Nevertheless, he read dutifully on and after a while realized that it was having a marked effect on him.

The story itself was strange. Abel, the hero, is a Venezuelan nobleman and revolutionary who, after a failed uprising, escapes up the Orinoco River to Guyana, finding refuge with a native tribe. He explores a forbidden forest in which he is accompanied by a mysterious song, at once birdlike and human. Although warned that the voice is an evil spirit, the Daughter of The Didi, he returns, fascinated, again and again.

"I dropped on my knees and kissed the stony ground, then casting up my eyes, thanked the Author of my being for the gift of that wild forest, those green mansions where I had found so great a happiness."

For some reason, on reading these words, Fred had begun to cry – or, rather, without his feeling any emotional disturbance, water had poured out of his eyes, as if something inside him had sprung a leak. There in his lodgings, mug of cocoa forgotten on the bedside table, he had read on into the night.

The singer is revealed: Rima – no demon but a wild girl of the forest. Tiny, beautiful and chaste, loved and trusted by all the creatures of her realm, her moods shifting from rapturous enthusiasm to inexplicable terror. Hudson's writing was, Fred could see, most inventive – Rima's skin was neither white nor brown, her eyes red, her hair seemingly every colour in turn – but he had still felt a sense of anticlimax when she finally appeared. Perhaps the ineffable should remain always on the point of becoming visible? He recalled an uncanny moment when he had been alone down in Heaton Woods. He had suddenly shivered, as if sensing an unseen presence, and had felt the hair rising on top of his head. Then he had run in panic – although whether towards it or away from it he had never quite decided. Perhaps it had not been Pan but Rima, or some similarly inquisitive spirit of the place?

He found it hard to visualize her but perhaps that had been Hudson's intention?

"I mentally cried, oh why has nature, maker of so many types and of innumerable individuals of each, given to the world but one being like this?"

It was astonishing how slowly he progressed, when he could speed through and retain whole government reports. He found himself re-reading sentences or inexplicably hanging between them for minutes on end. It was not a comfortable feeling – as if everything was simultaneously speeding up and running down. Perhaps reading fiction was like drinking and you had to build up a tolerance to it? He had, however, put the book aside over the weekend. Without her saying anything, he was aware that Emily disapproved.

A note pinned on Epstein's door directed Fred to a studio round the corner where another note directed him to a second studio in Emerald Street. The entire mews appeared to be derelict: only one rusting door displayed a scarlet symbol like a pair of staring eyes or an overturned figure of eight. With a crash it fell open, resting on one precarious hinge, and he saw that a large boot was raking it back. Stepping forward, he was confronted by a shockingly bulky figure, its face obscured by strips of cloth and a pair of motorcycle goggles. A night-soil man! – he almost fled but the accompanying smell of chemicals, burnt wood and rotting apples was somehow reassuring.

"Yes, it is me under all this." Epstein's accent was American, not Polish. He was almost square, with overdeveloped arms and shoulders: although he was panting his chest did not appear to move. "In my trade, Minister, you have to watch out for your eyes." He wore filthy blue overalls, their crotch held together by safety-pins, and a matching peaked cap, ridiculously too small, was perched on top of his head.

In dim light filtering through holes in the ceiling, Epstein led the way down a narrow corridor. He moved in an unusual fashion: it was as if that chest and belly were throwing themselves forward with the rest of the body being dragged reluctantly behind. Fred became aware that the walls were lined with objects carved out of dark wood. There were war-clubs and spears, bowls and long spoons, grotesque masks – part-human, part-animal – and weird-ly-shaped blocks with holes and apertures that suggested musical instruments to be beaten or blown.

"Where do all these things come from?" asked Fred.

"Portobello Road," Epstein began to unwrap himself, "Originally from Benin and Gabon."

"Very nice," said Fred.

The chest and belly swung back towards him, followed by Epstein's face, which looked nothing like the caricatures. With those clear eyes and ruddy cheeks he resembled a gentleman farmer.

"But would you consider them to be works of art, Minister?"

"I think I would call them implements," said Fred, "But very beautiful ones."

Now they had plunged into darkness. Fred had the sense of having entered a vast cavernous space. "Make yourself at home," came Epstein's voice, "I'll brew us some tea although I'm afraid there's no biscuits." There was a distinct echo as he stumped away. "In fact, I'm not sure whether there's even any milk . . . or sugar."

Fred was reminded of when he had met the King. How hard some folk tried to make an impression on you! Perhaps if the lights went up he might find himself back in Buckingham Palace once again? Now that his eyes had adjusted he saw to his left a faint and flickering glow. The carpet felt at one step threadbare but at the next luxuriously deep: invisible objects crunched and crackled under his feet. There was a new smell, like hot bread and embrocation, but still with that sickly-sweetness behind it. The light emanated from two candle stubs on the point of guttering out. Something caught the back of his legs and he fell into an armchair: he had the impression that a small animal had tracked him across the room, awaiting its moment.

Directly opposite, beyond the candles, was a dark and glistening shape, not unlike the African carvings but larger and more solid. A statue – but not of wood or even of stone: pale shadows rippled across it. It was, Fred realized, a life-sized representation of a naked woman, recumbent, leaning forward but with the neck pulled sharply back, one knee raised and the other leg flat to the floor.

"You don't look very dangerous to me," the lips of the figure had not moved but in the slitted eyes Fred caught a flash of green. With the angle of her head he could see right up her nose: she did not appear to be breathing but the nostrils were fringed with hair.

"Where is your gun? I thought Socialists were supposed to be dangerous." She put a lot of extra R's into the word.

"I suppose we're no more dangerous than anyone else – not individually, at least," said Fred, "And I'm afraid I haven't got any guns."

"I am dangerous," said the woman, "I am a model. And Epstein is a sculptor, so he is dangerous too . . . Very dangerous, very very dangerous," the words ran together to become a sort of electrical purring, "Everyone is dangerous . . . except for you."

Fred's laughter seemed to come bursting out through his chest rather than his mouth. When had he last laughed like this? When had he *ever* laughed like this? He hoped that he did not look as ridiculous as the King.

"Aha," she said, when he had finished, "So you *might* be dangerous, after all." Her expression had not changed. In fact, she still had not moved a muscle. "I used to be friends with your Victor Grayson" – she savoured the R's in the name – "Do you know where I can find him?"

"I'm afraid I haven't seen him since before the war," said Fred, "Is it an urgent matter?" The green eyes widened.

"As urgent as anything else."

"I see you've met Dolores," came Epstein's voice, "Or should I

351

say Rima?" There was a blaze of white light and Fred shielded his eyes from the naked bulb swinging just above his head. Dolores, he noticed, did not even blink. Now he could see that they were in a long, low-ceilinged warehouse, its windows boarded up. Draped figures of various shapes and sizes clustered around two large tables piled high with miscellaneous debris. Fred's chair was the only one in the room. Epstein was carrying a tray laden with blue and white china and milk in a jug, sugar with tongs and a plate of neatly-cut bread and butter. "I met Grayson once," he sat down on a three-legged stool, his great bulk seeming to ingest it. "I thought he might be a pansy."

Dolores snorted. "He was a proper gentleman . . . but danger-ous, of course, as dangerous as you can get." She showed no sign of embarrassment, nor did she adjust her immodest and surely uncomfortable position.

She was only the second woman that Fred had seen naked – and he had only caught partial glimpses of his own wife's body which he had pieced together, as it were, over the years. Apart from an unexpected episode after papering the front parlour, he and Emily had only ever made love in pitch darkness. He realized that he was looking at Dolores without the least arousal. He did not think of her as being naked: it was as if she was somehow fully clothed in her own skin.

The body fascinated him. She was evidently tall and slender but despite the tension of her pose the ribs did not show through the flesh. The face and neck were markedly paler than the rest as if she had been living in a very hot climate, unclothed except for a wide-brimmed hat. What Fred had taken to be a shadow behind her was, he realized, the main mass of the hair, pinned halfway up to create a great dark hallo: its coils appeared to be writhing, as if full of static electricity. Torso and limbs were berry-brown but the elbows and knees were almost black, while pink lines like thin cords criss-crossed the wrists and throat. Her breasts were small and almost square with pronounced and very red nipples which could be seen to be quivering, as if they were somehow taking the strain of the body's stillness. The insides of her thighs were purple, as if from deep bruising, and the pubic hair was thick and marmalade coloured, trimmed into a perfect triangle.

Although Hudson's heroine had not been a woman but a young girl, innocent and nervous and only four and a half feet tall, Fred still felt that he was looking at Rima. In trying to imagine her he had only thought about the face but now he realized that every part of a human body could be equally expressive.

Epstein's enormous hands had each been simultaneously rolling two cigarettes: there was something uncanny about the dexterity of those bloated fingers. He lit up, then inserted one between Dolores' unresponsive lips. Although she did not seem to have inhaled, twin streams of smoke came bursting from her nostrils.

"Let me show you my new ideas," said Epstein, after extricating himself, not without difficulty, from his seat. Leading Fred to the far end of the room, he whipped off one of the drapes to reveal, balanced on an orange box, a small rectangular white stone carving. Against an elaborately patterned background, a naked girl was running forward, her hair blowing behind her, her arms outstretched. "This is what The Ministry rejected – thank God! It's very fine, of course," he ran his thumb along the nose, "But not quite there. The birds, for example, are lost among those leaves: I widened the wings but it only made them look like bats. And the figure is too lumpish: I might as well have put a hockey stick in her hand. I wanted to show her flying, while also remaining in touch with the earth but it can't be done. I can only resolve the paradox by cutting her off at the waist" – he dug an elbow into Fred's ribs – "Or, rather, just below it. Now take a look at these."

Fred had already seen some of the drawings but now they made sense. Rima *did* look surprisingly threatening but perhaps the rest of *Green Mansions* would explain this. There was study after study of a human ear. In the final one, the lobe was squared up to taper into the neck, while the ear itself became an open mouth, screaming.

"That's the one!" – A huge forefinger flicked the paper – "Got it right there! You can see from the maquette that a relief just can't go deep enough to give her a proper forward thrust. You can only really get that from a free-standing figure. But if I take off her legs, turn her sideways and tilt her back, I open up the whole line of the jaw and ear. And I'll get rid of all that fussiness behind and cut the birds to just two - bloody big ones, mind, with very long beaks." Epstein nudged him again. "I wanted to give her a gorilla as well but Graham says they're only native to Africa."

"What about a coati?"

"What's a coati?"

"Coatimundi," came Dolores' voice, "Like a racoon but with a big snout. Dangerous but very sweet."

> "Ist denn, liebliche Dolores –
> Also singt in ihren traum."

In a surprisingly high voice, Epstein had begun to sing, while his feet shuffled in a curious dance.

> "In der muschel deines ohres
> Fur kein, perienwortchen raum?"

Fred had picked up some of the language in the mills of Little Germany: this seemed to have something to do with dreams and pearls.

"Fuck off, Eppy," a perfect smoke ring rose to quiver in the air, "And fuck off, Brahms."

"She hasn't moved since we came in," Fred whispered, "Are you sure she's all right?"

"Don't worry. It's a matter of professional pride. Even when I nip out for a couple in The Lamb, she's still holding the pose when I get back."

It was evident that Dolores could have given even Admiral Horthy lessons in immobility.

"She has the most wonderful hair," said Fred.

"If I had my way, I'd shave off everything except for the eyebrows. The shape of that skull! And as for those ears - well, the whole world will go mad if it ever sees her ears."

"Just one question," Fred cleared his throat, "Why is Rima naked?"

"Because she is a wild jungle girl, unashamed and free of hypocrisy and cant."

"But she isn't naked in the book, is she? At least, not before page 127."

Epstein's pale blue eyes rolled like marbles in their sockets. "Isn't she?"

"Haven't you read it?"

"They did give me a copy but it's buried somewhere under all this mess" - he waved an arm - "so if she's not naked, out there in the jungle, what on earth *is* she wearing?"

"A high-necked, calf-length shift," said Fred, "Woven for her by the fine floating lines of small gossamer spiders."

"I'd like one of those!" Dolores called.

"I think the book might get in the way now," said Epstein, "I've got a pretty good idea of the sort of thing they're after and I've got a pretty good idea of what I'm going to do. Besides" - he gave a great sigh of relief - "If it wasn't nakedness they wanted they wouldn't have asked me."

Fred was shown various other works-in-progress. There were three portrait heads - all of the same woman, long-necked but definitely not Dolores - and another of Bernard Shaw. Despite its dark bronze Fred felt this might be the man's own severed head and so he replaced the drapes before it could begin to talk. "I did him as Laocoon," said Epstein, "Being crushed by the snakes of his own remorseless cleverness, but when I told him so he merely clapped his hands and laughed." There was also a crouching female nude - that Egyptian-looking woman again - next to an emaciated Christ, peering through his crown of thorns to meet Fred's gaze.

So this was art. Fred recalled how he had used to quote Kipling's dismissal of Morris and his 'sacred smut'. And now it appeared that it had been he himself who had been missing out for all these years – although whether on the sacredness or the smut he was not quite sure.

Epstein removed the cigarette stub from Dolores' mouth, then brushed the ash from her breasts.

"Goodbye, Minister of Works," her left eye slowly winked, "When you do see Victor again, say 'hello' from me."

"What is the young lady's surname?" Fred asked in the corridor.

"She's just Dolores," Epstein smiled, "Like Rima or Lilith or Eve. What use would she have for a second name?"

"Where did she come from?"

"She claims to be Creole, from Martinique, the love-child of a French count" – Epstein yanked the front door clean off its final hinge – "But I have it on good authority that she was born just round the corner" – he pointed – "In Doughty Street. And that she was christened Noreen."

Fred left him there in the mews, contemplating the metal door, turning it this way and that, making it flash like a burnished shield in the sunlight.

Going back to The Ministry, Fred again passed the Cavell statue. How feeble it now appeared! Instead of advancing towards him, the figure seemed to recede, as if seen through the wrong end of a telescope. The way the tiny head had been stuck on top of that solid block – pleated to suggest a floor-length cape – implied that the Germans had buried her in cement. It was impossible to imagine a human body under there: those two vertical grooves were presumably her arms, hanging limply by her sides. For the first time, Fred noticed that two other figures – a blandly mediaeval mother and child – were peeping apprehensively over the rim of the main block. Whatever were they doing up there? The whole thing contrived to be skimped and overblown and fussy and crude all at the same time. It was as if it had not been erected but had instead fallen unexpectedly from the skies: he was surprised not to see a pair of legs sticking out from underneath. 'NO HATRED AND BITTERNESS': once more he ran his hands over the words. They had indeed been cut deep, as he had instructed, but cut even deeper and in letters three times as high was the main inscription: 'FOR KING AND COUNTRY'.

Now Fred just could not stop looking. Surely Admiral Nelson was far too small and his column far too large? It was a monument not to the man but to the stone. And as for all those miserable-looking lions, it was quite impossible to imagine them stretching themselves and getting to their feet, yawning or roaring or even flicking the tip of a tail. He wondered what an Epstein lion would be like: Trafalgar Square would probably be strewn with human bones.

It wasn't only the statues: he was seeing everything as if for the first time. How many pretty girls there were walking down Whitehall! And how animated they were, chattering away to each other, pushing dauntlessly through the crowds! One even smiled and bumped her hip against his. How beautiful the traffic fumes were, hanging blue on the air! And how was it, he wondered, that a discarded black shoe, there in the gutter, should be full of fine white sand?

He paused in front of The Cenotaph. Some folk at The Ministry were afraid of it: four years after the unveiling, the Portland stone remained dazzlingly white - no grime seemed to adhere to it. The stark and unadorned face was undeniably moving but Fred had a sudden revelation of what this war monument should have been. For an instant, he even saw it there: Dolores - sitting in this afternoon's pose, innocent yet knowing, utterly unimpressed, eyes narrowed, legs apart, a cigarette in the corner of her mouth, blowing smoke rings towards the Houses of Parliament.

When he reached his office, he was still elated. Although he did not like to use the telegraph, he called in a secretary - even prettier than the girl who had bumped him earlier - and dictated a cable.

Dear Cunninghame Graham,

Rima commission perfectly acceptable. New designs not in the least controversial. Official confirmation follows.

Jowett.

Commissioner Of Works.

⁂

Everyone had a different tale about Grayson, each unlikelier than the last. He was with De Valera and the Irish rebels, or working for Trotsky in Russia. He had died in Melbourne during a bar brawl or had joined a silent order of monks in Maidstone. He was in Deauville, squiring the young wife of an American millionaire or running a furniture shop in the East End of London. He was often seen on the tube – usually the District Line, heading west – invariably accompanied by beautiful women.

"He must be dead," said Snowden to Jowett. "I can't imagine him hiding away for half an hour, let alone for years. Benedictine monk be blowed! That man would have started a riot in an empty cloister."

"I'm not sure," said Fred. "I feel that he *is* dead but somehow without being so. Suppose all those stories are true and that death has merely split him up into dozens of different Graysons?"

Philip decided to ignore this. His friend had picked up some curious notions since he went to The Ministry of Works: you would have thought that it would have had the opposite effect.

The most credible account had come in a letter from George Flemwell, a New Zealand artist. He had known Grayson during the war and had drawn him many times. Two days after the gener-ally-agreed date of the disappearance, he had been visiting London. While sketching on the bank of The Thames, he had seen an electric canoe containing Grayson and another man heading for Ditton Island. Keen to see his old comrade, he had hired a boat and rowed across. The canoe was moored in front of a white bungalow with the nameplate, 'Vanity Fair'. Flemwell kept knocking until the door was opened by a handsome dark-haired woman in a dressing-gown, dishevelled and short of breath. She said that she had never heard of Grayson and slammed the door in his face. "She was obviously lying," Flemwell wrote, "But, knowing Victor, I just assumed that some sort of orgy was going on. I merely felt miffed that I had not been invited to join in." What kind of man, Philip wondered, could so casually commit such a statement to paper? "I did not know, of course, that Victor was supposed to have disappeared. I returned to New Zealand and thought no more about it until I saw a piece in the *Maori Star.*"

On making further enquiries of Henderson at The Home Office, Philip discovered that 'Vanity Fair' belonged to one Maundy Gregory and was lived in by Edith Rosse, believed to be his mistress. According to Norman, however, this man had been employed by the secret service and was known to be a close confederate of Lloyd George. By the expression on his face, Philip knew not to pursue the matter further.

Communication between Norman and himself was increasingly unspoken: a raised eyebrow, a languid wave of the hand, a pained clearing of the throat or a whistled snatch of Brahms . . . 'All Flesh Is Grass' from *The German Requiem*, for example, meant that it was time to be leaving. Graham, who did not speak the language, would look from one to the other in bewilderment. Once you were in power, you entered a completely different world. Snowden had long remarked how MacDonald and Baldwin would look at each other across the chamber. Their expressions were identical – complicitous but also rather sinister, as if they had together committed some unspeakable but as yet undiscovered crime. Now that Philip was a Privy Counsellor, Baldwin regarded him in the same way: he hoped that he was mirroring it acceptably, even though he was unsure what this shared knowledge might be. Even Lloyd George's manner had changed: he treated

Philip not with respect exactly, but with a more refined level of contempt.

According to Norman there were only forty people in Britain who mattered, and perhaps two hundred in the whole world. It was, of course, vitally important for them to approve of you – and Philip had been deemed to be 'up to it', while MacDonald, alas, had not. Out in society, the new PM seemed to believe that the prettiest woman must also be the most influential person in the room which was, perhaps regrettably, not usually the case. Nevertheless Mac boasted that one tete-a-tete with a strawberry blonde had enabled him to scupper Admiral Beatty's grandiose dream of a naval base in Singapore.

The forty men of power had more in common with each other than they could ever have with constituents or even ministerial colleagues. A cabinet meeting, with full agenda and minutes scrupulously taken, would be of less significance than a few seemingly inconsequential words exchanged in passing through some Mayfair salon. So much that mattered was in code! Norman and his cronies, while ostensibly discussing the respective merits of Woolley and Hendren, would not really be talking cricket at all. On his friend's recommendation, Philip was currently reading John Stewart Mill, Immanuel Kant and Helmholtz's *The Sensations Of Tone*. They all got mixed up together in his head – but, according to Norman, that was the very point.

Those bankers really were a rum lot – especially the Americans. They preferred to meet at night, entering and leaving by the back entrances, faces muffled, car headlights switched off. Once, during a perfectly routine discussion, there had come a knock at the door and the chairman of Chase Manhattan had ducked behind Philip's night screen and taken refuge under his bed. Who would have thought that the Treasury – composed, as Ethel put it, of jumped-up shopkeepers – would have such a cloak-and-dagger atmosphere?

The forty people who mattered only cared about what the other thirty-nine might be thinking. They were like those Maidstone

Benedictines: a closed order. Being in office was somehow incidental. Snowden was fascinated by how Asquith, outmanoeuvred and
marginalised by Lloyd George, was still consulted and deferred to
even in matters surely well beyond his competence. Norman would
repeat the man's mumbled non sequiturs as if they were holy writ.
Sometimes it felt as if actual events were irrelevant, that reality
itself was merely a projection of the forty's meditations. During
that seemingly informal initiation ceremony with the King, Philip
had the sense that something momentous was taking place. This
was no mere formality: who could tell what subtle changes were
being wrought on body, heart and soul? "I know you are not a
Privy Counsellor," he said to Jowett, "But you're still a Minister of
The Crown. Didn't you feel that you were somehow different after
you'd seen the King?"

"I didn't and I don't," Fred had replied but Philip was not
convinced. Fred would never have lied, of course, but perhaps there
were certain things that he could not admit even to himself? He had
grown increasingly terse since Philip refused to back that private
members' bill on Widows' Pensions. But why on earth should he
undermine his own authority by putting himself in a suppliant
position when the Liberals were never going to support it? "Next
time, Our Fred, why don't you bring along some loaves and fishes?"
he had snapped but then, seeing the eyes blinking behind those
dusty glasses, had added: "But have no fear! The day of the widows
is rapidly approaching but it has not yet dawned." Fred seemed to
draw little consolation from these words. That same day, Ethel had
been officially presented at Court. With ostrich feathers in her hair,
a gown of jade marocain, a train of emerald and silver and a peacock
fan, she had made quite a stir. "I wished to choose a dress that
would be as simple as possible and yet adequate to the occasion."
She had informed the goggling journalists. It was generally agreed
that she had put Sarah Bernhardt and Lola Montes to shame. The
Snowdens had shared the front page of *The Standard* – he for an
intransigent speech he had made on war reparations, leaving the

more emollient MacDonald, over at the Dawes Conference, high and dry.

Afterwards, in triumphant mood, they had dined with Lloyd George at Churt.

"If you owe something you have to pay it back," said Philip.

"Well, you do if you're German," laughed Lloyd George.

"They didn't borrow it from us," Ethel's feathers dipped dangerously close to the candles. "It was a punishment for losing the war – as if all those millions of dead were not punishment enough. Jingoism is forgivable during wartime but afterwards it is ugly and vulgar and counter-productive."

"I am not a jingo" – Philip smiled – "But Britain must always come first. Whether we like it or not, the Socialist International or even the League of Nations will never supplant the individual nation state."

"There are more important things than one's country," said Ethel quietly.

"Such as?" – enquired Lloyd George.

"Surely I do not have to remind you, of all people, that Universal Love knows no territorial boundaries." She closed her peacock fan then crashed it down on the table. "That is why it is Universal."

There was a long silence, broken only by Lloyd George apparently choking on a fishbone.

"There is that, of course," said Philip at last.

After this, the conversation became rather desultory, especially when Ethel had cut herself a slice of stilton, rather than spooning it out of the well – venting her spleen on the innocent cheeseboard.

So it was with some relief that Snowden and Lloyd George finally left the ladies and stepped out into the starlit garden to enjoy their cigars.

"I understand that you have been making enquiries as to the whereabouts of Victor Grayson," said L-G.

"Some of my constituents have become concerned about his

welfare. Beneath our gruff exteriors, we Yorkshiremen are a sentimental lot."

Lloyd George leaned forward and deposited two inches of ash
on his antirrhinums.

"Tell them not to waste their time looking for him" – the silver
mane shook violently – "At least, not in *this* world." The tongue,
long and red, lolled out of the grinning mouth, while the eyes
glowed with a disturbing lambency. For the first time Philip saw
what Ethel might have meant when she said that L-G was other
than human.

Rima was dead. Fred could not believe it. On first leafing through
Green Mansions, one illustration had struck him as being out of
place: an ominously stippled pall of smoke drifting through trees
into a black sky. 'Burnt to ashes' read the caption and he had vaguely
wondered what might have been burned. And now, on page 279,
he knew: it had been the wild girl herself. The native tribe, having
pursued her through the forest, at last trapped her at the top of
the tallest of her trees. To prevent her escape, they felled the others
surrounding it and then set it ablaze. The women and children were
described singing and dancing in the clearing while she burned.
Fred imagined the smell of roasting flesh and the sound of the poor
coati's fur crackling in the flames.

Surely the point of fiction was to provide the readers with a
happy ending? But even after Rima's death, Abel, the narrator,
in the grip of what he himself called 'moral insanity', stirred up
the neighbouring Indians to slaughter in revenge the entire tribe.
Fred was particularly distressed by the death of Cla-Cla, a harmless old woman who had, throughout the book, been the butt of
much good-natured humour. The description of her corpse, with its
'tangled white locks drabbled in blood', haunted him. 'Drabbled' – a
little voice kept whispering inside his ear – 'Drabbled'.

What kind of monster had this Hudson been? According to Graham he had died bitter and disillusioned: well, it had served him right. Fred had begun to dream about Hungary again. It was as if the book, having banished the nightmares, had now conjured them all back again. He recalled how Paul Pronay had liked to tell his victims that they were about to be released, only to have them conducted to a neighbouring cell where he would be waiting, with new instruments of torture already in his hands.

He realized that, all along, he had been dreading that The People would hurt Rima. It was what they would do. Why couldn't they see how good and beautiful she was? Why did they consider her closeness to the animals and birds to be a reproach to themselves? Why did anything different scare them so much? If only Hayhurst could have come along on his bicycle and sorted them all out before things got out of hand! But perhaps it was also, to some extent, Rima's own fault? What if she had greeted them rather than scaring them away? What if she had taken an interest in their lives: perhaps even – without losing touch with the natural world – devoted some of her time to rudimentary sanitation and public health?

The press had got word of the Epstein commission. It was suggested that Rima would be depicted with a bun in one hand and a banana in the other or seated on a lavatory reading *Das Kapital*. They had also discovered the identity of the model. 'None other than the notorious Dolores: whose name is a byword in Soho.' The reporter had not seen fit to reveal what it might be a byword for.

Epstein was now working on the figure in his new studio on the edge of Epping Forest. How many studios did one man need? He was like a fox with a dozen earths, always one step ahead of the hounds. Baldwin Hill, although only twenty minutes from London by train, seemed remote and forbidding. It was said to command a wonderful view across the city but whenever Fred visited everything was shrouded in fog. For reasons that were unclear even to himself, he made his way out there three times a week. As he approached, along the narrow track, he would hear the chisel biting into the stone with fast irregular strokes, creating a metallic twittering like the song of the skylarks, high above.

"If you're looking for Dolores," said Epstein, "You'd be better off trying The Pillars of Hercules - in the public bar. She won't be coming out here: her work is done."

Not only had Fred never thought about seeing her again, he somehow felt that it was not even a possibility, as if she had been a mirage impossible to recapture or replicate. He found it hard to imagine her in some smoky dive, knocking back her favourite tipple - a pint of wallop, whatever that might be.

"Do you mind my watching you at work?" Fred asked.

"Not at all" - Epstein replaced his goggles - "I won't even know you're here. Just let yourself out when you get bored."

So it was curious how - without knowing he was there - the man would hold forth for hours on the nature of stone. Fred had previously thought of it as mere inert matter but according to Epstein it was changing all the time, like the sea or the sky. He was carving Rima out of monochromatic oolitic limestone. "'Oolite' is my favourite word," he said. "You try saying it." "Oolite" - Fred had a momentary vision of cool green waters through which, without a ripple, long snakes silently moved.

The sculptor had some curious habits. Sometimes he would throw down his implements and pluck up some wet clay - which seemed to be there for no other purpose - and then pace back and forth in front of the relief, arms held at full extension above his head, passing it from hand to hand. After a while it disappeared: presumably he had worked it into his palms. Often he would burst into song - usually a Hungarian gypsy tune by Brahms, all about the River Rima. Fortunately he sang in German, not Hungarian.

> "Hoch geturmte Rimaflut, wie bist du so trub
> And dem unfer klag ich laut nach dir mein lieb!"

When he grew particularly excited, the thick hair would rise on top of his head, causing the little blue cap to fall off, at which he would kneel to retrieve it then press it back into position. There seemed no point to his wearing it but Fred guessed that this must be a vital accessory to the rhythms of his toil.

Epstein often talked of his war experience. He pretended that it had all been a great joke but it had obviously affected him deeply. He had been called up in 1917, after the introduction of conscription, but had applied for an army commission as an official artist, with the remit – from the Imperial War Museum – to depict all the different races that had come together to fight under the Union Jack. This had been vetoed, however – by none other than Sir George Frampton – and so he had instead found himself a Private, assigned to a training barracks near Plymouth. "My feet were aching from their boots, my brain was splitting from their noise – the shouting, the swearing, the incomprehensible orders! I couldn't sleep or eat, and they all laughed at me because I couldn't urinate in front of them. When we went on manoeuvres to Dartmoor I lost my platoon, then the regiment, then the battle itself. So I just started walking. I wandered round in circles for three days. When they found me they were going to shoot me as a deserter but then they decided I was mad and kicked me out instead. I heard later that someone had said to Frampton, 'But suppose Epstein were to be killed?' And do you know what he replied? 'Then the suffering of millions will not have been entirely in vain'."

"What do you think of his work?" Fred asked.

"I don't like it, of course . . . But then I don't dislike it either. It just doesn't register with me." His cap fell off but, with a supple twist, he caught it in mid-air. "I wouldn't call him a sculptor at all but I don't want him killed" – he plonked the cap back on his head – "Maiming would suffice."

"Aren't you upset that so many people are against you?"

"Not at all. It bothered me once but now I positively thrive on abuse: it's a sign that I'm still going in the right direction. With your line of work, I suppose I could ask you the same question."

"Yes," said Fred, "But it still hurts. I've never got used to it and I suspect I never will."

"The day I'm going to start worrying," Epstein took up his chisel once more, "Is when they come with their knighthood and shake my hand and tell me I'm the Grand Old Man of British sculpture." He swung the mallet in a savage arc which culminated in the most delicate of taps.

When Epstein had gone to make tea, Fred stepped forward to pass his fingers over the half-formed figure of a bird. He was expecting the stone to feel rough or jagged but instead it was smooth and cold. And there was the very faintest vibration, like a heartbeat or a pulse.

"You're going to say it's nothing like, aren't you?" Epstein was returning with the customary well-laden tray. Fred was pleased to see that there was seedcake today.

"Nothing like what?"

"Rima. Or Dolores. Or the Eternal Feminine. Or your good lady wife or your dear old mum. Or nothing like anything at all – neither up to your hopes nor down to your fears."

"I haven't really seen it," said Fred, "When I do catch a glimpse it's all out of focus, as if it doesn't want to be looked at yet."

Epstein looked hard into his eyes: "Why do you come here?"

"To get some fresh air into my lungs. There's always tea and cake. And it's interesting to watch you work – although there's surely no point in looking at the figure before it's done? I mean, won't the very last line that you carve alter all the others, establishing the meaning or the feeling of the whole thing?"

"Yes," said Epstein, "That's what it should do."

"And I have no expectations about what it should look like. All I know is that her eyes should be blue, like the sky."

"In case you haven't noticed, Minister, this stone is white, so there will be no colours in it."

"But surely the colours will be . . . implicit, if that's the word.

They will be in the lines and the shapes. I see many statues in my job and when I recall them, they're always in colour - like people but more vivid and alive. Watts' horse in *Physical Energy* is cast in bronze but I see it as pure white. Isn't that the way it's supposed to work?"

"Yes, although Watts got the legs all wrong. And, if you recall, Dolores' eyes are green. What colour are Rima's, in the book?"

"They vary," said Fred, "Different shades of red."

"Good God!" - Epstein dropped the sugar tongs - "It's just as well I didn't read it! But you're right about colour, you know. Everyone goes on about the Elgin Marbles - their classical purity, their dazzling perfection - but originally they were all painted. I mean *really* touched up, like a bunch of tarts going out on a Saturday night."

Fred noticed that he was being unusually generous in his cutting of the cake. "Are you aware that you keep sniffing, like Sexton Blake's bloodhound, looking for clues?" - Epstein handed him the larger slice. "I'd offer you a mask but whatever you wear the dust will get through."

"It's your drains," said Fred. "There's leaf blockage and I'm sure there's a broken pipe underneath. But other smells do come through. Oolite: I've never smelt freshly-worked stone before."

"My sinuses are all clogged up," said Epstein, "Tell me what it smells like."

"It's hard to put it into words," said Fred, "Something between rusting metal and freshly-baked bread . . . a sort of hazy brown, but sharp too, as if you might almost cut your finger on it."

A great paw reached over and took Fred's hand. "Unusual hands for a politician."

"I used to work in the mills," Fred smiled at the pride in his own voice, "As a loom overlooker."

"Looming . . . and overlooking," Epstein murmured, "But I suppose it wasn't as exciting as it sounds."

"It got me fit," said Fred, "And it set me to thinking about things. These days I never have time to think properly. Nothing concentrates the mind more than monotonous physical work for low wages, to no useful end."

"You are a very curious man for a minister" – the cake-knife was cutting yet another slice – "Tell me, do you ever see colours when you listen to music?"

"I don't hear much music, as a rule. Sometimes, when we were singing 'The Red Flag', I'd shut my eyes and everything would go red but I suppose that's what would happen anyway. We never sing it now, you know. MacDonald says that it sends out the wrong signals."

"I came across him the other day," said Epstein. "I was down in Canterbury doing a portrait bust of Conrad and he called by, with a set of the complete works to be signed. He wanted to put him up for a knighthood but he wouldn't accept it. MacDonald was almost in tears afterwards. 'Oh well', he finally said, 'I suppose he *is* a dying man' – as if that somehow explained everything. Dolores tells me that he's dangerous but if he is it could only be in a sentimental sort of way. He seemed rather too nervous a type to be PM: a beautiful head, of course, but there's only so much you can do with Noble. Now if I was to do you, Minister, it would be as an enormous nose, with a little eye on one side and a little ear on the other, like a Picasso."

"The Prime Minister has been having a difficult time." Fred had many criticisms of MacDonald and Snowden but whenever anyone outside the movement said anything he would spring to their defence. "McVitie and Price gave him some shares which he could cash in to buy a Daimler, and he gave their managing director a knighthood. But then *The Daily Mail* found out and he had to return it. He almost resigned over the matter."

"I think these biscuits are McVities'," the sculptor passed the plate. "Very tasty. What's a Daimler?"

"A sort of car. Very nice, I should imagine, but evidently too good for socialists." Fred dunked a Garibaldi in his tea. "I fear that we will not be in office for very much longer. Don't worry – your commission cannot now be rescinded. I understand that you have put in an application to extend this shed . . ."

"I just can't see properly in here," growled Epstein, "I've got to go outside and peer through the window and even then I can't get low enough. I need at least another twenty feet. Ideally, I'd like to be able to get behind her as well, so I can jump out and take her unawares."

"How much do you need?"

A crafty look came into Epstein's eyes. "Fifty quid," he said, "To do it properly."

"Forty," said Fred, "And the Department will, of course, be requiring receipts." He took out his official chequebook and wrote. "There's an extra seven pounds ten for those drains. For the time being, put down a cup of disinfectant every evening, followed by two kettles of boiling water."

"I shall miss you," said Epstein. They shook hands. "Everybody will."

He returned to his work but Fred lingered in the doorway for a while. It was fascinating how the man would chip away at one corner and then move over to the other, or tap high just once and then again low, singing the Rima song at the top of his voice. Fred suspected that Sir George Frampton would not jump about all over the place but would start at one end and silently and implacably work his way across to the other, then lay down his tools and march off to his club.

Outside, Fred took a final look. He had a curious impression that Epstein was no longer alone: it was as if he was dancing or even fighting with an invisible partner. For a moment Fred thought he glimpsed the shadow of a second figure, following the sculptor's movements, as if trying to negate the effect of each stroke . . . And surely he had seen, atop a long neck that struck out like a snake's, the bland features of Paul Pronay?

He turned away. Dusk was falling and through the trees he could see the lights of Loughton flickering and, beyond, an enormous glow in the sky above London. Looking back, he saw that the fog had not completely lifted but was now confined to Epstein's house and shed. Indeed, it seemed to be actually emanating from them. Fred could feel the hair rising on top of his head: if he had been wearing a little blue cap it would most certainly have fallen off.

⁂

"Wake up, you bloody fool, we're buggered!"

In fact, Snowden had been sitting on his bed for the last two hours, working on his speech. He had become increasingly afraid of drying: although he had never yet needed to consult them, he liked to have the papers in his hand.

"Open this door, Philip, those red bastards have done for us!"

He and Jimmy Thomas were staying in Slaithwaite with his agent, Whiteley. This morning they would tour Colne Valley, then go on to Huddersfield market square, to finish with a torch-lit rally in Leeds. He always enjoyed general elections, even when he knew they were going to lose.

What on earth had the Liberals been playing at? With their disastrous by-election results it was obviously in their interests to prop up the government for as long as possible but not only had they refused to support that bill on non-payment of rent but also talked out the subsequent amendment. Lloyd George and Asquith – who normally never spoke – made a point of sitting together, whispering and laughing. A furious MacDonald had to be talked out of dissolving parliament on the spot.

Thomas had given up shouting and was rattling the door handle. Snowden always locked every room he entered. At home he wore a large sporran of keys: "This is supposed to be Eden," Ethel would say, "Not Armley Jail." Now Jimmy was moaning and scraping his fingernails down the wood. Perhaps the house was on fire? There was indeed a burning smell but surely it was only Mrs Whiteley's toast? Taking up his india-rubber, Philip erased a joke about Mr Baldwin's pipe.

Ridiculous and avoidable scandals had finally brought the government down. Just after the Daimler affair, MacDonald had instructed the attorney general to drop treason charges against the radical journalist – and disabled war hero – J. R. Campbell. "How can a man with no feet be subversive?" he had asked, which prompted Ethel to enquire how a man with no brain could be Prime Minister. Tories and Liberals had combined to demand a Committee of Enquiry. The government could have hung on – the worst that could have happened would have been a reprimand – but MacDonald declared that he would not have his honour impugned. What honour might that be? Philip could not bear to hear that word issuing from such a mouth. Yet again, everything had been ruined by one man's egotism. If only he could say all this in his speech! With his silver propelling pencil he reinstated the pipe joke.

On finally opening the door, Philip choked on the aroma of brilliantine, shoe polish and French cologne. Thomas was dressed in an immaculate pearl-grey suit with an onyx tie-pin and links. Thank God he had mislaid that dreadful monocle! 'Gentleman Jim', the Tories called him, and the poor fool took it as a compliment. Being a gentleman had not improved his language, however: his new swell friends loved to hear him swear.

With a sort of whimper he thrust a *Daily Mail* into Philip's hands. The front page was soggy with spilt tea.

GREAT SOCIALIST PLOT DISCOVERED! MOSCOW'S
CIVIL WAR ORDER TO OUR REDS!

With three days to polling day, Philip had been expecting something like this. The new Conservative wall-posters had gone up, depicting a ragged British working man standing next to a booted and fur-hatted commissar.

"I need work," says the Briton.

"I wantski £40,000,000!" sneers the Russian.

He flicked idly through the text. A secret letter from Grigory Zinoviev, head of the Comintern, written to unnamed British stooges, had conveniently come into the newspaper's possession. "'Firing squads to be set up'" – he read aloud – "'Their Majesties primary targets . . . blood will flow, sinews will be strained, nerves will be stirred . . . no stones will be left unturned . . . the British Proletariat will pronounce its weighty word' . . . it doesn't sound very Russian, does it, Jimmy? A bit too orotund: it's probably written on Blenheim Palace notepaper. I can just imagine Churchill and The Beaver knocking it off after a good lunch – it reeks of port and cigars."

"They wouldn't do that," said Thomas, "He's a bloody gent, is Winston."

"He's a sharp politician with a sense of humour" – Philip gave his nastiest smile – "The fact that this is utterly unconvincing is its whole point. If there had been names, addresses and dates, bags of gold and crates of high-explosive, there would have had to be repercussions. As it is, not one person in the country will really believe this but it will suit them to pretend that they do. Before we hit the buffers, we were making a real go of it: we deserve another chance but the voters are nervous. Socialism in power: it still sounds wrong, even to my ears. This rubbish merely gives everyone an excuse not to do the right thing. But in three months we'll be winning by-elections again and in five years, who knows? And the problem for Baldwin is that you can only play the Red Scare card once. Next time everyone will laugh, even if the Red Army is marching down The Mall."

"Someone must tell the King," said Thomas, evidently on the point of tears. "He would never let this pass."

Snowden recalled how, after MacDonald had announced the government's resignation, the Clydesiders had begun to sing 'The Red Flag' and Thomas had threatened them with clenched fists.

"Stop that row!" he had yelled, "Consider His Majesty's feelings."

"I have, of course, communicated my decision to the King," MacDonald had continued, "He seemed most anxious on one point. He put his hand on mine" – the idiot had stared at his own right hand, as if in disbelief – "And said 'Prime Minister, you *have* found me to be an ordinary man, have you not?' and I was able to reassure him that we all considered him to be the first among all the ordinary men in his kingdom . . . Three cheers for His Majesty and may we soon be able to serve him once again!" Even Maxton and his pals had joined in the applause – everyone, Philip noticed, except Fred Jowett.

"Never mind the King." With his cane, he prodded Thomas back along the landing. "What you're going to do now is apologize to Mrs Whiteley for your foul language."

"But she's out," wailed Thomas, "Walking the fucking dogs."

"You've turned the air blue," Snowden said mildly, "While you were a guest in her house." He brought his face up close and opened his eyes as wide as they would go. "It would be best for you to apologize." Gentleman Jim turned pale and began to stammer. Philip was always amused that strong and virile men not only cowered at the lash of his tongue but seemed physically afraid of him as well.

Hyde Park in the Spring! Fred Jowett was in London for the first time since the election. He was no longer an MP: the Tories had withdrawn to give his Liberal opponent a clear run and he had lost by sixty-six votes. In contrast, Philip's majority had doubled while, in Aberavon, MacDonald's had halved. Overall, their vote had gone up by a quarter but Baldwin was back with a majority of 200. Nevertheless, Fred remained cheerful: surely this must be the end of the Liberals, who had lost three quarters of their seats? And he did not miss the travelling: there really was nothing like peace at home. Even now he was on a return ticket: after the unveiling of the Hudson Memorial he would have dinner with the Snowdens and then catch the midnight train.

How he wished that Emily was with him! He would have loved to have shown her the House, then walked arm-in-arm down Whitehall, dropping in on his friends at the Ministry of Works, before crossing Trafalgar Square then heading down The Mall past the palace. But she would never come. Perhaps Philip and Ethel were the problem? Emily seemed fine with them in her own home but he had often seen her head turn sharply, with a flash of something like irritation in her eyes. And sometimes she seemed to be stifling a yawn, almost as if she might be bored by the conversation.

The train arrived late and the Central Line was closed, so he was forced to hail a cab. Rather to his surprise, the driver had recognized him. "If you want, I'll take you back to Bradford afterwards," he said, "You've given me thirty pounds a year now that I can drive through The Park. Any cabby will tell you: Comrade Fred always travels free." He turned out to be a lifelong Conservative supporter but no admirer of Baldwin. "This pretending to be an ordinary chap: who's he trying to fool?" They drove in triumph through Cumberland Gate. "We want toffs and kings to be like toffs and kings, not bloomin' bank managers!" The crocuses and daffodils were fully out: everything was three weeks in advance of Bradford. Fred was overdressed: against Emily's instructions, he unknotted his muffler. The cabman kept sounding his horn. "Bloomin' nursemaids! Bloomin' prams! Where do they think they are – Hyde bloomin' Park?"

And so, rather than being late, Fred had arrived early and in unaccustomed style. He forced a shilling into the driver's hand: "It's not the fare, it's a tip," he insisted. Hardly anyone was about. A few small boys were lugging enormous toy boats towards The Serpentine and a limping, ragged man was being pursued by a uniformed park keeper, who also limped, but with the other leg. Behind them came Bernard Shaw and Cunninghame Graham, their bearded chins raised at identical angles, haranguing each other.

The Memorial was draped by a greasy tarpaulin behind an incongruous red velvet curtain. Leaning insouciantly against the railings was Stamfordham, presumably representing the King. He was definitely not wearing Moss Bros seconds.

"His Majesty would like to invite you and Mrs Jowett to his next garden party, although I warned him that you would probably not accept. He says you're the only one that really believes in Socialism."

"We all believe," said Fred, "We just have different ideas of how to bring it about."

"Ahdidanahdo!" – Cried Stamfordham. "His Majesty is always saying it. Particularly as it seems to irritate the Prime Minister no end." An expression almost of terror appeared on his face: Philip and Ethel were coming down Rotten Row. "I must be going, Fred. Remember that you have powerful friends, should you ever choose to call on them." Vaulting the railings, he made off into the trees.

"We haven't seen one single bird since we entered the park," said Philip, "Perhaps they have a sixth sense about such things." Knowing the Snowdens' opinion of contemporary art, Fred wondered why they had decided to attend. "Wasn't that Stamfordham?" Ethel enquired, "I was talking to his aunt only yesterday. A kindred soul, a fellow toiler in the vineyards of Love."

Philip was looking well enough but remained inconsolable at being out of office.

"I had the most beautiful budget lined up" – he waved his single cane – "It would have been my Eroica: I was going to get Tommy Beecham to conduct it."

"You'll be back, Philip."

"Yes, but what mischief might Churchill get up to in the meantime? I'm not sure that even Norman can control him. We've got to get back on The Gold Standard as soon as possible. That was to have been my centrepiece, you know" – he began to sing – "Back to the Gold! Back to the Gold! . . . We had our chance and we threw it away – or rather MacDonald did. Have you heard about his latest stunt? He thinks he's Moses now."

After the election, MacDonald had once again disappeared into the mountains. "Friends fail you," he wrote, "But the hill road never does. When you are up it never blames: it has no grievance if not put in a cabinet and its ruts are not made in reverence . . . And when you are down it does not attribute its misfortune to you." Ethel had made a series of speeches promoting Henderson as leader but when Mac finally descended – without the Ten Commandments – he had been re-elected unopposed.

"Next time I suppose he'll be having a cabinet of mountains," said Phil, "Seeing how we humans keep letting him down. I'll be all right, of course, but it'll be Ingleborough for Home Secretary, Whernside at Health and Pen-y-ghent at the Ministry of Works."

Fred had often wondered why Phil himself would never stand. He suspected that being openly defeated by MacDonald would be too much for his friend to bear.

By now a couple of hundred had gathered. Epstein appeared, out of breath, as if he had run all the way from Bloomsbury. Even in good tweeds, white shirt and MCC tie, he still looked a mess.

"No sign of Dolores. I told her that there'd be plenty of press and photographers and that if she put in an appearance it would add to her notoriety." Epstein sighed, "But these days she's off with Nina Hamnett to the wilds of Sussex or Kent. They come back stinking of cider, covered in bruises and singing the most horrible folk songs which they claim to have 'collected'. They're working their way through the ruralist composers: those boys think that they are corrupting them but I'm afraid the rubber boot is on the other foot. Ah, women!" He turned away, rolling his eyes in Ethel's direction, "Women! Wherever would we be without them?"

"I am not an anti-semite," said Ethel, watching him go. "In fact, I have often been denounced for my Zionist sympathies. Nevertheless, I do agree with Mr Chesterton that our Jewish visitors should be obliged to dress in eastern robes so that we can more easily recognize them."

"As a sort of declaration of interest," said her husband, "To put it in parliamentary terms."

Fred was sorry that Dolores had not come. He had not quite understood what she was doing in the countryside but he hoped that she was having a pleasant time.

Now the guest of honour came shuffling by. The Prime Minister himself would be unveiling the memorial. Fred had to admit that the cabby had a point: Baldwin was wearing dirty galoshes and a threadbare suit. His cheeks were ruddy and full but his throat was pale and baggy, as if he had sprung a slow leak. A short-stemmed pipe was clamped between his teeth. As he passed, he contrived, in one single gesture, to nod to Snowden, bow to Ethel and pointedly ignore Fred. When he finally reached the dais he sprang up with unexpected vigour.

"He never used to smoke," said Snowden, "There's no tobacco in that pipe. It's just a prop."

Fred was relieved when Shaw did not rise to make the speech. Instead a man from the RSPB droned on about our feathered friends and our passerine pals, making a series of jokes incomprehensible to anyone outside the bird protection fraternity, periodically breaking off into alarmingly convincing whistles and trills, to which there came no response. He did not mention Hudson or Epstein. It struck Fred that the ornamental pools did not seem to be working properly. Surely that drain was too small and wrongly situated, and its metal ring had already begun to corrode? And however would the birds manage to reach the water from a ledge that was fully eight inches above? Only cormorants or herons would be able to drink or wash.

At last someone tugged the back of the speaker's jacket and, as the echoes of his final call faded, Baldwin stepped forward. Phil had been right: no matter how much he puffed at that pipe, no smoke issued from its bowl. At least he had taken it out of his mouth for the ceremony itself: he pulled at the tasselled cord but nothing happened. He pulled harder and it came away in his hand. Two men in overalls stepped up and began to discuss the situation while Baldwin, with a martyred air, stuck the pipe back in his mouth. Then Shaw, elbowing them aside, kicked the curtain to the ground and grappled with the tarpaulin until, almost wholly enwrapped, he had borne it away.

There was utter silence, save for a hissing sound that might have been coming from Ethel. Then Baldwin's pipe fell, to land with a crack on the stone step below. He did not bend to pick it up, however, just continued to stare, slack-jawed.

Although Fred had approved the designs and watched the work in progress, the finished article still came as a shock. He realized that he had only ever seen it by artificial light: now, out in the sun, there was no glow to the stone but instead a chilly blue radiance, as if the forms had been hacked out of ice.

In the shed on Baldwin Hill, Fred had formed the impression that Rima would be dancing but now he could see that she and her attendant creatures were launching themselves into flight. Two more birds had been added: despite their long sharp beaks, they also combined elements of reptile and fish.

She was naked and inescapably sensual: it was evident that Epstein had never opened the book. The long thick tendrils of hair, stretching behind her, seemed to writhe like snakes. The right hand was open, as if ready to slap, the other closed, as if to punch. Although she was in profile, one eye was fully visible, rolling wildly upwards: it was hard to imagine Dolores abandoning her self-possession to such an extent. Epstein had decided to drive the world mad: he had revealed the ear. To Fred's eyes, it resembled a coiled serpent. The overall effect was ecstatic but vengeful: very dangerous indeed. But it was not Rima, nor even Dolores – in fact, it was like nothing Fred had seen before but also somehow deeply familiar . . . he recognized it and it recognized him.

The figures appeared to be on the point of breaking free from the slab: it was hard to conceive of any force strong enough to hold them there. Nevertheless, they did not move . . . but Fred still felt that something wonderful and terrible had been loosed into the world. She was Nemesis, the spirit of just retribution – and, as for the birds, weren't there supposed to be four horsemen of the apocalypse? He imagined the shadow of their wings falling over Buda Hill. In the British Legation, the teacups would begin to rattle, while in the Palace Admiral Horthy would spring sobbing from his throne and, before his bewildered retinue, rip the decorations from his uniform.

In Hyde Park the silence persisted until Shaw, having at last extricated himself from the tarpaulin, raised his hands above his head and began to clap, very loudly. After a few seconds, everyone followed suit.

"I don't call that a statue," said Snowden.

"It's not a statue, Our Phil, it's a relief."

"Well it's not a relief to me," said Ethel, "Typical Asiatic brutishness without an atom of Love in it."

Baldwin, having retrieved his broken pipe, was already leaving. One hand was over his mouth, as if he might have been injured in some way: although there was no breeze, his voluminous trousers were flapping wildly.

"An utter waste of public money." said Snowden.

"It was all raised by subscription," said Fred, "676 donors, including a couple of tramps who gave sixpence each."

"What was Epstein paid?"

"Five hundred and twenty-five pounds, I believe."

"*How* much?" Ethel almost squeaked.

"They offered him five hundred guineas but he insisted that artists, like tradesmen, should always be paid in pounds."

"If it was a statue you wanted why didn't you get Frampton? Anyone would have told you that he is the only man for such things."

Epstein, Shaw and Cunnighame Graham came past, laughing,

"Did you see Baldwin's face?" crowed Shaw, "It was like a halibut on a slab being struck by a bolt of lightning. I could swear that there was almost – almost! – a flicker of life! I suppose he was expecting a saucy little popsy in an off-the-shoulder slip."

Fred had long since revised his initial opinion of Shaw as being harmless. He had not, of course, seen any of his plays but he felt that if The Devil had ever existed, then he would have looked and sounded like this man. He was, however, disappointed at the attitude of the other two: it was as if they had set the whole thing up just to spoof the Prime Minister.

"I'm no admirer of Baldwin," said Snowden. "But the office itself deserves some respect."

Except when it's held by MacDonald, Fred thought, but he held back the words. You couldn't blame Philip, cheated of his 'musical budget', for feeling disappointed.

A group of reporters approached.

"Do you really consider such a sculpture to be suitable for a public place frequented by ladies and young children?" asked the man from The Yorkshire Post.

"I did and I do," said Fred.

"What of the opinion, held by many, that it is downright ugly?"

"Well, Mr Epstein's panel represents Rima, who lives a wild, free life among the animals of the field and forest. There may be some persons who think that such a being could be represented by a composition on angelic lines, pretty and perfect in every way, but their idea is not mine."

"So you are entirely unrepentant, Mr Jowett?"

"Entirely."

"And your opinion, Mr Snowden?" Philip merely winked and wagged a bony forefinger.

"It is an outrage to womankind," said Ethel – slowly, so that they could take down every word. "This is not Hudson's Rima: it is more like the soul of a Shoreditch poulterer's wife being conducted to Hell by two frozen hen-turkeys."

"Thank you, Mrs Snowden," said the men, "That was perfect."

Fred strongly suspected that she had composed her reaction before she had actually laid her eyes on the stone. Besides, Rima now had four attendant birds, not two. Perhaps her new friend Chesterton had written it for her.

Most of the crowd had drifted away. Fred saw that the park attendant and his former quarry were now sitting together on a bench, perhaps comparing the circumstances in which their injuries had been sustained. Then, with a rush of air and a mighty twittering, a multitude of small birds came flying low over their heads.

"I fear that they are in for a severe disappointment," said Ethel. Fred hoped that he had been wrong about that drinking ledge.

Fred's cabman and the others at the North Ridge rank began to sound their horns and cheer. Ethel beamed and, removing a glove, raised her hand in acknowledgement.

"I suppose one should be annoyed," she said. "But I cannot help but feel that they mean it as a compliment - not to myself, of course, but to the mighty and inscrutable powers which I serve."

Fred looked down at her feet: they were still touching the ground but perhaps only because her husband's arm was wound tightly around her waist.

CHAPTER ELEVEN

JOWETT HALL (1927)

"COMRADES" – JAMES Maxton spread his arms like a great ragged crow – "Here tonight, in Bradford, we are privileged to witness the delivery of the first instalment of the Co-operative Commonwealth. Here are meeting rooms, games rooms, a great auditorium, a library with over fifteen hundred volumes and not merely one piano or even two but three! A piano, Comrades, on every floor! (Cheers). A wee peek into a golden future: The People's university, The People's symposium, The People's athe-naeum! (More cheers).

"But this new hall of ours is no mere club – except in the sense of being a weapon with which we may belabour our enemies. Argument and ideas are our chosen ways, persuasion and conversion are our means, but if sweet reason should fail" – he brandished a large tome above his head "Then *Das Kapital* here is heavy enough to bang some sense into even the thickest skull." (Laughter and applause). "And now let us remember the Great Men of the ILP who led us to this place. Too many of them – Hardie, Glasier, Maguire – are no longer alive but Fred Jowett marches indomitably on and it is fitting that we honour him today. When he mounted Chapel Street on his way to found our party, thirty-four years ago, he could never have guessed that one day this would no longer be the Temperance Building but . . . Jowett Hall!" (Loud cheers and applause).

Everyone was looking in Fred's direction: his own head had turned, as if to see what was happening behind him. He could have sworn that he glimpsed a couple of mill owners – and wasn't that Fenby, the Liberal who had beaten him in the last election? Whatever were *they* doing here? The cheering went on and on: he could feel the sweat prickling his cheeks. There was something disturbing about such enthusiasm: some folk, not known for their sentimentality, were nearly in tears. In these dark days since the General Strike, everyone was desperate to find something to celebrate, as if that failure had left a deep wound that blighted every aspect of their lives.

"I have here a telegram," Maxton continued, "From Comrade Philip Snowden, who, of course, resigned from our party last month. (Boo-ing, some cheers). It reads:

'My dear and notorious Fred,

Many congratulations on becoming a Hall. Madame Snowden, however, suggests that, for continuity's sake, you should adapt your own name to the building's previous use. The Honourable Frederick Temperance, I'm sure you will agree, has a fine ring to it.'"

Much to Fred's relief, the catcalls had given way to laughter and applause. It was inconceivable that the ILP could ever really turn against Our Phil.

He slipped away into the empty library. There was a gap on one shelf where Maxton had plucked down Marx for his rhetorical effect. He had never felt at ease in libraries: the books seemed to be looking askance, as if taunting him with all the things that he would never know. Who would have thought that there could be so much poetry in the world? It took up an entire wall. Opening a volume at random, he discovered that the print was tiny and crammed right up to the edge of the page: there was even more poetry than it had appeared.

Shaw had insisted on donating his *Complete Works*. "We couldn't turn him down," the librarian had said, "But we've stuck 'em up on top so you'll need a long arm and a head for heights." *Plays Pleasant and Unpleasant*, *Volumes of Theatre and Music Criticism* and scores of socio-political works: how busy he had been! *Common Sense And Municipal Trading*, *Common Sense About The War*, *Peace Conference Hints*, *How To Settle The Irish Question*: Shaw had opinions on everything. He had sent a bakers' dozen of his latest, entitled *Translations And Tomfooleries* – which seemed to Fred to sum it up. But suppose the man really *did* have solutions to every problem and nobody took them seriously, coming from such a source?

Although Jowett Hall smelt heavily of wax polish and fresh paint, Fred remained suspicious of its drains. It had taken years to raise the money. "It was a funny thing," the Committee told him. "We'd just done the sums and found we still needed seven hundred when a cheque arrived for that exact amount. When we made enquiries it wasn't from our Russian friends, but from the ABC Foundation, which belongs to some rich American, one of those oil typhoons. We think they've confused you with a different, theological Jowett, in Oxford University, but we're not going to look a gift horse in the mouth."

From the auditorium there came a dreadful sound. Maxton had found one of the pianos and was banging out his party piece.

> "Oh better far to live and die
> Under the brave black flag I fly
> Than play a sanctimonious part
> With a pirate head and a pirate heart."

Jimmy's own head seemed to be unscrewing itself from its neck. Fred wondered if his frequent illnesses could be caused by the rigours of such performances. The audience were singing along but that tuneless roar drowned them all out.

> "For I am a pirate king!

And it is, it is a glorious thing
To be a pirate king!"

Maxton leaned back on the piano stool and raised his enormous dusty boots to block out the final chords. How could Philip's hero Brahms call Britain a land without music when we had Gilbert and Sullivan?

Now the crowds were flowing out of the room. Fred felt his arms being seized: bowing to the inevitable, he allowed himself to be borne down the stairs.

The basement bar was half the size of the auditorium but twice that of the library. He shaded his eyes as the light from a dozen gas lamps flared off the polished oak and brass: the gleaming mirrors were stippled with the name of the brewers who had generously provided the fixtures and fittings. Judging by the scrum, they would be getting their money back on the first night. Above the beer pumps, the shelves were crammed with exotically-labelled bottles. There was evidently just as much alcohol as poetry in the world: perhaps the two were somehow related?

He couldn't help thinking that the Snowdens had a point: once something had been christened, it should keep its name for ever. What had become of The Temperance Movement, formerly one of the moral foundations of Socialism? He looked around: there was a nasty, vaunting feel to all this carousing. Now the few remaining teetotallers had become their enemies – life-denying killjoys – while Joshua Tetley and Sons were their boon companions.

He was jammed up against Willie Leach at the bar. Willie had a glass in either hand, from which he was taking alternate gulps. When George V had started drinking again, after the war, he had not abandoned his own reverse pledge. He never seemed drunk but nor did he ever seem quite sober.

"Congratulations, Fred. A hall is better than a street or a road or even a statue. Personally, I'd like to be a pub – one day The Queen's Arms will bear my name."

"Here's your usual," said the barman, presenting Fred with a half of dark mild. He winked. "On the house – on *your* house, you jammy dog!"

Joseph Southall, the painter, joined them. "I'd like to be a main line railway station," he clinked glasses, "Perhaps even a junction."

They led him to a table where Maxton was already seated, dipping his beak into a tall glass brimming with dark liquid. It looked as if it might be some hideous cocktail of absinthe, blood and chemicals, rather than what it was – dandelion and burdock.

Fred sipped his beer. It had been a curious day. This morning, for the first time in thirty years, he had gone down to Heaton Woods, to find that the reality was even worse than the reports. The Parks Department had culverted the stream into a series of paddling-pools: the trees had been felled, the hyacinths and marsh-marigolds all rooted up. Wherever would the dippers and wagtails be nesting next Spring? There was no sign of the copy of *Heroes and Hero-Worship* that he had once pitched into the bushes. The bushes themselves had gone. He had hardly ever given them a thought but now he realized how important it had been that the woods were still there, unchanging from generation to generation.

He could only see this as another personal attack. Having lost his parliamentary seat, he had decided to stand once again for Bradford Council – but in Tong rather than his old Manningham ward. He had anticipated a low-key campaign and a fairly comfortable victory, but it had not turned out that way. 'What can a Little Hortonite ever know of Tong?' demanded the Liberal leaflets – as if Tong lay west of Suez, rather than the other side of Sticker Lane. Then the *Telegraph and Argus* had reproved him for 'picking up metropolitan airs', the anonymous writer having taken offence at his perfectly ordinary shoes. And then Alderman Pullen, leader of the Liberals, had claimed that when he had succeeded him as Chairman of the Health Committee, twenty-five years ago, he had found it 'a cesspit of drunkenness and corruption'. Fred knew who he meant: Dr Arnold Evans – the sainted man had long since drunk himself to death, and was thus in no position to defend himself. Fred had lost by 243 votes: after the count, the Liberals had celebrated by singing 'The Red Flag'.

"Attaboy," said Willie, "Have another." Fred was startled to see that his glass was already empty. "Pint this time!" and before he could demur, the smirking barman had slammed it down in front of him. And so it was that he made the momentous discovery that – even though it had been drawn from the same pump – a pint of dark mild actually tasted twice as good as a half.

Southall's own drink had remained untouched while he toiled away at a sketching pad, his eyes never leaving Fred's face. He had been doing this for years but the long-threatened portrait was yet to appear.

"Missed it – again!" The artist threw down his pencil and drained his glass. "That look – it was there – I had it and then it was gone."

"Tell us when he's doing it again," said Maxton, "And we'll grab hold of him."

"Epstein said that he would do me as an enormous nose," said Fred, helpfully.

"That wasn't quite what I had in mind." Southall took a dim view of modern art. He had recently become reconciled to the Impressionists only for the Post-Impressionists – or the "Pimpressionists," as he called them – to once again blot out the light. "It's funny, you know" – he took another drink – "The face quivers, then goes into flat planes that sort of shuttle about. He reminds me of someone but I don't know who it is."

"Just another wee peek into the future, perhaps," said Maxton, finishing his dandelion and burdock. Even over the hubbub, you could hear his bones creaking as he rose from his seat. Tomorrow morning he had a speaking engagement across the Pennines in Chorlton-cum-Hardy. "Hail and farewell, Comrade Temperance," he said. The whole bar applauded his slow and painful exit: he had learned a lot from Snowden.

"Bastard!" said Leach, "He wouldn't dare to twit Philip to his face. Did you hear the way they booed him?"

"It was the strike," said Fred, "Philip disappointed us all."

"What did you expect him to do? He knew that it was doomed and that our enemies would use it as a stick to beat us with. He's not one of those who blunder along from day to day, he plays the longer game. So even when he seems to be wrong he always turns out to be right."

The barman, collecting the empties, paused: "If your Snowden took you to the edge of a cliff and told you to jump, what would you do?"

Leach flapped his arms: "I'd get ready to fly."

Nevertheless, it was sad that Phil was not here. He had resigned from the ILP when its conference refused to nominate MacDonald for the honorary post of Labour Party Treasurer, a formality that it had observed for the last fifteen years. "I will not tolerate gratuitous insults to our leader," he had announced, even though he himself insulted MacDonald on a daily basis. Fred had hardly seen him since the General Election and when they did speak on the telephone, Phil would rant as if addressing a public meeting. "Those Clydesiders are destroying the ILP," he shouted, even though membership had doubled since Maxton became Chairman. Philip was now a national figure: queues would stretch as far as Westminster Bridge whenever he and Churchill were due to clash over financial affairs. He was said to be about to form a new party with Lloyd George: why else would his wife be spending so much time at Churt?

When the strike began, Philip had taken to his bed. The old trouble had flared up again, leaving him paralysed, flat on his back, too ill even for visitors. When Lady Wimbourne and the Archbishop of Canterbury had invited him to join them in interceding with the government, Ethel had turned up instead, insisting that if the strikers and the mine-owners would only love one another then all would be well. It was rumoured that her husband had been spotted round the corner, feeding the ducks in St. James' Park. When Fred rang, an unwary parlour maid had informed him that the master and Sir Montagu had gone to Covent Garden for *The Marriage of Figaro*. Saturday night seemed a curious time for a wedding but presumably this was one of Norman's foreign banker friends.

Philip finally rang back a full week after the strike had collapsed. "Such things never do anyone any good," he said, "In industrial disputes both sides are always equally in the wrong."

"How did Mr Figaro's wedding go?" asked Fred.

"Wonderful! It was naughty, I know, but who could resist Frau Lehmann and Fraulein Schumann – to say nothing of Maestro Walter. Brahms and Mendelssohn notwithstanding, I do believe Mozart to be The Gold Standard of the musical world."

Sometimes Fred had no idea what his friend was talking about.

"I've just been for a walk in Hyde Park," Philip continued, "They've been at your statue again. 'Death To Jew Miners' in red paint: that Epstein gets even more stick than we do."

The next day, Snowden had risen in the House and excoriated the government's handling of the strike. And when they introduced their Trade Disputes Bill, making secondary strikes illegal, he had torn it apart in a ninety minute tour de force of remorseless logic and sarcasm. Apparently Churchill – against all parliamentary practice – had been seen applauding at the end. How Fred loathed this hypocritical cameraderie! Before the strike, Churchill had claimed that prominent ILP figures had been deputed to blow up strategic bridges and railway lines. If Baldwin had allowed it, he would have rolled out the firing squads. As it was, he had commandeered tank squadrons to deliver his anti-strike rag, *The British Gazette*. When faced with such vicious inanities, however, Phil had merely laughed: "Good old Winston!"

Fred became aware that someone was tapping him on the

shoulder. "Hail the conquering hero!" said Alderman Pullan. Fenby, also grinning, was standing by his side. "Allow us to buy you another drink."

"I've got one," said Fred.

"Well, let us at least congratulate you."

Fred stared at the proffered hand. Why ever did the man wear two wedding bands?

"I fear Mr Jowett is still a little miffed," said Fenby, with what seemed genuine regret. During the strike he had called for the suspension of habeas corpus.

"Oh, come off it," said Pullan, "All's fair in love and politics. You'd have done the same to us."

"No I wouldn't," said Fred.

"Then more fool you," said Pullan, "And it's you who's the hypocrite - playing the Holy Joe when you're here knocking it back with the best of them."

"I'd like to congratulate you," said Fred, "For ruining Heaton Woods."

"We've cleaned them up" - Pullan's face was turning puce - "No more scratchy brambles, no nasty snuffling badgers, no squawking jaybirds, just good straight gravel paths and lovely paddling-pools, regulation fourteen inches deep. Everything neat and tidy and perfectly safe: innocent fun for all the family. I thought you'd be pleased, the way you're always maundering on about the kiddies." Fenby took his arm and drew him away. "Anyroad," he shouted over his shoulder, "This will be Jim Pullan Hall before we've done."

"Nay, Fred," said Leach. "It's not like you to refuse to take someone's hand."

"Who invited them?" asked Fred.

"I did. They were only being polite and now you've hurt their feelings. We've got to be able to work with these people: Pullan will be Mayor next year."

Fred drained his glass. "I see things differently since the strike."

The General Strike had only lasted for nine days but to Fred they had felt like weeks, months, even years. In contrast, the Great War had flashed by mercifully quickly: in his memory, it and the strike had assumed a curious equivalence. How eerie was the silence on that first morning when no trams or buses ran! Even the birds and insects had held their peace. Many folk had left as usual for their early shift only to find themselves locked out: the mills had been closed for fear of machine-breaking. "It's come to something," they complained, "When the bosses walk out before we do." On the back of his son-in-law's motorcycle, Fred had traversed the region from Wakefield to Halifax but found few opportunities to express his solidarity. It was like when the Old Queen died: most people remained inside their homes.

On the second day, the atmosphere was different. There were rumours that some trams were operating in Leeds: Fred unsuccessfully tried to turn back a mob setting out to walk the fourteen miles along the canal towpath. The expressions on their faces reminded him of Grayson's Keighley audience: it was as if they were consumed with hatred for everything – even for each other and themselves. Many had bulging sacks slung over their shoulders. "But won't there be any stones in Leeds for you to throw?" he had asked. "Nay," came the reply, "It's a funny place, is Leeds."

It had been immediately apparent that the government had stockpiled coal, oil and food ready for the strike, whereas the unions' leadership, fearing to appear intransigent while negotiations continued, had made no preparations at all. Russian offers of financial support had been declined: it was better to lose than to be thought of as unpatriotic. As always, the working-class movement had played scrupulously fair, while its opponents blithely ignored all their own rules. They would bribe and threaten, forge letters, smash windows, arrest the innocent on trumped-up charges, traduce the living and the dead and then, when they had triumphed, come forward, smiling, wanting to shake your hand.

It had to be said that Snowden was not the only prominent figure to come badly out of the strike. MacDonald had spent his time trying and failing to get on the radio to address the nation. He blamed Ethel Snowden, who was now on the Board of the BBC, but what could he have said that would have made any difference? Walter Citrine and the TUC had made no secret of their lack of enthusiasm, and Maxton had been ill once again. Fred had dashed about, seeking sympathetic printers for local strike bulletins, to provide some correctives to *The British Gazette*. It was apparent that the further south you went, the less effective the strike became.

In Manchester he could have sworn that he had seen a tram being driven by none other than Victor Grayson, in a white wool sweater, with a briar pipe clamped between his teeth. "That man is capable of just about anything," said Leach, "Not only did he fight in the war, he actively recruited for it . . . But I don't think he'd ever wear a roll-necked sweater."

The strike had ended ingloriously. Jimmy Thomas, acting as a go-between, informed the union leaders that, if they called it off, the government would then implement Lord Sankey's compromise report. Subsequently, of course, they had done no such thing. Everyone flounced around, claiming to have been betrayed, but they had known all along what was happening, only pretending to be fooled. The rest of the movement had then watched as the miners hopelessly fought on until winter. And when they did march back to the pitheads, it was to discover that, for a third of them, there were no longer jobs to be had.

Fred saw that Leach had produced his notorious leather hip-flask. It was the sort of thing that explorers would carry into a desert. Although his inside pocket had been reinforced, the weight still pulled his shoulder down. New acquaintances took him to be a hunchback.

"What is it?" Fred had expected whiskey or brandy or fire and brimstone, not this delicious fruity taste.

"Vodka" – Leach pronounced the 'v' as a 'w' – "From Gomersal, distilled by genuine White Russian refugees. Mixed with blackcurrant cassis. I call it The Zinoviev Letter, because it saws you off at the knees."

Fred felt - curiously - both agitated and relaxed. How odd to be toping after all these years! Now he understood: drink brought out the best and worst in you, then made you feel that there wasn't a ha'porth of difference between them. It had also temporarily relieved his deafness. He could now hear everything that was being said, although little worth the hearing. A group of Labour Councillors had joined them: why was it that these people seemed to take a dimmer view of their comrades than of their enemies? Most conversations began and ended with MacDonald: no-one had a good word to say - perhaps that was why he kept being re-elected as their leader, unopposed?

Leach's latest bugbear was Oswald Mosley. It was a long time since anyone had made such an impression on the movement. "He combines the amorality of Grayson with the immorality of MacDonald" - Snowden had said - "Without the charm of the one or the weasel cunning of the other." Fred wondered if this antipathy stemmed from Mosley also being a handsome man and, by repute, even more romantically inclined than his predecessors.

"Philip is right," Leach topped up their glasses, "He's a man on the make."

"I rather like the sound of him," said Southall, "Isn't he a guild Socialist, like Morris?"

"More like a gilded Socialist," said Willie, "But not a gelded one."

"Shaw thinks that he might be The Superman, the one we've all been waiting for."

"I've not been waiting for a Superman. Have you, Fred?"

"All that matters is that Mosley is against the Gold Standard and for a proper Incomes Policy." Fred was about to agree when he realized that it was his own voice he was hearing. "And, unlike MacDonald or Grayson, if he says he's going to do something, he does it. I saw a lot of him during the strike: he made dozens of speeches, poured his own money into the miners' fund, even bought his own newspaper to counter Churchill's lies. He claimed – and I believe him – that he didn't sleep a wink for the entire nine days."

"What I don't get," muttered one of the Councillors, "Is what's in it for him. He's a rich man and a toff and he's MP for Smethwick. Where are the bloody coalmines in Brum?"

"I was talking to a comrade in Birmingham," said Fred. "Apparently Mosley was at a strike committee meeting when the police arrived to arrest them. They waited outside until he had left before they moved in. When challenged about this, the Sargent replied, 'Did you see that suit? How can you arrest a chap dressed like that?' but he got the impression that they were actually physically intimidated, afraid that he might cut up rough."

"Ah, so he's just one of them that likes a good scrap," said the relieved Councillor, "There's plenty of our lads like that."

Fred had last seen Mosley when they had been guests of honour at the Durham Miners' Gala. Perhaps because of its cancellation the year before, it had seemed larger and louder than ever. The banners of every union and affiliated organisation fluttered defiantly against an unnaturally blue sky. Brass bands were stamping about, all playing different tunes: sometimes it was an advantage to be deaf. Fred had already taken his place under the faded standard of the Dyers, Bleachers, Finishers and Textile Workers when Mosley had swept past, without acknowledgement. Not even the Devil himself would have dared to molest him in that suit. Introduced as 'The only man in the parliamentary party who had the guts to stand by us', he received a standing ovation before even opening his mouth. The speech that followed had been competent enough but afterwards Fred could recall little about it, except that he had invoked humanity and justice in furious tones, while the direst of threats had been accompanied by a merry laugh. And, halfway through, after a particularly strenuous passage, he had produced a handkerchief of the most dazzling whiteness. He flicked it open with a conjurer's flourish, revealing that it was at least twice normal size. Then – without blowing his nose or mopping his brow – he refolded it and replaced it in his top pocket. Grayson himself could not have done it better. Afterwards, that handkerchief had been the talk of the Gala: "Did you hear the sound it made? Like a peal of thunder – it must have been *starched!*"

Before returning to Bradford, Fred had visited Chester-Le-Street. Somehow, even before his train pulled into the station, he had known that something was wrong: he could smell the misery in the air.

And there they were, those metal shacks and lean-tos, those coops of wire and board, with even their doors and window frames now gone, chopped up for fuel. His ministerial edict had been countermanded or ignored. Hoards of black-pad beetles swept to and fro, like murmurations of starlings. The drains were clogged with filth, greyish water dripped from rusty stand pipes and, even in the heat, the mud was almost impassable. The place resembled a long-neglected farmyard: Instead of these pallid and unshaven men and these women with bruised faces, he almost expected giant bedraggled hens to appear. Everyone walked with their heads bowed, as if ashamed to meet his eyes. Their children were dirty and half-starved, at once feral and apathetic: many had rickets.

"Don't blame yourself, Fred," said the union man, "You've always done your best. We knew the strike was hopeless but we had to do *something*, didn't we? Otherwise, we'd have lost our self-respect." He waved an arm at the desolation around them and then, to Fred's bemusement, began to roar with laughter.

For some time, Joe Southall's unsteady hand had been misdirecting his beer down his shirt front. "Shorry," he said, "Sheem to've losht the may to my wouth." Leach's head was tilting further and further back as he attempted to smoke a whole cigar without disturbing its ash. Either the barman had dimmed the gas or the smoke was clouding Fred's vision. The place was already fuggy and disreputable, its walls yellowed by nicotine. Without his noticing, it had emptied, except for their table and a little knot of Liberals who were singing an obscene version of 'Adeste Fideles'. He had not previously realized how horribly Pullan's backside protruded: it had parted his coat-tails and was now peering around. Leach stood up, only to slide to the floor in a great cloud of ash. Fred and Southall went to help, only to find themselves sprawling next to him. "Sawn off at the knees, Comrades," Willie cackled, "Sawn off at the knees!"

Fred had little recollection of the next two hours. Unless drunkenness enabled you to magically project yourself from place to place, his faithful legs had, presumably, carried him home. Nevertheless, he had a hazy impression that at one point he had been hovering high above the city. Emily had informed him that his coat was torn up the back: perhaps it had caught on the Town Hall spire? His toes were throbbing and he could not dispel the dreadful suspicion that he had booted both Fenby and Pullan up the backside. He felt that he had kicked them simultaneously – which was impossible, unless he had indeed been flying at the time. Most likely nothing had happened: surely, at sixty-two, it was too late to be entering your name in the arse-kicking stakes, unless some natural law demanded that, if you were sober and responsible in your early and middle years, you must become – in your dotage – sottish and absurd. Perhaps everyone had their quota of imbecility to fulfil?

Emily had not been impressed by his explanations. Although she had declined to attend the ceremony, she had been waiting up for him. Her finger pointed to the clock: Fred, squinting, saw that it was ten to one, or was it quarter to two? He began laughing because he had never before noticed that the clock's hands ended in two tiny fists. At this, Emily had gone up to bed, but not before saying something terribly hurtful which he could not now recall. When he tried to follow, he was unable to negotiate the stairs.

Since then he had been dozing on the kitchen chair. He felt to be constantly falling asleep when he already was, then waking up from being awake, as if consciousness and unconsciousness were made up of alternating and infinitely thin layers. Then something began to cruelly squeeze his bladder and he found himself back on his feet. He had not visited the lavatory all evening – the barman had dubbed him 'the camel' – but now he just had to go. As he tore at his fly-buttons, he realized that he would never reach the w/c across the yard. His other hand jerked up the sash-window and, bending his knees, he leaned forward over the sill. At first, nothing seemed to be happening but then he heard the drops slapping the flagstones below.

He did not need to consult his watch: it was ten to four. The sky was full of stars: he could never remember their names or pick out the shapes of the constellations. There came a faint sound of breaking glass: from this distance it was like the tinkling of sleigh bells but how terrifying it would be if it was close at hand. "Broken bottles," he said aloud, "Bloken bockles, Comlade Glayson."

He had never known such relief. On and on it flowed, as if determined to wash the whole city away. A yellowish steam arose and there was a sustained hiss as if it might be eating its way through the stone. What if the neighbours awoke and saw him? Perhaps he could claim to be acting on Royal Authority? "There's nowt like piss at 'ome," he would say.

A stealthy movement caught his eye. Out of the darkness came a large brindled cat. Evading the stream it calmly lifted its tail and sprayed the bottom step to mark its territory. Now he understood why it had been months since he had seen – or even smelt – a rat.

Now something else was stirring. Three irregular white shapes were floating, seemingly independent of each other, across the earthed-over tump where the privy middens had stood. As Fred watched, these resolved themselves into the figure of a tall, pale-faced man in dark clothes and luminous spats. He appeared to be advancing and receding at the same time, as if taking two steps forward, then one step back. Even before he made out the features,

Fred had recognized Victor Grayson. He was not surprised, as if all the other events on this peculiar day had somehow been leading up to this point.

"It's nice out, Comrade Jowett" – the voice was distorted into a Yorkshire accent even worse than the King's – "But for God's sake put it away before someone sees it. And I'd close that window if I were you. Haven't you read *Tristram Shandy?* – Grayson reverted to his mellower tone – "We don't want any nasty accidents with that sash."

The upper body appeared stiff, as if bound in a corset, and the head was set at a quizzical angle but he was still smiling, as dapper as ever in a long overcoat of some shiny material.

"You're looking older, Fred . . . older and even wiser."

"And you're looking . . ." – Fred's voice tailed off. Grayson had reached the kitchen steps: it was now evident that he was soaked to the skin.

"Wet," said Grayson, "I'm wetter but no wiser."

"Has it been raining?"

"Wherever I go, it seems to be wet" – Somehow, his face and hair were perfectly dry – "I wouldn't say I was unlucky but the other day I unpeeled a banana and there were nowt in it."

Fred was not sure how to respond to this revelation.

"Sorry," said Grayson, "I thought that was a well-known Yorkshire expression."

"No," said Fred, "It's not. We don't see many bananas up here."

"Your rabbit seems to have escaped." The long fingers rattled across the empty wire cage.

"It's where the tortoise used to live."

"What an appropriate pet: that impregnable carapace, that slow but inexorable onward tread. I used to have a dog, one of those big silly Airedales, but my wife's parents took it after she died. I bet they've clipped the poor thing's coat. I called it Nunquam, after old Blatchford."

"That's what we called the tortoise."

"Forget cities, pubs and halls," said Grayson, "People naming their pets after you - that's immortality."

"Snowden told me that, in Colne Valley, the dogs that tried to bite him were all called Grayson, and that Victor the cockerel kept him awake the night before the election."

"It's nice to know that - if only indirectly - I can still trouble the slumbers of decent folk."

"What brings you to Bradford?" Fred was buttoning up his fly.

"Didn't you call me? I distinctly heard my name and something about broken bottles."

He still smelt the same: Fred had always taken it for the scent of women but now realized that he must be perfuming himself. Grayson paused halfway up the steps and extended his leg sideways. It hooked itself over the sill, to be followed, in one impossibly fluid movement, by the rest of the body. "How much sweeter life would be," he trilled, "If everyone came and went by windows rather than doors."

Fred followed him through to the living room.

"Very bohemian," Grayson whispered, "Not at all what I expected. But isn't it time you repapered those walls?"

"Can you speak up?" Fred cupped his ear.

"I was trying not to wake Mrs J." - Grayson leaned against the mantelpiece - "You do have a problem if you can't hear what your own hallucinations are saying." Even indoors, his breath was still condensing. "Are your daughters at home?"

"Only the eldest: I don't think she's your type."

"Oh, I haven't got a type." From his inside pocket he produced a flask even larger than Leach's. It had not, however, affected the lines of his coat. "Where do you keep the good glasses?"

"There's just those," said Fred.

Grayson half-filled two chipped tumblers with a cloudy, yellow-ish liquid. "None of your bathtub hooch. This is the real stuff, what Hyndman used to call 'The Necktie Of The Gods'. It takes you beyond inebriation to that happy land where Falstaff and Savonarola play leapfrog, while Queen Victoria and Messalina sit comparing notes. There's too much nonsense talked about the demon drink: it's no worse than any other habit. Did you ever see Keir Hardie when there wasn't a cup of tea to hand? I remember him sweating and shaking outside a closed Lyons Corner House, like an opium-addled Lascar. I had to knock on doors, begging the goodwives to brew up for the Lion of the Proletariat . . . Cheers!"

The nectar of the Gods turned out to have no taste whatsoever but it smelt like the gobstoppers that Fred had loved as a child. Grayson immediately refreshed their glasses. "Yes, my magic flask is always full, no matter how much you imbibe."

"Never again, after tonight," said Fred.

"But it's already tomorrow morning. One little tip: always drink standing up, keeping your feet well apart. Breathe in deeply to a four count, then exhale to a five."

They stood in silence for a while, breathing in and out together. Fred was relieved to observe that his companion was reflected in the mirror.

"You don't seem particularly surprised to see me," said Victor, at length.

"No. You are the only person I know who might appear in such circumstances."

"So you didn't take me for a broken-hearted night-soil man, haunting the scenes of his former happiness?"

"No, but I'm still not sure whether you're really here or not."

"Are we ever really anywhere? Even as a child, I felt that I didn't belong – that I'd taken a wrong turning and couldn't find my way back. I've tried pretty much everything but even dying hasn't helped. At least I get some peace now: you're only seeing me because of the drink – I do not deign to manifest myself before the sober."

"Didn't I see you in Manchester, driving a tram?"

"Not I" – Victor brushed the water off his lapels – "There are three things a man should never do: board a tram, smoke a pipe or cross a picket-line. I played no active part in the strike, although I did follow it with interest. I always thought that the rank and file would never come out but they turned out to be as keen as mustard. It was their leaders who got cold feet and left them in the lurch." He threw back his head. "Cold feet and mustard in the lurch! Bring me my soapbox, I've still got the gift!" He leaned across to clink glasses. "But tell me, after everything that's happened, do you still believe in the triumph of Socialism?"

"I did and I do," Fred half-choked on his nectar. If only he could stop himself saying that!

"Personally, I take pride in being the only man ever to be elected to parliament as a Socialist, with the word itself in brackets after my name: the first and probably the last."

"We'll win, all right: by weight of numbers and sheer persistence, we will wear them down, until – in the end – The People stand alone."

"And, as Pope puts it, 'Universal darkness covers all'."

Perhaps he had gone over to Rome? Fred was not particularly surprised. "I haven't seen you since before the war, when Philip and I witnessed your Keighley speech."

"Ah, my farewell tour! Those bloken bockles – how they lapped them up! Murder In The Red Barn just wasn't in it! Thick gammon slices, smoked and glazed, as Ruth used to say. What fun it all was! But I was dreadfully hurt by your response."

He had not appeared hurt at the time, nor did he now.

"Perhaps Philip was a little hard on you but his mother was gravely ill."

"I can't imagine Comrade Snowden having a mother: I always pictured him crawling out of the crater of Vesuvius and riding down on the lava flow. But it wasn't what he said that bothered me but your silence. While I stood awaiting excommunication, your mouth kept opening and then closing again." – Grayson made a popping noise – "Like a disapproving goldfish."

"I agreed with Philip and I still do. I was so disgusted that I could not trust myself to speak. He always felt some affection for you but I did not. The movement is still coming to terms with the damage you wrought, all the hopes you raised and then dashed – but I don't suppose you care about that."

"I didn't and I don't," Grayson picked up the seashell on the mantelpiece and held it to his ear.

"If I had enjoyed your advantages, I would have made better use of them."

"What advantages?" Grayson blew into the shell.

"When you entered a room – even unannounced – everyone would turn to look at you. And when you began to speak everyone fell silent. Presence, bearing, charisma: whatever you call it, it cannot be taught. You either have it or you haven't."

"If you don't need to work at something, you tend to undervalue it. And, rather like being double-jointed or able to wiggle your ears, it doesn't fit you for very much. When people are fascinated they stop listening to what you say and when they want to fuck you, of course, they don't hear a word. Perhaps it is not a blessing but a curse. And you can't turn it off: when I tried to be self-effacing, they went into an absolute frenzy."

"I have to be self-effacing," said Fred, "But lately I have wondered if I might not have been too single-minded."

There was something curious about Grayson's face. Most people had just one smile, a simple indication of pleasure that appeared at appropriate moments but with him, it was a continuous flow from one smile to another – from merry to mocking to flirtatious to cruel. If smiling was your habitual expression, could you really be said to have a smile at all? The eyes never blinked and the teeth remained concealed: in Keighley, Fred recalled, they had been on permanent and threatening display.

"What do you think you might have missed?" The voice had a curious hollowness and whenever he used the letter 'S', the sibilance hung on the air. At least his breath was no longer condensing.

"I wish I'd seen some real mountains – the Alps or the Himalayas – and perhaps even scrambled up one or two. And I'd like to have had a proper garden and known about flowers. And to have been able to go into a library, shut my eyes, and take out books at random, to follow wherever they might lead. There's shelf after shelf of poetry, you know, but I've only read our lads – Morris, Blatchford, Turner and Maguire."

"It has to be admitted," said Grayson, "That Keats, Shakespeare and Milton have the edge."

"And then there's painting and music, and my family and the old friends I never see. But all these remain as nothing compared to my duty to serve The People."

"Ah yes, The People," Grayson's smile now stretched from ear to ear. "They don't deserve even to be led. They're not worthy of their Napoleons, Cromwells and Luthers, let alone their Jowetts."

"Are you laughing at me?"

"Perhaps you are laughing at yourself? It's never too late to develop a sense of humour."

"I suppose I should have laughed at you."

"Yes, you took me far too seriously. But as for what I represented – well, you never took that seriously enough."

"And what exactly did you represent?"

"Joy! Joy!" Grayson sang. Dropping to his haunches, he began to hop like a frog. "Fun! Fantasy! Freedom! Universal Love!" – his Ethel Snowden impersonation was all too accurate – "And change, change – always change!" Having circled the room, he resumed his indolent pose. "And to be constantly amazing one's friends, one's enemies and oneself. Well, doesn't the revolution call for a new human type?"

Fred sighed, "I suppose you think that you are the Superman."

"Of course" – Grayson refilled his glass – "The Superman of The Bottle."

Fred saw that the level of his own had also risen. "I've never read Shaw or any of those German chaps. But I threw Carlyle into the bushes forty years ago and I won't be fishing him out again. The idea that change will be accomplished by a single man – like oneself, of course, only bigger, stronger and louder, is a fantasy best left in childhood."

"Strangely enough, my most enthusiastic following was among the very old," said Victor. "Those who get to seventy usually realize that their years of so-called maturity were utterly wasted and that reality resided solely in the dreams of their youth. Nothing can ever happen without people like me . . . Although, of course" – he raked a hand through his hair – "there will never be another *quite* like me . . . Without others who are determined to be themselves. And our message is very simple and very pure: let's smash everything up! The merry tinkle of breaking bottles might even get The People off their knees. And we will not only destroy our enemies and their institutions but also each other and ourselves. If we ever do blunder into Utopia, we'll smash it up in its turn. That's the fun – the tragedy and comedy – of it all! That's what *real* men and women – not Heroes or Supermen or The People – are put on earth to do."

"You have always treated The People with contempt."

"With as much contempt as they wanted me to feel."

"You have never understood them. You do not take them seriously enough. When I speak of The People, I am talking about the future. At present, they are sleeping, but tomorrow, when they awake, who knows what they may become? Their potential is limitless, whereas you and I – in our different ways – can only ever be ourselves. The People still retain their innocence. Many were shocked when MacDonald said that he wanted to put The People to sleep until we had properly arranged things for them, but I knew what he meant. It is our job to preserve and guard them until they can claim their birthright, until the air is fit for them to breath."

"But whatever is this wonderful innocence? In what new forms will it be manifesting itself?"

"That belongs to the future, but I think I caught a glimpse of it once, in Epstein's *Rima*."

"What, the statue?"

"It's not a statue, it's a relief. There was something in her eyes

- or rather in her eye - that frightened but thrilled me, as if she was looking into parts of myself that I did not know existed. And it seemed to me that she was at one with everything in the world while remaining utterly independent and free and I had the curious notion that when The People awake they will not walk but fly."

"For me, innocence is the only sin," said Grayson. "To be guilty is to be alive, to have lived, to be fully human. How do you expect The People to turn from brutes into angels, with no stages in between?"

"Because they do not need to change - only to fulfil what they already are. Every man and woman knows the difference between good and bad, right and wrong. The difficult thing is to face this, then to act on it."

"Absolute truths do not exist. There is no such thing as right or wrong, there is no good or evil. There are only patterns shifting into new alignments, rising and falling, waxing and waning. The People will slumber for ever: the day will never dawn when you draw their curtains to awaken them."

The door swung open and Emily, carrying a neatly-folded blanket, entered the room. They had not heard her descending the stairs. Although Grayson was evidently invisible to her, Fred still found the sight of them together utterly grotesque.

"Don't pretend to be asleep," she said, "I could hear you chuntering away to yourself."

"Perhaps I was snoring," said Fred.

"*Bellissima!*" Fortunately Emily could not hear Grayson either. He rolled his eyes, kissed the tips of his fingers and vanished.

"Are you all right?"She demanded, "The back window is open and there's a very funny smell."

"I was shooing off a cat."

"A cat," said Emily, flatly.

"A tom cat." Fred subsided onto the sofa.

She shook out the blanket expertly, like Mosley with his handkerchief.

"I don't know what's got into you these days. First it's story-books, then it's statues, now it's beer. Whatever next, I wonder?" She swaddled him in the scratchy material, then tucked it under his chin. As so often these days, her face wore what he thought of as her 'That Dolores' expression. Now he remembered the subject of their earlier conversation, if not the exact words she had spoken.

He had only mentioned the woman once, in passing, but Emily, ever since, would not let it go. Perhaps it was impossible to utter the name 'Dolores' in an innocent fashion?

"That Dolores," she said, "What did you say she was wearing?"

Fred had never told her that Dolores had been naked: it was as if she had somehow intuited it.

"I didn't notice. It was dark in the studio."

"Was she beautiful?"

"Epstein thought so but she was what they call his muse. She looked sulky – a bit vicious, I suppose: the newspapers call her notorious."

"That's what they call you and all," Emily put the seashell back in its appointed place: she could not see Grayson's silver flask.

"Do you dream about her?"

"You know I never dream," said Fred, "Or if I do I can't remember."

Emily said no more. Her descent had been silent but her return journey shook the foundations of the house.

"Sulky and vicious, indeed!" Grayson was back at the mantel-piece lighting a cigar. "You don't know much about women, do you, Fred?"

"What should I have said?"

Grayson put on that dreadful accent again: "Oh, she were bonny, right enough. If you like that sort of thing." He was now wearing a suit, black with a thin grey stripe, but was just as wet as before. "You *are* a dark horse: who is this Dolores?"

"Epstein's model. She was looking for you: I got the impression that you and she had been good friends."

"I can't quite place her. Ruth was always keener on that Bohemian set than I was. We used to know a lot of models – good girls trying to be bad, bad girls trying to be respectable. But then, of course, I was never all that bothered about women."

"But they're what happened to you! Chasing women and drinking: they're what destroyed you!"

"I never chased a woman in my life." Grayson helped Fred to extricate himself from the blanket's coils. "Or a man, come to that. Some boys, perhaps, when I was younger. People were always chasing me and I didn't like to disappoint them. I admired their persistence, but women didn't do much for me. I never met one I could really talk to, except for Ruth and she wasn't really a woman at all."

"What was she, then?"

"She was Ruth." Grayson relit his cigar. "Sex, you know, is a basic need, like sleep and food: it only becomes a problem when you can't get it." He blew three huge smoke rings. "It's funny, because every time I went to bed with someone, I used to think of you, although I don't think you will appreciate the association. That slogan of yours – 'Bun, Banana, Beverage' – is the perfect rhythm for fucking. Put it in with a good firm thrust – 'Bun!' – then move it in a long, slow circle – 'Banana!'" – he drew the word out, giving it, for some reason, a Spanish inflection – "Then pull it out long and slow" – his upper body shook, setting his voice quivering – "'Beverage!' And then, when I was getting close to ejaculation, I would mutter those words under my breath to slow myself down. And when I finally did come, I'd be bellowing them at the top of my lungs. You should try it with your Emily – just remember not to call her Dolores."

Now Grayson had picked up the night-soil men's little key. He inserted it into the seashell and began to rattle it about.

"Women like to be idealized, but they've too much sense to idealize themselves. Any woman – yes, even Emily – would smile at your squeamishness. They *do* give birth, you know, and generally nurse the sick and the dying. And, as far as love goes, I have never ceased to be surprised by their demands. Men are all too predictable but no two women are alike. You would be surprised just how free and easy even refined young ladies really are. Not only are they not deterred by fluids and emissions, they are in their element. By the way, did you know that piss is good for the complexion? Turning to the mirror, he patted his cheeks, "There, that's my secret out."

"I'm afraid I didn't hear any of that." Fred cupped his ear but Grayson went remorselessly on.

"The most meaningful human communication, I have concluded, is through the fundament. A tongue reaming an arsehole: that's how you really learn about people. I cannot now recall most of the names and faces, but I never forget a bum. If your Dolores were to bend over, it would all come flooding back to me – those days of wine and roses, the laughter and the tears. I have even begun to suspect that our arseholes are our souls."

"All this is incomprehensible to me," Fred's hands had clenched themselves into fists. "I can only presume that you are trying to shock me. It is impossible that people could behave like that, except perhaps at moments of drunken abandonment or extreme despair. I accept that an isolated individual might, in certain circumstances, become so debased but it is beyond credulity that he would so easily find partners or accomplices with similar inclinations."

"There are thousands of us, millions. We have our cities and countries. This is our world. It is you, my undebased comrade, who is an isolated individual, the man born out of his time. It is true that the majority do not yet dare to openly act out their desires but they think of little else and are overwhelmed by them in their dreams."

"I never dream," said Fred, "Unless I'm dreaming now."

"We are both dreaming," said Grayson, "At least, I hope so."

Fred had refused the offered flask but his glass was replenished once again.

"However did you think that you could achieve anything in politics when your head was full of such filth?"

"For that very reason. Because I realized that there was nothing to be afraid of. While you were freeing people from poor sanitation I wanted to free them from shame."

"If there's nothing to be ashamed of, then what about torture? Would your refined young ladies be as free and easy about that?"

"Torture is a funny thing," Victor flicked his cigar stub into the fireplace. "Mostly it's just play-acting - light spanking and granny-knots - but there are some who want to kill or to be killed or both, preferably at the same time. What is interesting is that sadists always look like Unitarian ministers - so stiff and po-faced that all you can do is laugh. Perhaps that's why they like blindfolds and gags: one word, one smile would annihilate them. They are utterly ridiculous - although this is not much consolation if you happen to be in their power. He took out his cigarette case: whenever he flipped it open, there was just one left. "But they remain our brothers and sisters. We're all in the same boat: '*Inter faeces et urinam nascimur*', as St. Augustine says. Why do we always consider him an authority, I wonder? 'We are all born between . . .'"

"I know perfectly well what it means," Fred interrupted, "But being born between . . . urine and . . . faeces . . . doesn't mean that we have to spend the rest of our lives there."

"I love the way your mouth prunes up when you say those words." When Grayson laughed, it seemed to issue from his stomach rather than his mouth. "What's wrong with good old piss and shit? Wherever would we be without them? Why should we care what goes into or comes out of our bodies? Shit is the very stuff of life: why do you think farmers spread it on their fields?"

"I don't mind animal manure. The smell of the stable or the sty is innocent and sweet. It's only human . . . excrement that stinks."

"Except yours or mine: no-one's shit smells bad to their own nostrils. Personally, I have always been proud of my stools: I feel closer to them than I do to my so-called comrades. We are all standing on a dunghill, Our Fred, but only so that we can get closer to Heaven. That's not St. Augustine, it's one of my own. There's been much theological debate, you know, about whether Christ, when hanging up there on the cross, felt any pain. The Jew Ahasuerus was cast out for all eternity after suggesting that those tears and groans were merely for effect. But that does not interest me – nor do I care whether he was fucking the disciples and the Magdalen. What really matters is – did he sleep? Did he dream? Did he piss and shit?"

"I am not a religious man," said Fred, "But that is a disgusting thing to say."

"Pissing and shitting are merely bodily functions. Are you also disgusted by food? There's no obvious reason why we shouldn't eat out of a toilet bowl and then, in convivial company, shit on the dining table. Don't look at me like that, Fred" – he wagged a finger – "I just caught you pissing out of the window.

"Do you remember the night-soil men? I saw the way you were looking at them in Keighley – like a dowager hearing rats scuffling behind her escritoire. Your nose was twitching, as if it could smell them clear across the hall. Were you afraid that handling your shit had given them some power over you? It was just a job to them, you know, so habitual and familiar that they didn't think about it anymore. I always rather admired them: strong, sturdy chaps, labouring in the darkness, shunned and reviled merely for performing a necessary task. They should have been there in *Heroes And Hero Worship*, instead of *Frederick the Great*."

"I pitied them, of course," said Fred, "But they were utterly brutalized. Now there is at least hope for their children."

"So you cast them out, you pious devil, just for earning a crust. You talk as if it was all their fault – like blaming doctors for sickness or undertakers for death. It wasn't their shit, you know, but yours, mine and everyone else's. In any sane world they would have been the most respected, the highest paid, clad in magnificent uniforms with medals and epaulettes, brandishing shovels of solid silver, inscribed with St. Augustine's immortal words. What is this hope that you are offering their children? – A world of perpetual constipation, perhaps?"

"I find it hard to believe that anyone can be truly indifferent to sanitation." said Fred.

"Let me put it this way. If Hell had existed and the afterlife had been an eternity of burning lakes of piss and shit, I would merely have yawned at the sheer predictability of it all."

"In terms of appearances, Grayson, you always struck me as being fastidious to a fault."

"No-one's hands are clean – a politician's, least of all. Can you imagine a privy midden as filthy as Lloyd George's post-war administration? And has it never struck you that the way you look at the night-soil men is the way The People look at you? They like to pretend that politics has got nothing to do with them-a dirty trade beneath their notice. As if their own street is the only reality and all that truly matters are Dad's bunions and the goings-on of her at No. 69."

Fred had indeed noticed, in recent years, a new hard look in the eyes of his constituents. And, sometimes they even seemed to be sniffing the air. Perhaps it was he himself that had begun to stink – of politics?

"Why didn't they look at you in the same way?"

"They thought that I wasn't really political at all: when, in fact, it was merely politics of a different type. Politics is everything, you know, just as everything is shit. Fortunately, I had cast myself into the darkness before they could realize their mistake."

"Tell me," said Fred, "If you really *are* dead . . ."

"I'm dead-ish," Victor interrupted, "People are never properly dead until everyone has forgotten them."

"Tell me what the afterlife is like."

"I don't want to spoil the surprise. And although you'll understand it drunk, I'm not sure what you'll make of it after you've sobered up."

"Do they have Socialism in the next world?"

"Next worlds," corrected Grayson, "Yes, but they call it something else. Don't let the cat out of the bag, when your own time comes."

"Do you eat? Do you sleep? Do you do everything we do?"

"Yes, but in a different way. Shit and piss, for example, are a form of currency or security. I don't really understand the physics or the metaphysics, let alone the economics of it all – it's rather like The Gold Standard."

"Can you foretell the future?"

"Not really. But before I go back into my bottle, like a genie in *The Arabian Nights*, I can grant you one wish – or at least, I think I can. Depending on what it is, of course, and over a reasonable period of time."

Fred raised his glass. The flavour of the nectar was beginning to come through: it was as if his feet were somehow tasting it.

"I want to see Bradford the City Beautiful."

"But isn't it that already?" Grayson clinked glasses. "Just give all that sandstone a good scrubbing and, when the sun comes up, it will look like Florence."

"No, I want it to be not only beautiful but an ideal – like Athens or Paris, New York or Moscow."

"Leave it with me," Grayson pocketed his flask, "And I'll see what I can do."

He extended a hand. Fred expected it to be freezing cold but it was quite normal, if rather damp.

"We should have had this conversation twenty years ago," he said.

"It wouldn't have made any difference."

"Perhaps, but I still wish we'd had it."

Without Fred noticing, they had moved through to the kitchen, so that instead of leaning against the mantelpiece, Victor was at the open window with his legs already over the sill. Behind him, a thin yellow band ran along the horizon.

"Where are you going now?"

"Back to bed," said Victor, "Back to the river bed . . . Bradford the City Beautiful . . . I'll see what I can do."

He turned and seemed to walk out into the empty air: there was no sound of his hitting the ground. When Fred reached the window, the receding figure had already crossed the middens.

"Remember," came a faint voice, "Remember to forget me . . . Tell them all to forget me."

"Nay, Our Victor," said Fred, "How could anyone ever forget you?"

Fred was sure that he had not dreamed the last few hours. "I peeled a banana and there were nowt in it": he was quite incapable of imagining such rubbish. Nor could he have generated all that sexual vileness, especially not in such a casual tone.

Now the parlour was illuminated by light reflecting off the attic window opposite. Despite Grayson's words he could see nothing Bohemian about it: the wallpaper appeared to be holding up perfectly well. He ran his finger along the mantelpiece: there was no dust, even though he had never seen Emily actually cleaning it. His reflection in the mirror was unclear: its glass was smeared with greasy fingerprints. He saw that the little key had gone.

From over his head came the sound of those paddle feet hitting the bedroom floor. He knew that, when Emily appeared, all the previous night's misunderstandings would have been forgotten. Truly, there was nothing like peace at home. In pride of place on the mantelpiece were half a dozen stones, which had been chucked through their windows during the war. One, the size of a baby's head, was covered with lichen and feldspar: someone must have carried it down from one of the Lake District peaks. There were pebbles and sea-shells from Bridlington beach, flint arrowheads picked up on Baildon Moor, a glass vase filled with unusual bird feathers, and two china dogs which looked more like seals. The Nectar of the Gods, dripping from Grayson's flask, had bitten into the wood: Fred did not like to think of what it might have done to the lining of his stomach.

He did a little shuffling dance, swinging his head from side to side, but the room no longer whirled. Then he leaned forward, bending at the waist until his fingertips brushed the floor. He had not done this – or even felt the need to try – since the turn of the century. The shock of it caused him to break wind before, in a series of creaks, he resumed the vertical. Then he reached above the mirror until he could feel the rough material of the replica banner that the Dyers' Union had presented to him. In the few months since the Miners' Gala, it had assumed the same consistency as the faded and tattered original. Underneath its rainbow arch, some words had been brocaded in letters of gold.

WE DYE TO LIVE

All ye who try
To do the same
Must join us
Or just live to dye
Organize! Organize!

Fred's eyes misted over. Whatever Grayson might say, here was true poetry! Here was a Gold Standard worth marching under!

12

TWENTY-THREE MINUTES (1931)

T HE NARROW CORRIDORS of Savoy Hill were full of young men in dark tweed three-piece suits – improbably tall and thin, stooping and twisting their necks so that they were almost looking at you upside down. Wherever did the BBC find such people? Ethel claimed that they were all pansies but she said that about most men, these days. She had even begun to speculate about MacDonald.

The one who conducted Philip to the studio had a curiously shiny face: he could see his tiny convex reflection on the bulb of that nose. The man's manner was respectful but the eyes were cold: during her five years on the Board of Governors Ethel had made many enemies. He did not address Philip as Chancellor but, with heavy emphasis, as *Mister* Snowden, as if he had got wind of the impending ennoblement and strongly disapproved.

He had broadcast several times before but had never got used to it. The studios kept changing: there were always new pieces of menacing-looking equipment. This windowless room – with its lowered grey felt ceiling, wires and furniture bolted to the floor – reminded him of his pre-war visit to America's Sing Sing Prison, where the governor had proudly displayed their electric chair. They were hanging the microphones from the ceiling now: the shiny head swayed like a cobra before his eyes. How he missed that big metal funnel into which Dame Nellie Melba used to sing! It was a strange feeling to be speaking to no-one and yet to millions at the same time. The only difference between the Chancellor of the Exchequer and some madman jabbering away to himself was this microphone.

"I would like some time alone, to prepare." As always, he was early.

"You have exactly twenty-three minutes," said the man. "And then this light" – he indicated a glass bulb on the far side of the table – "Will turn red. And ten seconds after that, from inside the control cubicle, I will silently count you down. Please speak in a normal conversational tone and keep your mouth eight inches from the microphone. Try not to hiss your 'S's' or pop your 'P's', and whatever you do, don't sneeze. Should you feel it coming on, please throw yourself to the floor. When you raise your voice, lean back until your crown touches the headrest: should you wish to whisper, let your chin drop onto your chest. Otherwise, keep your head still: the Prime Minister, you know, bobs about like a prize-fighter."

"Why should he change the habit of a lifetime?" asked Philip, but the man was already closing the door behind him.

He took his papers from his beloved red briefcase. Although this would no doubt appear both garish and dilapidated to those that did not understand its significance – handed down from Chancellor to Chancellor – it was what he would miss most when he went to The Lords. This morning, Ethel had observed how it matched his eyes, no longer merely bloodshot but an even crimson, and changed his tie accordingly. Red eyes, red tie, red box, red light – but he would certainly not be concluding his little talk with a rendition of 'The Red Flag'.

With his silver pen, he struck out the first lines of the speech then wrote in firm letters: 'In front of me, as part of the wireless arrangement, is a red light, and a red light is a warning of danger to be avoided. I am going to give you this warning tonight.'

How often it happened that, when you were stuck for ideas, life would provide you with the very thing! For a while, this afternoon, his speech had seemed to make no sense at all. Even the statistics no longer added up. Those long sleepless nights of the financial crisis had sorely tired him: perhaps he was cracking up, like poor

Montagu Norman, and was about to spew utter gibberish into millions of unsuspecting homes?

'It is only common sense' – the pen crossed out the words. He had developed a habit of repeating himself. 'Simple arithmetic' . . . 'The figures never lie' . . . 'Two plus two, whether we like it or not, can only ever equal four.' This was fine for getting a point across, but if a phrase worked too well it could be hung around your neck forever, like 'Bun, Banana and Beverage' or 'Broken Bottles'. He himself squirmed when anyone now mentioned 'Come to Jesus', even though it was usually meant kindly enough.

'It's only common sense' – there, the pen had put it back in, for what else could you say? Everything he had done in the last two years had been exactly that: no other course of action had been possible.

It had to be admitted, though, that common sense could land you in some curious places. In a Labour government, for instance, that saw millions thrown out of work, then cut unemployment benefits and sat waiting for American bankers to tell them what to do next. It had been common sense to form a National Government with your lifelong political foes and to be branded traitor by your former comrades. No-one could have predicted such an outcome but now, looking back, it had all been logical and inevitable. He was sure that tonight the people – no mere abstract mass but individual men and women – would recognize common sense when they heard it.

'These are not ordinary times. However anxious we may be to advance the social services we cannot do it when the resources from which the cost must come are drying up.'

The sound of his own voice reassured him. He often spoke to himself, especially in Tilford, under the pretence of addressing Spot the terrier. These days, Ethel was usually away and, besides, Spot's grasp of political economy was superior to hers. Nevertheless, there were teeth marks all over his speech: he had kept retrieving its pages from the corners of the study. Evidently Spot, unlike himself, had retained a vestigial loyalty to the Labour Party. The servants had put the little dog out into the garden and then, when he would not stop barking, had locked him in the potting shed.

'Unless it wants to be landed into bankruptcy, a nation, like an individual, cannot go on increasing expenditure when income is falling.'

It still seemed a little flat. Perhaps he should chuck in some of the good old 'Come To Jesus', after all? He could still remember it: 'The way to the Earthly Paradise is by the old hard road to Calvary ... through persecution, poverty and temptation, by the agony and the bloody sweat, by the crown of thorns and the agonizing death ... And then the resurrection to The New Humanity – purified by suffering, triumphant through sacrifice.' How peculiar all that Biblical stuff now sounded – about two thousand years out of date.

He was sure that his voice and his nerve would not let him down, but his bowels just might. He was afraid of farting during the broadcast. Ever since his Emergency Budget, he had been constipated. First the bladder, then the bowels: old age was coming on. Every half hour or so, he would emit a prolonged blast of air – mercifully odourless, to his own nose at least, but always accompanied by a foghorn blare – Meteorism, the doctors called it. At least he could now urinate without discomfort but the sound of his stream hitting the toilet bowel kept resolving itself into a querulous and accusing voice – female but not Ethel's. To drown it out, he would loudly hum 'All Flesh Is Grass'.

After the bladder operation he had almost resigned. His sticks were no longer for show: for a while he had needed two in each hand. His second budget had been delivered in dreadful pain, although he prided himself that no-one could have guessed. Willie Graham had been ready with a copy of the speech in case he broke down: the man had kept leaning forward to lightly press on the base of his spine an encouraging hand. But if he *had* gone, who would have replaced him? Not Willie, for MacDonald followed the principle of Buggins' Turn: Jimmy Thomas, probably, who, drunk or sober, would never be up to the job. He would ruin a healthy economy in three months, let alone an ailing one. It was rumoured that he had been sent to Monte Carlo to pay off a blackmailing mistress of MacDonald's, but had instead gone into the Casino and gambled the hush-money away.

On the way here, Philip had glimpsed the latest election poster. MacDonald, dressed in nautical cap and reefer jacket, was dauntlessly standing on a storm-lashed bridge.

'THE CAPTAIN WHO STUCK BY HIS SHIP!'

He had almost asked the driver to let him out so that he could write underneath:

'AND WILL STEER IT ON TO THE ROCKS'

One thing was certain: throughout the crisis, while he himself had acted out of duty and common sense, the PM had, as always, been driven by cynical calculation and reckless whim. Whatever anyone might say, they were definitely *not* in the same boat.

It was curious – in this, the twelfth General Election of his political life – to be no longer barnstorming the country but remaining, nice and snug, at home. He gave interviews and wrote articles for the *Express*, *Mail* and *Times*, and this afternoon he had put his signature to a letter that would be delivered to every voter in a Labour-held seat. 'If you do not want to see our country go to the dogs,' it concluded, 'Vote for the candidate that supports the National Government'. He was not standing for Colne Valley: MacDonald, in contrast, had insisted on fighting his Seaham seat against a Labour candidate – he would be torn to pieces, with any luck. In the event of a coalition victory – almost certain, in the circumstances – Viscount Snowden of Ickornshaw would be donning the ermine of the House of Lords. How they would hate him in Cowling for taking his title from the poorer side of town!

Perhaps he should, in Jack Payne's popular catch-phrase, 'Say it with music'? Unfortunately, the piano on the other side of the studio was locked. He was learning to play the Three Intermezzi, Op. 117: 'Lullabies of my sorrows', Brahms had called them but they sounded jolly enough to him. He had even found himself whistling the andante as he watched Henderson and Dalton making fools of themselves in the last finance debate. There were only twelve pages of music, which would last perhaps fifteen minutes when he finally had them down. And in a year or two's time, after he had dashed them off, he would contrive to give his audience the impression that the whole repertoire was at his fingertips. He had heard that Norman was an accomplished oboist: perhaps they could spend their retirement playing duets? But his friend had been uncharacteristically embarrassed, blushing as he denied the suggestion.

Poor old Monty! How were the mighty fallen! It had to be admitted, though, that none of it was his fault. He had been the sole survivor of The Big Four who had regulated world finance for over a decade. Now, with Strong, Schlacht and Moreau all gone, the Americans, the Germans and – especially –the French had made a fearful hash of everything.

"It is being said that the National Government has failed to save the pound. It is true that we have been driven off The Gold Standard and the external value of the pound has fallen" – he snapped his head back, for his front teeth had clashed against the microphone – "But its internal value has not depreciated. The purchasing power of the pound in your pocket is still twenty shillings."

How hard it was to sound positive about this! Norman's proudest achievement, under the last Conservative administration, had been the return to The Gold Standard. "Churchill kept pretending he thought it was a horse race," he had said, "So I told him, 'No, Chancellor, that is The Gold *Cup*, for which I would recommend Ballinode, with Ted Leader up.' Winston was so pleased when it won that the rest was bound to follow."

Philip had realized that his friend was becoming ever more

idiosyncratic. Each January, he would decline a peerage with the words, 'Definitely next year.' And he claimed to be able to walk through walls: "In one's own home, of course, it is relatively easy, but the real test is to encounter, on one's travels, an unexpected wall, a wall to which one has not been properly introduced and then, without so much as a by-your-leave, to toddle straight through it." If he did not get his own way, he would faint, upsetting a great deal of furniture while contriving to do no damage to his person. He had keeled over at the unveiling of his own portrait by Augustus John. "He has made me look like a syphilitic Don Quixote. Why didn't we get Orpen or McEvoy? I should have remembered what he did to Willie Yeats." To Philip's eyes the painting was a perfect likeness: when Monty looked in the mirror he probably saw, smiling back at him, his ten year old self.

Whenever he was up before the Finance Committee he was even more sullen than before.

"Don't you think that raising the Bank Rate will cause an increase in unemployment?" Keynes had asked.

"No."

"Do you believe that your sole function at the Bank of England is to maintain The Gold Standard, after which it is industry's job to make itself competitive?"

"Yes."

"Are you going to answer 'yes' or 'no' to every question I ask?"

There had been a pause. "Perhaps," said Norman at last. He would never forgive Keynes for calling The Gold Standard "a barbarous relic".

"I've lately begun to suspect that all along we've been playing in quite the wrong key." He said to Philip afterwards. He whistled something unrecognisable: "Do you see what I mean?"

At the end of an all-night session at The Treasury, just after the full crisis broke, Norman's secretary, a pleasantly excitable young man, had burst into the room. "Here it is!" From a brown paper bag he produced a shellac disk. "Solomon Cutner playing the B Major Rhapsody! *That* should cheer us all up!"

"Oh, bugger Brahms," groaned Monty. That had been the final straw. Nervous exhaustion, the doctors had said: they had virtually dragged him down to the dockside and on to the "Duchess Of York" for a month's recuperation in Canada. Philip had recommended that nice hotel close by Niagara Falls before recalling that it was said to have – along with Westminster Bridge – the highest suicide rate in the world.

"The Labour Party tells you that we have money enough to go on spending to our hearts' content" – he did not need to read this, he had it by heart – "Which is either appalling ignorance or wilful deception. Our country's resources are indeed great but they cannot be mortgaged for current expenditure."

How the comrades had wept and wailed and gnashed their teeth! They had not even liked his initial steady-as-she-goes budget, when he raised Surtax, top rate Income Tax and Death Duties and put a penny on a gallon of beer. Jowett had jibbed at the higher interest rates to be paid on government stocks: "You're taking with one hand and giving back with the other," he complained – as if that wasn't the whole point of finance! They all said that he had betrayed his past: well, what about his legislation for estate valuation, which would lead to the Land Tax he had dreamed of ever since hearing Henry George forty years ago? How many of the Red Clydesiders had even heard of Henry George?

"If you are in debt, with a sinking fund of £50 million a year, then you cannot embark on new expenditure until you have paid it off."

It was only common sense but a whole cross section of folk, from Lloyd George to Maxton, from Mosley to Keynes, seemed incapable of grasping it. Had they never, as children, observed the way their mothers ran the household? "As long as I hold this position," he had told the Committee, "I am determined, however burdensome it may be, that this country shall pay its way by honest measures."

He had seen Keynes, Stamp and Pigou all sniggering behind their hands: that was what came of using the word "honest" to so-called intellectuals. "I will not leave my successor to pay my bills." He had feared that Keynes was going to fall off his chair. Norman had been right about him: whatever happened, Keynes always claimed to have predicted it. He kept proposing huge capital projects – aimless digging and delving – in order to "raise animal spirits," as he put it. And he exhorted British housewives to spend not save: even Grayson, at his most depraved, would never have dared make such a suggestion. And he claimed that all statistics were meaningless – "like trying to paint the clouds" – because, by the time you had finished your counting, the whole situation would almost certainly have changed. He might have had something there: it was said that three million were unemployed, but there did not appear to be any increase in the number of people hanging about in the streets.

When everybody criticises you, it is a sure sign that you are doing the right thing. The Tories claimed that higher tax payers would be driven abroad, without revealing where they might be going. The rich would never stir until a way could be found for them to take Ascot and Epsom, Lords and The Oval, and their clubs, grouse moors and golf courses with them. Protectionists predicted that the duties he had repealed would destroy traditional crafts, but Philip suspected that they would still be manufacturing lace in Nottingham centuries from now. And although it was currently undercut by French appropriations from The Ruhr, our coal industry would surely soldier on. All those miners and lace-makers – were they just going to vanish into thin air?

At the end of the budget he had announced that there would be no further increases in Income Tax and Surtax for the rest of the Parliament. Jowett had remonstrated with him for tying his own hands, without realizing that he did not wish to have them free. History had moved on, but Our Fred had learned nothing. There he sat, outside his cobwebbed cave, gnawing away at a long-since meatless bone. At the election, he had beaten his Liberal opponent,

Fenby, by a surprising margin in a two-way fight. Nevertheless when MacDonald, with the Liberals' grudging support, had formed another minority government, only two men from 1924 were not reappointed. Memories of Wheatley's bowler hat had outweighed his record as Housing Minister: regrettable, but the man's own fault. And, as for First Commissioner of Works, the PM had told Fred that they needed a younger, more energetic man and then appointed Lansbury, six years his senior. At least MacDonald could not be accused of lacking a sense of humour.

These two had joined Maxton and his rebels in opposing Margaret Bonfield's every proposal at the Ministry of Labour. They insisted that all manifesto commitments be honoured, even though the Liberals would veto any such attempt. They had little support in the ILP itself, let alone the wider Labour Party and became even more marginalised when they purged themselves of three-quarters of their own membership. Only 17 MPs were left – Clydesiders, most of them, who shouted incomprehensibly and fought the attendants when they tried to remove them. One had even tried to run out of the Commons with the ceremonial mace.

Throughout that budget speech, Snowden could hear Jowett chuntering away to himself. Afterwards, Willie Leach revealed that he had been saying, "I am not satisfied" over and over again. That night, when he was slumbering in his usual chair in a corner of The Map Room, some party loyalists had tipped a bag of flour over his head. "Are you satisfied now?" They enquired, but Fred had wordlessly dusted himself down and gone back to sleep. Noticeably deafer and unsteady on his feet, he cut an increasingly pathetic figure. He had recently fallen over in the toilets: "I've broken my dentures," he was informing everyone. "What am I going to tell my wife?"

Nevertheless, he had still been able to pick apart, clause by clause, the Anomalies Bill on Poor Relief, wasting a full day of government time. They had only placated him by promising a few extra pennies to short-term workers. Then he had made an even bigger fool of himself at the beginning of the autumn session, when he had risen after the King's Speech and proposed a Socialist alternative. After an interminable catalogue of heartrending but factually inaccurate comparisons between the lot of the poor and that of the Surtax payers – however could the wool companies be giving 85% dividends on ordinary shares? – Fred had concluded with what he styled, 'a homely simile'. "An accumulation of wealth in a country is like manure. If it is all heaped up in the wrong place it is a pernicious nuisance but if it is spread and distributed it is a fruitful source of new and better life." When it came to a vote only ten supported him: most of his fellow-rebels had not even bothered to attend.

Such a charade could have been a serious embarrassment to the administration but, fortunately, His Majesty had been magnanimous. "I have considered abdication," he said, "But I fear that Comrade Fred is too busy battling with manure to be able to take the crown. Nevertheless, I think we all know who the true King of England is. How proudly I recall that day when he so graciously bestowed on me the seals of office."

Jowett had formed an unlikely alliance with Oswald Mosley. How incongruous they looked: stooped, broken Fred and that strutting Don Juan, plotting together, with their heads touching – one snow white, the other raven-black with brilliantine. Mosley had been made Chancellor of the Duchy of Lancaster, outside the cabinet but with the wide brief of tackling unemployment. Apparently, he was expecting to put the whole country back to work and still be in time to bag his favourite table at the Cafe Royale. It had to be admitted, though, that Macdonald was a shrewd judge of talent, so Snowden had tried to take the man under his wing.

"Don't worry about depressions," he told him, "They have often recurred in my lifetime, only to pass away again. Trade is like a pair of lungs, contracting then expanding. Times change: for instance, when I was a boy, negroes did not ride bicycles: now they do and workers in Coventry are employed to manufacture them."

"My constituency is in Birmingham, not Coventry," Mosley's eyes had bored into his own, but he had yet to meet the man who could stare him down. "And I am not a nigger and nor do I ride a bike." Why did young people take everything so literally?

A month later, Mosley's six-point memorandum had landed on MacDonald's desk. It had been predictable: mass public works, bank controls, extended credit, the school leaving age up and the pension age down. Sheer wildcat finance: "Counter-cyclical deficits can never work," he had warned Mosley. "If you swim against the tide you will only drown." When the measures were rejected, the man immediately resigned his post: if he had really believed in his ideas, he would have stayed to fight. He still had followers in the constituency parties, however, and at the Llandudno Conference, he and Jowett had nearly sneaked through an anti-government motion, while the union representatives were in the bar.

Now Mosley had left the party altogether to form his own, which he called The New Party. Surely he could have shown a little more imagination? Why not The Moustache Party? – his acolytes sported copies of his own, like caterpillars crawling along their upper lips. Perhaps Philip should form The Snowdenites, all limping on alternate legs, supporting themselves on golden crutches to signify their adherence to sound finance? Peculiar little parties were appearing everywhere. Last week, a member of the Green Shirts – fascist boy scouts, apparently – had thrown a brick through the window of Number Eleven. It seemed to have been painted green but, when cut in half, was revealed to be the same all the way through. Was it a fossil or some sinister meteorite, like in a story by Wells? Did all these curious folk hail from a different planet altogether? Their deficit finance and social credit theories might work on the moon, where the laws of economics – as well as those of gravity – presumably would not apply.

At least Grayson had never taken himself entirely seriously. Whatever Lloyd George might say, Philip suspected that the man was still alive. Perhaps, like King Arthur, he was sleeping – not under Glastonbury Tor but in some Limehouse opium den – awaiting the hour of his country's call, when he would arise, take up his sword and buckler, slick down his hair and make an awful mess of everything once again? Thomas claimed to have recently encountered him on Albemarle Street, arm-in-arm with two large negresses – no doubt looking for their bicycles.

The latest rumour was that Grayson was really Queen Victoria's favourite grandson – also Albert Victor – supposedly dead at the age of five but, in reality, cast out after displaying, in the nursery, unmistakable signs of Socialism. When the adult Grayson discovered his true identity, they said, he had been kidnapped and imprisoned, with his features concealed behind an iron mask. Many thousands of parents, however, had also christened their children after this unfortunate infant. Nobody ever said such things about Albert Victor Alexander, who had risen from The Co-Op to become First Lord of The Admiralty, but then poor 'AV' – with his droning voice and pendulous nose – was no Victor Grayson.

Philip had resigned his parliamentary seat by letter. What a relief it was never to have to return to Colne Valley! On his last visit, his reception had been almost hostile. At the constituency meeting, Ernest Marklew, one of the 1907 gang, had insisted on reading out, in full, Philip's electoral address. "Public works, higher dole, higher pensions," he had concluded, twirling his eyeglasses on a long scarlet ribbon. "It sounds like The Mosley Memorandum to me."

"Of course we would like to do such things," Philip had patiently replied, "But economic realities are not bound to honour the pledges of a Labour manifesto. If we even tried, then capital would go flying out of the country. Our only course is to work diligently within the existing system until we have either converted the powers that be or are in a position to finally confront them."

"Victor would never have let them get away with it," grumbled Marklew.

"No, he wouldn't," Philip agreed, "He would have got them drunk and then borrowed money from them."

The audience had actually booed these words, even though they had known their truth. And now Marklew, with his ribbons and ridiculous white hat, was his own replacement as their parliamentary candidate. Perhaps, in this broadcast, he should give the fellow a special mention?

"The Hero of The Hague," Marklew kept calling him, to appreciative sniggers. But those Reparations Conferences had been no laughing matter. Philip suspected that – his stewardship of the economy notwithstanding – *this* was what he would be remembered for. And hadn't he been just a little heroic – or steadfast, at the very least? The situation itself, of course, had been most unfortunate. The war should not have happened but it had. Punitive reparations should not have been imposed on Germany but – thanks to Lloyd George and Clemenceau – they were. Now all he could do was to look out for British interests. France and Italy, it was proposed, would be paid out of the unconditional annuities, while our portion would come dribbling through from the conditional share. Norman – out of loyalty to Brahms, Beethoven and Bach – had argued for suspension or at least some easing of the rate, but if the French merely grabbed everything, how would that benefit the Germans?

The heat at the August Conference had been unbearable. Opening the windows of the chamber had made no difference, only admitting clouds of midges, mosquitoes and shiny flying ants. Fortunately they had known better than to bother the British representatives but they crawled all over the French, especially their chief negotiator, the fat and sweating M. Cheron. Perhaps because of this, his arguments had been incomprehensible both in French and in translation, and he waved his arms and stamped his feet in an increasingly agitated manner. In his reply, Philip had described this as 'ridiculous and grotesque' – at which Cheron had risen from his seat and waddled out of the room, followed by the rest of his delegation. Perhaps something had been lost in translation, although '*grotesque et ridicule*' sounded right enough. After a day's impasse, with Philip naturally refusing to apologise, they had reconvened, with the unfortunate interpreter saying that he had mistranslated the words, which should have been rendered as '*Amusant et original*'. "No," Philip had said, "The fault was mine. I should have said 'vile and insane'. '*Affreux!*'" – his index finger had jabbed at his temple – "*Et fou!*"

M. Jasper was the only one of the French who did not require a translation. "You are hard, hard," he said to Philip afterwards, "Much too hard. I have never met anyone like you before. You are a new human type."

"Nay," said Philip, "We're all like this in Yorkshire. I'm one of the reasonable ones."

In truth, he had rather surprised himself. He had always been a Socialist, a Pacifist and an Internationalist, but when he sat down in a foreign country, with a little flag on the table in front of him, his spine stiffened and a tightness in his stomach rose to his throat until he feared that he might choke with pride, and he became as fierce as any jingo in the land. As MacDonald observed, with his usual cynicism, when you are in trouble domestically, the best thing to do is to pick a fight with foreigners – preferably the French. Whenever Snowden appeared on the newsreels in Paris cinemas, riots ensued.

At the next conference, Henderson, as Foreign Secretary, had been deputed to keep negotiations at what MacDonald called 'a more civilised level'. As it was, he had not once dared to open his mouth. Was it Philip's fault that no-one else ever seemed to have been properly briefed?

"So I might as well go home, then?" Henderson had asked at breakfast on the second morning.

"That's about it, Arthur," said Philip, without looking up from his papers. At the end of proceedings, not only had he increased Britain's share by £1,500,000 but also bullied the Italians into buying £1 million of our coal!

There had been one strange thing: on the final day one of his civil servants had entered the room.

"Whatever is that fellow Grayson doing here?" he had asked.

"You mean Graham, don't you?"

"No, Grayson – the revolutionary chap. I saw him outside and he winked at me. Smelt like a French tart's boudoir but I'd like to meet his tailor."

He had obviously been mistaken but Philip was left with the nasty feeling that Grayson was always there, shadowing him. Often, when working late at the Treasury, the columns of figures would blur and then part to reveal, for an instant, that familiar face with its unsettling smile. And when he was coming round after his bladder operation, he had a vivid hallucination: Grayson, having somehow materialized outside the third-floor window, was ogling the nurses. Perhaps it was being neither dead nor alive but missing that gave the wretched man such all-pervasiveness?

On their return from the Conference, he and Ethel had been driven in an open carriage, through streets lined with flag-waving crowds, to receive from the Lord Mayor – "In recognition of your heroic stand for the interests of our nation" – the Freedom of The City of London. Then they were invited to Sandringham, where Their Majesties had presented them with a bookstand and a tea-table, fretworked by the gardeners of the estate.

"Now that we have the friendship of the King and Queen," said Ethel, as they journeyed home, "We have no further need of political parties" – she waved, regally, at a field of cows – "That was certainly a great triumph, darling" – she had not called him 'darling' for seventeen years – "But always remember that L-G won the war."

He was hardly likely to forget L-G. Six years ago, when he had expressed, in the course of some financial debate, guarded approval of the Liberal's land policies, Neville Chamberlain had accused him of "giving Lloyd George the glad eye." There had been an intake of breath and then the whole chamber had erupted in merriment. He knew why they were laughing – L-G was not called 'The Goat' for nothing – but they did not understand Ethel. The more she admired a man, the less corporeal he became in her eyes. When she spoke of Love, she did not mean what ordinary people meant. What *had* always worried him was the way that – although she scowled whenever MacDonald appeared – her head would turn, as if against her will, to watch him go. When a woman claims to hate a man, he had heard, the truth is usually quite the opposite. So perhaps she secretly hated L-G or even Philip himself? It was all so confusing.

Over the last two years MacDonald had offered Lloyd George, now isolated from his own fractious party, a series of government posts – all of which he had turned down. "Once the dust has settled then we'll talk," was his unvarying response. Well, now Baldwin and Samuel would veto any such suggestion and the dust would indeed be settling . . . on the grave of Liberalism itself.

Philip had observed vain men who strove to maintain a deceptively youthful appearance – he was particularly suspicious of MacDonald's moustache – but why ever had L-G dyed his hair that blinding albino white? He still scurried about like a man half his age: perhaps that very incongruity was the secret of his appeal? Ethel had commissioned a copy of the recent Orpen portrait: when in Tilford, she would carry it from room to room. One evening, joining her for supper, he had discovered it balanced on the arms of his own chair. The Welsh Wizard had been depicted seated at his desk, looking up from his correspondence. The eyes were wide, as if some mystic vision had just been vouchsafed unto him. The right hand held a pen, awkwardly wedged between second and third fingers, but the left was at his side, cupped and curled backwards in a curiously furtive gesture. Perhaps the Angel Gabriel was slipping him a few quid for a peerage? Never trust an artist! Orpen had got the measure of his man. Philip would never allow himself to be 'done': unless, perhaps, in a sculpture – just the head, and definitely *not* by Epstein!

"Don't you think there's something odd about his expression?" he had asked Ethel.

"Oh, he often looks like that" – she picked up the picture and danced it round the room – "Especially when he's feeling a bit rompish: just like Spot, when he fetches his own lead."

Over the years, Ethel had gradually become more solid – statuesque was probably a better word – but she had not lost her charm. Who else could have prevailed upon Chaliapin, at an Opera House fundraiser, to perform the full death scene from *Boris Godunov* right there in the drawing room of Number Eleven? Afterwards, all the carpets had needed to be re-laid.

What he liked most were their evenings, when they would sit together in the summer house as the daylight faded, with Spot gnawing at the fretwork table or snoring rhythmically in his basket. Ethel had her own way of sitting: gradually the shoulders would slump while, as if to compensate, the chin rose, fully stretching and displaying that long pale throat. He often recalled the first time he had seen her – not the day they met but the first time that he had really *looked at* her. He had just spoken at The Drill Hall – to a full and enthusiastic house –but, as they were walking back to Keighley station, the wind had taken her umbrella and the rain had soaked them to the skin. There had never been a storm like it. They had been forced to take shelter in the terraced house that he had once shared with Horner and his crew. Fortunately, some of his clothes were still there, including that embarrassingly-frogged dressing gown. He had thought that she would be lost in its folds but, if anything, it appeared to be too small. The frontal 'v' kept deepening, as if pulled by invisible hands and the cord loosened itself, so that first one leg, then the other, emerged through the vent. He could have sworn that there had even been a flash of white knee. She had put her wet stockings on the mantelpiece, weighted down with two candlesticks, so that they hung before the fire, which was blazing away as always, irrespective of the season. In that filthy sitting room, before an audience of half a dozen inebriates, she had expounded her philosophy of Universal Love. Never before had he heard anyone – no, not even Bradlaugh – who spoke in perfect sentences, paragraphs, even chapters. Those blue eyes had gradually turned black, while her hair, which he had only seen pinned up, dried into a great red-gold halo, full of dancing sparks. Her bare toes had been digging into the well-clinkered hearthrug: their tiny nails kept changing colour, from white to rose to mother-of-pearl. The other men in the room were also hypnotised, although they were not looking at Ethel but at the firelight flickering through the gauzy stockings. Horner's huge hands cradled a tumbler of gin which, for a full two hours, they neglected to raise to his gaping mouth. Perhaps they had a bet on which stocking would be the first to catch alight: the left, as it happened.

The studio manager had appeared in his control booth: evidently there was a second, external entrance. He was adjusting dials and mouthing silently to himself.

"Can you hear me?" Philip asked. The man raised a hand: somehow the sound-proofing was only one-way.

"In July our own financial difficulties were aggravated by panic on the continent." He paused but the man did not look up. "I need not go into that story: it has been told to you often in the last few weeks."

The economy had been in steady decline since The Wall Street Crash but a full crisis was precipitated by the collapse of Austria's Kreditanstalt, followed by a number of German banks. It spread to London, where Norman had to bail out Lazards, Kleinworts and Schroeders. Then the May Report forecast a deficit of £120 million for the year and £170 million for 1932. With the rise in unemployment, the insurance fund was borrowing £1 million a week: Paris and New York were threatening to call in their short-term loans. He could not raise taxes or suspend the Sinking Fund, for what sort of impression would *that* give? And MacDonald's favoured option of a 10% import tariff was absurd – whoever would we trade with when the crisis was over? Expenditure cuts were the only sensible option. It was regrettable, but when the world realized just how far he was prepared to go – when they saw the rigours inflicted on ordinary people and how uncomplainingly they bore them – they would know that the Labour Party – or, at least, its Chancellor – had to be taken seriously.

In August he had stayed at his post while everyone else went on holiday. When the run on gold began and poor Norman had left for Canada, they all came scuttling back. MacDonald broke off from chasing Lady Londonderry through the whins and brooms of Morayshire; Baldwin, Chamberlain and Samuel quitted their grouse butts; and even the King returned from Balmoral.

At the cabinet meeting everyone had been so long-faced that Philip could not help but laugh. "None of this is difficult for me," he told them. "I am naturally of a saving temperament." After nine hours, they had agreed to cuts of £56 million but he still insisted on another twenty, half of which would be drawn from unemployment benefits. He persuaded them at least to find out whether this would be acceptable to their American creditors.

Then they had waited, all day and long into the night, for a response from Harrison of the New York Federal Reserve. It was so warm that they even took off their jackets and wandered round Number Ten's garden. The night was unusually clear and full of stars: the general silence was only broken by Jimmy Thomas picking them out. He managed to locate Cassiopeia in three different parts of the sky. The telegram, when it arrived, offered merely a short-term loan of $10 million and that only if the French were prepared to match it. Harrison also demanded assurances from the Bank of England and other City institutions that they were in full accord. Although The Cabinet voted by eleven to nine in favour of this proposal, it was evident that they would no longer have any real control of financial policy and that those voting against – including, to Philip's surprise, Willie Graham – would immediately resign. It was impossible for the government to carry on.

"I'm off to The Palace to throw in my hand." MacDonald's left hand gripped his right wrist, as if to indicate that he would indeed be wrenching it off and tossing it into His Majesty's lap.

"I'm going back to bed," said Philip, "Tell the King that his fretwork bookcase has collapsed."

"Better not, in the circumstances," said MacDonald.

The shiny-faced young man had emerged. He was now wearing white gloves, like some black - faced musical performer on Brighton Pier: either his hands were enormous or the gloves were heavily padded. He placed a carafe of water on the table, well away from the microphone, and then half-filled a tumbler, wide-bottomed and weighted to prevent spillage.

"I have always been a strong party man, and I never expected to find myself in the political company I am keeping today. But I do not have a shadow of a doubt about the common sense - no, about the wisdom and rightness - of my actions."

The prime minister had returned with the news that he was going to form a National Government, with a mixed cabinet, appointed not as party politicians but as independent individuals acting solely in the interests of the country. There were Baldwin and three other Tories - not including Churchill; two Liberals, neither of them Lloyd George; and, of the present government, Sankey, Thomas and Philip himself.

It had always been obvious what MacDonald was going to do: he was not hard to read, providing you had a strong stomach. Philip had never been sure just how far the man's self-knowledge extended: perhaps he had genuinely believed that he would resign until he heard his own voice acceding to the King's request? Even when he did show some common sense, he still contrived to present it as a wild, semi-supernatural impulse. He claimed to have been deeply moved by the interview.

"I said to him, 'Your Majesty, do you truly believe that I am the only man to see the country through?' and then he put his hand on my shoulder" - he attempted to demonstrate but Philip moved out of reach - "And do you know what he said to me?"

"No," said Philip.

"He said, 'I did - and I do!'"

This sounded like one of King George's private jokes. MacDonald never knew when he was being laughed at.

"Tomorrow, when the news is announced," he continued, "Every

436

duchess in London will be wanting . . ." – he rubbed his hands together with an abrasive sound, then sprang across the room to whisper, in Philip's right ear, "To kiss me!"

Ugh, he had actually felt the spittle running down his cheek! MacDonald stuck out his tongue, rolled his eyes and cut a little caper: a revolting display – especially for a man of sixty-five. What was particularly vile was that he had meant something else, something far worse than 'kiss'. What on earth could that Monte Carlo woman have been blackmailing him with, what reputation did he have left to lose? He was indeed 'an Ibsinite out and out' and 'the state could not understand him even though it tryed'. 'Wy I Am Anakist,' it appeared, had always been his secret credo.

Philip went back to bed but slept fitfully. He dreamt of a queue – extending the full length of Downing Street – of stately dowagers in their corsets and stays. Lady Londonderry was at the head, of course, with Lady Sackville not far behind, but somewhere towards the middle Philip had glimpsed his own wife's face.

Since that day, MacDonald had lost the few wits he had ever possessed. He seemed to think that the crisis demanded a series of interminable and meaningless speeches to the nation. "We shall go on and on," he would say, "We shall go up and up" – here he would pause dramatically – "We shall go on and on and up and up." His metaphors ran wild: somehow, he was simultaneously setting a course for calmer waters, clapping his spurs to his valiant steed and leaving no stone unturned. Nevertheless, the value of the pound rose after each faltering broadcast. Last week in the House, while addressing an innocuous question on the Sinking Fund, he had broken off and stared into space for a full half minute. "You know, there is absolutely no logic in the conduct of human affairs," he finally muttered, then shook himself – like Spot emerging from the lily-pond – and resumed his obfuscations.

A white glove waved to attract his attention, then pointed to the clock: six, no, seven minutes left. Philip saw that a tiny money-spider was frantically swimming on the surface of his water: fortunately, he was not thirsty.

"I know that the economies we have had to make are disagreeable. It has been no pleasure to impose them. They were necessary to prevent a far more serious reduction in working-class conditions."

A week after the Government's fall, a letter from Jowett had arrived at Tilford. Philip had taken to loitering by the mail-box: he suspected Ethel of intercepting his post - to spare him, no doubt, although he had no wish to be spared.

"You are aware of my personal views" - Fred's copperplate was as firm as ever - "But I want you to know that I have no doubt about your sincerity in the course of action that you have adopted."

How Philip hated such bland, unshakable benevolence! His own sincerity or otherwise was utterly irrelevant. It had all been a matter of simple common sense: to have acted in any other way would have been madness - and the sincerity or insincerity of madness was surely beside the point. He had even begun to suspect that a deep and deadly sarcasm ran through Fred's every utterance. "Mr Figaro's wedding," indeed!

". . . And had it not been you and MacDonald who wielded the scalpel, it would have been Baldwin and Churchill with the axe. History may even conclude that you have mended more than you marred."

Philip had responded immediately, by telegram.

"Jowett -
    In the unlikely event of my requiring absolution I shall obtain a priest.
    Snowden"

Downright hostility was much easier to deal with. Uncle Arthur trying to snarl was an absolute joy, as was the sight of Leach haunting the corridors, waiting for Philip to appear, so that he could cut him dead. Most of the party took this line, except for

Ben Turner, who had trotted up with his old friendly grin, then begged him to contribute a Foreword to his forthcoming Collected Poems.

"Tell me, how do you sleep at night?" Lansbury had enquired.

"Like a log," he had lied. "Instead of counting sheep, I count the unemployed."

Only the other day, Glasier's widow had crossed Regent Street to stare into his face. If looks could kill! It had taken all his self-control not to burst out laughing. How could she imagine that the Chancellor of the Exchequer would be discountenanced by some wretched harridan giving him the evil eye?

He felt an almost physical aversion towards his former comrades. 'A lot of blethering easie-oosie asses': for once, he had to agree with MacDonald. Now, on the other side of the chamber, he could see them for what they were: those mad, twisted faces, the mouths full of rotting teeth – he could actually *smell* the decay. A convulsive wave periodically passed through their ranks, as when a wind blows over a field of ripe corn. Only now did he understand that he had always stood alone, representing no-one and nothing but himself. What people called Socialism had actually been whatever Philip Snowden was doing at the time. The irony was, of course, that he should now be joined at the hip to the man whom he always hated above all others. MacSnowden: one of Fate's little jokes: how his mother would have appreciated it!

"May I say a word to my old friends in the Labour movement? Although my recent action may seem to them inconsistent with my past, I can assure them that it is not."

His emergency budget had met the crisis head on: not only cuts in wages and the dole but also an increase in Surtax and a suspension of the Sinking Fund. When the new opposition accused him of breaking his own pledges, he replied that these had been made by a Labour Party Chancellor and thus could not be binding on a National Government one. "Now I have balanced my budget," he said, folding his arms. He had not merely covered the £170 million deficit – he had actually arrived at a £1.5 million surplus! Although it was true that statistics never lied, they could sometimes be prevailed upon to fib a little.

He had ended the speech with some lines from his father's mildewed copy of Swinburne. *England: An Ode* – as well as the usual underlinings and exclamation marks, the margin had been decorated by the wobbly outline of what appeared to be a hen. Philip took this to indicate Dad's heartiest assent.

> "All our past proclaims our future
> Shakespeare's voice and Nelson's hand
> Milton's faith and Wordsworth's trust
> In this our chosen and chainless land
> Bears witness – come the world against Her,
> England still shall stand."

He would have liked to have said something more directly about the Americans and French but could not, lest they withdraw their loans.

Labour's new leader, Henderson, and Willie Graham, now Shadow Chancellor, were seldom seen in the chamber during the subsequent five-day debate. Willie had lost weight and walked like a broken man. "Where is the member for Edinburgh Central?" Philip kept asking – then, after a felicitous slip, "Where is the member for Head-in-hands Central?" He hoped that Graham did not take this too hard: in politics you had to exploit your opponent's weaknesses, whatever your personal feelings might be.

Dalton had proved to be his most dangerous antagonist, pointing out that those earning £5,000 a year would lose 3% of their income, those on £500, 5% and those under £50, 10%. "Is that The Chancellor's idea of equality of sacrifice?" he had enquired. It was a good point, effectively made – those *were* the figures, right enough. There was no use arguing: at such moments, personal abuse was the only option. "The Honourable Gentleman," he had replied, jabbing that lethal finger in whose occult properties he himself had almost come to believe, "Is nothing more nor less than a Bolshevik!"

Whatever could someone like Dalton - late of Eton, Cambridge and the LSE-know of sacrifice? It was something you had to learn: there were examinations to be sat and qualifications to be gained. What was now called poverty was nothing compared to fifty years ago. Ordinary people, though, had not forgotten what it had been like. They still remembered how to cope with privation. It was only common sense that *they* should make the sacrifices, rather than those who had known only security and comfort. And wasn't it easier to economize when you could actually *see* your pennies lined up in front of you, rather than having them in stocks and bonds and such like? The people knew what Philip Snowden had done for them: why shouldn't they trust him now? This would only be a temporary setback: austerity might even be pleasant, in a nostalgic sort of way. Long cosy evenings spent by the fireside although, admittedly, with no fire in the grate.

He did not need to inform his listeners of the necessity for sacrifice: nor would he be praising and flattering them as Baldwin and MacDonald did. Unlike the rich, the poor would be proud - with a mixture of patriotism and fatalism - to be making the sacrifices necessary to get their country back on its feet. How else could you explain the donations that were rolling in? Even children were sending the contents of their piggybanks and yesterday a beggar had gone into The Treasury to empty on to the table his capful of ha'pennies, farthings and buttons.

The real question - which such as Dalton refused to answer - was what good it would do if capitalism were to implode before there was a working alternative - whether Socialist or even Snowden-ite - ready to take its place. Philip had never forgotten what he had seen from the train crossing the Rocky Mountains: that benighted soul sitting alone amidst utter desolation, reduced to using books for fuel. His former comrades did not seem to realize how easy it would be for the world to relapse into such a state. To employ Jowett's 'homely simile', someone had to take up a shovel, put a peg on their nose and clean the whole mess up. He was under no illusions that he would be thanked for it. Even his current popularity in the country, he suspected, would be as short-lived as His Majesty's fretworked gifts. For when the crisis had passed, all the old fantasies and illusions would come flooding back, and the easie-oosie asses would take up their bletherings once again. But one thing was certain: the name of Philip Snowden – whether as hero or villain – would never be forgotten.

Despite the budget, however, the Bank of England had still been losing millions of pounds a day: since the crisis began, a full billion had vanished from their coffers. Now the foreign assets held in London exceeded available gold reserves: if they paid out any more, the security of the currency itself would be jeopardised. There was only one course left: to leave The Gold Standard – if only until international confidence was restored.

The Bank's officials decided to warn Norman of their impending action by telegram. He was a day out from Quebec on the return voyage home: they had found him on the ship's manifest, travelling under his usual alias. In order to avert premature speculation and panic selling, they employed what seemed to Philip to be a rather obvious code, using the Bank's nickname, 'The Old Lady of Threadneedle Street'.

"Dear Prof Skinner," the telegram read, "The Old Lady goes off at midnight."

"At a complete loss," was 'Skinner's' reply, "Has something happened to my mother?"

Norman had remained in ignorance until, after disembarking at Liverpool, he read the newspapers on the Euston train. He had stormed into the Bank in a blind fury but soon saw the humour of the situation. "This sad and sinful world," he had sighed, "Is not yet worthy of The Gold Standard." As a penance or forfeit, he swore that he would never again wear a hat – not even the one with the bee embroidery. "It was either my hat or my trousers," he said.

The pound fell in value but twenty-five other countries had followed their example and, almost immediately, export markets began to pick up once more. Keynes, of course, claimed to have predicted the whole thing. And a second letter from Fred Jowett had arrived. "I know that you must be grieving over this latest turn of events," he wrote, "But who knows, it may prove to be - in the short or even the long term - all for the best." Philip had not dignified it with a reply. Only this morning, however, he had discovered that Emily Jowett had died on the very same day that the country had come off The Standard. One of Ethel's maiden aunts had read a notice in the local paper. For some unaccountable reason Fred had not mentioned this in his letter.

The BBC man was waving again, holding up two fingers. Philip reached for his water glass but then remembered the spider. Against all probabilities, it had reached the side and crawled up the sheer face, for now it was perched on the rim, considering its next move. Although this could only be a good omen, it had come too late to be worked into his speech. Besides, parables and metaphors could so easily go horribly wrong.

Perhaps tonight he should revert to t'owld Yorkshire doric? Last year he had heard his mother's voice eerily emanating from his radio cabinet. She had been recorded by dialect researchers just before her death. "A remarkable survival," the announcer had said, "From an obscure and atavistic Northern hamlet." *That* would have gone down well in Cowling!

"Ayup," he said in his uncle's voice, loudly cracking his knuckles, "It's the scurvy gouger." Perhaps he had better not - the shiny head behind the glass had swivelled sharply - for that would surely tax the microphone worse than any sneeze.

How long ago it all seemed! How merrily he had whistled, the scurvy gouger, as he cycled away from the humiliated shooting party. "This is sansculottism run mad!" What a heartless little tyke he had been and how little he had understood the world! Why on earth had he refused Sir Walter's money? It had been considerably more than the fines that the men had paid. Although their paths had subsequently crossed, in the House of Commons, Long had never once mentioned the matter but his face would always take on a curious expression. He did not smile – indeed, the line of the mouth would tighten, as if in disapproval – but his eyes could only be said to be twinkling. Up until then, Philip had taken this to be purely a figure of speech. When he had attended the man's funeral, it had been deeply moving – all sorts and conditions of people had been there, most of them visibly upset.

"The Labour Party programme is the most fantastic and impracticable ever put before the electorate. Derelict industries will be taken over by the state with you, the tax payer, shouldering the losses. Banks and financial houses will be run by the TUC and your hard-earned savings and investments will be appropriated to fund these madcap policies."

After these words he had left a gap. Something needed to go there, he felt, even though he had no idea what it might be. Now it had come to him – the perfect line, the killing thrust. Once again he took up his pen.

"This is not Socialism," he wrote, "This is – BOLSHEVISM RUN MAD."

Although he had put the three words in capitals, he was not going to shout. He would deliver them in a neutral tone, delicately stressing the syllables – Bol-Shev-Ism – and then pause for three seconds before eliding RUN and MAD into one single word. And in that silence every single listener – even those who had never seen him in those countless market squares, temperance halls and party platforms – would know that he was smiling his very sweetest smile.

BOLSHEVISM RUN MAD . . . as he savoured the words, he had a vision of Fred Jowett – wild-eyed, lips flecked with foam, clothes drenched in blood, brandishing a mutilated baby like a club.

"This one's for you, Our Fred," he whispered. Viscount Snowden of Ickornshaw was not a man to be too lightly forgiven.

"Ready?" The radio man's voice boomed unexpectedly.

Philip nodded. The spider had now vanished: even though the water looked cloudy, he drained the whole glass. The red light came on. He had expected the glare to scorch his eyes but it was feeble and closer to pink. The white gloves began their counting down. He leaned forward so that his lips were exactly eight inches from the microphone, then lifted one buttock and expelled, in one continuous blast, all the air that had built up in his alimentary canal. He did not look towards the control booth: why should a Chancellor of the Exchequer care what anyone thinks? There was now no possibility of his disgracing himself before the nation – the last white finger disappeared – Everything had been simple common sense.

CHAPTER THIRTEEN

ICKORNSHAW MOOR (1937)

F ROM THE BURNLEY Road it was a two-mile walk across the moor to the place where Philip Snowden's ashes were to be scattered. There were at least a dozen parked cars along with three – no, four! – charabancs: the narrow farm track was obscured by a slowly-ascending crowd. "He'll be getting a good send-off," Little Emily shouted into her father's ear, "In terms of numbers, at any rate."

As a young man, Fred Jowett had feared blindness but now here he was, going deaf. He had been so busy worrying about his eyes that he had neglected his ears. That horrible dead feeling – as if the canals and tubes had been stuffed with dirty cotton wool – had recurred at ever-shortening intervals until it had become almost an habitual state. Last year, the doctor had syringed out basinfuls of honey-coloured wax but it had made no difference. He suspected that Grayson's Drill Hall speech had started it: he had almost seen the germs swarming about in the foetid air. Two days later, he had come down with an infection that had seemed as much moral as physical. Now he would often lose the external world altogether, to become aware of a low humming which set the bones of his face vibrating in an almost unbearable way. He was sure that it was the late King George saying "Peace at 'ome . . . Peace at 'ome," over and over again.

There had been some short periods of remission. If he was out in a strong wind, a series of clicks in his sinuses would sometimes presage a return to his pre-Keighley state, although he would always relapse before the day was out. And now his sense of taste was increasingly affected: he didn't enjoy food if he couldn't hear himself eating it. Evidently it was not true that if you lost one sense then the others became more acute in compensation: his vision would still blur in the evenings, although his nose remained as keen as ever. It was almost as if his ears were bored: if anyone said something interesting or significant, they would hear it all right – they had only heard the telephone ring when it had been Snowden on the other end of the line.

At least his legs and lungs still worked: they began their climb. His life had been, by necessity, an indoor one – from mills to meeting houses to council chambers to committee rooms. He had always promised himself that, at the last, he would retire to the countryside but apparently his were the kind of politics that you never could retire from. Whenever he visited his youngest daughter, up in the dales, he would walk out to Coniston Dib and back. Each time it took him five minutes longer. Everything seemed so clear and simple up there: the white limestone outcrops stood out like the bones of long-extinct monsters. When he finally returned to Kettlewell, he was always surprised not to be greeted with the news that capitalism had, in his absence, finally succumbed. Last week he had gone down to Heaton Woods and found that the paddling pools had been filled in and the gravel paths removed. As if by magic, Red Beck had returned to its former course. He had gone to the Town Hall but no-one seemed to know anything about it. Perhaps Grayson had begun to deliver on his parting promise?

Little Emily was mouthing at him again. It suited folk for him to be deaf as if it provided a convenient explanation or excuse. For a while, she had even employed a small blackboard on which she would chalk 'SLIPPERS ON!' or 'ANOTHER CUP?' – but Fred had just stared in silence until she took it away.

"Pull up your muffler, Dad" – she finally shouted – "You'll catch your death." Once again her hands were at his throat, knotting the wool far too tight. "Ne'er cast a clout till May is out." This was one of her favourite sayings, along with "She's her own worst enemy" and "Some people don't even know they're born." She closely resembled her late mother, except that she was over twice the size and her tongue had a sharp edge that was all her own. She had been bitter and disillusioned long before the world had let her down.

How dreadful it was to find that you were now dependent! "He's spent his whole life looking out for other folk, so you can't begrudge him now," she would say, in a distinctly begrudging tone. First she and her family had moved in next door, then her great lummox of a husband had appeared, in a shower of plaster and brickdust, through Fred's parlour wall. Now, whenever the connecting door swung open, he felt as if something terrible – even more terrible that Little Emily or The Lummox – was about to appear. Why couldn't she just come out of her own front door, take two steps and walk through his? "I'm saving me feet," she explained.

His Emily had died when the labour movement turned against itself: he suspected that this had been the cause. She had been in tears when Willie Leach had spoken what had turned out to be his final words to Fred. "It was all your fault – you and Maxton and the rest. You made them leave, with your sniping and carping and ridiculous demands. You drove MacDonald into the arms of the Duchesses."

"This will *kill* your father," she had said to Little Emily, but it was she herself who had died. And, of course, it had been that death – and not the political reverses of the day – that had come close to killing him. It had never crossed his mind that she might be worrying: not once had she complained about his absences – in fact, she has always endorsed his commitment. And while he was away he was perpetually aware of her invisible presence at his shoulder, gentle and calm, happy and proud. The idea that she had been suffering on his account was hardly to be borne. Only when she was gone had he realized that she had been what really mattered in his life. For the last six years, although clinically still alive, he had been, to all intents and purposes, a dead man.

The real catalyst for his grief had been a letter of condolence from Blatchford. "Surely you do not think that Death is the end?" He had written. "That would be defeat indeed!" Nunquam, of all people, had renounced Socialism and taken up table-tapping and similar mumbo-jumbo . . . And now he and those smirking daughters of his had joined Mosley's British Union of Fascists. When Henderson had won the Nobel Peace Prize for his work on the League of Nations, Blatchford had proposed that he should be hung instead, and that for any Englishman even to utter the word 'peace' should be a capital offence. *The Clarion* newspaper was no more: all that remained was its cycling club, an enormous phalanx to-ing and fro-ing in perpetuity across the Sussex Downs.

A hawk flew low over their heads: too big for a peregrine but too small for a buzzard – its barred tail was familiar but he could not recall its name. It had been as if he had *felt* the bird's presence before he actually saw it – almost as if it had come fluttering out of his own chest. The rain was lashing into their faces but the dirty black clouds were keeping pace with them. Moorland weather was unfathomable: there even seemed to be a third wind, blowing clean through his head, setting his ears clicking, unlocking his hearing once again.

This moor was different from those above Haworth and Keighley, with no bracken or ling, only cotton grass, mosses and particularly cloying ground – more like Lancashire mud than Yorkshire. And its bees were unusual, striped black and red, making a crackling rather than a buzzing sound. And the sheep looked almost *too* healthy: local blackfaces had been crossed with fuller-fleeced and chubbier Southern breeds. Fred had never quite trusted sheep since Colne Valley. He could imagine them, on rare fine mornings, bleating 'Grayson weather' to each other.

Attending funerals and memorial services was taking up more and more of his time. All his old council colleagues had gone and so had Henderson and even the Red Countess of Warwick. None of her radical friends had been invited to the ceremony – the aristocracy had ruthlessly reclaimed their own. Only last month, Kathleen Glasier's eldest son, a boy of great promise, had died after a rugby ball struck him above the heart. The mother's hair was grey now but her expression had never changed: it was as if, back in 1893, she had already been anticipating the suffering that lay ahead. By far the best attended had been Gustav Behrens' interment in Undercliffe Cemetery, with convincing demonstrations of grief from the surprising number of millworkers who attended. Perhaps they had been put on time-and-a-half for the day?

Pulled up beside a crumbling barn was a black and silver limousine. It made the Countess of Warwick's famous cars look like black-beetles. Although the engine was turned off it still seemed to be giving out a low purr of satisfaction at its own mechanical perfection. No mud besmirched its bodywork and a briar bush was bending its thorny branches away: even nature knew its place. Fred rested a hand on its bonnet: the gleaming chrome did not deign to show its reflection.

Ahead of them, the crowd had halted at a stile, as if afraid to approach three incongruous figures. A very tall young man in a chauffeur's uniform and cap, an old man in a wheelchair and a slender girl dressed in black silk. Her hair was exactly the same shade as the old man's, but the effect was very different: Fred guessed that this must be one of those 'blonde bombshells' that the newspapers were always going on about. She and the chauffeur were helping the man out of his chair, useless on the increasingly rutted ground. He was wearing a coat of dark fur with an old-fashioned top hat and carrying two cork-tipped walking canes. The eyes were hidden behind black-lensed spectacles but he did not appear to be blind. His face looked as if it had been baked too long in an oven and was now beginning to crumble: a startlingly red tongue kept licking at the parched lips. Nevertheless, with that sivery mane and dangling moustache he had an impressive air, only slightly offset by his markedly bowed legs. If he were to encounter a pig in a passageway, Fred reflected, he would not be able to stop it.

"It must be Beaverbrook!" said Little Emily but Fred shook his head. It was not the newspaper editor, whose fastidiously clean-shaven features looked as if they had been crushed in a vice. Emily, having spotted a couple of her cronies, scuttled over to talk to them. The old man handed his canes to the chauffeur, dropped to his knees and then, with surprising alacrity, crawled through the Jowett Hole next to the stile. The young woman followed but with more difficulty. Once she was on all fours, her hips seemed to be spreading wider and wider.

It was the first time that Fred had ever really looked at a bottom, as if it might be a separate thing in itself. Blatchford and Hyndman, he recalled, often talked as if the constituent parts of women had been laid out for them on trays, as in a butcher's shop. He had never understood this: Emily, for example, had been . . . Emily – why ever would he want to anatomize her? But now he could not help himself: it was the only part of the girl that was visible. She seemed to be stuck: should he offer to help? Now those hips had begun to roll alarmingly, simultaneously up and down and round and round. Through the tight black material a pale glow seemed to be emanating, like the moon about to emerge from behind a cloud. Then, in a flash she was on the other side, head thrown back, laughing delightedly. She turned and bobbed a little curtsey: Fred realized that he was not the only man who had been transfixed.

"What a shameless little baggage," said Emily, returning. "You wouldn't catch me dressing like that – no, not even for a million dollars. She's supposed to be his secretary, though you might call it other things."

But Fred was struck by the way the girl looked at her employer. Surely such affection could not be feigned? Nor did her expression change when the old man looked away. Sometimes life was not as simple – or as crude – as Emily liked to think. Fred was even inclined to believe that the colour of the girl's hair was perfectly natural.

"They're Americans," Emily continued, "Or at least they say they are. No-one seems to know why they're here."

After a respectful pause, the chauffeur took two long strides and effortlessly vaulted the wall. Fred felt inspired to follow: left foot up to the step, then a sideways turn, right foot over, then twist and down to land on both feet, with the wall behind him. I can still do it after all, he thought, just before the pain came stabbing through his heart and kidneys. While he fought for breath and Emily scolded, the girl and the chauffeur were moving on. Having linked arms with their employer, they were both bowing their legs – not, Fred was sure, out of mockery but in sympathy or solidarity. The girl's perfume, sweet but pungent, lingered on the air: it made him think of Heaton woods on a spring morning and, also, of Epstein's model, Dolores – not of her smell but of the woman herself. He had not seen *her* bottom, he recalled, for she had remained seated through-out their brief interview.

Three years ago, he had received a postcard from Epstein

Dear J,

Thought you should know that the Notorious D has passed. They found her in a basement off Praed St. No susp. circs. Models are like elephants, you know – when their time is up they leave Soho and drag themselves to Paddington to die.

– Ep.

Fred had not known quite what to make of this: in the end, he had not replied. Epstein was still a prime target for the Beaverbrook and Harmsworth newspapers. Recently Ethel Snowden had got up a petition against his commission from Coventry Cathedral – *Ecce Homo*, a squat and agonized male figure suspiciously reminiscent of The Beaver himself. And Rima and her birds, despite Hyde Park's railings, were regularly vandalised. She had been tarred and feathered, stained by permanganate of potash, daubed with crude slogans – 'GOD SAVE OUR KING AND BRITAIN FROM THE CANCER OF JUDAH', and the like.

The ceremony was to be held on a plateau about three hundred yards short of the summit. Philip's body had been cremated in Surrey and its ashes brought up here. Fred had not received an invitation to the official Commemoration Service, to be held at St. Margaret's Westminster in three days' time. He was taken aback by today's crowd – at least two thousand, and in foul weather, too. He suspected that they were mostly locals. "Don't all the older ones look like Uncle Phil?" observed Emily, "They're even more inbred than the Sax-Coburgs!"

And here was Ethel, perching on a large, toad-shaped rock, and there, cradled in her lap, was a small rosewood box. She was dressed in a cape of greeny-black bombazine but the rain, held in suspension on its shoulders, gave off a silvery light. Her face was obscured by a smoky veil that reached almost to her waist: "Perhaps she's taking up bee-keeping as a sideline," said Emily. Then, dramatically, the gauze was thrown back to reveal the face. How pale she was! – but the eyes were as wide and bright as ever and that little secret smile was still tucked away in the corners of her mouth. It was as if she was posing for some inspirational painting entitled 'Faithful Unto Death' or 'The Fair Relict'. She observed their approach and lowered her eyes. Putting the ashes aside, she produced a small golden penknife and began to scrape the mud from between the treads of her walking brogues. "At least we're still worth cutting," said Emily, "Just watch her work her way around the congregation, ignoring them one by one."

Fred remembered one of Philip's final telephone calls. "The funniest thing, Our Fred," he had begun. "This morning, at break-fast, My Lady Snowden suddenly threw down *The Times* and announced, 'Cynthia Mosley – in her overweening arrogance – has left a vacuum in society which I intend to fill.' Then she walked straight out of the house – still in her best slippers – and the last I saw of her she was running in the direction of the railway station.

Ah, women, Fred, women! Wherever would we be without them?"

"Precisely where I *have* been for these last six years," Fred had been tempted to reply. Our Phil could be most insensitive at times.

An elbow dug into his ribs. "Don't forget to remind her about his desk," growled Emily, "If you don't, I will."

Viscount Snowden of Ickornshaw had spent his last days in his study, at his hexagonal oaken desk, staring out of his bay window at the rolling Surrey countryside. It had made him feel, he said, like a captain at the wheel of some great ship: as if he could have set a course for anywhere in the world but chose instead to remain anchored at Eden Lodge, until the end. Whenever his spine plagued him and he had to repair to the day-bed, he would have the nurse carefully position a full-length mirror so that he could still see 'his' view. He had once told Fred that he liked to imagine that the lawns hedges and trees, the birds and squirrels, even that particular patch of sky, would perish along with him.

How Fred coveted that desk! He did not expect to find a hidden drawer containing some revelatory diary: it was as if, by merely sitting at it, he might come to understand everything that had happened. Besides, he had never become accustomed to his own writing-table: whenever he forgot himself and crossed his legs it would give his left kneecap an admonitory crack.

Phil had been nominally employed as a journalist, paid £2,000 a year to write – for the *Chronicle* and *Express* – weekly columns that almost no-one read. "Lloyd George's pensioner," they were calling him, and Fred could tell that his old friend's heart was no longer in it. He simultaneously opposed and supported both Roosevelt's New Deal and L-G's abortive British version. In one paragraph he would convert to Keynesianism, only to return to free trade orthodoxy in the next. The German National Socialists, he maintained, could not be taken seriously because of their vegetarianism: he seemed to be under the impression that Herr Hitler dressed in robes and sandals rather than military uniform and boots.

"Somehow, Fred, I always knew that at the end of it there would be a wide desk, a comfortable chair with a grand view and" - there had been an audible gulping sound - "A plentiful supply of good champagne."

"But you took the pledge, Phil," he had protested, "All those years ago in Cowling."

"Champagne isn't alcohol, Our Fred - at least, not in the way that brandy, whiskey or beer are. Just as a stalking panther is not a snoozing tabby and the Brahms *Requiem* is not a Music Hall song. And I challenge you to show me a single working man whose life has been ruined by champagne."

He had been swimming with some very strange fish. His near-neighbours, Beaverbrook and Harmsworth, kept plying him with gladioli, cumquats and Verve Clicquot. "I eat the flowers and put the fruit in water," Phil wrote - presumably, he still drank the champagne. "I think they're courting me. They're after something but I don't know what it is." One evening he had taught them 'The Red Flag'. "Fred, old friend, I am not joking when I say that it was most affecting. I had tears in my eyes and so did they: I have never heard it sung with such fervour as by those two deep-dyed reactionaries. 'We feel positively shriven, Comrade Snowden', The Beaver said, 'Now let us storm The Crystal Palace!'" Even Philip had wondered when he heard, a few days later, that this building had subsequently been burnt to the ground.

Fred heard angry voices: an argument had broken out between local factions as to whether Philip's title had been properly bestowed.

"'E never were Ickornshaw. 'E were Cowling born and bred."

"I suppose he thought that Ickornshaw had more of a ring to it. Cowling's a good place, right enough, but you must admit it sounds a bit, you know . . . docile."

"Nay, nay," said a dangerously intense-looking man, "'E's not Ickornshaw but 'e's not Cowling neither. 'E's a bloody Middletonite, right in between."

What a difference a few hundred yards could make! This debate was obviously going to continue for some time. It was still unclear whether these men were trying to claim or disown Snowden, whether they took pride in him or were ashamed.

Now the hymns had started and Fred wished that his deafness would return. The tunes were pleasant enough but the words were usually absurd. He had never believed in some easy correspondence between the values of Socialism and Christianity.

> "Praise we the peaceful men of skill
> Who builded homes of beauty
> And, rich in art, made richer still
> The brotherhood of duty."
> "Builded" – what kind of word was that?

After Snowden and MacDonald had left the party and formed the National Government, Henderson and Lansbury had chosen to blame the ILP. It seemed absurd to punish those who had warned what might happen and tried to prevent it, but they nevertheless insisted that Fred and Maxton and the rest accept the standing orders of the main party, thus effectively abolishing the ILP. And so, in July 1932, at Jowett Hall, a special conference had voted to go it alone and disaffiliate. The ILP had maintained its independence – if being utterly devoid of power and influence could be so described. Fred had been the treasurer for the last decade: it looked as if this might be a lifetime position – there were precious few funds to treasure. It was like being back in the days of the Impudent Little Party, except that the few remaining members were far from impudent, taking instead an all-too fatalistic view. As for Jowett Hall, ownership had reverted to the Labour Party who first banned Fred from the library – even though every book had his name stamped in it – then sold off the fixtures and fittings and leased it to the Civic Theatre. Soon afterwards, it was gutted by a fire – started deliberately, it was said, to collect on the insurance.

"Your friends are the people who will betray you," MacDonald had said to him over breakfast when they were up in Aberdeen trying to break the seamen's blockade. "The only ones you can really count on are your enemies." Fred had paid little attention to this at the time – MacDonald had been notorious for waxing paradoxical while salting his porridge – but now it seemed significant. "Don't tell your pal Snowden – it would only upset him – but he, above all other men, is my Simon Peter, my rock . . . Even though he hates me – no, precisely because he *does* hate me, so single-mindedly, steadfastly and reliably." At this point, he had smeared the porridge onto a kipper – "I sometimes wonder whether such hatred might not ultimately be a purer and nobler emotion than love."

For a while, Philip and Fred had almost lost touch. Their infrequent exchanges were increasingly formal: one letter had actually begun 'Dear Jowett' and ended 'Yours, Snowden'. Then, one afternoon, Fred had once again heard his telephone ring.

"Dead, dead, dead," came a voice, "Dead, dead, dead."

It *was* Phil – but choking, as if in a seizure. Obviously, someone or something was dead but, for a while, he had been uncertain whether it had been Lady Snowden or the dream of Socialism. At last he realized that it must be Spot – a mangy terrier who bit everyone except Ethel – who had been run over and killed by Vere Harmsworth's limousine. Hitherto, he had taken the sobbing references to long wet tongues and paddy paws to be merely figurative. After a while, the sorrow had abated: having blown his nose, Phil proceeded to inveigh against MacDonald for the next half hour. Unfortunately, all this intensity had rekindled Fred's own grief: he had not slept for many nights afterwards.

From then on, the letters and calls had been incessant. Sometimes Phil reminisced and occasionally even expressed regrets. "I wish I'd never got into Parliament: I should have stayed a missionary. How I wish I were back on t'owld stump, givin' 'em that red-blooded Socialism, hot and strong! Those were the best times!" Fred doubted whether he truly meant any of this. Mostly, however, he talked of MacDonald. "What a spectacle! Ramsay's downfall is greater than even his worst enemy could have wished for. I hear that in the House he is regarded with universal disgust . . . If he were not lost to all sense of decency, he would seek some obscure retreat where he might hope to be forgotten. My utter contempt for him cannot be expressed in words."

There was something disturbing about this. Fred recalled what Shaw had written about Philip's autobiography, which had dismayed even his admirers with its shrill and self-exculpatory tone. "It reads like something that a slighted lover might dash off in the heat of parting, with Ramsay MacDonald as the errant swain".

But perhaps Philip needed his anger to keep himself going? He had been positively incandescent when, at the last election, Earnest Marklew, still sporting Grayson's white but now unrecognizably battered hat, had won back Colne Valley for Labour.

"I thought we'd seen the last of chaps like that. A sort of milksop Grayson: at least you could never have accused Victor of being wishy-washy!"

"It's funny, Phil, but I've been thinking lately that everything went wrong after we lost Grayson."

"On the contrary – the defeat of Graysonism was one of our finest moments. It was a narrow escape from anarchy – or worse than anarchy, whatever that might be . . . Sheer brutishness, I suppose. Anyway, we didn't lose Grayson, he lost himself."

"I know he would have been a disaster . . . But suppose it might have been a disaster that led to something else, perhaps even something remarkable? Suppose Graysonism was a stage that we needed to go through, a trial that we needed to endure?"

He had expected Phil to blow his top at this but there had instead been silence on the line. He almost hung up and redialled but then realized that he could still hear the sound of ragged breathing.

"Phil," he said at last, "Why didn't you stand up to the bankers? It was your great chance. Norman was your friend: he might even have backed you."

"It was all too complicated, too big a job for one man. I still don't understand what happened and I haven't the least idea what I could have done differently" - there came a long, whistling sigh - "Nay, Our Fred."

"Nay, Our Phil," said Fred. Then, from Snowden's end, there was the soft click of the receiver being replaced.

Despite the wind and rain, the Colne Valley lads were obviously having a whale of a time. Their charabancs had stopped at every pub between here and Slaithwaite and would be stopping again on the way back. "It's how he would have wanted it," said one, having downed in a single gulp a bottle of brown ale. They were not talking about their deceased former representative nor of their current champion, Marklew - they were talking of Victor Grayson. There had evidently been more sightings: he was back in Manchester, somebody said, running a tobacconist's in Miles Platting with a spot of bookmaking on the side. No - he was working as a wall-of-death rider in New Zealand! No - he was a mountain guide in the Swiss Alps! "I can just see Victor in one of them cocky hats with a feather in it". They were all laughing but Fred saw that their eyes were hopefully sweeping the fringes of the crowd.

Some of them were taking bets with the locals as to whether Ramsay MacDonald would be attending the Westminster service.

"Here's two bob says he won't, even though he does live just around the corner."

"What odds on Victor turning up riding a white charger and waving Excalibur?"

"No - coming down the Thames aboard the Flying Dutchman, under a black and ragged sail!"

"No - arm-in-arm with Jesus himself, both of them pissed!"

Mercifully, the children's choir drowned them out:

> "In peace their sacred ashes rest
> Fulfilled their days' endeavour."

How healthy these young people looked! Perhaps they too had

been crossed with fuller-fleeced southern breeds? And how loudly and enthusiastically they sang! Fred had noticed that, in every choir, there was always one child – whether male or female – of an almost supernatural beauty. Not merely of face and form but seeming to emanate a sort of spiritual radiance. And he could always pick out their individual voice – higher than its fellows, with a piercing note more like that of a bird's. He had wondered whether, through some divine providence, an angel had been smuggled in to ensure that everything went well. There was one here today, centrally positioned: a boy whose freckles and protruding ears only seemed to enhance his otherworldly appearance. The head was tilted back so that the eyes gazed straight up: a small patch of blue was opening, as if that innocent gaze had burnt the clouds away. Such a child could not have been born in these villages a generation ago. How Fred wished that some of his old foes from the Council or the Commons were here, so that he could point a finger and say to them, "There! That's what bun, banana and beverage can do!"

> "They bless the earth and they are blessed
> Of God and Man forever."

But something about these children worried him. Their heads sat proudly on long straight necks but the faces wore complacent, even smug expressions, not unlike those on the government benches that he had sat opposite for so many years. It was becoming more difficult to distinguish between rich and poor: soon, perhaps, everyone would *look* the same, while all other inequalities remained. He had noticed that the eyes of the choir, bright and unnaturally wide, hardly ever blinked. Where was Philip's dark fire or MacDonald's bull-like glare or those curious eyes of Victor Grayson, that changed colour even as you looked at them? And those teeth, strong and white, seemed to be biting off the words they were singing. They were full of calcium, vitamins and cod-liver oil, their clear skins attesting to days spent in the open air rather than the mills – but did they have the least idea that what had been gained could be lost, that what had been conceded could just as easily be taken away? Would they even notice when their milk was watered, when the buns were stale, when they unpeeled their bananas only to find that there was nothing inside them?

Whatever would these songsters have made of Snowden if they could have seen him in his prime, up on t'owld stump, before a wildly enthusiastic crowd? They would probably wonder what all the fuss was about. Philip - and Hardie, MacDonald, Grayson and the rest - would seem like actors without a play, hawkers with nothing to sell, comedians who told no jokes. Now, when politicians wanted to communicate, they went on the wireless. "I am an Englishman," Baldwin had said last night, after yet another rise in unemployment - "And you are English men and women. Which means that the more difficult times are, the more cheerful we become." More people had listened to this twenty minutes of tosh than had heard Fred in his whole life.

And how they lapped it up! Sometimes he wondered if The People, whom he had lived to serve, no longer needed him. "For Heaven's sake, Dad," Emily would burst out, "Do stop going on about the blessed 'People' all the time, as if they're drawn up in lines, wearing Phrygian caps, with pikes and torches in their hands! . . . They're just separate men and women trying to make their way through this world. All they want is some peace and security in which to raise their families, to have a little fun and to be left alone by folk like you with your great causes." To hear her talk, it was as if The People had never existed at all.

Perhaps it was because Philip had always seemed like a dying man that his actual death had come as such a shock. He had suffered a heart attack in the middle of the night and died before the doctor could arrive. Ethel had been away, attending the Grand Ball that followed the Coronation of King George VI. She would have been comforted, Fred imagined, by the length and respectful tone of the newspaper obituaries that appeared - even though none of them had seemed to be about the man he had known. All that had signified, it appeared, were Phil's official positions, his election triumphs, the speeches in Hansard, the Conferences and Committees, the budgets and financial statements and the judicious or pawky assessments by prominent colleagues and opponents. James Maxton, the gentlest and most forgiving of men, had come closest to the reality. "It is the end of an epoch," he had written, "Whatever Snowden might have done in 1930 pales into insignificance beside the effect his presence and voice made on me one afternoon in Edinburgh . . . In a quarter of an hour he had changed my life. There are thousands like me and we will never be able to repay that debt." This had brought tears to Fred's eyes but it was still not enough. Why had nobody asked him to write something? After all, he was Philip's oldest friend and one of the few original ILP men left alive. Why had he not been asked to speak today? There were things that needed to be said and he was, perhaps, the only one who could have said them.

Fred suspected that his own consistency counted against him. Former comrades apparently considered him to be either a fool or a living reproof to their own compromises – even both at the same time. There was no doubt that the world had changed but he had found no reason to adjust his own views or way of life. He still lived in the same house and still paid his monthly dues to the ILP and to the Overlookers Union – even though he had not overlooked a single loom in fifty years. If he could still scramble over a stile, however, then perhaps he could handle those warp beams? Were there some things that you could never forget?

He observed the secretary's continual solicitude for the old man. Having retrieved the wheelchair, she had wrapped him in a tartan rug. She never looked at the chauffeur and he never looked at her but Fred could sense an affinity between them, a total awareness of each other's presence and proximity. Surely people who looked like that could never be classed as servants or even employees? At that moment, the girl met his gaze with a dazzling smile, but Fred, abashed, turned away.

"They say he was a sort of tramp who struck lucky," Little Emily was saying, "He was prospecting for gold but found diamonds or he was looking for water and struck oil instead. He didn't find what he was looking for but something else found him. It's funny how often things turn out like that – in the telling of the tale, at any rate."

Would it have made any difference if he and Grayson had been able to compromise and Snowden and MacDonald had been slightly less biddable? Philip had been seduced by the doctrine that everything was terribly complicated, that there was a secret, higher science of politics and economics, known only to a few initiates. "It's not algebra or even maths, Our Phil," he used to tell him, "It's just sums." But Snowden would always give that snickering laugh that he had picked up from Montagu Norman. Grayson, of course, at the other extreme, had believed everything to be too simple. He had imagined that all he had to do was to stand up and announce himself, then strike a pose and rake his fingers through his hair, in order to bring the great halls and palaces crashing to the ground.

Was there anything Fred could have done? Could he have kept MacDonald out of the arms of the Duchesses, got Grayson off the whiskey, rescued Philip from Norman's chilly spell? Probably not – but it troubled him to think of just how ignorant and opinionated he had been in his earlier years, how quick to dismiss things about which he had known nothing at all. Through Epstein and Rima, he had come closer to understanding what the Grayson affair had been really about – something deep and troubling that was at the root of art and religion and, it seemed, even politics as well. Fred Jowett had always been right . . . but only as far as he went. Now he knew that there were things to which his remit had not extended. If Blatchford had been correct about reincarnation, then he would certainly be making them his priority, next time around . . . Unless, of course, there was no-one else available to take up sanitation and public health.

There was a smattering of applause: an elderly man in a grey morning suit was getting to his feet. He looked like a fatter and more corrupt version of Ben Turner. No, it really *was* Ben Turner – or rather, Sir Benjamin Turner OBE, CBE. He no longer looked much like the most dangerous man in Britain: as MacDonald said, he was now only a danger to the à la carte menu. Turner muttered something, then fished a slim volume out of his pocket, from which he began inaudibly to read.

"Don't worry, Dad," boomed Emily, "No-one else can hear him either. I think it's a poem of some kind."

Poor old Ben! His poetry had always been a standing joke in the movement. MacDonald had frequently employed sections of *Pieces From A Yorkshire Loom*, to considerable comic effect. Once, however, in a break from a particularly fractious NEC meeting, Turner had taken Fred aside. "You know, Comrade Jowett, I *will* be remembered – not as a politician but as a poet!"

The locals were still wrangling over the Cowling or Ickornshaw question and the Colne Valley contingent seemed to be working themselves up to a sing-song, but Fred felt that it was of vital importance that someone should be listening to Turner's words. Even though, as far as he could recall, the man was among those who now refused to acknowledge his own existence. By minute inclinations of his head, as if tuning the temperamental radio in his parlour, he managed to isolate then amplify the weak and quavering voice.

> "It wod be grand – aye varry grand
> If yo' an' me could see,
> A growin' happiness i' th'land
> An' gentle pleasantry
> An' what's to stop it? Nowt! Nowt! Nowt!
> There's ivvarything we need,
> If we'd be neighbourly i'thowt
> An' neighbourly i'deed."

Only Fred applauded at the end. He had no idea whether this

would be considered good poetry and it did not seem particularly applicable to Philip, but the pride and pleasure in the author's face, despite the rain and tears pouring down his ruddy cheeks, were surely all that mattered. A local minister followed but all he had to offer was more platitudes. Fred wanted to interrupt, to tell them how Phil should be remembered for all those little things – that were really big things – that everyone had taken for granted and about which, by the end, he himself had probably forgotten. He should be remembered for the Post Office clerks.

To reduce wage costs, it had been the Post Office's practice to employ teenage clerks and then sack them on the day before their twentieth birthdays. There had been something so petty and mean-spirited about this that it had really got Our Phil's goat: Fred recalled how, when he talked of it, his friend's eyes had seemed to be on the point of starting out of his head. Between 1906 and 1912, he had waged an unrelenting campaign against it: nothing but sheer thankless toil – gathering evidence, writing thousands of letters, pamphlets and articles in the press, appearing before Committees, tabling parliamentary questions, raising points of order on the flimsiest of pretexts. Nor had he accepted any help: "Nay, Our Fred," he would say, grinding his teeth frightfully – "I want all t'glory for myself." He had bullied the weak, made deals with the corrupt, flattered or cajoled people that he despised and who despised him in turn. And he had never let up until the government had been not so much persuaded as worn down. They had given Snowden his clerks just to shut him up. That had been the difference between them: Fred would trudge along until the political weather changed, but Phil could make things happen by sheer force of will.

But who cared about any of this now? Today's Post Office clerk would know nothing of it: his twentieth birthday would only mean – if he was lucky – a cake with candles on it. Ethel, he knew, had considered it a waste of Philip's valuable time, having absolutely no bearing on the cosmic currents and inscrutable purposes of

Universal Love. But she had been mistaken, just as MacDonald had misunderstood the nature of Phil's indignation: for only Love could, for so long, have provided the fuel for so bright and fierce a flame as Philip Snowden's.

Now Ethel arose and, with a curious swooping motion, handed the little box to an elderly man. He was one of the few locals who did not resemble Philip but was, apparently, his cousin Tom. Having prised open the lid, he seemed unsure of what to do next, staring at the ashes as if surprised at what he saw. Then, instead of scattering or pouring them, he swung his arms forward, as if extinguishing a fire with a bucket of water. By some trick of the winds, however, the released ashes remained in suspension for a few seconds, forming the rough outline of a human figure. "That's the best colour I've ever seen him," observed Little Emily, before there came a great howl and the remains of Philip Snowden were dashed back into the faces of the congregation and then off in the general direction of Skipton. Fred wondered whether they were making for that beloved garden at Eden Lodge.

Naturally, it was to be the angelic boy and the prettiest of the girls who were to scatter the flowers – bluebells, wild orchids, primroses and poppies. The girl was fascinated by the orchids: she lowered her face to one, inserted the tip of her nose into its cup and sniffed, then sneezed violently and blushed. Unlike Cousin Tom, the boy was making sure that the flowers were laid out just right: what seemed like random scattering was, in fact, a composition of some art . . . And then, of all people, Willie Leach was suddenly there, trampling over the bright carpet, carrying a bulging briefcase in his hand. He seemed to be trying to give the impression that he was coincidentally passing through this isolated spot on the way to somewhere else. Without stopping, he yelled something that Fred could not catch, then yelled it again. His eyes were red and running with tears, but perhaps they were only smarting from the ashes, for his whole face was smutted and streaked with black.

"Now all that's done with, the sun's coming out." Little Emily was unfastening the top button of her coat. Fred was shocked by her mordancy: she had once been so fond of her Uncle Phil. Now she was fumbling with a second button: "Why, it's almost Grayson Weather!"

What wonders in the sky! Those big fluffy clouds, like white horses, were dragging behind them a great expanse of blue. One horse's head broke off and turned into a mallet, which decapitated each of its fellows in turn, then the blue just soaked them all up like a sponge. Fred's wife had always maintained that the skies of Yorkshire were more beautiful than any others on earth. As she had rarely set foot outside the county – only once to London and never abroad – it was hard to know how she could have justified this radical conclusion. But perhaps she had been right: once something reached a certain level of beauty, surely there could be nothing beyond it?

At the very top of the moor, large birds were taking off and landing. "Hen harrier," he said aloud, and Little Emily gave him a sharp look. *That* was the name of the hawk he had seen earlier! If death was not the end it would be pleasing to think of Phil soaring aloft, looking down on his own funeral, free of pain, no longer harrying his foes with sarcasm and invective but with sharp talons and beak. But wasn't it the females who were brown with a barred tail? The male hen harriers, as far as he could recall, were smaller, silvery and much more delicate in appearance.

If only nature could be all there was to life! Whenever he felt grass – or even mud – beneath his feet, he knew that he had come home. But he could never forget that there were still a quarter of a million houses officially designated as unfit for human habitation – although, as the Tories liked to point out, if there were humans actually living in them then it followed that they must, after all, be fit for habitation! The crumbling back-to-backs remained, their water supply trickling from a rusting communal pump and – in parts of Manchester and Liverpool – there were even some surviving privy middens, shared by up to a dozen families. Yet the government were, year by year, whittling away the slum clearance subsidies!

Nevertheless, Fred had recently seen the future. At Quarry Hill, right in the centre of Leeds, the council was building blocks of flats based on the Karl Marx House in Vienna. He had been shown the plans and had walked among the foundations, imagining the great wedges of wood, metal, glass and stone shooting up into the heavens. A thousand working people would be living, like gods, in the sky. Looking down, they would see and understand everything that had previously been kept from them and then they would no longer be just people, they would be The People once again. Hydraulic lifts were to be installed and the finest plumbing and, in the kitchens, with their Garchey System, vegetable peelings, bottles and cans would be disposed of through a hole in the sink. And the interiors would be revolutionary as well: some German scientists were attempting to eliminate the need for furniture – soon, the tenants would be sitting or reclining on columns of rising air. Once The People were hovering it would not be long before they began to fly: they would step off their balconies and let the wind bear them northwards to the Pennine Hills. Poverty, suffering and need – all would be forgotten. No more sickness, no more sorrow and one day perhaps even mortality itself would be going down the Garchey Hole.

Now, rolling and twisting in mid-air, Fred's hen harrier was fighting another bird, as big as itself but with a longer and straighter beak, a crow or a raven. But perhaps they were not fighting but playing, enjoying – like Snowden and MacDonald – the pleasures of hating and being hated? Another bird passed between them, going straight up like a skylark, except that is wasn't singing. He almost expected it to burst like a firework but it kept on going until he could not see it anymore and his neck began to ache.

The children's choir came past. Even the littlest ones were in step, although not so much marching as traipsing. They flowed across the ground as lightly and easily as the shadow of the final cloud. Many trials and tribulations awaited them but, at least, thanks to Philip, they would not be suffering the lot of the Post Office clerks.

Fred recalled how his own working life had begun: being lined up, at eight years of age, to be passed fit by the doctor at the mill. It was the merest formality, for the man had never been known to turn anyone away. Fred was to be a part-timer: a six and a half hour day, with school in the afternoon, until the age of thirteen when he would graduate to a sixty-hour week.

The man's hands had been cold as he set Fred on his knee. Beneath the reek of dark tobacco and peppermint, he had smelt horribly unclean. He liked to assess children by their teeth, like a gypsy buying a horse. Fred could still remember that those two stubby fingers had made a squeaking sound as they slowly rubbed across his teeth and gums. At the last, they had tugged at his tongue, as if about to pull it out by the roots. How many times he had tried to picture that doctor's face! The closest he could come was King George V.

Neither Fred nor Emily had heard Ethel approaching: it was as if she had descended from the sky. As always, Fred found himself checking whether her feet were actually touching the ground.

"I am so sorry, dearest Frederick," she began, "About Philip's desk. But Mr Lloyd George is such a close neighbour of ours – a mere two fields away. And besides, it would never go up those blessed stairs of yours. Above all, though, L-G's need is pressing indeed. Great plans are afoot" – she made a cupping gesture – "He is holding the future in his hands."

Fred hoped that he had successfully concealed his disappointment. He was assailed by the image of Ethel and L-G, one at each end, lugging that great oaken desk through a herd of inquisitive Fresian cows.

"She's always liked to have him rummaging through her drawers," Little Emily hissed in his ear.

"I knew that you would understand, Fred. I think we have both long been aware of what an incomparable privilege it is for such as we to recognize and serve the greatness of others."

The secret smile had been growing broader and broader until

it had become a jack o' lantern grin that threatened to split her face in two. And Fred saw that this unfathomable and formidable woman was in the grip of a grief and despair perhaps even deeper than his own.

"And don't worry." Ethel laid a hand on his arm – the strength of her grip was alarming. "I've burnt all his letters and personal papers."

Whatever did she mean? What on earth could there have been for him – or anyone else – to be worried about?

"There will be a great statue on this very spot," Ethel announced, "Raised by public subscription. And, upon the plinth, the inscription will read, 'HE WORKED FOR THE POOR'!" Rolling her eyes ecstatically, she walked – or rather glided – backwards, to be swallowed up by the departing throng.

"I can just imagine it," said Emily, "Uncle Phil in marble, holding forth in full 'Come to Jesus' style. He'll be twenty foot tall all right, but he'll be perched on Auntie Ethel's palm." To demonstrate, she extended her own right hand and then slowly closed it into a fist.

Fred suspected that the grand monument would never be built but even if it was, it would surely be left unvisited and unremarked until it had crumbled away. Unlike *Rima*, no-one would even take the trouble to vandalise it. The men of the ILP had come and gone and would not be remembered. There would be no paintings or sculptures, no statues or plaques, no rechristenings of towns and streets: Leach would never be a pub, Southall would never be a railway station. Perhaps the names Snowden and MacDonald might serve as examples of betrayal, long after anyone could remember just what it was that they were supposed to have betrayed. But he himself would be utterly forgotten, which was just as it should be. He took great comfort in the thought of his own replaceability: the next chap would do everything just as well, if not considerably better.

"Good afternoon, Mr Jowett." It was the chauffeur, respectfully inclining his frame so that he leaned into Fred rather than towering over him. "My employer did not know Viscount Snowden well. In fact, they met only once – a fleeting but memorable encounter just outside Leadville, I believe." He spoke without any trace of an accent, not even an English one. "But he has long been an admirer of your work and would be grateful if you would grant him a couple of minutes of your time." Fred could see that the old man and his secretary had begun to move towards them, against the flow of humanity, very slowly, riding their invisible ponies.

There was a sudden commotion and then the angelic choirboy came dashing back up the path. He shouldered Little Emily aside, without upsetting her balance. Fred saw that the lad's previously beatific expression had undergone a wild alteration.

"Stop him, somebody," came a woman's harsh voice, "The little bugger's off again!"

But the boy was already twenty yards further on, dragging out from behind a rock a scarlet bundle lashed to the end of a long and sturdy stick. Running-away clothes and food: his escape had obviously been well-planned. Now he was running again, ignoring the winding track and cutting up through the heather and gorse straight for the summit cairn. Fred turned and began to follow, stumbling at every other step. Surprisingly, he seemed to be making up ground but he was not really trying to catch the lad: he too wanted to see what lay on the far side of that hill.

ACKNOWLEDGEMENTS

THANKS TO THE helpful staff at Bradford and West Yorkshire archives, Huddersfield University, The British Library, The Museum of Labour History, Tate Britain and many other selflessly interested parties.

To Tom Bailey and David Rose - who always believed in the book - and to Steve Garnett's Unplanned Obsolescences Consultancy - 'We can see problems where others merely see solutions . . .' And to Simon Geoghan for photography and hi-lo tech support.

To Annette Green and David Smith - my dearest agents.

To The Hawthornden Foundation: "Oozolem Foozlem" section written at The Castle, 2013.

To Beck Mills, Clayton for providing office space.

To the Royal Literary Fund for financial support - and much more.

This book has been typeset by
SALT PUBLISHING LIMITED
using Neacademia, a font designed by Sergei Egorov
for the Rosetta Type Foundry in the Czech Republic. It
is manufactured using Holmen Book Cream 70gsm, a
Forest Stewardship Council™ certified paper from the
Hallsta Paper Mill in Sweden. It was printed and bound
by Clays Limited in Bungay, Suffolk, Great Britain.

CROMER
GREAT BRITAIN
MMXXIV